FIRST CONTACT

Patrick Woodrow was born in 1971. He graduated from the University of Cambridge with first class honours in English before working as a management consultant in London, Seattle and Singapore. He is married and lives in Oxfordshire. *First Contact* is his second novel.

Also available by Patrick Woodrow

Double Cross

FIRST CONTACT

PATRICK WOODROW

arrow books

Published in the United Kingdom by Arrow Books in 2009

1 3 5 7 9 10 8 6 4 2

First published in the United Kingdom in 2009 by Arrow

Arrow Books
The Random House Group Limited
20 Vauxhall Bridge Road,
London SW1V 2SA

Addresses for companies within The Random House Group Limited can
be found at: www.randomhouse.co.uk/offices.htm

The Random House Group Limited Reg. No. 954009

www.rbooks.co.uk

A CIP catalogue record for this book
is available from the British Library

ISBN 9780099478621

The Random House Group Limited supports The Forest Stewardship
Council (FSC), the leading international forest certification organisation. All
our titles that are printed on Greenpeace approved FSC certified paper carry
the FSC logo. Our paper procurement policy can be found at
www.rbooks.co.uk/environment

Typeset by SX Composing DTP, Rayleigh, Essex
Printed and bound in Great Britain by
CPI Bookmarque Ltd, Croydon, CR0 4TD

for Sally-Ann

PART I

One

The helicopter leaned on its side, entangled in the jungle. Its dislocated rotor blades were covered in moss. The windscreen was black with lichen. Creepers snaked over the tail boom like the tentacles of some rapacious green beast. Underneath, the skids had sheared off in the crash and were now hidden among the roots on the forest floor. The aircraft's paintwork was only visible in a few places and it took Mark Bridges a couple of seconds to realise what he was looking at. As he pieced it together, he sighed with relief. The wreckage was a God-send. It might just save their lives.

'Are you OK?' he asked.

Melanie nodded. 'I think so. You?'

'Don't worry about me.'

'Do you think it's got a radio?'

'Yes,' Mark replied, checking the sun's descent through the trees. 'But I doubt it's working.'

The light was fading. Trepidation about a second night in the jungle grew as the shadows lengthened. They had no food, no water and no guide. The mosquitoes were swarming, and their antimalarial tablets were back in the lodge, more than fifteen miles away.

They had been lost for twenty-eight hours.

Mark pressed forward, parting the foliage with lacerated hands. As he drew closer, he saw that the helicopter was a commercial aircraft, perhaps thirty-five feet long. In the air it would have been sleek and fast. But not any more. Down here it was prey: a metal fly enmeshed in a big green web. Mark battled through the vines, energised by the prospect of what they might find inside. Food and water were unlikely but what about a map, a compass or fuel to start a fire? Better still, what about a first-aid kit to treat their cuts?

Back home in London, Mark had just completed his training to be a doctor. He had seen photographs of tropical ulcers in a course book: lesions the size of saucers, erupting from just an infected scratch or bite. Melanie was in a far worse state than he was. Ignoring his advice she'd insisted on wearing shorts and a T-shirt. Now her limbs were covered in angry red lines. A wait-a-while vine had ripped a furrow along her thigh, its spines as sharp as a barracuda's teeth. If the wound wasn't dressed soon it would begin to fester.

Gunnera plants had grown up beside the helicopter's cabin, concealing the pilot's window.

Mark tore at the leaves until he exposed the door.

Melanie watched from a log, too exhausted to help. 'Shit, I'm thirsty. Be careful, Mark.' She closed her eyes briefly. *Careful?* When had her brother been anything else?

Mark had spent the day holding back branches, steadying logs, and occasionally offering his hand or shoulder. They had only covered four or five miles but he hadn't taken a single step without checking to see where he was putting his foot. Melanie couldn't remember a time when he'd slipped: an incredible achievement for a man his size. Six feet six, eighteen stone, and there he was with hardly a scratch on him. Not because he was hesitant or precious but because he was so damn . . . *diligent*. There! That was a word he'd be proud of. He was calm too. It was her fault that they were in this mess but so far he hadn't reproached her. She knew that he must be seething and wondered what it must be like to have his self-control.

Mark pulled the door handle but nothing happened. Lack of water had made him weak. He pulled again, harder. This time there was a sharp crack as the rust around the hinges split. The door fell open. He staggered back. A black fog rushed towards him and he ducked. A colony of bats exploded from their lair, their wings scraping his neck as they flew into the dusk. Mark raised his head and immediately wished he hadn't. Behind him, Melanie screamed.

The pilot lay scattered around the cockpit. His flesh had long since decomposed or been devoured by the jungle's many hungry mouths. With no muscle to support it, his skeleton had collapsed. He had been thrown forward on impact with the ground and his skull rested on the dashboard, a pair of headphones still clamped uselessly over absent ears. A fly buzzed in his eye socket. His shirt rippled as an army of ants marched along his ribs. Moths had eaten patches out of his clothes, which now served as a rotten sack for his bleaching bones.

Mark looked closer, his revulsion diluted by curiosity. A body decomposes quicker in the jungle than anywhere else. But even allowing for additional moisture, warmth and wildlife, he guessed that the skeleton had been lying there for at least a year.

Mark cursed and hauled himself into the cockpit. Lost in the rainforest somewhere in the middle of Papua New Guinea, this was hardly the kind of holiday that he'd planned. They had come in search of birds of paradise. Now, for the second day running, they'd found trouble and death.

Somewhere behind them Peri and Gile, their native guide and boatman, lay dead in the mud. Butchered in a fight with four warriors from a neighbouring clan. Mark hadn't been able to follow the argument but the repetition of a woman's name had provided a clue to its subject. He and Melanie had walked away at the first sign of trouble, calling for Peri and Gile to follow. But it had been too late. An accusation had met with an insult; a shove in the chest returned with a punch. Then the axe, hacking into bone as white as the sago bark for which it had been designed. Mark had intervened only to find himself threatened with a machete. The warriors had never seen someone his size before and fear fuelled their aggression. If he hadn't backed off, he and Melanie would have been next.

The killing had been over in a flurry of blows. Then, thinking only of Melanie's safety, Mark had pushed her into the jungle and they had run. Not *to* anywhere; just *away*. Escape rather than retreat, with each step taking them further into the forest. Hulale was the last known settlement before the vast uncharted jungle between the Fly and Aramia rivers. Its warriors could have hunted them down in minutes, but the tribesmen had been content to chase them deep into the forest, where the spirits would do the rest.

Since then there had been plenty of birds all right, but as Mark put his hand on the back of the pilot's seat, paradise was a very long way away.

It was *his* fault that they were here. He should have put his foot down. Peri had told them that they would see plenty of wildlife within a few miles of the lodge, but Melanie had been determined to break new ground. Birdwatching had never been her thing. She'd wanted adventure. Papua New Guinea was the final frontier – one of the most biologically diverse and least explored countries on earth. She hadn't flown all this way not to see a crocodile, so she had offered Gile double to ferry them upriver in his pirogue. And Mark, against every instinct in his body, had said nothing.

He had always been the sensible one. The brake, the safety net. And it was a role that he was tired of playing. But Melanie had been adamant. She was going through a difficult time and he hadn't had the heart to argue. She had always been impetuous and irresponsible, but divorce from Zak after only six months of marriage had left her even more reckless than usual. *A few hours exploring the tributaries of the main river and back in time for dinner*. It hadn't sounded dangerous, but word at the lodge was that the Hulale were among the more primitive clans in the area. 'Excellent!' Melanie had said, reassured by Gile's assertion that he had a 'special friend' there. Mark had raised his eyebrows and shrugged. His fault. Definitely *his* fault.

The cockpit was damp; the air rancid. Mark's bulk left little room for manoeuvre. He immediately began to sweat. There was no sign of a fire but a hole in the roof showed a large crack where the cowling met the fuselage. Mark guessed that the helicopter had come down more or less as it was supposed to, only too fast and in some of the densest jungle on the planet. The pilot had stood no chance.

One look at the instrument panel was enough to tell him that the radio wouldn't work. Mark removed the headphones from the pilot's skull and tried it anyway. With one earpiece cupped against the side of his head, he began twiddling the dials on the receiver.

Nothing. No lights, no noise. Not so much as a crackle.

Mark tried a few more switches on the instrument panel, more out of curiosity than hope; but the battery was dead and the circuits broken.

Satisfied that he had done all he could, he squeezed through the door to the main cabin. The wall on his left bulged inward, grossly dented by the trees outside. Its window had smashed, providing an entrance for the bats. A metal strut pierced the ceiling by his head, popping through the trim like a hernia. Anxiety rose in Mark's throat. He was claustrophobic. This was like being on the inside of a crushed can.

It was dim inside but Mark could still see the bones of the flight's only passenger, heaped in the middle of a three-seat bench. The man's skull had toppled to the floor, where it stared vacantly at a large rucksack. Mark hurried forward then dropped to a crouch. He grabbed the nearest strap and slid the pack towards him. As he did so, he noticed two small keys, rusting on a leather cord amid a pile of collapsed vertebrae.

Curious, Mark looked again, peering into the gloom on the far side of the passenger's remains. He had missed it the first time but now it was clear what the keys were for.

There on the bench, hidden among the shadows: a black briefcase, still handcuffed to the bones of the guy's right arm.

Two

Mark looked from the handcuffs to the keys and then back to the briefcase. It was much like any other: steel-frame, leather trim, with two chrome-plated clasp locks either side of the handle. The lid was firmly closed. Freed in the crash, a stray fire extinguisher had wedged itself between the top of the case and the helicopter's crumpled wall. Mark briefly wondered about drinking the extinguisher's water. Then he noticed four white letters, printed on the canister's side. AFFF. Aqueous Form Filling Foam. Not very tasty.

Ignoring his thirst, Mark turned his attention back to the briefcase. Papua New Guinea had a terrible reputation for crime and the passenger had not been taking any chances with his luggage. But what could be so valuable that it had to be handcuffed to his wrist on a flight with no other passengers? Cash, perhaps? Drugs? Commercial, political or military secrets?

Passwords, stolen goods or jewellery? Mark felt his hand reaching towards the fire extinguisher. He would need to dislodge it before he could use the keys. Contracts, forgeries, photographs? Accounts or presentations? The possibilities were endless.

Mark placed the heel of his hand against the fire extinguisher and pushed. It didn't budge. He tried again but to no avail. Years of strength training meant that there weren't many things that he couldn't move when he put his mind to it, but the cylinder was stuck fast. It had come to rest upside down, its plastic grip pinning the briefcase to the seat. No way was it going to shift. For a split second he thought about using his foot so that he could exert more force but the idea vanished when he heard Melanie being sick outside. She was dangerously dehydrated. Vomiting would only make her condition worse.

Mark made his decision instantly. He was wasting precious time. The briefcase could wait. Whatever was inside was unlikely to get them out of the jungle in any case. If there was food or first aid to be had, he would find it in the bergen. There was something nefarious about the handcuffs anyway, and Mark wanted no part of it. He didn't care who the guy was or what business he'd been on. Right now, his sole concern was to care for his sister. He grabbed the passenger's rucksack and hauled it backwards out of the helicopter, leaving the briefcase untouched.

Melanie was standing with her hands on her knees, spitting the last of her vomit into the ground. Her hair, normally auburn and straight, was flecked with mud and bedraggled with sweat. Mark gave her a worried look but knew better than to make a fuss of her now. Leave her and she would be more likely to accept his help when she had regained her composure in a few minutes.

'What have you found?' she asked, her eyes watering.

'This,' Mark replied as he hefted the rucksack on to a fallen tree. 'Start praying it contains something useful.'

'Who to? God left this place a long time ago.'

Mark unclipped the bag's top pocket and began searching the main compartment. A pair of waterproof trousers came out first, followed by a matching jacket. Both were in a military camouflage print.

'Great,' Melanie said. 'An anorak.'

Mark ignored her. He was unpacking things quickly now, his confidence increasing as he extracted first a torch and then two ziplocked freezer bags. He tossed one to Melanie who made no attempt to catch it. Mark opened the seal on his. 'You're wrong,' he announced as his fingers closed around a slab of dried apricots. 'There is a God.'

Melanie raised her eyebrows and stooped to retrieve her bag. Within seconds her mood had changed, a smile lighting her features for the first time in more than a day. 'Come to Mamma!'

'What is it?'

'Glucose tablets. And they're still dry.'

Mark sat next to her and they swapped foods, gorging themselves. After a few seconds he put his hand on Melanie's arm. 'Better save some. We don't know how long we're going to be here.'

Melanie stopped, considered the advice, and slowly lowered the packet of apricots from her mouth. 'Bloody spoilsport!' she said. 'So what now?'

'You unpack the rest of the rucksack while it's still light. I'm going to see if I can find some fuel to start a fire. Extra points if you can find me a lighter.'

'What was it like in the helicopter?'

'Not good. I can't say I'd recommend it.'

'How many?'

'Just the pilot and one more. Both very dead.'

'Anything else besides the rucksack?' Melanie's mouth may have been parched but her tone was as importunate as ever.

Mark hesitated. 'A briefcase.'

'A briefcase? Why didn't you bring it out?'

'I couldn't.'

'Why not?'

Mark sighed. Melanie was heavily in debt and there was no way that she would have shown his restraint in the face of such temptation. Then again, she would need the constitution of a coroner to get past the skeletons and a sledge-hammer to dislodge the fire extinguisher. 'Because it was handcuffed to a dead guy's arm.'

Melanie was momentarily speechless. 'You're kidding? What do you reckon's inside?'

'None of our business.'

'Something valuable, don't you think?'

'I don't know,' Mark replied. 'Ask someone who cares.'

Melanie clucked her tongue, frustrated by her brother's apathy. 'Do you think anyone else knows about this?'

'The briefcase?'

'The crash.'

Mark paused. He had been wondering the same thing. The helicopter may have been a write-off but surely someone would have come to retrieve the bodies had they known where to look. 'No chance,' he said, picking up the torch and trying it. He was surprised when it emitted a weak beam. Maybe their luck was changing.

Wading through stinging nettles, Mark walked around the helicopter towards the fuel tank. If they could start a fire the smoke might – just *might* – clear the canopy. Dietmar and Beatrice Katzer, the Austrian couple who ran the bird-watching lodge at Teraruma, would know that they had been missing since yesterday. And if they saw the smoke, they would use it as a beacon to guide their rescue mission. But as Mark rounded the helicopter's tail boom, his hopes diminished.

The starboard flank had taken the full brunt of the impact. The bodywork was twisted and torn; sheet metal ripped like paper by the force of the crash. A eucalyptus tree had entered the under-carriage at eighty-five degrees, piercing the chopper's midriff like an arrow. Mark whistled under his breath. The tree trunk had been invisible from inside but it could only have missed the cabin by inches. Mark located the fuel cap and crawled under the fuselage, breath-ing deeply to control his claustrophobia. Being the same height as an upright grizzly meant that clambering into a confined space was an unwelcome task.

It took only a moment to confirm his fears. The fuel tank had been punctured by the tree.

Not ready to concede defeat Mark stretched his hand inside the hole's jagged edges. There was still some liquid in the sump but when he scraped his fingers along the bottom he scooped up a handful of earth. Quite how it had got there was anyone's guess. Then, when he withdrew his fingers and smelled them, it became clear that any residual fuel had been heavily diluted with rain. A fire was out of the question.

This time Mark knew that he was beaten. The drops of water on his fingertips had only reminded him how thirsty he was. He crawled back out from under the helicopter and stomped back through the vegetation to Melanie.

'What have you got, Mel? Give me some good news.'

'More toys than a Christmas stocking. Look at these: a lighter, a fleece, a machete, a washbag . . .'

'Does the lighter work?'

'Not exactly. It's completely rusted. I can't even turn it.' She handed it to Mark, who tried to spin the flint wheel before tossing it back into the bergen in disgust. He wasn't sure if he could face another unsuccessful night of grinding a dry stick against a sheet of bark.

'What's in the washbag?' he asked.

'Toothpaste, soap and a packet of pills.'

'Pills?'

'I dunno. Some sort of medicine.'

Mark picked up the washbag and unzipped it. He ignored the other items, going straight for the small plastic pot in the main compartment. He was hoping that it might contain antimalarials but analgesics would do.

'And look at this,' Melanie was saying. 'A notebook. I found it under his clothes. Why are you smiling?'

Mark rattled the tube. It contained something far more useful than medicine. 'Always read the label!'

'Huh?'

'Not pills, Mel. Water-purification tablets. In our condition these are more valuable than an entire pharmacy.' He paused. 'Assuming we can find some water to purify, that is.'

Mark glanced doubtfully at the trees. Surely there was some nearby? The Fly was the

17

country's second-longest river, discharging a similar annual volume to the Danube, Niger or Zambezi. Its waters permeated the landscape. He and Melanie had wandered far from its banks but he could sense it all around them, its bends circling the forest like a python's coils.

They hadn't discussed the fact that they might die out here but Mark had acknowledged the possibility within a few hours of becoming lost. The density of the jungle had mocked their attempts to retrace their route. They had shouted themselves hoarse in the hope that the Hulale would return and guide them back to the river, but their cries had only startled the birds. Since then there had been no paths and no high ground. No water other than muddy puddles. And with every step they had dropped more sweat. Now their bodies were husks.

Melanie was still brandishing the passenger's notebook at him. 'You haven't looked at this yet.'

'Is that the last thing?'

'Nearly. I haven't unpacked the side pockets. It feels like an empty water bottle in one, and there's something heavy in the other.'

Mark held his hand out and took the notebook. He noticed that Melanie had begun to shiver. The sooner he could find some water and use those tablets the better.

'I'm fine, Mark. Take a look and tell me what you think.'

Mark gave the notebook a cursory glance. It

was A5 with a comb binding along its short edge. He riffled through the pages. There was still just enough light to see that they had been filled with detailed sketches of flora, fauna and indigenous tribes. Each drawing was accompanied by a paragraph of explanatory text. The pictures of people generated far more commentary than the animals and plants. Mark turned to the inside front cover to see if the owner had written his name there. He hadn't.

'His drawings are almost as good as Grandad's,' he said as he tossed the notebook back to Melanie and began exploring the rucksack's side pockets.

'No way!' Melanie scoffed. 'He's not even in the same league. Anyway, who do you think he was? Some sort of naturist, if you ask me.'

'Naturalist,' Mark corrected. 'And no; I don't think he was.'

'Why not, Einstein?'

'Because of this.'

Melanie's mouth opened long before she spoke. 'Shit the fucking bed!'

Three

It was a pistol. Which meant that the guy had been a soldier, a cop, or some sort of government agent. Or a criminal. But not a naturalist. If a naturalist had needed a weapon he would have chosen a rifle, which offered greater range and accuracy for shooting animals. Pistols, meanwhile, were designed exclusively to shoot *people*. The passenger's camouflage clothing meant that he had probably been a soldier, but that still didn't explain the commercial helicopter, the notebook or the briefcase. So maybe he was Special Forces on a covert mission. To do what, though? Draw pictures of the plants? It didn't make any sense.

Sheathed in a webbing holster, the pistol had been well protected from the damp. Mark unfurled the belt and carefully withdrew the gun. It was black and heavy in his hand. This was the first time he had held a firearm and he was careful to point the barrel into the bush. He tilted it on its side, first left then right, until he saw what he was looking for.

'Wow!' Melanie exclaimed as she stood beside him. 'Do you think it works?'

'I don't know,' Mark replied. 'And I've got no intention of finding out.'

'Let me have a look.'

'What for?'

'To see if it works.' Melanie flashed her brother a smile, the excitement causing her nausea to pass in a flash. When the smile wasn't returned she held up her hands in mock surrender. 'OK! OK! I promise I won't shoot you! Now gimme the sodding gun!'

Mark shrugged. Then he passed the pistol to his sister. She was twenty-two. Plenty old enough to know what a loaded weapon could do. He watched her, intrigued, amused, envious even. Life must be so much more fun when you didn't give a damn.

A yard to his right, Melanie braced her feet at shoulder width. She held the pistol two-handed in anticipation of the recoil. Then she pulled the trigger.

It stopped. She tried again, repeatedly. 'Bastard's jammed!' she said. 'There's a tiny bit of slack, then it won't go any further.'

Mark sighed. 'Fancy that.'

Melanie looked at him accusingly. 'You knew it wouldn't work, didn't you? Otherwise you wouldn't have given it to me.'

'I'm going to find you some water.' Mark took

back the pistol and placed it in its holster. Then he returned the weapon to the rucksack. 'Put the rain jacket and trousers on; they'll protect you against the mosquitoes.'

Melanie scowled at the clothes on the ground. The adrenalin from handling the pistol was wearing off. She felt ill again. Mark was right. In the last few minutes the air had become thick with mosquitoes. They formed clouds at head and ankle height, fizzing in short aimless bursts. Melanie swiped the air and blew one away from her lips. Her hand brushed her calf and then pinched her earlobe as the insects attacked. She watched as one settled on her forearm: legs splayed, shoulders hunched, ready to plunge its needle into her flesh. She waited just long enough to wonder if it carried malaria then slapped it dead.

Melanie grabbed the waterproofs and pulled them on. 'How will you make sure you don't get lost?' she asked.

'I'll stay within earshot,' Mark replied. 'I'll call out once every minute. You holler back and that way I'll be able to keep my bearings.'

'But it's almost dark!'

'Which is why I'm going to hurry. Mosquitoes hatch near water so there must be some nearby.'

Melanie looked unconvinced. Night was falling fast. The whoop of nesting birds had been replaced by a constant trill of insect song. A breeze rustled through the canopy and somewhere in the distance a booming toad called for a mate. A heavy blanket of cloud had descended on the forest. Soon it would be pitch-black. Any minute now the undergrowth would begin to rustle as the night's predators went looking for prey. There were no big cats to worry about but there were plenty of snakes. According to one book back at the Katzers' lodge, this area was home to at least fourteen venomous species, including the death adder and taipan, both of which could deliver fatal bites. Mark's assurance that the snakes were more afraid of her had been a blatant lie.

Mark smiled and held up the water bottle that he had found in the rucksack's remaining pocket. It was a military canteen, made of tin. 'If I can't find water within ten minutes, I'll come straight back.'

'No rush,' Melanie replied. 'You just told me there's a cute-looking dude with a pair of hand-cuffs back there. We may just have ourselves a party.'

Mark winced but said nothing as he collected the machete and disappeared into the bush. He had already decided that he wouldn't go far. There had been times during the day when he had felt as though they were still being followed, but the crashes they'd heard in the jungle had probably been made by a cassowary. Still, with night falling, the risk of getting lost was simply too great.

Mark sniffed. *Lost?* Who was he kidding? They were already *lost*.

'Mel?' Mark checked in after thirty metres. He was walking in a circle around the crash site. If he went anticlockwise then the helicopter would always be on his left.

'Over here!' Her voice came back from directly behind him. So far he hadn't ventured off course. He swung the machete at a thicket of bamboo shoots and then made the left turn that would put him on his circuit around the wreck.

It was heavy going as he threaded his way between the trees. In some places the jungle was impassable. The machete made his passage easier but every blow sapped his strength. Mark blinked as a mosquito flew into his eye. He and Melanie had been taking Malarone, the market's best antimalarial drug, since before their arrival in Papua New Guinea ten days ago. Their bodies might have stored a reasonable dose of the drug's prophylactic agents, but without more pills their protection would only last for another two days. Still, malaria was only going to be a problem if they got out of the rainforest alive. The incubation period for the disease was usually between one and two weeks. If Mark didn't find water they would be dead in a day.

'Mel?' He had come another thirty metres. He was fighting an ongoing battle not to give in to his own exhaustion. But he knew that he had to stay strong for Melanie's sake. For all her pluck and bravado she was still emotionally fragile. If they fell out or if he showed signs of defeat, her resilience could easily shatter.

'Here!'

Mark pressed on around his imaginary clock face. His thoughts now returned to the helicopter. How much use was it really? It clearly hadn't been discovered before, which meant that it was probably invisible from the sky. There was no fuel or functioning lighter to start a fire and the radio was useless. The rucksack had given them a lifeline but what good would it do them to remain at the crash site? He would have to remove the skeletons before they could use the cabin as a shelter. And then what? Learn to hunt and make fire and spend the rest of their lives in the jungle? *No thanks.* He was going to get them out of this place or he was going to die trying.

'Mel?' He had reached the nine o'clock position on his tour. Still no water, but he could see what looked like a steep gully ahead. It would take a while to force a path through to it and then several minutes to follow it down, by which time it would be dark. Then again, this was the first real gradient they had seen in hours and it whispered a half-decent chance of finding water at the bottom.

'Mel?' He called again. Louder this time. Where was she? Had he walked out of earshot already? He glanced in the helicopter's direction but it was hidden behind an impenetrable tangle of creepers and vines. For once his height was no advantage at all.

'M-E-L!' This time Mark really yelled: a futile action that only tired him further. His throat was dry. His voice cracked. His thirst meant that he could muster no more than half his usual volume.

Still no answer.

Was she all right? Maybe she had already passed out, which was why she wasn't responding. Mark stopped. He could press forward, explore the gully and perhaps find water. Alternatively, he could return and hope that the glucose tablets had given Melanie enough sustenance to make it through the night. She was in desperate need of rehydration, but there would be no point in filling the canteen if he couldn't find his way back. The more he thought about it the harder the decision became. A thunderstorm was a possibility, in which case they might be able to catch enough liquid for several mouthfuls each. In the meantime, whatever moisture was left in their bodies would be commandeered to break down the apricots that they had eaten earlier. Six of one; half a dozen of the other.

Then, suddenly, a shot shattered the dusk. It was a sharp, clear crack that seemed to reverberate in his gut. Shockingly loud, it was instantly followed by the whine of a ricochet. A cockatoo shrieked. A flock of parakeets burst from the trees. Then silence. Even the cicadas had stopped singing.

Mark turned on his heels and ran.

Four

Melanie had found the pistol's safety catch. At least Mark *hoped* it was Melanie. But what the hell was she shooting at? He was now four hundred yards from his sister and there was a jungle assault course between them.

Mark threw himself at the vegetation, crashing into it like a startled bear. As he ran, his mind immediately turned to the Hulale. Had the tribesmen been following them, after all? Perhaps they had changed their minds. Yesterday the warriors had murdered two innocent men, so it would make sense to eliminate the witnesses to their crime. In his mind's eye he saw Peri then Gile fall to the ground, their black skin awash with blood. Saw, too, the power in the warriors' legs: a freeze-frame image that captured the brutality of the slaughter. Quads taut, hamstrings braced, their calves bulging as they stooped to dismember their foes. These were strong men, exacting revenge in the most primeval way. God alone knew what they would do to Melanie.

Mark felt something stir within him. He wasn't a brawler; he'd never needed to be. Troublemakers had always given him a wide berth on account of his size. He tightened his grip on the machete nonetheless. It felt good in his fist, releasing another wave of adrenalin. Suddenly he was running with renewed purpose; the instinct to protect rousing him for the fight. God help them if they'd laid a finger on his sister.

Mark ran. He didn't need to see where he was going. Forearms in front of his face, he rammed the undergrowth with all his strength. Vines snagged his shins. Thorns raked his arms. But the forest was powerless in the face of such momentum. He tore on, ignoring the damage that he was inflicting on his body. There had been only one shot. Mark didn't know if that was good news or bad. If there had been a conflict then it was already over. Either the Hulale had run off or . . . *Melanie! No. It wasn't possible.*

It took him four minutes to return to the crash. Bursting on to the site, he saw his sister bent over the rucksack. Her hands were rummaging deep inside the main compartment as she repacked some of the contents. There didn't appear to be anything wrong.

Mark stopped. He was panting hard. 'What happened?'

Melanie looked up.

Mark saw her blanch, heard her gasp. Something had startled her.

He spun around in case someone was behind him but all he saw was an emerald-green fern, swaying in his wake. 'What is it?' he asked, unsure whether they were in danger.

'Your face,' Melanie replied. 'It's bleeding.'

'Sod my face, Mel! What were you shooting? Are they here?'

'Who?'

'The bloody Hulale!'

'Oh Christ!' Melanie brought her hand over her mouth to stifle a laugh. 'You thought I was being attacked?'

'Weren't you?'

'No. Shit! Mark, I'm sorry. It was just a possum.'

'A possum?' Mark looked around. Dread had turned to confusion. 'You shot a possum?'

'No. I missed. I hit the helicopter instead.' Melanie indicated the aircraft with a nod. There was now a small hole in the cabin wall.

'Where's the gun?'

'Over there.'

'Is the safety on?'

'Yes. Why didn't you tell me about it?'

'Why were you shooting a possum?'

Melanie swallowed. 'After you left I heard something making a noise in the bushes. I was scared so I went to get the gun. You weren't surprised when it didn't fire earlier so I knew I must have missed something.' She grinned nervously.

Now Mark's confusion was rapidly turning to anger. He had only lost his temper twice in his life. On both occasions it had been with Melanie. Once, aged fifteen, when she had defaced their grandfather's sketchbook. Then again on her sixteenth birthday when he had arrived to meet her off a train, only to find that she had been arrested two stops earlier for being drunk and disorderly.

'Damn it, Mark! I was scared. I thought it was those fucking savages. Don't you dare have a go at me.'

'You could have shot me. You could have hurt *yourself* for God's sake!'

'Hardly!' Melanie scoffed. 'You know what I'm like. I couldn't hit the floor if I fell out of bed. Besides, you were somewhere off in the other direction.'

'Another few minutes and I would have found water. Christ, Melanie! A possum! They're not exactly dangerous.'

'Oh, great! So now it's my fault we're going to die of thirst, is it? Screw you, Mark! We can't all be as perfect as you. Anyway, at least we now know we've got a gun that works.'

Mark sat down in the dirt. He was too angry to reply. Too exhausted; too dry to form the words in his mouth. Instead he looked at Melanie, hard, until she lowered her eyes. He had been hoping that this holiday would bring them closer together. At twenty-eight he was six years older than she was. As kids that age gap had always been too big for them to be close. Now, as adults, there was an opportunity to get to know each other. To become friends as well as siblings.

It had been his idea for Melanie to join him. He thought that the break would do her good after everything she'd endured with that idiot Zak. And the truth was, he liked his sister. She may have been irresponsible and crude but she was wilful and brave. She still had plenty of growing up to do but she was fast becoming her own woman. As a doctor, he liked the fact that she questioned everything. Melanie would rather make a wrong decision than no decision at all, and she was prepared to learn from her mistakes. She was carefree. She lived life in the moment. And there were times, many times, when Mark wished that he could be just a little more like her.

He tossed the empty water bottle to the ground. Melanie was probably right about the pistol. They were undoubtedly safer with a gun that worked. 'Let's sort a few things out for the night,' he said.

'Like what?'

'Receptacles to catch rainwater; in case we have a storm.'

'There's only the water bottle.' *Receptacles!* What kind of a stupid word was that?

'We'll put the apricots in with the glucose tablets. That way we'll have another bag. Even if it doesn't rain, we should manage to trap some moisture. Plastic's great for that.'

'And which of your three A-levels taught you that?' Melanie sat hunched under her waterproofs, swatting mosquitoes. Fucking hell, she could be a cow sometimes! Mark deserved better than this. He really did. Never mind that he made her feel immature and thick. That was *her* problem, wasn't it? Here he was, cutting his face to ribbons to see that she was all right, only to be thanked with her petulance. She was only still alive because of him. Of that she was quite sure. What a way to repay his generosity! Mark's training at Imperial had left him with debts of £28,000, but he had still paid for her to come here. What was it he had said? A trip to the tropics was as good a tonic as any for the pain and humiliation of her divorce from that idiot Zak. *Tonic!* That was the word he had actually used. As if some concoction from Jeeves could sort out a marriage! Forget the bloody tonic, she'd told him. Give me the gin instead.

She watched as he went about his work. He was unhurried and meticulous as he mixed the apricots in with the glucose tablets and then hung the empty freezer bag on a nearby tree. He bent a twig to hold the mouth open and to provide extra stability in the wind. Now the bag was secure, ready to catch the rain. He may have been her brother, but Mark never ceased to fascinate her. This giant of a man, with the body of a decathlete, hands like spades and the dexterity of a Swiss watchmaker. Mark sank to his knees and began smearing his face with mud.

He applied it thick, all the way down his neck. He was especially careful to coat his eyelids. Soon he was completely masked.

'What the hell are you doing?' Melanie asked. 'You look like one of those Asaro mudmen we saw in the highlands.'

'A repellent against the mosquitoes. You should do the same. It'll help to block our scent. It's not much but it's better than nothing.'

Melanie pursed her lips. Slowly, she reached out a hand and grabbed a fistful of dirt. Her brother was incredible. Where had he learned that shit? She'd always thought of him as an academic, yet here he was giving her lessons in jungle survival like he was some sort of SAS instructor. The guy's brain just never stopped working.

Ten minutes later they did their best to make themselves comfortable for the night. Mark had chopped the leaves from the gunnera plant by the helicopter and laid them down to make a groundsheet: protection of sorts from the centipedes and ants. Their spat had passed. Now they sat in silence, battling their thirst.

Melanie was thinking of home: of their parents, tucked up in their redbrick semi on the edge of Ealing. It was now December but winter had already arrived when they'd left England. She remembered her father, grumbling about the rise in oil prices as he'd driven them to Heathrow. Then her mother, with her nervous laugh, reminding her to take her Malarone. Melanie didn't feel especially sad to think that she might never see them again. Just weird. Really *weird*. Unprepared. As though her life had been an exam and the invigilator had just said 'Stop writing!' So many things she could have said if she'd tried harder but time was now up and what could she do? Would they hold a memorial service? What would they say? What *grade* would they give her? Mark would get all the plaudits of course, but what adjectives would they use to describe *her*? And her stuff! What would they do with all her stuff? She'd recently moved into Mark's flat in Kilburn and had barely unpacked. That would make life easier for them! Would they sell it, she wondered. Keep it? Give it away?

A flash of lightning was followed by a distant peal of thunder. It rolled over the forest with malignant intent. Melanie was grateful for the passenger's waterproofs. Grateful too for Mark's enterprise with the second freezer bag. She glanced at it, erect and sturdy in its bracket. It made a damn fine receptacle. Maybe they would get their drink, after all.

'I wish I had my iPod,' she said. 'Those owls freaked me out big time last night.'

Mark smiled sympathetically. Music was Melanie's passion; US punk her specialist subject. Somewhere along the line Zak had introduced her to the voice of disaffected American youth and it had struck a chord. *No*, Mark grinned. That was unfair. Many of the songs that she had played him had at least three chords.

Bands like My Chemical Romance, Bowling for Soup and OPM. Some of their stuff was really quite good. But none of it was a patch on the hoot of a southern boobook.

'You'll be reunited soon enough,' he told her. 'The battery would be dead by now, anyway.'

'So what's the plan for tomorrow?' Melanie asked, conceding that her brother was probably right.

'First we're going to walk to that gully I spotted earlier, check it for water, and fill up the canteen, if we can.'

'Then what?'

'Then we're going to follow it. All the way to the sea, or . . .'

'Or what?'

Mark rolled on to his back and laced his fingers behind his head. He had been thinking about the briefcase handcuffed to the dead guy's arm. And the notebook with its sketches of jungle plants and naked tribesmen. He had been thinking about the pistol, and had failed to make any sense of it at all.

'Or what?' Melanie insisted.

'Or until we drop; whichever comes first. Do you think you can sleep?'

'I can now, you reassuring bastard!'

Mark smiled and shifted his weight. Then he put an arm around her shoulders: an instinctive gesture born out of the bleakness of their situation. It was the first act of affection between them in years.

'A vulture gets on a plane, carrying a dead possum under each of its wings.'

'Vultures can fly,' Melanie protested. 'Why would it need a plane?'

'It's a joke. A peace offering.'

'It better be good.'

'And the stewardess says, "Sorry, sir! You're going to have to put one of those in the hold. It's strictly one carrion per passenger."'

Melanie made a sound through her nose, somewhere between a scoff and a snigger. 'Have you just made that up?'

'No. It's taken me a while.'

'That's awful, Mark! Truly awful!'

'Thank you. Personally, I didn't think it was as good as that.'

This time Melanie laughed and relaxed her head on her brother's shoulder. Then she closed her eyes and tried to ignore the sounds of the jungle waking in the dark. The rustle in the foliage might have been a snake or it might have been the wind. Melanie was too tired to care.

Five

Sandwiched between the equator to the north and Australia to the south, Papua New Guinea forms one half of the third-largest island on earth. Home to the greatest expanse of rainforest outside the Amazon, it remains one of the few places in the world that has not been fully explored. Its jungles are thought to contain thousands of animals and plants that are still unknown to Western science. New species of orchids, ferns, frogs, birds and insects are discovered here every year. And while most people in the northern hemisphere would struggle to locate it on a map, many could tell you that Papua New Guinea was home to two of the planet's most extraordinary inhabitants: cannibals and birds of paradise.

Mark Bridges had come in search of the latter. He had wanted to visit Papua New Guinea (or PNG, as it was commonly called) ever since he was a small boy. The country's pull was in his blood. His grandfather, inspired by the success of three Australian brothers, had travelled here in the 1930s to try his hand at gold prospecting. Noel Bridges had returned a year later, empty-handed and shaking with malaria, but he had brought with him a sketchbook filled with colourful drawings of exotic birds. The explorer had even claimed to have discovered a new species, which he had named the King of England's bird of paradise, in honour of George V. However, in the absence of an authenticating photograph or specimen, the sighting had remained unofficial and the sketch in his book dismissed as fantasy by the ornithologists at the Natural History Museum.

The sketchbook would later become a source of fascination to Mark, who vowed to see the birds for himself one day. Now, after completing his medical training, the dream had finally come true. The itinerary that he had put together had been designed to give him the best chance of seeing as many of the thirty-eight endemic species of Paradisaeidae as possible. The rarity of some and the inaccessibility of others meant that a full house was out of the question, but Mark had still been hoping for double figures.

Earlier in the holiday he and Melanie had visited the Tari cloudforests in the centre of the country, where Sir David Attenborough had filmed several documentaries. There, they had spotted seven species, including the ribbon-tailed astrapia and the King of Saxony bird of paradise, with its antennae-like feathers and a cackle that sounded like static electricity. A week later they had flown to Daru in the southwest and then inland to Suki, where a motorised canoe had ferried them the final thirty miles to the Katzers' lodge at Teraruma.

Here, on the banks of the great Fly River, the landscape was a unique patchwork of swamp, savannah and gallery forest. Greater and king birds of paradise were the main attractions, but, on their second day, Peri had pointed out a twelve-wired bird displaying on the upper branches of his lek tree. The sighting had justified Mark's decision to venture further inland. Most visitors to the region made straight for the luxury of the Bensbach Wildlife Lodge two hours north of Daru, but Mark and Melanie were on a tight budget and Teraruma had promised a more authentic experience. Besides, this was the area in which their grandfather had claimed to have discovered the King of England's bird and Mark still harboured a fantasy that one day he would validate the sighting.

Experiences didn't come much more authentic than the one that Melanie woke up to on Wednesday 9 December. The storm had missed them but it had still rained during the night. She was damp and cold. The gunnera leaves had ripped under their weight and her waterproofs were covered in mud. She had a headache. Her vision was blurred. Despite the rain she had been too exhausted to wake up and open her mouth.

Her tongue had swollen in the night and now felt like a crust of bark. She tried propping herself up on her elbow only to collapse back. As she did so, her hand rocked the water bottle. The canteen teetered but remained upright, heavy enough to withstand the knock. Last night it had been lighter.

Water! The thought alone was enough to galvanise her. This time Melanie managed to sit up. Within seconds the canteen's lid was unscrewed, the tin cold against her cracking lips. She allowed a small amount of liquid to trickle into her mouth, where it was immediately absorbed by her tongue. More followed, pooling in her palate until her cheeks bulged. She held it, marvelling at how cool and soft it was. Then she swallowed. A little at a time because her throat was sore. She tasted chlorine and knew that it was safe. Mark, wherever he was, had made sure of that. She wiped her lips, gasped for air, and then drank the remaining water in one go. It was, she decided, the most pleasurable moment of her life.

The effects were immediate. She was like a character in a video game, given a new life by a gourd of magic potion. She blinked and fancied that she could feel a little more moisture around her eyes. Her vision was clearer now. And there was Mark, standing stock-still some twenty yards beyond the helicopter. He was peering into the trees, apparently looking for birds. Melanie smiled. The big bear was incorrigible!

She stood up and nearly puked. Then, after

several deep breaths, she found that she could walk without stumbling. For the first time she became aware of her surroundings. She heard the whoops, cackles and whistles of the dawn chorus. She had learned much from her brother on this trip and fancied she could discern the caw of an electus parrot amid the cacophony of other birds. All around her the jungle steamed in the rising sun.

They were lost. They were alone. And it was eerie. Mystical. Magical. Downright bloody beautiful.

Mark heard her coming. He turned, smiled, and put a finger to his lips. He still had mud on his face but Melanie could see the excitement in his eyes. She crept towards him, aware that he must have seen something cool. She hadn't been interested in birds before this trip but her brother's enthusiasm had begun to rub off after the first few days. Now she was blessed with all sorts of useful knowledge. Until eight thousand years ago Papua New Guinea had been attached to Australia, so it shared much of its neighbour's wildlife. There were marsupials, but the absence of placental mammals such as squirrels, monkeys and cats meant that there was little competition for the insects and fruit that proliferated throughout the forest. Small wonder then that its birdlife was the richest on earth.

'What is it?' she whispered.

'A magnificent riflebird. You can just see his blue throat.'

'Where?'

'Go to that clump of pandanus trees and he's in the third one from the left. About half-way up, on a forked branch. Look! He's swaying to catch the sunlight on his feathers.'

'I still can't . . .' Melanie caught her breath. 'Wait! With the black back and two wispy plumes along his sides?'

'That's him. *Ptiloris Magnificus*.'

'Is he a bird of paradise?'

'Most definitely. He's one of only three species to be found in Australia too.'

'He's not the one I drew on in Grandad's sketchbook, is he?'

'No. That was the magnificent bird of paradise. This is a magnificent riflebird. Similar names but two different species.'

Melanie looked at her brother. His eyes blazed with something akin to rapture. This might turn out to be their last day alive, yet she had never seen him so happy. Birds. *Bloody birds!* If only he'd show more interest in the non-feathered kind. Mark could name all thirty-eight indigenous birds of paradise, could describe their habitats, mating rituals and calls – but could he attract a decent mate of his own? Could he, hell! Quite what he'd been doing with plain Jane Donahue for so long was anyone's guess. Jane had been what their mother called a 'sweet' girl, but Melanie had always thought she'd had the charisma of a cold flannel. It had been a huge comfort to her when Mark had finally broken off their relationship earlier in the year. Since then Melanie had taken it upon herself to find him someone more exciting but the jungles of PNG were not proving a target-rich environment.

He didn't know it, of course, but underneath all that mud, Mark was handsome. Devilishly so. His colouring, Melanie realised, was not unlike the riflebird's: jet-black hair and iridescent blue eyes that flashed whenever he smiled. Usually clean-shaven, he now wore six days' worth of stubble, which made him look decidedly rugged.

Melanie had seen the way that women looked at him: a mixture of approval, respect and sexual curiosity. Sometimes even fear. Her friends at school had all fancied the pants off him, all wanted to know if he was proportionately equipped. He could have had the pick of them if only he'd shown more appetite. Maybe he'd shagged his way through those final terms at med school, carving a hundred notches in his bedpost since his split with Jane. But Melanie didn't think so. He was too cool for such sluttish behaviour. Far more likely that he had resisted the offers and stuck to his natural game. Mark was a romantic. And he would wait with the patience of Job.

'How did you sleep?' she asked.

'In fits and starts. Probably a couple of hours in all. You were out most of the night.'

'You've been to the gully?'

'Yes.'

'How does it look?'

'Full of running rainwater. The jungle's pretty thick but the ground falls away quite steeply. I'll be amazed if it doesn't drain into something bigger.'

'Like a river?'

'Hopefully.'

Melanie nodded. 'Done your exercises?'

'Not this morning. The tank's running a bit low and I need to conserve my energy.'

This time Melanie grimaced. Mark *always* exercised. Every morning. Whether he was on holiday or not. He exercised on Christmas Day. He exercised when he was hung-over. He exercised if he was ill, away from home or late. He'd even exercised on the flight over: two hundred press-ups in the aisle at the back of the plane. The fact that he had passed this morning – the first such time that Melanie could remember – told her just how serious he considered their predicament to be.

'Oh,' she muttered, unsure what else to say in the face of such an omen.

'You should eat something first,' Mark replied. 'And drink more. I filtered the water through my shirt but it's still pretty muddy. Won't do you any harm, though.'

'I've already finished the bottle.'

'Good. Now drink the stuff in the freezer bag.'

'What about you?'

'I've had over a litre already. I'll have some more when we get to the gully. We need to get going if we're going to make full use of the daylight. Do you feel up to a little stroll?'

'I'll just pack my stuff,' Melanie replied. 'Ta-da! Ready when you are!' She chuckled, pleased with her joke. Then her face clouded over. 'Do you think they're looking for us?'

'The Katzers?'

'Anyone.'

'Yes,' Mark replied. 'Definitely.'

'So why haven't we heard a helicopter?'

This time Mark sighed. He didn't have an answer to that. It had been troubling him for the last twenty-four hours but he hadn't wanted to mention it for fear of scaring Melanie. Why *hadn't* they heard a helicopter? It was a damn good question. 'We will,' he told her. 'Soon enough.'

They left the riflebird to his courtship and walked back to the rucksack. Mark hoisted it on to his shoulders and pulled the machete from a nearby log. Then they turned their backs on the clearing's horrors and began walking, deeper into the wild.

Six

The stream in the gully was two feet wide. It ran fast with last night's rain. The water was tan, having collected mud and silt on its way through the forest. Mark and Melanie stopped to drink another two litres each. It was a lengthy process, which involved pouring water from the freezer bag to the canteen via the filter of Mark's cotton shirt. This was followed by a ten-minute wait which allowed the purification tablets time to dissolve. By the time they had repeated the process twice each, it was eight o'clock in the morning.

Progress through the jungle had been slow yesterday. Today it was even slower. The vegetation grew thicker close to the stream and while Mark had the machete, he also had the rucksack. The additional weight was inconsequential but the extra bulk meant that he became snagged more often. Conditions underfoot were treacherous. Any exposed earth had turned to mud.

Branches, roots and logs, meanwhile, were as slippery as ice.

Mark had decided during the night that it would be prudent to mark their trail as they walked. Not only would this allow them to find their way back to the helicopter if they really *did* need to make a camp, but it might also tell them if they were travelling in circles. With the canopy so dense, navigation by the sun would be hit-and-miss. As he went, he hacked a cross into the tree trunks at regular intervals: one every ten steps. The wood was white and juicy under its bark. His crosses stood out as clearly as if they had been painted on by a forest ranger.

It wasn't long before they had to make their first difficult decision. Melanie was still wearing the passenger's camouflage waterproofs. The Gore-tex was excellent protection against the brambles and leeches but it was also making her sweat. All the liquid that she had just taken on would soon be expelled, leaving her in a similar condition to last night. In the end, Mark convinced her to take them off. Cuts and leeches were unlikely to prove fatal, whereas dehydration might. Now that they were following the stream they could refill the canteen at any time but frequent stops would slow their progress. Besides, the water-purification tablets wouldn't last forever. From now on they would have to be rationed along with the glucose and apricots.

By ten o'clock the jungle was largely quiet. The songbirds had finished courting. Now the only sounds were the shriek of parrots and the occasional crash as a cassowary loped through the bush. Mark and Melanie made as much noise as possible, beating the undergrowth with their machete and stick. Their aim was to scare the snakes but if they attracted the attention of a nearby tribe then so much the better.

Mark's assertion that they would follow the stream all the way to the sea had been somewhat melodramatic. Teraruma was two hundred miles inland and they would be dead long before they could walk an eighth of that distance. Meanwhile, his theory that the gully would drain into something bigger was looking more credible with every step. It was now midday. The gradient had eased in the last half-hour but already the brook was too wide for Melanie to step across.

They walked in silence to conserve their strength, stopping only to clear a path or check that the other was all right. They strained their ears for the sound of a searching helicopter but heard only their own footsteps. Melanie occasionally whistled a guitar riff to make up for the absence of her iPod, announcing over her shoulder that it was by Green Day or Blink 182. She knew that Mark didn't care but that didn't stop her from believing that he should. The way she saw it, she was doing him a favour. It was part of his education.

At two o'clock they broke for another snack but still neither spoke. There was nothing to say. Either they were going to find a river soon or they were going to die here. Maybe not today. Perhaps not even tomorrow. But soon enough after that. Instead, they communicated with their eyes. Little messages of reassurance, encouragement and hope.

By late afternoon the birds had become more active again, fleeing through the canopy at the sound of approaching footsteps. Mark caught flashes of brilliant blues, alarming reds and shocking greens. Under normal circumstances the sheer abundance of species would have been captivating. Orange-breasted fig parrots, rainbow lorikeets, Papuan flower-peckers, blue-winged kookaburras, honeyeaters, shrikes, fantails, sunbirds, cisticolas, and spangled drongos. Mark could name them all. But every sighting brought a stab of guilt. It didn't seem right to be enjoying the wildlife at such a precarious time.

On one occasion he thought he saw a flash of pink in the spread of a cajuput tree. Pink was an unusual colour in nature. Humans had it. So did pigs, squid, flamingos, the odd cockatoo and ibis. But that was about it. Except, of course, for the King of England's bird of paradise, the new species that his grandfather had painted. The bird in the sketchbook wore an iridescent pink collar: gaudy contrast to its otherwise black plumage. The bird in the cajuput tree, meanwhile, had disappeared long before Mark could focus on it.

'Why have you stopped?' Melanie asked.

'Nothing. I thought maybe I'd just seen the King of –'

'Forget it, bro! It doesn't exist.'

'Wait a minute! Listen!'

'Oh, do me a favour! That stupid bird was a hoax all along. Always has been, always will be. Either that or the old boy was smoking dope when he painted the picture.'

'No, seriously. I can hear something.' Mark put a finger to his lips and held his breath. Then his eyes flashed as a smile burst through his beard. 'It's a river, Mel. It's a bloody river!' And before she could reply he picked up the machete and hurried on.

They hadn't seen the helicopter until they were almost on top of it. It was the same now with the river. Only when they were ten metres from its edge were they aware of the additional space and daylight beyond. They pressed on, stepping carefully around the mangroves. They both wore hiking boots but the ground was flooded. Already they were ankle-deep in water. Then, with a few more swipes of the machete, they emerged blinking into the afternoon sun.

The river was far bigger than either of them had anticipated. It was fifteen metres across, upstream and down. And it was full. Very full. It wasn't much to look at: a tepid rush, the colour of stewed tea. The landscape was equally featureless. Thick rainforest grew on both sides as the river snaked its way to the sea. But the sky!

The sky was a different story. They hadn't seen much of it for the last two days. Now it opened above them, as blue as a kingfisher's back. Released from the claustrophobia of the jungle, Melanie looked at it and felt a surge of hope.

'Well done, Mark. You're a fucking genius!' And for once she meant it.

'OK,' Mark smiled. 'That's the first phase complete. Let's take a break and get some more liquid down.'

'Where do you think we are?'

'I don't know. It's not wide enough to be the Fly, I'm afraid. But it could easily be the tributary we travelled up from Teraruma.'

'If we ever get out of here alive, I swear to God I'm going to make up for all those times I've been a bitch to you.'

'You've never been a bitch to me, Mel.'

'Don't say that! You know it's not true.'

Maybe it was exhaustion, maybe it was her relief at finding the river. Maybe it was a genuine goddamn epiphany. Whatever it was, Melanie found herself starting to sob.

'Can't you push back just once in your life and tell me what I need to hear? I might have turned out to be a better person if you hadn't been so nice to me the whole time.' Suddenly she was crying, heaving noisily as the stress of the last two days came pouring out. 'I'm a bitch, Mark! And you know it. I'm sorry. I'm so sorry!'

Mark swung the rucksack off his shoulders and laid it on a dry patch of ground. He wrapped her in his arms and held her close. At six feet six he was eight inches taller than she was and he pressed her face against the base of his neck. Her hair and T-shirt were wet with sweat. 'We're going to get out of here, Mel. You know that, don't you? But you need to conserve your strength.'

She sniffed and nodded. When he tried to pull away, she wouldn't let him go.

'If only I'd listened to you,' she spluttered, 'I would never have got involved with that idiot Zak. Then I wouldn't have needed to come to PNG and we wouldn't have got in this mess in the first place. Married at twenty-two, for fuck's sake! What was I thinking?'

'Mel, you're talking nonsense. Deep breaths, OK?'

She nodded again.

They stood like that for another twenty seconds until Melanie suddenly stiffened in his arms. Something was wrong.

'What is it?' he asked.

'What would you say if I told you I could see smoke?'

Mark broke from her clutch as though they'd been fighting and spun round to face the river. 'Where?'

'About two miles upstream. On the other side. Three plumes rising from somewhere in the forest.'

Mark brought his hand up to shield his eyes from the sun. Melanie was right. The trails were unmistakable. 'My God!' he whispered. 'It's a village. I think it's a village!'

Melanie clapped her hands and suddenly they were hugging again, dancing a frenzied jig as the implications of their discovery set in. All thoughts of preserving energy were washed away downstream. They whooped, hollered and bounced: a display far stranger than any bird's. Then, suddenly, Melanie's mood darkened.

'What if it's Hulale?' she asked. 'Maybe we've walked in a massive circle.'

'I don't think so. I've been trying to keep us on a south-easterly course.'

Melanie glanced at the sun. Then she turned through ninety degrees, muttering a mnemonic for the points of the compass as she oriented herself with her brother's bearing. 'Never-Eat-Shredded-Wheat. Oh yeah! Nice one! Well, we've got to get across, then. How deep do you think it is?'

'I don't know,' Mark replied. 'Those fishermen we saw the other day were using punt poles but this might be a different river. Besides, I'm more worried about the current. It's going ballistic after all that rain. First things first, though. Let's have tea. How does the sound of a dried apricot and half a glucose tablet grab you?'

'Mmm! My favourite! Can't we eat the whole lot, now that we know we're safe?'

Mark shook his head. 'That village – if it is a village – is at least two miles away, which could mean another three or four hours' walking. A lot could happen in that time. Besides, we've got two hours more daylight at most so we might not even get there. We hope for the best but we plan for the worst.'

Melanie nearly made a caustic remark but stopped herself just in time. Mark was right. Again. 'What about the rucksack? How are we going to get that across?'

'I'll carry it on my head.'

'What if it's too deep?'

'Then it's going to get wet.'

It took ten minutes to eat a quick snack and to filter some more drinking water. Then they were ready to address the river. A quick glance left and right told them that there was little point in searching for an easier crossing. The river was the same width for as far as they could see in either direction. They could have walked upstream until they were opposite the smoke but it was clear that the village was set deep within the forest, well back from the water's edge. Besides, Mark was keen to get the crossing out of the way while it was still light. This was easily the most difficult and dangerous obstacle that they had encountered so far. He wanted to tackle it while Melanie's enthusiasm was still at its peak.

Melanie wrapped what was left of their food in the waterproof clothing and stuffed it deep into the pack. Then Mark picked it up and hoisted it on to his head, using just one hand to hold it steady. The other still clasped the machete.

They shuffled awkwardly into the water. Mark

went first. Melanie followed, her right hand clamped firmly on her brother's shoulder. The first few steps were easy. Then the water became faster and deeper. Now they could only crab forwards a few inches at a time.

Upstream and out of sight, a pair of menacing black eyes scrutinised their progress.

Seven

Contrary to popular belief, most species of crocodile are normally shy and wary of humans. The New Guinea crocodile is no exception. Primarily nocturnal, it prefers to stay in the water during the day. All its sensory organs are located on the top of its head, which means that it can still monitor its surroundings whilst leaving ninety-five per cent of its body submerged. This was precisely the reason why Mark hadn't spotted the large male lurking fifty yards upstream from where they had entered the river.

He had been aware of the risk, of course, but hadn't wanted to say anything for fear of spooking his sister. It was imperative that they reached the village, regardless of the danger from the local fauna. He had checked left and right but since the river didn't really have any banks, it had been impossible to eliminate the threat. The water stretched well beyond the trees. For all he knew there could have been a hundred crocs lurking in the mangroves directly opposite.

It was December: the mating season. The crocodile's behaviour had changed. Shyness and wariness of humans had been replaced by territorial aggression. This particular crocodile, all three and a half metres of him, was defending both food and females. Two beats of his massive tail had propelled him downstream for a closer look at the intruders. Now he lay no more than twelve feet ahead. The two creatures advancing towards him were far larger than normal prey but they were clumsy in the water and that made them fair game. The element of surprise was his greatest asset. His sixty-eight teeth could exert a bite of nearly five thousand pounds per square inch: twelve times stronger than a great white shark and five times more powerful than a hyena. With armour plating that had been sixty million years in the forging, he was a formidable weapon.

'I don't like this, Mark! The current's too strong.' They were almost halfway across and Melanie was scared. The water reached up to her armpits. It pushed against her left side and pulled away from her right. Its power was uniform, immovable. She looked behind. They had come so far. It wouldn't get any easier if they tried again later. Not unless they waited another four months for the dry season. Each movement required a huge effort but at least the river bed was flat underfoot. It didn't feel as though it was going to get any deeper.

Melanie gripped her brother's shoulder with

all her strength. It was the risk of crocodiles that was really freaking her out. She knew that they must be out there. She'd seen Mark scouring the river and had instantly known why. *Crocodiles!* The word alone was enough to send shivers down her spine. She hadn't said anything; hadn't wanted to be a wimp. Mark hadn't needed to spell it out for her, either. That village was the difference between life and death. They had to reach it, come hell or high water. The irony, of course, was that it had been her desire to see crocodiles that had taken them away from the lodge in the first place. And now look where she was! *You stupid, stupid cow!*

'A few more steps and we'll be halfway there,' Mark said over his shoulder. 'It should start to get easier again after that.' He stopped suddenly. Was it the current or had he just seen something? A shape under the water? A shadow above it?

He looked up, hoping to see a bird, but the sky was clear. He peered again into the murky water. It was impenetrable. Maybe he was imagining it. And what the hell could he do, anyway? He held the machete in front of him, his arm cocked for a downward strike. No way was he going to turn back now. The only way on was forward.

He took another step. His leg would barely move. It was like shifting a heavy weight in the gym. As his foot came up, so the river dragged him off balance. It was impossible to walk in a straight line. Every step was a stumble down-stream followed by a drunken correction. It would have been easier without the rucksack and without Melanie holding on to him for support, but he didn't want to lose contact with either. If Melanie let go now she wouldn't have the strength to withstand the flow. She would be gone in seconds.

Mark tried another step and knew instantly that it was one too far. His balance gone, he felt the rucksack slide from his head. He weighed up his options in a fraction of that first second. He could dive forward and save the bag or he could anchor himself to the river bed.

No contest.

His spare arm scooped violently at the water as he jammed his foot into the mud and braced with all his strength. The rucksack continued its slide, hitting the water just as the crocodile launched its first attack.

The river in front of Mark erupted like a muddy geyser as the reptile lunged. He saw its black eyes and the white of its throat. Teeth over an inch long slashed at his shirt, falling just short as the rucksack crashed between them. Mark cried out and staggered back, fear injecting his legs with new-found strength. A blur of brown-grey scales was followed by a massive splash. Water splattered Mark's face, blurring his vision. It tasted brackish. A metre in front of his balls, the croc thwacked the river with its tail and righted itself for another assault.

Melanie didn't need to see what was going on to know what had happened. She screamed and began to retreat. In her panic she tried to move too quickly. Her legs were swept from under her. She flew sideways, clawing her fingers into Mark's shirt. A second later she screamed again as the river broke her grip. And suddenly she was moving, buffeted sideways like a paper bag in a gale.

'Mel!' Mark made a desperate lunge for her outstretched hand, only to see her spiral out of reach. 'Mel!'

In front of him the crocodile sensed that the easier target was now drifting downstream. It swung its snout in her direction.

'No!' Mark screamed. He wanted to use the machete but the crocodile was out of reach. He could only watch as it flicked its tail in pursuit of his sister.

Then, amid the chaos and the spray, Mark saw something to give him hope. The crocodile hadn't moved very far. One of the rucksack's shoulder straps had snagged on its jaws, creating a considerable drag. Mark didn't need a second opportunity. He dived forward and grabbed the sinking pack with his spare hand. He gave it a sharp tug and cackled triumphantly as the croc's head turned towards him.

The strap was stuck fast, hooked around one of the beast's lower maxillary teeth. The reptile worried its head from side to side but could find no purchase on the obstruction. Crocodiles tear their food. They can't chew. There was no way to grind through the heavy Cordura nylon. Mark saw what was happening and took a step back. The crocodile followed, confused now by the weight on its jaw. It had lost all interest in Melanie.

Mark glanced to his right. Mel was already more than thirty metres away, racing down the river at seven or eight knots. He could just make out her head and then a flailing arm as she fought the current. 'Swim, Mel! Try to get to the bank!' He was aware, even as he shouted, what a stupid thing it was to say. As if she hadn't thought of that herself! Besides, it looked as though swimming was out of the question. Her only option was to go with the flow. Mark screamed in frustration. He was powerless to help her. In another twenty seconds she would disappear around a bend and be lost from sight.

Mark continued to stumble backwards, his eyes now fixed on the crocodile. It had a long, broad snout and a gormless grin. Its back was plated with a series of triangular scutes, which eventually tapered into its saw-blade tail. He wasn't sure if he was dragging the beast towards him or whether it was pursuing him out of choice. Suddenly it opened its jaws and hissed: a thick, guttural sound full of prehistoric menace. It was frighteningly loud, a rasping wet threat that briefly silenced the river. Mark turned his head as the stench of rancid breath hit his face.

He didn't know what he was going to do when he reached the trees but already he could feel the water getting shallower. So too could the crocodile. It sensed that it was in danger. Now it just wanted to get away. It hissed again and then thrashed its head from side to side. When neither of these actions freed the rucksack it boiled the water with a barrel roll. Mark saw the flash of its white underbelly; saw too the claws on its squat, ungainly legs. On the second roll, the rucksack at last came free. And with a flick of its mighty tail the animal shot below the surface and was gone.

Mark finally felt the water draining off his thighs. Suddenly his movements were freer again. He turned and ran to the mangroves, dragging the pack behind him. Five metres into the trees he found solid ground. But there was no time to rest. The rucksack was sodden. He hefted it on to a nearby branch where it could drain in the sun. For a moment he considered taking the pistol from the side pocket but dismissed the idea in a flash. The gun would be drenched: dangerous to shoot, if not already useless.

Melanie had gone. There was no way that he could catch her on foot. He had to find her again. The machete was in his fist. And as for the crocodile; well, just let it bloody try!

Mark was operating on autopilot: action at the speed of thought as he plunged back into the river.

Eight

Mark waded back to the middle of the river as quickly as he dared. It was easier without the pack but he still took care not to slip because he wanted to start his descent from the same place as Melanie. If he was going to catch her then he would need to be on the same trajectory. There was no sign of the crocodile. No doubt there were others in the vicinity but Mark's adrenalin was flowing as fast as the water around him. He wanted his sister back. And this was the only plan he had.

He let himself go a few yards later. He simply bent his knees as though sitting down and the current swept him up. Its strength was phenomenal. It rushed against the small of his back, barrelling him on to his front. He was pushed forward as though in a crowd, powerless to alter his course. He made small corrective strokes with his hands in an attempt to keep himself facing downstream. But the river had other ideas. It spun him in its eddies, then picked him up and spewed him forward. He was flotsam.

Mark reached the bend in less than thirty seconds. For a moment he felt as though he was going to be washed into the trees. Then the river dragged him around the turn. The slack water in the apex remained several metres away. There was no sign of Melanie.

The new view was a carbon copy of the last: a big brown river, meandering through swamp forest. Mark didn't recognise this new stretch of water although admittedly there wasn't a whole lot to recognise. It was looking increasingly likely that this morning's creek had drained into a different water system from the one at Teraruma.

So where the hell was he?

Mark scanned the mangroves. Melanie had been wearing a black T-shirt: not the easiest colour to spot among the lattice of branches that fenced the river. She was a strong swimmer but for all her fighting spirit she would have been no match for a crocodile. Mark began to feel sick. His adrenalin was fading. Now panic and despair flooded his veins. He glanced over his shoulder. The smoke from the village was almost invisible.

'M-E-L-A-N-I-E!' He screamed at the top of his voice, beating the water with his fists. The anonymity of the place only added to his desolation. He had been in the river for five minutes and there had been no change in the current. Every now and then he managed to plant a foot and spin himself around so that he was facing downstream. He would land again, several metres further on, and then spring left or right to keep himself in the centre of the flow. It was exhausting work. Each leap sapped the strength from his calves.

Then, as Mark approached the next bend, the river suddenly deepened. When he put his foot down, there was nothing there to support it. He gasped in surprise. Water rushed into his mouth as he sank beneath the surface. His eyes were open and for a split second he saw thousands of dirt particles suspended in the current. Then he flapped his arms and emerged spluttering into the twilight.

He instantly began heaving for breath, wheezing like a seal as he sought to expel the water from his lungs. He tried the bottom again. He could just brush it with the toe of his boot but standing up to take stock of the situation was impossible.

Mark slowly regained his composure. He rounded another bend. Then another. Five minutes became ten. Ten became fifteen. Above him the light was fading as the day drew to a close. A comb-crested jacana trotted over an expanse of lily pads to his right but there was still no trace of his sister.

What would she have done? Would she have had the strength to have swum to the sides? Would she have wanted to? Why not stay in the water and drift for as long as possible? That had been the plan, hadn't it? To follow the river all the way to the sea. What better way to do it than this? They were travelling five times faster than they could on land.

Mark was growing more tired with every minute. Had he not been searching for Melanie he would have floated on his back to conserve his strength. He couldn't accept that she had drowned; or been taken by a crocodile. *No!* Melanie was a pugnacious character, too damn truculent to succumb so soon. She was somewhere up ahead. Just out of reach – like so many other times in his life.

For the last twenty-two years Mark had been the one in front. Life changes quicker during childhood, and the six-year age gap meant that they had rarely shared the same new experiences together. When he had been allowed out after dark, Melanie was already in bed. When he had been choosing films with an 18 certificate, she had been restricted to tamer material. He had been learning to drive; she had been riding her bike. When he had started university, she had still been struggling with spelling and arithmetic. And the day he'd moved into his own home, Melanie had run away from their parents' house.

An hour ago, Melanie's tears had bridged the gap between them. Her remorse may have been stress-related but nonetheless it might have marked a turning point in their relationship. It may not have happened in the way that Mark had planned, but, for a few minutes this afternoon, Papua New Guinea had brought them together after all. And then, just when they were closest, she had been snatched away from him. Some bloody holiday this had turned out to be! They were supposed to be going home in a few days, but nothing was certain now.

The river flowed on. As Mark drifted around yet another turn, he saw a mudflat directly ahead. It was roughly the same size as his parents' garden in Ealing. An irregular shape perhaps forty feet long by fifteen wide, it formed an island in the middle of the waterway. The current forked either side of it: wider to the left, narrower to the right. Mark took one look at it and knew that he needed to rest. He sagged forward on to his chest and then kicked hard for the right-hand channel.

He wasn't a strong swimmer. He was too damn big to be buoyant. His boots were full of water and felt as heavy as dumbbells. He thrashed his arms in his best front crawl, the water churning in his face. The pull from the left-hand passage was immense. He was like a spider being sucked towards the plughole in a draining bath. But then, with a roar of sheer determination, he swam into the shallower channel. Mark felt the river bed under his feet and waded, panting, on to the mud.

He collapsed immediately: a bedraggled creature, gasping for air like one of nature's first amphibians. The island was barren except for a sturdy-looking branch that had been washed up some time before. Mark raised his head and glanced downstream. The mudflat was the only obvious landmark since they had first entered the river but Melanie wouldn't have had the strength to reach it. Mark pressed his face into the mud, hoping that the discomfort would usurp further despair. It was the not knowing that hurt most. His sister might be dead. Then what?

For a while he was overcome with grief. He lay there on the mud, chest heaving as he sought to control his dread. He was a doctor, damn it! He was supposed to save people; supposed to make things better. But no amount of medical training had prepared him for a situation like this. He imagined himself breaking the news of Melanie's death to their parents. Imagined their faces creasing with anguish. Heard the questions. *How? Where? When?* Then saw himself shaking his head, unable to provide a single answer. He imagined the story reported in the tabloids, the press factual but implicitly critical of them as though they had only themselves to blame. It was too unreal. This sort of thing didn't happen to the Bridges.

Mark rolled on to his back. The sun had sunk below the trees. The mosquitoes were gathering in their thousands. If there were villages in the area, as the smoke had implied, then he was at risk from a whole spectrum of vector-borne diseases. He was up to date with his inoculations against typhoid and hepatitis A, but what about schistosomiasis and lymphatic filariasis? What about Japanese encephalitis? And as for malaria, well, he was assuming that he'd already been infected with *that* particular disease.

Mark thought about returning to the water, where the mosquitoes could only bite his head, but he knew that the strategy was flawed. The crocodiles would be more active by night and he didn't have the strength to withstand another encounter. More importantly, he wouldn't be able to spot Melanie if he continued his journey in the dark.

In the end he decided to spend the night on the mud: a tough choice with harsh consequences. The mosquitoes were a constant plague. Squadrons of little stealth fighters that came with the dark, each carrying a potentially lethal payload. Twice he was forced to defend his island from crocodiles, driving them off with the driftwood. At other times the night itself provided drama, his solitude mirrored in stars, and echoed in the hoots of owls.

Memories of Melanie played through his mind like a roll of film. Family holidays in Cornwall. Teaching her the basics of chess. Visiting her in hospital when she had broken her leg. Melanie had been a rebel, a thorn in the family's side for as long as he could remember. But she had been cherished, her misdemeanours forgiven on account of her lust for life. She'd always cheered them up as quickly as she had riled them in the first place.

Mark called her name every ten minutes but he knew that he would not be answered.

It was the sun on his face that woke him. Weak from lack of food and water, he must eventually have drifted off to sleep in the early hours of the morning. Mark licked his lips. They were dry and tasted of dirt. His first thought was that he was lucky to be alive. Miraculously the crocodiles had not returned. He couldn't understand why.

Then he opened his eyes. The explanation stood a few inches from his face.

A pair of feet.

And they weren't Melanie's.

Nine

The feet were black and broad. The toes were splayed and the arches had collapsed, maximising the soles' contact with the ground. The nails were gnarled, broken or missing altogether. They may have been ugly but the man's feet were an evolutionary triumph. Passage through a muddy rainforest would be much easier with his weight spread over such a wide surface area. And with skin as tough as leather, he would never need shoes.

Mark kept very still, unsure if this latest development spelled good news or bad. He had been found, but if the feet belonged to one of the Hulale warriors then he might be seconds away from a brutal death. He raised his eyes as high as he could. The man's legs were muscular but scarred with cuts and welts. The skin around his knees sagged as though he had developed an extra thick layer for protection when kneeling.

Mark planted his palms on the mud and

pushed himself up – the closest he would get to a press-up this morning. He moved slowly, arriving in a squatting position as though performing some sort of yoga. He raised his head and was instantly grateful for his caution. An arrow pointed at his face. It had been hewn from bamboo, the tip slotting into the shaft so that it would break when pulled from its target.

The man was no more than five and a half feet tall. He wore a cassowary quill through his nostrils. A necklace of pink feathers covered his throat. His skin was the colour of roasted chestnuts; his hair short and thick. He had a beard and a moustache, both tinged with grey. His left hand gripped his hunting bow. The right lay against his cheek, motionless despite huge tension on the string. His mouth was sealed, his lips drawn thin in an expression of intent. Mark had no doubt that the tribesman would use his weapon at the slightest provocation. But the look in his eye offered a glimmer of hope. It was awe not fear. As though the tribesman had seen white men before, only none so big as this. As though Mark should be revered. Like he was some sort of God.

Mark learned a lot about the man in those first few seconds. He was primitive; far more so than the Hulale or the other tribes that he and Melanie had encountered in the highlands. The Hulale had worn grass skirts and penis gourds. Some of their younger children had even worn cast-off T-shirts: gifts from the missionaries who occasionally stayed at the Katzers' lodge. This man was naked. It also occurred to Mark that he might be important. He was probably in his mid-fifties and carried himself with pride. He hadn't run off and he hadn't attacked. The bow and arrow were clearly just for self-defence. It was as though he felt some responsibility to find out what was going on. The brilliant pink feathers around his neck, meanwhile, seemed to bestow him with some sort of status. A tribal elder or shaman perhaps.

Mark looked at the feathers and immediately thought of the painting in his grandfather's sketchbook. Birds of paradise had long been revered by the indigenous population, their colours and customs integral to tribal culture throughout the country. Mark felt a flutter of excitement. Was it possible that the King of England's bird really *did* exist? Was that the species that this tribesman was dressed to emulate? Mark smiled. He couldn't help it. With his half-sighting yesterday, the evidence was mounting in his grandfather's favour.

Two yards away the hunter saw Mark smile and slowly lowered his bow. Then he smiled back. Neither man had spoken but they were already communicating. Mark smiled again, letting the display of friendship tear across his face. It was forced, but its message was genuine. The tribesman smiled back, rapidly nodding his head. He was missing several teeth. The poor condition of his gums was noticeable even from Mark's inferior position.

The hunter uttered a few words and gestured for Mark to stand. His voice was quiet but there was urgency in his tone. Mark climbed to his feet and wiped his hands on his trousers. He dwarfed the tribesman. His muscular frame was utterly different to the elder's pot-bellied compactness. It was another beautiful morning. Behind him, the forest rang with birdsong. Above him, the sky blazed blue. He experienced a sudden pang as he remembered Melanie but his dread was instantly tempered with hope. The tribesman was a friend: a potential ally in the search for his sister. Food and fresh water would be easier to come by now. There was no doubt about it. The situation had improved dramatically.

With all sense of hostility gone, Mark felt encouraged to try an introduction. English, Hiri Motu and Pidgin – or Tok Pisin as it was called locally – were the three official languages of Papua New Guinea. Mark had picked up a smattering of the latter from his guidebook. He tapped himself on the chest. '*Nem bilong mi* Mark.' My name is Mark. '*Husat nem bilong yu?*' What's your name?

The tribesman looked at him bemused. Mark laughed, embarrassed by his accent. It was hardly surprising that the man didn't understand him. The vast rivers and steep mountains that characterised much of the country meant that many tribes had never left their own valleys. This enforced parochialism accounted for Papua New Guinea having more than eight hundred recognised languages: twelve per cent of the world's total, and far more than any other country on earth.

'I'm lost,' Mark said. 'Lost.' He raised his eyebrows, shrugged his shoulders and then looked left and right. It was a terrible piece of acting but it seemed to do the trick. The elder smiled and nodded again, the feathers on his necklace glinting in the sun. Then he began jabbering away in his own language. He pointed first at Mark then at the rainforest while making a walking motion with his fingers.

'That's right,' Mark said, encouraged by this apparent breakthrough. 'But my sister is still lost.' He put a hand to his head while he tried to remember the phrases in his guidebook. There was one about a lost wallet that he could adapt. '*Mi lusim sista bilong mi. Dispela em wanpela imegensi.*' I lost my sister. This is an emergency.

Again the tribesman looked baffled. Mark may as well have been speaking Greek. There was no point in persevering. He was clean out of things to say anyway. Unless he wanted the bill or to ask the way to the toilet, neither of which was appropriate right now.

For a few seconds they stood in silence, wondering what to do. Then the hunter turned and waded into the river. He chose the channel to the left of the mudflat where the water ran fastest. After several yards he beckoned for Mark to follow.

Mark hesitated. He didn't want to leave the

river. The waterway was his only link to Melanie. To leave it behind would be to admit that they were finally on their own: that she would have to survive without him. But on second thoughts, what choice did he have? If the elder led him to a village, his escape from the rainforest would be almost guaranteed. The tribe might lend him a canoe or, better still, guide him back to Teraruma. Communication was going to be an ongoing problem but the plan of action was now as clear as the sky. There wasn't a moment to lose. Mark walked forward and waded boldly into the water.

The hunter was standing stock-still, apparently impervious to the current. He reached out his bow. Mark grasped it and felt himself being pulled towards the far edge of the river: away from the helicopter, towards the village. Twenty seconds later he clambered through the mangroves and followed his guide into the forest.

The jungle was dark and instantly claustrophobic. The huntsman set off at a fast walk. Mark found that he needed to trot to keep up. He had no idea where he was going, taking it on trust that the elder would help him. They turned left towards the village.

After a hundred yards Mark knew that they would have to slow down. There was no way that he could maintain this pace. He had always been fit. He had played rugby at a high level in his teens. But this wasn't a game. It was serious. Deadly serious. He had eaten next to nothing in the last three days. He hadn't drunk anything for nearly fifteen hours. He was perspiring and there was fever in his sweat.

'Wait!' he called. 'Slow down!'

The tribesman loped back through the vegetation to offer him a hand. Mark held his palms up to say no thanks. He wasn't sure why, but it struck him as being important that he gained the hunter's respect. He didn't need help walking, just a slower pace.

Twenty minutes later they changed direction. Mark had been keeping track of the sun through the breaks in the canopy. Now they were turning east, away from the river. The village lay to the north, somewhere up ahead. This new departure didn't feel right. Then again, this might simply have been the path of least resistance.

Path? There was no path. Not that the tribesman required one. He was moving through the jungle as though he knew every tree. He didn't need a machete either. He simply picked his way between obstacles as though they didn't exist.

Mark fell for the first time a few yards further on. He threw his hands forward only to receive a splinter in his palm. Somewhere in the trees a red-cheeked parrot shrieked at his misfortune. He sat there, disgusted with his weakness. His body temperature was too high. He felt sick. When he had stopped for a piss earlier, his urine had been pungent and brown. He knew that he was ill with fatigue but knew too that he couldn't afford to be. He didn't have time. Melanie was out there somewhere. She needed him.

Mark picked himself up. Sweat stung his eyes. He felt something warm on his calf. When he lifted his trouser leg he saw a fat black leech gorging itself on his blood. He stooped and peeled it free, twisting it carefully to remove the head from his flesh.

The tribesman watched him with an expression that was somewhere between amusement and approval. Mark stood up and immediately staggered. His condition was deteriorating rapidly. He had been in the forest for almost four days now and his body was telling him that enough was enough.

The tribesman came forward and ushered him to a log. He checked underneath it for snakes and muttered something unintelligible. Mark caught the gist of it from the man's hand signals. He wanted him to stay there. Mark was reluctant to stop but he knew that the rest would do him good. He stared blankly ahead as the hunter disappeared into the bush. The guy was out of sight within seconds. He was running hard but Mark never heard him. He was a ghost, gliding silently through the forest.

The elder was gone for nearly forty minutes, giving Mark plenty of time to worry about Melanie. Then, just as he thought that he had been abandoned, the tribesman returned. He was carrying a white root in one hand and some sort of black fungi in the other. The latter looked like truffles.

The fungi had obviously been growing under-ground because their flesh was covered in earth. The tribesman sat down next to him and began dusting off the dirt. He stank of sweat and smoke. When he had finished he smiled and offered the growths to Mark.

Mark stared at the strange offerings in the elder's hand. Each one was an irregular black mass, soft and shrivelled like a small marsh-mallow. They looked disgusting, if not poisonous. They looked exactly the sort of thing that he shouldn't eat.

The tribesman held them up, jerking his palm towards Mark's mouth. Age had creased his face with wrinkles but the lines around his eyes suggested kindness and warmth. Mark scooped up the truffles. He was running on empty. He needed sustenance fast; couldn't help Melanie without it.

He ate.

The truffles tasted bitter, as though they weren't yet ready. Mark left some for the tribes-man but his guide insisted that he eat them all. Mark smacked his palate with his tongue, trying to generate some moisture with which to dilute the taste. He needn't have bothered. To his right the tribesman snapped the root and passed it over. Mark took it and held it to his mouth. Water trickled on to his tongue. It tasted sweet, as though it might contain sugar.

After five minutes the elder started walking again. He was smiling incessantly now as though something had tickled him. Mark stood up to follow. He still felt weak and giddy. The truffles had done little to revive him and he suspected that they were far less nutritious than the apricots and glucose sweets that he had eaten before. He couldn't notice any discernible effects from the meal.

Not for the first twenty minutes, at any rate.

Then, suddenly, strange things started to happen.

Ten

Mark's energy levels started to rise. It was a feeling that seeped through his stomach and spread up through his chest, like a warming dram of whisky. He stopped, immediately suspicious of the sensation. His heart was beating faster; far faster than it should have been: rapid palpitations hammered his breast like a woodpecker drilling for bugs. *Shit!* Mark giggled. This wasn't good; wasn't good at all.

But it *was* good. It was bloody amazing. And it was moving with phenomenal speed.

He experienced another surge of energy: a wave of euphoria that washed over him like a warm breeze. *The truffles.* What had been in those damn truffles? Mark put his fingers to his temples, aware now that he had been drugged. He took several deep breaths to reduce his pulse rate. *Control.* He needed control. He needed to work out what the hell was going on. Had he been tricked? Or had the tribesman been trying to help him? What had he taken? A sedative to render him vulnerable, or a stimulant designed to expedite his escape from the forest?

He glanced up. The tribesman was twenty yards ahead, apparently oblivious to the change in his condition. 'Hey!' Mark called. 'What the hell have you done to me?' He tried to sound angry but couldn't summon any aggression. His voice was breathless. He heard himself laughing and was momentarily furious. But then that too became funny. 'You bastard!' he challenged. 'What have you done?'

This time the tribesman turned. He grinned gleefully at Mark as he leaned against a tree. Then he flexed his biceps as though confirming that the truffles could increase one's strength. Mark saw the lines in the elder's face and thought his smile was the kindest thing he had ever seen. He had a sudden urge to be with his guide; wanted to hold him; wanted to bask in the man's friendship.

Mark walked forward. The rushes came quickly now: wave after wave of bliss shooting through his arteries. He stopped. He couldn't let this happen. He wasn't safe. He had never taken drugs in his life but he had treated enough cases of abuse during his time as an intern in Accident & Emergency. He had seen, first-hand, what narcotics could do. A teenage girl who had suffered a cardiac arrest after mixing GHB with too much alcohol. An ex-soldier, destitute and homeless, who had taken to injecting his eyelids because there was nowhere left for the heroin to enter his veins. An insurance salesman who had snorted a gram and a half of coke before falling out of a first-storey window. The list went on: dozens of screw-ups every Friday and Saturday night.

Mark shook his head, trying to rouse himself from the daze. Common sense told him not to fight it. Whatever narcotic property had been in that fungus was deep within his system. And it was strong. Very strong. He was a big man with a high tolerance of alcohol but these truffles had overwhelmed him in less than half an hour. He walked a few more paces, aware that his movement was now effortless. Then he stopped. Was that a helicopter he could hear? He wasn't sure. The noise was very faint. Perhaps it was the blood in his ears?

Despite the rapture, some part of his consciousness still had a grip on reality. He bent over and forced his fingers down his throat. He retched but nothing came up. He tried again but succeeded only in coughing. The noise he had heard earlier sounded further away now. He stared up at the sky but his view was blocked by the canopy. *Had* it been a helicopter? Impossible to know. It was getting harder by the second to tell what was real. Harder to care, too.

Mark felt the tribesman's hand on his arm. The guy's touch was velvet. His guide was talking to him, reassuring him that everything was OK. Mark nodded. He couldn't understand what the man was saying but his words made perfect sense. Damn, but he felt good! It was like being wrapped in a big feather duvet.

The hunter was asking him a question.

'OK,' Mark replied. 'OK. Just don't tell Melanie, all right?' Then he giggled uncontrollably, saliva hanging off his chin like drool on a dog's jowl. It was no good. He couldn't fight it. He was a prisoner of a greater force.

The tribesman grinned and muttered a few more words, his voice cooing like a dove as he cajoled Mark into walking again.

'My man!' Mark said. 'We understand each other perfectly now, right? We are *wontok*, yes? *Wontok*? You, me: *wontok*! That's what I'll call you. It means *friend* in Pidgin. Wontok, like *one talk*: someone who speaks the same language as you. Like us! You get it? We're friends now.'

The hunter smiled and mumbled his reply.

'Excellent!' Mark grinned and took the man's hand, shaking it vigorously. 'And I'm Mark. And we're friends. You and me, Wontok. We're friends, you know that, don't you?'

This time the hunter didn't reply. Instead he turned and pushed his way through the jungle, leading Mark on to wherever it was they were going.

'Hey! Wait for me!' Mark set off in pursuit, laughing hysterically. 'You want to run, Wontok? Hey, I don't mind running. Let's run!' Mark lengthened his stride and immediately threw his arms out for balance. He had grown another metre in the last few seconds. His head was ludicrously distanced from his feet, as though he had been strapped into stilts. His face, meanwhile, was like a lens. It had detached from his head so that information streamed through it like light through a prism. His brain remained several inches behind, processing the images a few seconds later. Wontok had shrunk. He was a pygmy, a Lilliputian scampering through the trees.

Mark strode after him. He stooped to pet him but as he reached down, he noticed something strange about the back of his hand. The skin was moving. He could see every line, every fissure with telescopic clarity. His whole hand seemed to swell in size, shrink and then swell again. Mark stopped, utterly fascinated with what he saw. It was beautiful, mesmerising. It was like looking through an antique kaleidoscope as his skin erupted in fractals.

Wontok was somewhere up ahead again, calling for him to follow. Mark stood rooted to the spot. The air around him was as clear as snowmelt. Everything was magical. Everything was mysterious. He reached out a hand and pulled a leaf towards him. Its veins stood out like a branch of coral as the leaf melted into nothing. Nearby, an army of ants marched along a fallen tree. They were smiling at him. The little fuckers were really smiling!

'Hey, Wontok! Come and check this out!'

Mark felt the hand on his arm again. He was

being ushered away but he didn't want to leave the ants. He wanted to stay there forever. They were so cool. They were so funny. He pulled on his arm, trying to wrench himself free from Wontok's hold. The tribesman smiled and tightened his grip.

Suddenly Mark panicked. For the first time he saw that Wontok's teeth were as sharp as the crocodile's. His incisors were fangs, honed for tearing flesh. Mark knew then that he had been tricked. Wontok was a cannibal. Mark was going to be captured, cooked in a pot and then eaten. As if to confirm it, Wontok smiled, only this time his features twisted and contorted. When they unfurled he was wearing warpaint, his meta-morphosis into a jungle savage complete.

Mark ran forward, peering into the jungle for the means to escape. It was moving. The plants were alive. He cried out when he saw thousands of black faces peering back at him from behind the leaves. Mark knew instantly what was happening. The rest of the tribe was gathering for the feast.

Again he ran. Wontok was in front once more. How the hell had he got *there*? Mark threw himself to the ground. *Melanie!* How could he do this to Melanie? Had they captured her too? He stared accusingly at Wontok, convinced that the man's belly was swollen with food. Then, suddenly, the hallucination passed and Mark experienced another wave of euphoria. It was followed by a moment of clarity. This drug, whatever it was, would be worth a fortune on the streets of London. A hallucinogenic upper that could be grown at home. All you would need were some spores, a greenhouse and a decent mycologist, and you'd be well on your way to your first million.

Shh! Wait! Was that the helicopter again? Mark giggled and hid behind a tree. He hoped not. He didn't want to be found. He wanted to be with Wontok.

Time passed. So did the noise in the distance. Mark was aware that they were walking again, aware, too, that they were now travelling uphill. But despite the increase in the gradient, his movement remained effortless. He was a bird, flying over the ground with no restriction.

At one point the naked body leading him on belonged to Jane Donahue, his ex-girlfriend. Mark experienced the most intense sexual desire as he watched her move. Her hips swayed as she ran. Tiny droplets of sweat trickled down her spine, pooling on the slope of her arse. Her buttocks quivered, teasing him on. Mark hurried to catch her up, desperate for a glimpse of her breasts. He had never felt such lust. His desire, it seemed, was the sole reason for his existence. He wanted her: here, now, in every conceivable way.

He suddenly realised that he was touching himself but when he looked down, the erection in his hand was the crashed helicopter. Mark stared fascinated as the hallucination developed. The dead passenger opened a hatch and clambered out on to the shaft of his penis. And there was the briefcase, still handcuffed to his skeletal wrist. Mark reached down to open it whereupon a hundred tiny Melanies leaped out and ran off into the jungle.

Mark cried out, confused, horrified, elated. More hallucinations came and went. Some were amusing, others terrifying. He had lost all sense of time. What had it been? Five hours? Ten hours? Ten *minutes*? All he knew was that they were still walking. Up hills, over streams, through valleys. Still the truffles fuelled him, the energy they gave him seemingly endless. He did not notice that night was falling, nor that the jungle had begun to thin. He concentrated only on following the bird of paradise with the pink throat, until finally he grew too tired.

He lay down.

The bird flew off into the rainforest.

Mark was happy.

He closed his eyes and slept.

Eleven

Eighteen miles away, Melanie clung to a log and her life. Above her, a full moon bathed the swamp in theatrical light. The river lapped at her ear like a dog demanding attention. She was delirious, close to death. And all she could think about was Mark.

Her brother had saved her from that crocodile. She'd seen it with her own eyes as she'd flown down the river. Legs braced against the current, he'd somehow pulled the creature towards him. Mark had ceased to be Mark at that point: strength twisted his features into a bestial snarl. It had been like watching a wildlife documentary. Or one of those computer-generated special-effects programmes where they made dinosaurs come to life. Two giants, wrestling for supremacy in the land that time forgot.

Who had won? Where was he now? *Oh God!* she cried. *Please, Mark! Please don't be angry with me!* Her chest heaved as she sobbed. The forest had stripped away her outer shell. The river had washed away her bile. Gone was the bravado; gone were the bark and the bite. She was a young girl. Twenty-two, alone, and very, very scared. This, she realised, was the real Melanie. And she couldn't survive on her own. She needed her brother. Her strength.

Melanie felt herself slipping into unconsciousness. Her vision was blurred. Dehydration, exposure and exhaustion had drained her senses of their edge. Her body felt heavy. Her mind was a washout, plagued by the incessant trickle of water. It was like a tap that she couldn't turn off. And it was driving her slowly insane. She tried humming some Good Charlotte to block it out but she couldn't concentrate on the melody and it just sounded rubbish.

Driven to the bank, a hundred metres beyond the confluence of two rivers, Melanie's face was pressed against the reeds. Somewhere, in the fug of her brain, it occurred to her that they might support her weight. And in that instant, it became her sole focus to make a bed. A bed to lie on. A bed to die on. This was her fourth night in the jungle and there wouldn't be a fifth. She knew that very well.

Last night had been the longest of her life. After her separation from Mark, she had stuck to the plan, following the river for as long as she could. Ten minutes beyond a prominent mud-flat, the current had eventually slackened, allowing her to make it to the sides. Terrified of snakes, spiders, crocodiles and scorpions, she'd elected to spend the night up a tree but hadn't slept for fear of falling out.

She had returned to the river in the morning, this time with the support of a log for buoyancy. She had seen crocodiles but none had come closer than twenty feet. Progress had been agonisingly slow, interrupted by frequent breaks to relieve her nausea and diarrhoea.

She had heard the helicopter around midday. Heard it and wept with relief. Then, over the course of the next two hours her relief had turned to despair. The helicopter had remained many miles to her right, searching the area around Hulale. Melanie had stood in the river, waving at the sky. Waving and screaming at nothing more concrete than a distant throb in her ears. Oh, the frustration! The torture. The utter helplessness.

Slowly it had dawned on her that the helicopter wasn't going to come her way. She had cursed the pilot with the basest words she knew, goading him to find her. It hadn't worked. The stupid wanker hadn't been able to hear her. When the sound of the blades had eventually died, she'd feared that the search had been called off for the day, and had returned to the water. Then, perhaps twenty minutes ago, the tributary had widened, eventually spilling into a much bigger river, which she'd guessed to be the Fly.

She'd swallowed plenty of it in these last few

minutes. The waters at the confluence had boiled around her face before settling into a gentle simmer further downstream. Now it was time to get out. The log had made her sore under her arms. Her breasts were tender where the wood had pressed against her flesh.

Melanie closed her eyes, drew a deep breath, pushed the log away. Then she hauled herself out of the river.

Easy! A feat of sheer determination. Nothing but nothing had been going to stop her.

But even as she became aware that she had made it, she knew that it had been the final action of her life. She was breathless. Spent. She had nothing left to give. Game over. Thank you for playing. Better luck next time.

The reeds flattened under her weight. The water rose to make a comfortable mattress for her shivering frame. Melanie lay with her head on its side, staring at a cairn of stones, two metres in front of her face. Something was moving on it. Something black. An ant or a beetle. She tried to focus but her eyes were too full of dirt. She could feel the grit against her eyelids, scratching, itching; demanding tears that she was too dry to cry. The beetle moved towards her and then slid back. It did it again. Forward, back. Forward, flicker, back. Forward, flicker, flicker, flicker, back.

Melanie groaned. *Wasn't that just typical!*

Not a beetle. A tongue.

Not a cairn. A snake.

She scoffed; a half-laugh of desperate resignation. *Oh, well! What can you do?* Melanie had never quite known whether to believe in God but she knew instantly that this was retribution. How could she come to Eden, trespass, and not expect to encounter a snake?

It was an ugly beast. A triangular head with a short, stumpy body. A raised, horn-like scale over each of its orange eyes. Its pupils were vertical and black, staring at her as it tasted her scent with its tongue. Its body was brown. Or grey. Or charcoal. Melanie couldn't tell. Couldn't care. She was all cried out. Ready to go.

The adder moved. Its coils unravelled, its head probed the space between them, tumescent in the twilight.

The strike was coming.

Melanie closed her eyes.

And she knew that she would never open them again.

Twelve

'Aha! Welcome back, big fella! Howzit going? For a while there you had me worried. Thought we was gonna lose ya, mate! We've been trying to feed ya some water but you've been out like a light for the last three hours. Reckon you've been for a walk on the wild side, eh mate?'

Mark blinked again. Was this another hallucination? If so, it was the most real yet. He was lying on his back in some sort of vehicle. He had a slight headache and he was cramped for space. His knees were bent and almost brushing the ceiling. The jeep, or whatever it was, was bouncing around over rough terrain but the seat beneath him was leather and it cushioned the worst of the jolts.

'You was bloody lucky we came along when we did. You can thank Terry for that when you meet 'im. I said we shoulda gone down Karania way, but he said nah, the guys at Dugudugu were more in need of our help. Last time we were here they seemed to be doing OK. Looked like the nets we gave them had been working. Then we get down here at first light and find that eighteen out of twenty-six kids have got it. Eighteen out of twenty-six! Can you believe that, mate? Seventy per cent! It's a shame. It's a crying shame, is what it is. Reckon you'd appreciate that, you being a doctor 'n' all.'

Mark's neck was stiff. He rubbed it, then brought his hand in front of his eyes. His skin was caked in dirt but the flesh was no longer moving. His palm was in focus. It was the right size. This wasn't a dream. It wasn't a hallucination. The effects of the truffles had passed. He felt a wave of relief wash over him, sweeter than anything he'd experienced the day before.

'Can you sit up, Mark? You need to drink something, if you can.'

A woman's voice. English but with the trace of an accent. Spanish or Portuguese perhaps. How did she know his name? How did the other guy know that he was a doctor?

Still groggy, Mark shifted his weight on to his elbows and propped himself up. He was on the back seat of a Land Cruiser. It was light outside. Morning. The night was a total blank; Wontok a distant dream. The last twenty-four hours had passed in a narcotic flash.

'There ya go, mate. Jeez! I bet *you* got a story to tell! Eh?'

'Go easy on him, Steve.'

Mark nodded and smiled at the faces staring

at him from the front seats. Steve, the driver, was in his mid twenties. He had a thick russet beard and a gold stud in his left ear. He wore a baseball cap, the words *Save the Children* embroidered on the peak in heavy black stitching. Underneath it, his eyes were hidden by a pair of Oakley wraps. He was chewing a ball of gum, his lower jaw yawing left and right like a bullock grinding its cud.

The woman to his left was several years older. Early thirties probably. She was naturally olive-skinned but her face and arms had bronzed in the sun. A glossy mane of black hair cascaded from her head, curling behind her ears and billowing on to her shoulders. She held a large digital camera in her lap and Mark guessed that the rectangular object in her breast pocket was a Dictaphone. She looked at ease, as though a Land Cruiser in the middle of a Third World swamp was a familiar environment.

'Where am I?' Mark asked.

'*Now* you're on your way to our field camp just below Tidal Island on the Fly.' Steve adjusted his cap and grinned at his passenger in the rear-view mirror. 'You *were* on the other side of the river, about two miles north of Dugudugu. It was the villagers who found ya. Lying on one of their hunting trails. Christ knows what you were doing there, mate! It's the back of bloody beyond. Hasn't even been mapped properly. Anyway, they took you in, paddled you across the water, and handed you over to us as soon as we arrived. Guess how many of us it took to put you in the car.'

'Five,' Mark said, staring out of the window.

Steve was momentarily silent. 'Yeah. Five. How'd you know that? You were unconscious.'

'I didn't. You asked me to guess.' Mark weighed one hundred and fifteen kilograms: the same as a cast-iron bath. No way would they have got him into the Land Cruiser with fewer than five.

'Bloody lucky this didn't happen twenty years ago,' Steve continued. 'Why? You wanna know why, eh? They woulda eaten ya, mate! A generation ago this lot were all cannibals.'

'Here,' the woman said, passing Mark a bottle of water. 'Drink this.'

Mark thanked her, noticing for the first time that she had a tattoo on her left shoulder. It was of a small brown bird, possibly a lark, flying through the broken bars of a cage. The bird's mouth was open as though in song. It was clearly ecstatic to be free after years of captivity. The tattoo was a skilful piece of work: compact, colourful and unequivocally triumphant. Mark was intrigued, but right now he had more pressing matters to attend to.

He drank greedily, washing his throat, cooling the burning sensation in his chest. He put a hand to his brow. It was clammy with fever. Whatever ailments he had contracted would be made worse by his comedown from the truffles. As he sank back into the seat he caught a glimpse of himself in the mirror. His beard had grown. Above his moustache, his cheeks and forehead were splattered with mud. The scratches from the thorns had dried, the blood clotting into a lattice of tiny scabs. His eyes, meanwhile, had sunk deep into his skull. He stared vacantly at his reflection. He hardly recognised himself.

'How do you know my name?'

'You're a superstar in these parts, mate. You and yer sister have been all over the radio. Whole damn province is looking for ya. We knew who you were straight away. Mark Bridges. Twenty-eight years old. A British doctor, staying at the Katzers' place at Teraruma. Lost since Monday. Same goes for yer sister, only I guess she's not with you. What happened, mate? You get separated?'

'Yes,' Mark replied. 'We got separated. She's still out there.'

Silence followed. Mark stared through the windscreen. The Land Cruiser had a white bonnet. It rose and fell like the bow of a ship as it navigated the bumps in the road. Outside, the track was no more than a muddy scar on the landscape. Mark felt sick. With Melanie still lost it was impossible to enjoy his rescue. Besides, he still didn't know where he was or how far he had walked. The names Tidal Island and Dugudugu meant nothing.

'There was a helicopter,' he said. 'At least I think there was. I never saw it but I heard something in the distance yesterday.'

'The army,' Steve replied. 'Or, rather, the PNG Defence Force as they prefer to call it. The entire fleet was on exercise near Kavieng. Took a few days to free one up and get it down here but it flew most of yesterday. 'Sbeen up again this morning. We saw it a while ago, coming in from Suki way. You'll probably hear it if you wind down the window.'

Mark followed the suggestion. He strained his senses and heard it far away: the *dakka-dakka-dakka* of its blades was just audible over the growl of the Land Cruiser's engine. He sighed. That was good. Very good. But then again, how costly might the delay in scrambling it have been? Forty-eight hours to free up a helicopter? What the hell had they been doing? Rebuilding it from scratch? He shook his head and told himself to be positive. The Katzers had raised the alarm. People were aware that Melanie was still missing. People were looking.

'Listen,' he said. 'I'm really grateful. Thank you. Who are you guys anyway?'

'Steve's the name! I'm with Save the Children, mate. An Aussie if ya hadn't already clocked it. Carmen here's a Pom; same as you. Well, one half of her is, at any rate. Top half, if you ask me. Chilean mother; hence the accent. She's a reporter for a big newspaper in England. Whadizit again, babe?'

'The *Observer*,' Carmen replied. 'And actually, I'm freelance. They are just my client for this particular story. Oh, and Steve?'

'Yeah?'

'Don't call me *babe*!'

Mark winced. There was real fire in Carmen's rebuke. Nothing playful about it at all.

'The *Observer*. Right!' Steve winked at Mark in the mirror. 'She's doing a feature on our work down here. We're running a malaria programme: a joint task force between the Aussies and the Brits. PNG's a member of the Commonwealth, which is why both our countries still do their bit to help out. The programme's called the FRCHP. That's the Fly River Children's Health Project. You know much about malaria, mate?'

'Bits and pieces.' Mark ran his tongue around the inside of his mouth, searching for moisture. He was beginning to wonder if Steve would ever shut up.

'It's a bugger, is what it is. Malaria's endemic to one hundred and six of the world's countries. As far as communicable diseases go, it's second only to tuberculosis in terms of morbidity. It kills over a million children a year, but they reckon it affects up to half a billion people at any one time. What *we* do is work with the local communities, educating them on how to minimise the risk of being infected. We treat them when we can, but a lotta the time we're in the classroom or handing out nets and stuff like that.'

'Steve,' Carmen said. 'Let it go. Mark needs to rest.'

'He's all right! Eh, big fella? Tell you what; we've got another fifty minutes of this so why don't I shut up and you can tell us what happened.'

'Have you got a radio?' Mark asked.

'Yep, and you don't need to worry about it. We buzzed base as soon as we picked you up. They know Melanie's not with ya and they'll be updating the police as we speak.'

'Thanks.'

'Don't mention it, mate. Save the Children. Save the Poms. It's all the same to me!' Steve sniggered and winked in the mirror again.

'Ignore him, Mark. He is from the outback, somewhere near Alice Springs. He has not seen a sheep for three months so he is going slightly mad.'

Mark managed a smile. He wasn't in the mood for jokes but he was pleased to see that Carmen's mood had lightened. She had been preoccupied earlier, as though Steve's crassness hadn't been the only thing to have upset her. In the meantime, Mark knew that Steve wasn't going to let him sleep until he'd told them his tale. And talking was probably preferable to listening. To the Australian at any rate.

Mark began with the assault on his boatman and guide, explaining that Gile had probably been attacked for making a 'special friendship' with one of the Hulale women. He told them about their pursuit into the forest, their flight through the jungle and their discovery of the crashed helicopter. Told them about the brief-case, the rucksack and the gun.

'Jeez!' Steve said. 'What was in the briefcase?'

'I don't know,' Mark replied. 'None of my business.'

'You didn't look?'

'No. I couldn't open it.'

'Couldn't open it? I woulda smashed the bastard thing to smithereens! Whaddya reckon it was? Drugs, if you ask me.'

Mark shrugged. Why had Steve automatically assumed that the briefcase contained something nefarious? Boyish fantasy? Or gut feeling? Either way, Mark was finding it hard to match the Australian's interest in the passenger's luggage. The contents of the briefcase were inconsequential compared to Melanie's whereabouts.

He continued with a heavily abridged account of the last forty-eight hours, claiming that he had simply stumbled on the hunting trail a day after he and Melanie had been separated. He didn't mention the crocodile because he didn't think that they would believe him. He didn't mention Wontok or the truffles either. There were too many reasons not to.

It had been out of his control but Mark was still ashamed to have been tripping while his sister was lost. Ashamed too that he had been incapable of signalling to the circling helicopter. Many of the hallucinations had been sordid or sexual and he didn't want Steve's opinion on *those*. But there was another motive for being economical with the truth. Wontok belonged to a remote and primitive tribe, inhabiting an area that hadn't been properly mapped. He had avoided taking Mark to his own village, preferring instead to hike all the way to the edge of civilisation. Mark had been spirited out of the jungle by a potent dose of local magic. It had been administered by a sorcerer who clearly didn't want to be found. And Mark was happy to leave it that way. Wontok had saved his life. The least he could do was respect the tribesman's desire for privacy.

When he'd finished, Mark made himself comfortable and closed his eyes, signalling that he wanted no further questions. The car was warm and rocked him like a cradle.

He woke up just as they were pulling into the field camp. It was more like a small settlement, perhaps once a trading post for the surrounding villages. There were a number of tents, three or four huts made from bush materials, and one long concrete block, which Mark took to be a hospital. He estimated that there were between thirty and forty people in view, five of whom were Caucasian. The rest were local villagers, predominantly women and children. Many of the kids were naked. Cowed and emaciated, they clung to their mothers' hands or sucked forlornly on shrivelled breasts. Elsewhere, they huddled outside the food tent or on the hospital steps, patiently waiting their turn. An air of dignified acceptance hung in the air. No one seemed to be talking. Just waiting. And hoping.

One look told Mark that most of the people

here had malaria. The severe cases would be inside the hospital but those outside were clearly queuing for beds. He saw one child, a small boy of about five, hobbling away from the camp on a crooked stick. His scalp had been shaved to facilitate the entry of an IV drip and he was picking at the scab beneath a tatty dressing. His awkward gait, wobbly as a newborn foal, hinted at neurological damage: an unfortunate side effect of the intravenous quinine that had saved his life.

Before Mark knew it he was climbing out of the Land Cruiser. The instinct to help was overwhelming. For a moment he forgot all about Melanie. His only concern was to dress the boy's head and return him to his mother.

One of the Caucasians saw him emerge from the vehicle and waved. The man had been standing in a green field tent, talking to someone on a VHF radio. Now he hung up the receiver and made his way over, passing Carmen as she ducked inside the tent. The guy moved easily, perfectly at home in the heat. He was well built, his Save the Children T-shirt tight over his chest and arms. Mark knew instantly that he must be the project leader.

'Don't worry about Samuel! We'll take care of him.'

Mark glanced at the little boy, who had stopped to beat a puddle with his stick. 'He needs a new dressing.'

'He'll get one. I promise you.' The man

smiled. He was English, middle-aged but athletic in build. He wore bifocal glasses and had a bulbous nose, streaked with angry red capillaries. 'You must be Mark?'

'That's right.'

'They said you'd be big but I didn't realise they meant *that* big. How tall *are* you?'

'Six six.'

'Can you see the sea?'

Mark forced a polite smile. It was the same wherever he went.

'I'm Terry Landevelt,' the man said, extending his hand. 'I run the show here. I've just got off the radio with the district police.' He paused, the humour suddenly gone from his face. 'They've got some news.'

Thirteen

Mark's heart leapt. *News*. Did that mean good or bad. He wanted to speak but his tongue wouldn't move. In this instance the bad news could be *really* bad. It could be the worst. An image of Melanie flashed through his mind. She was snared in the mangroves, face down in the river. Brown water sloshed over her half-submerged corpse. Her hair streamed long and straight from her scalp, rippling in the current like a flag in a breeze.

'There's good and bad,' Landevelt said, as if reading his thoughts. 'The bad news is that your sister's still missing. The good news is that your parents were informed yesterday. Your dad's already on his way to PNG. He should arrive in Port Moresby tomorrow.'

Mark swallowed. The bad news had been predictable; but the good news? He hadn't been expecting *that*. He was momentarily disorientated. Mention of his father only reinforced the gravity of the situation. Until now it had been a local problem: *his* problem. Now, suddenly, it was something else. The police and Defence Force were involved. His father, Landevelt and the Katzers were involved. It was as though the situation had escalated to senior management because he had been unable to resolve it himself. Only it wasn't just a *situation* any more. Now that it was in the public domain, it was an emergency, a tragedy-in-the-making. It was a full-blown, no-holds-barred, right royal cock-up.

Mark sighed, exhaling loudly through puffed cheeks. Of course his father was coming. If he had been a parent he would have done the same thing. And it wasn't to take control of the situation like some sort of chief executive; it was to look for his kids. To be there when they were found. If he had left London yesterday he would still be on a plane now, ignorant of the fact that his son had been rescued. The poor man would be beside himself with worry.

'Are you OK?' Landevelt asked.

'Yeah, I'm fine.' Mark clenched his teeth, willing himself to stay strong. Now would be a good time to collapse and let the stress come pouring out. To admit how helpless and alone he felt. But what would that achieve? Exhaustion and self-pity weren't much good to Melanie, were they? 'Just a bit tired,' he said.

'I'm not surprised. Listen, the police mentioned a couple of other things. The Katzers say their guide and boatman are also missing. Do you know anything about them?'

'Yes,' Mark replied. 'They're dead.'

Landevelt raised his eyebrows but said nothing. It was the kind of look that doctors reserve for patients with fight- or drink-related injuries. Not critical, not sympathetic, just demanding of the facts.

'We were attacked.'

'That's right!' Steve had parked the Land Cruiser. He joined them, arms akimbo, shades wedged on the peak of his cap. He had heard a too-tame version of the story earlier. Now his eyes betrayed a thirst for gore. 'Helluva a mess, I reckon. Mark's not saying much but there must 'ave been blood everywhere, eh mate? Four against two, it was.'

'Steve,' Landevelt said with the trace of a scowl, 'Samuel's off on one of his little expeditions. See if you can't fetch him back and get that head cleaned up.'

Steve glanced down the track to where the little boy was still playing in the puddle. 'Sure thing,' he said, before trotting off, his boots squelching in the mud.

'Steve's our resident joker,' Landevelt explained. 'Verbal diarrhoea, but he's got a big heart. The kids love him.'

'I should talk to the police,' Mark said.

'We'll set you up in the office. You're a doctor, aren't you?'

'Just qualified.'

'Well, far be it from me to offer you advice but I think we should probably get some fluids in you. And a shot of chloroquine wouldn't hurt either. Mosquitoes have been making a meal of you, by the looks of it.'

Forty minutes later Mark was sitting at a desk in the main tent, talking to the police over Landevelt's radio. He had eaten two bananas and a bowl of rice. Carmen had brought him a mug of sweet tea and had now settled at a desk to write up some notes for her story. He had washed under a rainwater shower and was now wearing a clean pair of shorts and a fresh T-shirt that he had borrowed from Steve. Neither fitted. The T-shirt had ripped under the arms the moment he had put it on. The shorts, meanwhile, remained undone at the waist and were painfully tight around his crotch. Outside, his own clothes were drying in the sun.

An intravenous drip was pumping a litre of saline solution into his right arm. He'd had two shots in the left: one of chloroquine to combat malaria, the second a course of general antibiotics. Physically, he felt much stronger, his fever already cooled. Mentally he was still saddled with worry for Melanie. His stress was compounded by sporadic bouts of anxiety: a side effect, no doubt, of Wontok's hallucinogen.

Conversation with the police was laborious and unproductive. The duty sergeant in Balimo didn't speak English so everything had to be translated by Landevelt, who spoke passable

Pidgin. Mark gave brief accounts of the murders and his discovery of the crashed helicopter before asking what they were doing to find his sister. The answer was non-committal. The sergeant told him that he and his colleagues were doing everything possible to find Melanie but refused to elaborate on what that entailed. It didn't sound like very much. After fifteen minutes Mark was exasperated.

'Christ!' he said. 'The guy sounds like he's half asleep. Can't they get a second helicopter up or send a boat down the river?'

Landevelt placed the receiver back in its cradle and looked at him sympathetically. 'Mark, you're on the edge of an area known as the Middle Fly District in Western Province. It's twice the size of Wales with a population of perhaps sixty thousand people. Of those, I reckon maybe forty are policemen and *of those*, I imagine thirty are stationed in the townships of Balimo, Bamu and Nomad, none of which is within fifty miles of here. The entire Royal Papua New Guinea Constabulary has only one helicopter that I know of. It's stationed at Port Moresby and it's only recently come back into service after a two-year sabbatical, enforced by lack of funding. Do you see where I'm going with this?'

Mark flinched. 'There must be something they can do.'

'There is, and they've already done it. As soon as the Katzers realised that you were missing they called the police, who put out a mayday on just about every frequency possible. That's how we found out. The villagers at Dugudugu know and they'll spread the word to Karania, Ulaga and Waligi. The Defence Force has done its bit too. That helicopter is your best bet, right now. The Ok Tedi mining company would have sent theirs to assist but it's grounded with a technical fault and they're still waiting for the spare part to be shipped in. Beyond that, there simply aren't any resources for a coordinated search.'

'Then I'm going to have to go back in and find her myself. Maybe the villagers can lend me a canoe. I'll pay them to look for her. It's been nearly two days, for God's sake! If we don't find her soon it'll be too late.'

'I'd agree with you if we knew where to look. Hold still a second!' Landevelt removed the needle from Mark's arm and pressed a cotton gauze over the prick. The bag of saline was now empty. 'But the trouble is, you don't know where you were separated or how far you walked yesterday. Here, I want to show you something.'

Mark followed him to the other side of the tent, where Carmen was doodling in a notebook. She had pulled her hair into a ponytail, which twitched whenever she moved her head. She looked distracted, unable to concentrate on her work. She had been listening to their conversation and now wore the same pained expression that Mark had seen in the Land Cruiser. Behind her, two large maps hung from the roof poles on laminated boards.

'These are the best maps of the region that exist today,' Landevelt explained. 'This one was drawn by the Australian Army in 1964. The one on the right is a language map, produced by SIL International. It shows who speaks what and where. Now then; we're here, near Tidal Island. The Katzers' lodge at Teraruma is about twenty-five miles upstream. Dugudugu, where you were found, is over here to the right. Which suggests to me that the area you got lost in is here. Do you notice anything remarkable about it?'

Mark stared from one map to the next and felt his anxiety increase. 'You're kidding me,' he exclaimed. The two maps were very different in appearance but both depicted the area that Landevelt had been pointing to in much the same way.

White space. No topography, no symbols. Just blank paper.

The army map bore the words RELIEF DATA INCOMPLETE while the language map stated AREA UNINHABITED. Mark felt a nervous tingle down the nape of his neck. When Steve had said that the area hadn't been mapped properly, he didn't realise that it hadn't been mapped *at all*. Area uninhabited? Try telling that to Wontok.

'I reckon there must be a few places left in the world that haven't been commercially mapped,' Landevelt said. 'Parts of Borneo, West Papua, Antarctica, perhaps. Maybe the far reaches of the Gobi, Sahara or Amazon – but I'd be guessing. The satellite images on Google Earth aren't much help either. Obviously we don't have an Internet connection here but I looked at the area before I left England, and I can tell you that it's just one big green block once you get east of the Fly. Anyway, there's no point you storming back into the jungle if you don't know where you're going. We don't want to lose both of you. That helicopter's got enough work as it is.'

'I'm not giving up. I can't just leave her. She's my sister, damn it.' Mark turned. It wasn't fair to vent his frustration on Landevelt. The project leader was only stating the facts.

Desperate for some sort of progress, Mark examined the army map a second time. The area to the left of the white space was characterised by dozens of blue squiggles: a network of waterways, as complex and meandering as the capillaries on his host's nose. He found Teraruma and traced his finger north, up the Fly River. There were several tributaries leading off it. Gile could have paddled them down any one of them. 'Shit!' he said. 'Hulale isn't even marked.'

It was hopeless. Utterly hopeless. Mark felt his anger welling inside him. How could he have been so stupid? They should never have left the area around the Katzers' lodge. It was so unlike him too. The one time in his life when he'd said *sod it* and taken a bit of a risk, and it had back-fired completely.

'So what do you suggest we do?' he asked. 'It's only midday. We've got the whole afternoon to go looking.'

'Mark,' Landevelt took a step forward and put a hand on his shoulder. 'I know this isn't easy – God alone knows what you must be going through – but you're going to have to calm down. *We* aren't going to do anything. This may sound harsh, but I've got a programme to run here. Neither I nor any of my team has got any time to go looking for Melanie. There are lives here that we can save. Your sister's . . .' He didn't need to say any more. It was clear what he was thinking. 'Look, I'm sorry. Really I am. The best you can do is rest by the radio and wait for news. Let the army do what it can.'

Mark folded his arms and began chewing his lip. As a doctor he was familiar with the concept of triage: the process of prioritising patients according to the severity of their conditions. As far as Landevelt was concerned the kids in the hospital were urgent cases: probably Priority 2 on any of the global scales. Melanie, meanwhile, had been classed as expectant or likely to die, irrespective of intervention.

Mark sighed. There wasn't a damn thing he could do. To look for Melanie would be a futile risk of his own life. They had been separated nearly two days ago. If she was going to be found, it would have happened by now. But despite all evidence to the contrary, Mark refused to give up hope. How could he simply write off his sister's life like that? He could hear her indignation if she turned up alive and learned that he'd thought she was dead. *Thanks a lot, bro! What did you take me for? Some sort of loser?*

Mark sniffed. He was a doctor. He believed in biology, chemistry and physics, not the power of positive thought. But right now positive thought was all that he had to offer. For a moment he just stood there, willing her to be alive. Carmen caught his eye and gave him a sympathetic smile, telling him that she understood his pain.

'I am heading home tomorrow,' she said. 'Terry is giving me a lift to Suki in the morning, so we will ask if anyone has heard anything when we get there. You made it out, Mark. Melanie is made of the same stuff.'

'Mel and I are chalk and cheese.'

'Well, if she is chalk and you are cheese then she is harder than you are.'

Maybe, Mark thought. *But more brittle too.* Carmen's quip had been delivered with just enough warmth for him not to bristle. She had already proved herself to be a live wire but on this occasion she was just being optimistic. He liked that. It energised him, made him want to act. Sit by the radio all day and wait for news? When no one was out there looking for his sister? What was he thinking? He'd sooner swim with the crocodiles.

'I'm going back in,' he announced. 'Right now. I'll walk back to Dugudugu and ask the villagers to lend me a canoe.'

Landevelt shook his head. 'Two wrongs don't make a right. You might die out there.'

115

'Well at least it will be with a clear conscience. How would you feel if she was *your* sister? Could you live with the knowledge that you never even tried? Your own flesh and blood? It may not be much, but I'm the only hope she's got.'

Landevelt puffed out his cheeks. Sighed heavily and glanced at his watch. 'I'll get Steve to run you down. But that's the last time, OK? You change your mind, you're walking back. And I won't be wasting any more medicine on you either.'

'Thank you,' Mark replied. 'Listen, I know you're right but I can't leave her out there. I'm sorry. I just can't.'

Landevelt gave him a resigned smile. 'I'll lend you a map.'

They were halfway out of the tent when the call came through. Sergeant Pemba of the Balimo police, his voice deep and slow. 'Hello, Terry. *Yu kam nau. Mipela painim meri, pinis.*' Hello, Terry. Come in, please. We have found the girl.

Fourteen

Mark thought that he was going to be sick as Landevelt translated the message and picked up the receiver. *We have found the girl.* Did that mean alive or dead? He tried to read his host's expression but the project leader had turned his back.

Mark waited.

Landevelt listened.

Then, suddenly, it was all over. The aid worker spun round, grinning over his glasses. He gave Mark a big thumbs up and clapped him on the shoulder. 'She's alive! She's not very well, but she's alive!'

Mark closed his eyes and took three deep breaths. He felt behind him for the arms of the nearest chair and crumpled into it. For a few seconds he sat very still. His anguish had been a tumour in his belly: an ever-present knot since that moment in the river when they had been separated by the crocodile. He felt it loosen, then unravel altogether. He sighed, and the torment left him, expelled on his breath like an exorcised spirit. Melanie was alive. *Alive!* Mark smiled and buried his face in his hands. She was safe and that was all that mattered. It was the greatest feeling in the world.

He stood up. He had tears in his eyes but he was laughing now as his relief washed over him. Landevelt was still talking to Sergeant Pemba but Carmen was on her feet, hurrying towards him. The mood in the tent had been sombre and tense. Now it was light and euphoric. Suddenly Carmen was in front of him, throwing her arms around him. She too had tears in her eyes, the strength of her embrace confirming that she had been deeply moved by the whole incident.

'Thank you,' Mark said, appreciating for the first time how tall she was.

Carmen clapped her hands. 'I knew she would make it.'

Mark laughed with her. Carmen's reaction left no doubt as to which was her dominant half. Chilean passion versus English reserve? No contest.

Behind them, Landevelt hung up the receiver. He took a step forward and shook Mark's hand as though congratulating him on a fantastic achievement.

'I'm thrilled for you, Mark. That's terrific news.'

'What happened? Where is she? Is she OK?

How did she –' Mark had so many questions; he couldn't get the words out fast enough.

'An American film crew found her in the river this morning. It sounds like it was only a few miles north of here.'

'Christ!' Mark exclaimed. 'Had she been in the water all that time?'

Landevelt held his palms up. 'I don't know. All I got was the bare bones of the situation. I'm sure she'll tell you all the details when she sees you.'

'So where is she?'

'Well, it sounds like she's in a pretty poor condition so they've taken her upstream to Teraruma. The Katzers will collect her and give her some treatment back at the lodge.'

'How quickly can you get me there?'

'I can't,' Landevelt said. 'Not without a boat. But I can give you a ride to Suki in the morning when I take Carmen to the airstrip. You should be able to find someone to run you up the river from there.'

Mark was about to protest. Melanie needed him. He couldn't wait another day to see her. But then something occurred to him. He caught his breath and paused. 'Shit!' he said. 'I've just realised something. I can't have been thinking straight before. It's Friday, right?'

'Has been since this morning.'

'Well, Mel and I are supposed to be on that same flight. We've only got another two days before we fly back to England.'

'Me too,' Carmen said, leaning against her desk. 'Through Singapore on Sunday?'

'Yes,' Mark replied before a new concern gave him pause for thought. 'I hope Melanie's going to be well enough to travel.'

'Well, wait a few hours, and I'm sure you can talk to her yourself.' Landevelt waved at one of his colleagues outside the tent, tapping his watch to indicate that he would be there soon. 'In the meantime, Mark, *you've* got no choice but to be on that flight from Suki.'

'What do you mean?'

'Sergeant Pemba had another message for you. The police need a formal statement on the deaths. He's escalated the case to province headquarters in Daru. The Chief Inspector there wants to interview you personally. I forget the guy's name but he speaks good English, so communication shouldn't be an issue.'

Mark nodded. *Fair enough*. Despite the graphic nature of their end, it had been easy to forget that two men had been murdered. A moment ago, all he'd wanted to do was collect Melanie and get back to Port Moresby, where they could meet their father and fly home to England. Now he realised that he should spare a thought for Peri, Gile and *their* families. This little episode wasn't just about the Bridges. Others, less fortunate, were involved. A police interview in Daru would be a frustrating but essential delay.

Mark glanced out of the tent. Now that

Melanie was safe he felt his priorities changing. Wontok had saved his life but the people of Dugudugu had played their part too. Many of the village's women and children were right here. 'OK,' he said. 'Why don't you put me to work? I'm a doctor. Make the most of me while I'm here.'

Landevelt smiled. 'I was hoping you'd offer. I'll take you over to the hospital. Brian can always use an extra pair of hands.'

They left Carmen to her story and made their way to the hospital where Landevelt introduced him to Brian Selby. Dr Selby was another Brit: small, grey and angular but personable enough. They chatted just long enough for Mark to learn that he had been a researcher at the London School of Hygiene & Tropical Medicine before relocating to the Fly River Children's Health Project on its inception last March. He seemed pleased enough with Mark's offer of help but was far too busy to show any interest in his story. Mark was grateful for that. He'd told it twice already and that was enough.

The hospital wasn't really a hospital at all. It was more of a barracks, comprising a dormitory, an office, a storeroom and two plumbed toilets that relied on rainwater for flushing. A diesel-powered generator chuntered in the background, cajoling a few naked light bulbs to shine reluctantly down on the patients. There were no beds. The children lay on blankets, evenly spaced in two quivering rows. Some were comatose, others fidgeted. Many shivered, their limbs trembling with the cold sweats for which malaria was notorious. Their mothers huddled next to them, wide-eyed with despair. Somewhere in the gloom a young girl cried in pain as a million parasites multiplied in her liver.

Mark took it all in, not knowing quite what he felt. It was a harrowing scene, made worse by the overpowering stench of dysentery. It was sad but exhilarating, the enormity of the challenge daunting and inspiring him in equal measure. This was the bleeding edge of primary care: the front line in the battle against one of the planet's biggest killers. Mark wondered whether he had made the right decision with his career. Right now, the thought of becoming a GP in England struck him as a decidedly soft option.

'You can help me with my rounds,' Selby said. 'You start this end, I'll start over there. We're unlucky in that the mosquitoes here carry *Plasmodium falciparum*. That's the most virulent of the malaria parasites and the only one capable of attacking the brain. What you're looking for is signs of seizure or coma. First we grade the kids according to the severity of their illness, and then use that to prioritise treatment. Anyone in severe pain you can give a suppository to, but check on their notes first to see what they've had already. You'll find latex gloves and a mask in the storeroom. Here, I'll show you.'

Mark followed, eager to start work. 'How far off is a vaccine?'

Selby sucked in his breath. 'In my opinion, another ten years at least. There are more than ninety labs around the world trying to develop one and no one's managed it yet. It's one of the holy grails of modern medicine. Malaria's caused by a parasite, you see, not a virus, which makes developing a vaccine infinitely more complicated. The polio virus, for example, consists of exactly eleven genes, whereas *falciparum* has more than five thousand. GlaxoSmithKline has come closest in recent years. They've developed a drug called RTS,S/AS02 in collaboration with the US Army. They've been trialling it in Mozambique.'

'With what results?'

'Mixed. Sixty-five per cent of infants between the ages of ten and eighteen months who were inoculated remained immune over a three-month follow-up period. That's pretty damn good but it's not good enough.'

'So what's the answer?'

Selby shrugged. 'I still think a natural vaccine is more likely than a synthetic one but don't ask me where it's going to come from. Quinine, as I'm sure you know, originally came from the bark of the cinchona tree in Peru, so there'll be other therapies out there. We just haven't discovered them yet.'

They arrived at the storeroom, where they picked up their gloves and masks, then adjourned to the office to collect a clipboard of notes on each patient. Most, Mark noted, were under the age of six.

He spent the next four hours helping Dr Selby and his team of two local nurses. After checking the children's conditions there were injections and suppositories to give. There was water to distribute and there was bedding to change. He treated eye infections, ear infections and infections of the skin. By four o'clock in the afternoon he was exhausted, but most of the work had been done. There wasn't much more he could do until the drugs had played their part. Many of the outpatients had already begun the long walk back to their villages, disappearing barefoot into the bush. Some would hike for three or four hours, their only source of energy a sweet potato from Landevelt's kitchen.

Mark finally spoke to Melanie at half-past five, just as it was getting dark. Like him she had benefited from some sleep, food and basic first aid, and was already well enough to walk unsupported to the Katzers' office, where she'd raised him on the radio.

Their conversation was muted. No whoops of celebration. No verbal backslapping. Just quiet words of comfort and expressions of relief. Melanie was too drained for anything else. They'd come within inches of dying and she was too damn shaken to make light of it. She cried when Mark told her that their father would be in Port Moresby tomorrow.

There would be plenty of time for a full debrief later so they exchanged stories quickly. The snake had given Melanie a wide berth, slithering into the dark in search of smaller prey. She remembered nothing of the night and little of her rescue at dawn the next day. She was barely conscious when she'd been spotted by a film crew shooting a wildlife documentary for the Discovery Channel. The cameraman had hauled her from the water and then motored north in his boat to Teraruma.

Their chat came to an end with Mark explaining that the police had summoned him to Daru, whereupon Melanie insisted that she would be strong enough to join him. Mark wasn't convinced but decided not to argue. If Melanie shared just a fraction of his desire to get home, it would take more than malaria, dysentery and fatigue to hold her back.

Mark hung up and wandered to the mess tent, where the cooks had baked chicken in a mumu, or earth oven, in honour of Carmen's last night in the camp. It was a jolly evening, the expats ribbing their guests for returning to England and a life of comfort. Steve produced a few cans of beer to celebrate the day's extraordinary events. They toasted Melanie before Landevelt fetched his guitar and launched into his best Lynyrd Skynyrd.

Mark bedded down in the office at half-past eight. They had found him a spare roll mat and mosquito net. There was no sleeping bag, but Steve had salvaged a spare blanket from the back of the Land Cruiser. It reeked of diesel but Mark was too tired to care. He stretched and made himself comfortable. He imagined Melanie, tucked up in the lodge, listening to her beloved iPod. A smile tugged the corners of his mouth. They had made it. And tomorrow they were going home.

Somewhere outside a nightjar croaked in the trees. Mark closed his eyes. He would have been asleep in seconds had he not heard the tent flap open.

A visitor.

Sitting up, he peered at the silhouette in the entrance and knew instantly who it was.

Fifteen

'Mark, I'm sorry to disturb you. Do you mind if I come in?' Carmen stood in the doorway to the office, peering into the dark.

'Sure,' he said, thinking that she must have come to collect something from her desk. 'Help yourself.'

Carmen took a step forward. 'Actually, there was something I wanted to talk to you about. I know you are tired so I will make it quick.'

'That sounds intriguing,' Mark said. 'Go ahead.' He rolled on to his side and struck a match, lighting a candle on the floor. It flickered to life, bathing the tent in a soft orange glow. Carmen reached for the nearest chair and dragged it towards him. When it snagged on a cable, she changed her mind and settled cross-legged on the ground.

Mark had been too preoccupied with Melanie's safety to pay her much attention before. Then, over dinner, he'd found himself glancing in her direction. Carmen was tall and full-figured; a touch broad across the shoulders, perhaps, but still comely enough to look elegant in a sleeveless khaki top. She had laughed and sung when Landevelt played his guitar, as upbeat and free as the bird tattoo on her shoulder. Mark recalled the hug that she had given him earlier: a spontaneous embrace that was as innocent as it had been heartfelt. Now she sat opposite him, her expression friendly but businesslike. An attractive woman, entirely at ease in her own skin.

'I'm a journalist,' she began. 'I write features but I have a professional responsibility to look out for good news stories too. What happened to you and Melanie would make excellent copy. With your permission, I would like to write it up.'

Mark raised his eyebrows. He hadn't seen *that* coming. Not in a million years. 'For the *Observer*?'

'Initially, yes. Assuming they are interested.'

He paused. Thought it through. Couldn't see the point. 'Why?' he asked.

'You have had an incredible experience,' Carmen replied. 'You and Melanie were lost for over seventy-two hours in one of the most inhospitable environments on the planet. And you survived. It is newsworthy. Christmas is coming up and everyone loves a happy ending. It need not be very long.'

The candle flickered, casting shadows across

Mark's chest. English may have been her first language but Carmen still spoke with enough of an accent to sound exotic. Her voice had a natural lilting cadence, punctuated with a gentle Tonada beat. It was music to his ears. A song as thrilling as any bird's.

'Why would anyone be interested?' he asked. 'If we'd been missing for months or there was a bit of mystery involved I could understand it. But it's so damn remote here, no one even knows we were gone.'

'Well, that is not strictly true,' Carmen said. 'Anyone with a radio in the Middle Fly District knows. The police in Daru know, which means that the local press will probably find out anyway. And as for there being no mystery, what about the crashed helicopter and the guy with the briefcase?'

'You'd include that?'

'Why not? A helicopter crash is definitely newsworthy even if it did happen a long time ago. From what you told us this morning, no one knows where the wreck is. And it must have belonged to someone once, just as the pilot and passenger must have had families, friends or employers who would like to know where they are. There is a strong human element to all of this. Think about it! The story has got everything: murder, intrigue, survival against all odds.'

'Against all odds?' Mark asked, with a trace of a smile. 'That's a little melodramatic isn't it?'

Carmen's eyes flashed in the half-light. She leaned forward and picked a sliver of wax from the candle. 'I don't know,' she challenged. 'You tell me! I'm not sure how many people could do what you did. I mean, it is not every day that you walk across an area of unmapped rainforest without food or water and live to tell the tale. Besides, if you will excuse me for being frank, I think the story is probably more interesting than you are letting on.'

'Oh?'

'I get the feeling that there is some stuff that you are withholding.'

'Like what?' Mark lay back on his roll mat and laced his fingers behind his head. Carmen was sharp. He was impressed.

'I don't know,' she said, slicing through the wax with her thumbnail. 'One minute you slip while crossing a river and then, thirty-six hours later, it is like *hey presto!* You turn up on a hunting trail and get rescued. You glossed over the middle part of your story like there was stuff you didn't want us to hear.'

Mark saw her looking at him. She was trying to read his expression. Searching for a *tell*. Then her mouth tightened and her eyes narrowed as though she knew what cards he held in his hand.

'Look,' she said, before he could disagree. 'We are talking about a simple headline followed by three hundred words at most.'

Mark propped himself up again, wide awake now. 'What's in it for you?' he asked.

'At twenty-seven pence a word, not much. A pat on the back from my editor. Proof that I can write news as well as features. I am freelance. I live off scraps. The helicopter and the identity of the passengers could lead to a bigger story. It would be mine. Success in the media is all about access. I have access to you and that gives me an advantage if anyone wants to develop the story.'

Mark laughed. 'Access to me? Only because there's no lock on the door. You let yourself in.'

'No,' Carmen countered. 'That is not fair. You invited me in after I had asked. I'm trying to do this the right way, Mark. Asking your permission first.'

'As opposed to writing it anyway without my consent?'

Carmen shrugged. 'We journalists are not always renowned for our scruples.'

There was an uncomfortable silence, broken only by the nightjar celebrating the capture of yet more moths. Mark held his hand above the candle as though warming his palm on the flame. 'What if I said no? Would you write it anyway?'

Carmen flinched. '*Are* you saying no?'

'I'm not sure I want my name splashed all over the papers.'

She scoffed. 'Now who is being melodramatic? Or have you got something to hide? A few skeletons in the cupboard, perhaps?' Carmen rocked back, hugging her knees.

Mark found his eyes drawn to her upper lip: a perfectly stretched 'm' that arched over her mouth like a seagull's wings. 'The only skeletons, I can assure you, are those in the helicopter.'

'Look,' Carmen said, changing tack. 'They might not even go for it, and if they do, it will be buried in the middle of the paper where no one will see it.'

'Which begs a certain question, don't you think?'

'Or it could get syndicated to an Australian paper or to one here in Papua New Guinea, where it is a bit closer to home.'

Mark lay back down and ran a hand over his beard. The candlelight made his tan look darker than it actually was. He still wasn't sure that he wanted the story published but he was, he realised, enjoying the debate.

'I don't get it,' he said. 'I'm just an ordinary bloke from Ealing. Who the hell's going to care that I screwed up on holiday with my sister? The great British public has got more interesting things to worry about.'

'Ordinary people doing extraordinary things is usually a good formula. But listen: it is not important. I just thought I would ask. Sleep well.'

Carmen stood up and dusted her hands on the seat of her shorts. Mark was in no doubt that the conversation was over. She wasn't going to demean herself by asking again. Their tussle was finished. Honours pretty much even. Except her rather abrupt conclusion had left him feeling as though he was being unreasonable. Unnecessarily defensive. She'd shown him the courtesy of asking his permission, and he hadn't even thanked her.

'Your tattoo,' he said, keen now to delay her. 'What is that?'

Carmen stopped in her tracks. She had her back to him and she left it that way. 'A lark.'

'If there's one thing I can't stand, it's people who cage birds. Does it mean anything?'

'It's very personal,' she said, tucking her hair behind her ears. 'Good night, Mark. I am really glad you got your sister back.'

She was halfway out of the tent before he called her back.

'Carmen?'

'Yes?'

'Ask Melanie tomorrow if you can write *her* story. I'm sure she'll agree.'

She paused but didn't turn round. 'Thanks.'

'Sleep well.'

'You too.'

Behind her, Mark blew out the candle and swore at himself in the dark.

Sixteen

'You thought I was dead, didn't you?' Melanie punched Mark on the shoulder and laughed. 'Oh ye of little faith! I knew it! I just knew it! I made a bet with myself as I was floating down that fucking river that you'd assume I wasn't going to make it. That's the only reason I bothered to stay alive. Just to prove you wrong, you big lump!'

'Actually,' Mark replied, 'with you in the water, I was more worried for the crocodiles.'

They were standing outside Daru police station, waiting to be called inside. It was just after ten o'clock in the morning and a stiff breeze was blowing in from the Torres Strait. After the muggy confines of the jungle, the sea air was invigorating: auspicious perhaps for their journey home. A masked lapwing soared above them, wheeling away to harry a flock of lesser sand plovers that had strayed too close to its nest. Mark smiled to himself. Melanie's banter confirmed that their ordeal was now well and truly over.

Earlier that morning, Terry Landevelt had driven Mark and Carmen to the airstrip at Suki, where they'd met Dietmar Katzer and Melanie arriving from the other direction. After an emotional reunion, they'd boarded the plane for the short flight down to Daru. Melanie had brought their rucksacks from the lodge, giving Mark access to a much needed change of clothing. He had managed eighty press-ups and a hundred sit-ups before leaving the camp: a paltry tally by his standards but nonetheless he felt more invigorated than he had all week.

Melanie too was stronger for a good night's sleep but she still looked shattered. Her skin was pallid. She carried large bags under her eyes. Dietmar had administered intravenous chloroquine but she hadn't had the benefit of saline, which had rehydrated her brother. Mark had examined her at Suki. She was running a temperature but was well enough to continue her journey home. Their connecting flight to Port Moresby didn't leave for another four hours, which Mark hoped would be ample time for their debrief with the police. Dietmar would join them for the interview, leaving Carmen to explore the township and work on her article.

Mark was still annoyed with himself for the way he'd handled their meeting last night. First, he'd been unnecessarily guarded about the whole news thing. He wasn't proud to have been lost in such a dangerous place, but that aside he'd had no reason to be defensive about his name appearing in the paper. In the end, he had suggested that Carmen speak to Melanie because he hadn't wanted to back down from his original position. It wasn't in his nature to play games, but his resistance had created a tension between them that he'd found stimulating. Carmen had proved herself professional and polite but she'd also been witty and smart. Mark had enjoyed watching her as she'd pressed her case. But then there had been his gaffe with the tattoo. The lark was clearly symbolic of some event in her past and he knew that he'd touched a nerve with his question. He had apologised, but fourteen hours later he still felt narked.

'She's beautiful, Mark. Tall too. What do you reckon she is? Five ten? Five eleven?'

'Eleven,' Mark replied, conscious now that he had been looking at Carmen while talking to Melanie. She had been chatting to Dietmar, perhaps gleaning a few extra morsels for her story. Now she was twenty yards away, buying a coconut from a street vendor. She was dressed in shorts and walking boots, her black hair scrunched under a Save the Children cap that Terry had given her last night. She wore a sweatband in Rastafarian colours on her left wrist but her shades, Mark noticed, were DKNY. She was wearing earrings but no make-up, and while she protected her camera with religious zeal, she carried her cash loose in her pocket. She was tomboy and sophisticated lady at the same time. Elegant but with just enough grunge to give her an edge. A rare bird, Mark realised. One not easily classified.

'You're lucky,' Melanie said. 'You should've seen the guy who pulled *me* out of the river. Face like a bulldog chewing a wasp! Do you like her?'

'She's certainly interesting.'

'Interesting? As in you'd like to write a paper on her for *The Lancet*?'

'You're right,' Mark replied. 'That was a stupid thing to say. She's very natural; very caring. Incapable of hiding her emotions. She was genuinely moved when you were still missing, and almost as happy as I was when we heard that you'd been found. But I think she's troubled by something.'

'Troubled? You want me to find out what it is?'

Mark shook his head in disbelief. His sister had been married and divorced but at twenty-two she was still very young. 'No, Mel. I don't. Besides, she's the one who wants to interview *you*. Not the other way round.'

'Well she's going to have to wait. This looks like it could be our man.'

Mark turned towards the police station. It was an unremarkable construction with blistered paintwork and a corrugated-iron roof. The ground-floor windows were protected with grilles. A flagpole peeled in the sun. An officer in blue uniform stood in the entrance, waving for them to join him. He leaned threateningly in the doorway, his eyes concealed behind aviator shades. He had the build of a middle-distance runner, his sleek torso ending in a long neck and a thin black face. The badge on his breast pocket said that he was Inspector Kimpeau Kiuke, while the clenched jaw and drooping lips said that he was less than thrilled with the extra work that this visit was going to create. Mark remembered reading that in 2004 Australia had sent two hundred and thirty policemen to Papua New Guinea to help restore law and order. Most had been sent to Port Moresby, Bougainville, Lae, Mount Hagen and to stations along the Highland Highway, where gang violence had escalated out of control. Daru and the south-west had not been without their fair share of problems, but Kiuke was clearly proud to have held on to his job.

Dietmar trotted over and they filed inside, eventually arriving in a small room at the end of a dark hall. Kiuke's office was drab and functional, with few home comforts. The bin was overflowing and the desk swamped with paper-work. A fan rotated on the ceiling, causing the memos on his desk to fidget in the downdraught. The only splash of colour came from a large map of the province, mounted on the rear wall. There was no computer, just a single-line telephone and something that might once have been a fax machine. There weren't enough chairs so Mark elected to stand, leaving Melanie and Dietmar to sit down opposite their host.

Kiuke introduced himself as the senior investigating officer in Western Province. He spoke with a heavy accent, his English measured as he informed Mark and Melanie that their father had been met by a representative from the British High Commission and was waiting for them in Port Moresby. Then he asked Mark for an account of the murders.

It took about an hour to go through it twice. Melanie chipped in occasionally but for once she was content to let her brother do most of the talking. Mark struggled to give descriptions of the four Hulale tribesmen but thought that he would recognise at least two of them if he were to see them again. Kiuke nodded and stroked his chin but took few notes, leaving Mark to wonder whether he had any interest in bringing the culprits to justice. The Inspector's permanent scowl suggested that the whole episode was a major inconvenience.

On Melanie's right, Dietmar Katzer was growing increasingly frustrated. He had lost two members of staff, both of whom had been loyal friends and excellent guides. Peri's eye for birds had been second to none and his widow would struggle without his income. 'What are you going to do about this?' he asked, sceptical of Kiuke's commitment. 'The bereaved relatives aren't at all happy. I'm worried that it might escalate into a clan war.'

Across the desk, Kiuke sighed and made a steeple with his fingers. 'This sort of thing is always complicated, Mr Katzer. I doubt the Hulale even know that the police exist. The last I heard of them, they were only just aware of the outside world. I ordered a patrol there this morning, but I imagine we will have to rely on the clan elders to sort it out among themselves. My men will speak to the elders and try to ensure that the situation does not get out of control.'

'*This sort of thing*?' Melanie asked. 'You make it sound like it happens all the time.'

'It does not. But it is not unheard of. For the most part, the rural population is very friendly. But at the same time, many of the more isolated tribes can still be very territorial. You can bank on several conflicts a year. If it is not over women, it is over pigs or land. Now then, Sergeant Pemba also mentioned a crashed helicopter?'

'Yes,' Mark replied. 'About four or five miles from Hulale. I'm not sure in which direction. Probably east.'

'Show me!' Kiuke stood up and thrust his hands into his pockets. He turned to look at the map behind his desk. Mark joined him, while Melanie excused herself to find a drink of water. The map was the same Australian Army edition that Terry Landevelt had shown him yesterday. The helicopter was most likely somewhere in the white area, where the relief data were incomplete.

'You see,' Kiuke said, clearly unimpressed with Mark's lack of precision, 'commercial helicopters are a rare thing in PNG. There are a couple of charter companies in Moresby and the Ok Tedi mining company uses them, but if you exclude the military there are probably no more than seven or eight in the entire country. And no one has reported one missing at any time in the last two years. We have checked. We can account for them all.'

'So where did it come from?' Dietmar asked.

'Australia possibly. We are checking with their civil aviation authority now. The alternative is that it came across the border from West Papua, in which case it might have been smuggling contraband. The border with Papua is very – how do you say? Leaky?'

'Porous,' Mark corrected.

'Yes. Porous. A good word, I think. There is a lot of smuggling in both directions. Sometimes people. Sometimes drugs. Sometimes weapons, timber, exotic animals or birds.'

'Birds?' Mark asked.

Kiuke nodded. 'You like birds, do you not? The blue-eyed cockatoo is particularly popular. It can mimic almost any sound. In Europe and America people might pay $2,500 for such a bird. Even a black-capped lory is worth $500. It is the same with rainforests all over the world. In Brazil, I am told, they have a bird worth $12,000.'

Mark whistled under his breath. Probably a hyacinth macaw, the largest of all flying parrots and a must-have for any black-market collector.

He shook his head. His instincts had been correct all along. There had been something suspicious about that helicopter from the moment he'd seen it. You couldn't smuggle a bird in a briefcase but you could certainly smuggle its eggs. And if you handcuffed the case to your wrist, you would minimise the risk of dropping it, thereby safeguarding the contents.

Mark made room for Melanie as she re-entered the office with a bottle of water. Kiuke had sat back down at his desk. 'We need to discover if anybody saw this helicopter. It may have refuelled or taken off from an airstrip somewhere in PNG before making its return flight. I am going to need a better description than the one you gave Sergeant Pemba if we are to . . . What is the phrase? *Jot* people's memories?'

'Jog,' Mark corrected. 'Or jolt. I suppose I could look at some pictures and try to identify it that way.' He was about to ask if Kiuke had an Internet connection but realised that he would be wasting his breath.

'Yes!' Kiuke exclaimed. 'Some pictures. We think the same way, Dr Bridges. Here, have a look at these. They were faxed to me this morning by our headquarters in Moresby. I understand that these are some of the most popular types of commercial helicopter. Take your time. Try to be accurate.'

Mark took the pieces of paper, glancing doubtfully at the fax machine on Kiuke's desk. Clearly there was another one somewhere in the building. There were five pages in total, each one bearing six photographs of helicopters from a range of manufacturers. Mark sifted through the pages, then squatted next to Melanie so that she could see too.

Some of the names were vaguely familiar: Robinson, Sikorsky, Bell, MD, AgustaWestland. The quality of the pictures was poor but even so it didn't take Mark long to narrow his search. The Sikorsky and Agusta models were too big, while the Robinsons were too small. That left the MD and Bell models.

Mark looked again. The MD helicopters were characterised by round noses, and some lacked tail rotors. The nose cones on the Bell models meanwhile were semi-elliptical like a finch's beak. Mark placed the other pages on the desk and focused his attention on the Bells. Another ten seconds confirmed it.

'That's the one.'

'A Bell JetRanger?' Kiuke asked, peering at the fax. 'You are sure?'

'Positive. Two windows behind the flight deck and a bench seat for three passengers in the cabin. What do you think, Mel?' Mark passed the page to his sister, who was taking a sip of water.

'Close enough,' she agreed.

'Good,' Kiuke announced, taking back the fax. 'That is excellent progress. Better than I had hoped for. We will begin making our enquiries immediately. In the meantime, you and your sister are free to go.'

'Free to go?' Mark asked, surprised at the abrupt end to the interview.

'You heard the man,' Melanie said, leaping to her feet. 'What's not to understand?'

Mark hesitated. So far there had been no mention of the thing that he dreaded most. He didn't want to, but he knew that he had to ask a question that could significantly delay their journey home. Melanie wouldn't thank him for putting ideas into the Inspector's head but if they were going to be dealt a blow, much better to suffer it now before their excitement grew too great.

'When you say free to go,' he asked, 'do you mean we're free to leave PNG?'

Kiuke stood up behind his desk and placed his hands on his hips. His expression was still without warmth or humour. 'Of course. Unless there is something else you would like to tell me?'

Mark shook his head. 'I was just wondering if you might need us to identify the Hulale warriors. You'll need witnesses, if there's a trial.'

'*Free to go*, Mark. That's what he said. And I think now might be a good time, don't you?' Melanie nodded a goodbye to the policeman and pushed back her chair. 'I'll see you outside.'

Kiuke waited for her to go before giving his reply. Dietmar had stayed behind, clearly interested in the answer. 'If those tribesmen have any sense, Dr Bridges, they will disappear into the bush for six months. The chances of there being any arrests, let alone a trial, are virtually non-existent. If we can find the perpetrators, then we will put pressure on the clan elders to ensure that the victims' families are compensated with the appropriate number of pigs. That is how we do things over here. Do you find that . . .' He paused, while he found the word he wanted. 'Backward?'

It was a challenge, a trap that Mark had no intention of falling into. 'No,' he said, wondering how many pigs he and Melanie would have been worth if they'd been the ones who had been killed. 'I think it sounds very . . .' It was his turn to pause. 'Practical.'

'Goodbye, Dr Bridges.'

'Goodbye, Inspector.'

Seventeen

'He didn't tell you about the crocodile?' Melanie folded her arms and stared incredulously at Carmen.

'No, he didn't. But I'm not surprised. I am getting the impression that your brother is a very private man.'

'That's typical,' Melanie said, playing with the seat-table in front of her knees. 'Typical! He's so modest, it makes me sick! I bet he didn't tell you about the rugby either?'

'What rugby?'

'My point exactly. He played for one of the top London clubs when he was a teenager then gave it up to study. Can you believe that? If he'd shown a bit more aggression he might even have played for England – but all that became irrelevant when he decided he'd rather be a doctor.'

Carmen turned and peered over the headrest. They were flying with Airlines PNG on a Dash 8, about fifty minutes west of Port Moresby. Mark was dozing at the back of the cabin. The crew had given him one of the flight attendant's seats by the emergency exit: the only one with sufficient legroom. Carmen smiled. With Mark on board, it was a wonder that the plane had got off the ground at all.

'To be honest,' she said, 'the rugby never came up. We did not have a chance to chat very much.'

'I'm not kidding,' Melanie continued. 'He had to change schools and everything. He was at Northolt High, but they played football there and the PE teacher said he should try rugby because he was so big for his age. He was doing really well in class so they put him up for a scholarship to some posh place in Bedford where everyone was called Jeremy or Nigel.'

'My brother is called Nigel.'

Melanie froze. Then she put a hand over her mouth to muffle her giggle. 'Shit! I'm really sorry!'

Carmen rolled her eyes. 'Only kidding. I haven't got a brother.'

'Phew!' This time Melanie laughed. 'Anyway, he had loads of skill to go with his size and of course no one ever wanted to tackle him. Before we knew it, he was captain of the school team.' She stopped and glanced out of the window as though something had given her pause for thought. The sun was setting behind them, casting its rays over the Gulf of Papua so that the water glowed like molten lead. 'The trouble was, I don't think he was very happy there. All his mates were still at Northolt High. I think he thought that the change of school was a mistake, even though he ended up with a better education.'

Carmen glanced at her watch. At any other time she would have been happy to hear as much about Mark as Melanie could tell her. But their father was waiting in Port Moresby and this was her last opportunity to hear Melanie's story if her copy was to reach London in time for Sunday's paper. 'You were telling me about the crocodile?'

'Oh yeah!' Melanie said. 'Fucking huge, it was! It must have been lurking under the surface because suddenly there's this big explosion of water and the bloody thing's lunging at Mark, trying to take his head off. The next thing I know, I'm whizzing down the river like a demented Poohstick and Mark's dragging the crocodile out of the water. Nice tattoo, by the way. I'm thinking of getting one done when we get home.'

'Really?'

'Yeah. A surfer being attacked by a shark. Somewhere easily visible like the back of my hand. Every time I saw it, I could pretend it was Zak, and then I'd get this lovely warm feeling inside.'

'Zak? Who's Zak?'

'Zak – or "That idiot Zak", as we now prefer to call him – is my ex-husband. Surf bum, drug addict and professional sleaze. My biggest mistake.'

'You're divorced?'

'Yep. All done and dusted within six months. We'd been married for three weeks when I found him off his face on pills, and in bed with some bimbo from Newquay. *Our* bed, if you can believe it.'

'Ouch!' Carmen said. 'That's pretty low. But I would forget the tattoo if I were you.'

'You would?'

'Much better to be magnanimous towards your enemies. It is a sure-fire way of pissing them off.'

Melanie put her head back and roared with laughter. '*Magnanimous*? Ohmigod! That's such a Mark thing to say!'

Carmen felt her head turn towards the back of the plane but caught herself at the last moment. She knew that it was wrong to stare. Knew that *everybody* stared. But, bloody hell, it was hard not to when confronted with such a formidable man. Last night had been particularly difficult. At first she had found him rather cold, haughty almost. But then, as their conversation had developed, he had relaxed, gained a little confidence perhaps. At one point he had stretched out, bare-chested, with his hands laced behind his head. As though there was nothing unusual about a woman visiting his tent at bedtime. Nothing to be feared. Nothing to be gained. He had just lain there breathing like a bull in a pen, not an ounce of fat on his massive frame. And his arms! *Chuta!* As thick as her thighs!

'So?' she asked, suddenly aware that Melanie was waiting for her next question. 'What happened after the crocodile?'

They chatted for the rest of the flight. Or rather Melanie talked while Carmen battled to keep her in check with a series of polite yet firm questions. Melanie was an entertaining story-teller, her spontaneity and eye for detail reassuring Carmen that she couldn't be making it up. But by the time they arrived in Port Moresby, Carmen was exhausted. She had taken several pages of notes and was ready for some peace and quiet.

She hung back in the arrivals hall while Mark and Melanie greeted their father. Although she felt slightly awkward, she was unreservedly thrilled for them as they clung together in a tight three. When the hugging eventually stopped Mark beckoned her over and introduced her to his dad. Tony Bridges wasn't as tall as his son but still stood head and shoulders above every-one else in the airport. He was wearing shorts and a T-shirt, his white skin reminding her that it was winter back home. He had a handsome face, with strong features and a head of thick black hair. Carmen guessed that he was in his early sixties. The guy had aged well.

They said goodbye a few minutes later. Tony had invited her to join them for dinner but Carmen had declined, knowing that she was running out of time to submit her story. Besides, they would have nearly twenty-four hours together on their journey back to London tomorrow.

She took the courtesy bus to her hotel, where she checked in and retrieved her laptop from the concierge's safe. She hadn't taken it to the bush because she had only one battery and there would have been nowhere to charge it. Working with pen and paper demanded greater editorial rigour and had allowed her to travel unimpeded through the villages of the Middle Fly.

Back in her room, Carmen showered, closed the blinds, and then sat naked at the desk, revelling in the privacy of her own space after nine days in a jungle camp. Her feature on the Fly River Children's Health Project wasn't due for another week, which meant that she could focus her attention on Mark and Melanie's rescue. She felt a blush rise in her cheeks as she remembered some of the things she had told Mark last night. 'A professional responsibility to look out for good news stories.' Aiee! How pompous was that! It was a lie too. Being self-employed, her only responsibility was to herself, although she was actively seeking to change that. And what was it he had said about her asking his permission to write the story? 'As opposed to writing it anyway'? Carmen allowed herself a guilty smile. She had started making notes as soon as they had returned from Dugudugu.

Like many women her age, Carmen had

grown up wanting to be the next Kate Adie. Her own report on Save the Children's malaria programme was undoubtedly one of her better assignments: a story that was moving, inspirational *and* important. But when it was written she would be out of contract again, uncertain where the next commission was coming from. If she could find a staff job, she would have work every day. No more wondering what to do while she waited for responses to her latest pitch. She craved the cut and thrust of high-profile journalism. Two tourists getting lost in the jungle wasn't exactly the siege of the Iranian Embassy, but it might be a step in the right direction. Especially if she could learn more about the helicopter and its crew.

She flicked through her notepad. It was a chaotic miscellany of doodles, underlined words and half-completed paragraphs, a semantic scrapheap from which she would reconstruct her ideas. The trick was how to condense so much information into so few words. Concentrate on the facts: that was the answer. She could showcase her writing skills with next week's feature; right now her job was to answer six basic questions. Who? What? Why? Where? When? How?

She wrote the story in full length the first time, aware that a staff journalist would never have such luxury. Then she began cutting out the adverbs and adjectives, clipping away like a gardener pruning a wayward hedge. Sentences and finally whole paragraphs disappeared as she sought to bring it under control. The briefcase was among the casualties. Carmen had initially liked the suggestion of a mystery but ultimately she found it a distraction. Her story was about Mark and Melanie's survival, not the passenger's luggage. Mentioning the briefcase raised more questions than she could answer, and it was her job to deal in fact before conjecture. She highlighted the relevant paragraph and deleted it with a firm tap on her keyboard. The contents of the case, she told herself, had probably been nothing more sinister than everyday commercial documents.

It was a little over two hours before Carmen was finally happy with her work. The piece was still on the long side but, hey, that was what editors were for. She copied the document to her memory stick, dressed and hurried to the hotel's business centre, where she found a PC with broadband access to the Internet.

Carmen's story was three hundred and twelve words long: roughly equivalent to seven column inches of news or one page of a mass-market paperback. With London ten hours behind Port Moresby, it landed in her feature editor's inbox at 11.43 a.m. on Saturday 12 December. Simon Copenhagen read it once, acknowledged that the girl had the talent to go with her looks and sent it on its way, as per her request.

Forty-five seconds later it was picked up by Jez

Blackie, a subeditor on the news desk. Blackie read it twice, then rocked back in his chair while he scratched his stubble. The story was good. Very good. A double murder, a dodgy chopper with a couple of stiffs, a crocodile, and a happy ending. What more could you want? It took him eight minutes to edit Carmen's work down to two hundred and fifty words, whereupon he immediately emailed it to his boss.

Carolyn Greenspan, News Editor, liked it too. She chewed her biro while she pondered her headline, eventually settling on BRITISH BIRDWATCHERS FOUND AFTER JUNGLE HORROR. It wasn't great. A bit tabloid certainly. But the make-up editor on the copy desk was going to need as much time as she could give him to ensure that it received a prominent position on the page. Greenspan had been in the game too long to start tinkering with it. A good headline now was better than a perfect one in an hour's time. Things were going crazy after the publication of a cabinet minister's memoirs and she had bigger fish to fry. She forwarded the story a few minutes later, copying her email to the editor of Guardian and Observer News Services. The paper's syndication business would subsequently offer the story to a plethora of newspapers, magazines and online publications all over the world.

The article was duly set and the proofs checked. Later that evening the finished newspaper was uploaded to the print centres in east

London and Trafford Park, where three Rowland ColorMAN printers, comprising ten towers and two folders each, rattled off four hundred and thirty thousand copies in a little over five hours. The discovery of a crashed helicopter in a remote corner of Papua New Guinea was about to be made public.

Carmen's article would appear, unattributed, on page eight in the news section. And, as with all articles, some readers would be more interested than others. On Sunday 13 December, the *Observer* would be read, perused or glanced at by almost one and a half million people, two of whom would know what the others could not. That onboard the helicopter there was a black briefcase. And inside that briefcase there was something that could change the world forever.

PART II

PART II

Eighteen

He was sixty-four but he moved through the crowd with the ease of a college athlete. He wore a dark suit, white shirt and the blue oriole-print tie that his sister had given him for his birthday. A cellphone headset was hooked over his left ear. In his pocket, his right hand clasped the handset, his thumb poised to press any one of three speed-dial numbers that would connect him to his colleagues outside. He had arrived seventeen minutes earlier, on flight AA106 from Baltimore. Neatly groomed, with a black overnight case, he looked as purposeful as any of the thirty-seven other passengers who had stepped from the Boeing's business-class cabin.

He had slept for four of the flight's seven hours and that was plenty. This wasn't a dangerous job but it was certainly the most financially precious that he'd ever undertaken. With several billion dollars at stake and only one day in which to formulate a plan, he wasn't surprised to feel a trickle of adrenalin in his veins. Life in the private sector was comfortable, but he'd missed the cut and thrust of fieldwork.

The call had come through yesterday at 4.30 a.m. His boss had received a tip-off from an associate in England, and suddenly a project that had been dead for more than a year was once more very much alive. There could be little doubt that the helicopter was theirs. The newspaper article hadn't mentioned a specific location for the crash, but it had twice referred to the right part of the country. Now it was his job to find it, and to retrieve the briefcase that he knew was onboard. To do that, he was going to need some information from the only two people who knew where it was. And, if his research was correct, they weren't very far away.

He checked his watch as he passed through immigration. The flight from Singapore had arrived half an hour earlier and the information boards told him that its baggage was already in the hall. It was tempting, but he knew better than to rush. Speed attracted attention. It was one of the first things he'd learned about surveillance as a young CIA operative in Vietnam. Besides, if he missed them, Fletch would pick them up in arrivals.

He placed his case on the step below as he rode the escalator to the baggage hall. It was a little under a year since his last visit to England, and Heathrow hadn't changed much. He'd always thought that this airport was a disappointment, considering it was the world's second busiest. At 6.42 a.m., Terminal 3 looked as tired and dishevelled as its passengers. The floors were scuffed, the windows grimy and the carts poorly parked. But at least the security was tight. He spotted two officers from Special Branch posing as businessmen as they mingled with a group of passengers recently arrived from Riyadh.

The man stopped a few yards beyond the escalator. A quick check of the boards told him that luggage from flight SQ322 had arrived on carousel 6. The flight from Riyadh had been allocated to carousel 5, so he tucked in behind the cops and sauntered over, his eyes scanning the hall for his mark.

A mark called Mark. That was a first. Hard to believe that it hadn't happened before. The American's eyes narrowed as he racked his brains. No, he was sure of it. There had been a Marcus, a Marco, even a Greek hooker called Markita. But never a plain old Mark. Not that there was anything plain about this one. If the article in the *Observer* was anything to go by, then Bridges was bigger and more resilient than anyone he'd tailed in a long time.

The American was approaching carousel 5, when he saw them. There had been no photograph in the paper but he didn't need one to recognise his targets. Mark Bridges was over six and a half feet tall. He was dressed in jeans and a black V-neck sweater, and was pushing a cart towards the green customs channel. His father walked a yard to the right, one hand stabilising their rucksacks so that the straps stayed clear of the wheels. They were followed a few steps behind by Melanie, ostensibly tired after her journey from the other side of the world. She was turned, half towards him, waving a final goodbye to someone still at the carousel.

The American looked to his right and saw a young woman waiting for her luggage. She too was tall: five ten or eleven, perhaps. And what was she? Spanish? Mexican? He was confident that he didn't need to know who she was but he committed her face to memory all the same. Her features were beautiful in a sad kind of way, and her figure would have shamed most cheer-leaders. OK, she was kinda broad across the shoulders, but her curves kept her soft and feminine. A holiday romance? If so, Bridges was one lucky sonofabitch.

The American kept walking, tracking his quarry through the airport. He wasn't worried about being made. The marks were civilians who didn't even know he existed. Impossible for them to realise that they were being tailed. He caught up with them in the customs hall a few moments later. Several passengers were being searched, and a short line had formed while people waited to get through. The man now found himself standing directly behind Bridges. At six feet two, the American was no short-ass himself but the young doctor still had at least four inches on him. Outside, Fletch was of a similar build: slightly shorter and more barrel-chested, but equally imposing. What would it be like, he wondered, to see those two giants trading blows?

The man turned his head to look at a dog handler in the middle of the room. Not because he was interested but because Bridges had just glanced in the security mirror, encased in the wall on their left. It was a brief look: just enough to tell the customs officers behind it that he knew that they were there. Enough, too, to get a clear look at the American's face, had he not turned away. Then, suddenly, they were moving again, the sliding doors parting to reveal a packed arrivals hall.

The man kept his head down, watching out of the corner of his eye as Melanie ran to meet her mother. He passed them without breaking stride, jinking through the crowd of minicab drivers until he spotted Fletch, waiting for him next to an ATM.

'Welcome to London.'

'Thanks, Fletch. We all set?'

'Car's outside. The mother's driving a blue Renault. License plate DG52 TXJ. Level C in the short-stay car park. It'll take them ten minutes to get out. We'll pick them up as they come through the barrier.'

'You got the money?'

'In the car.'

'And the kid's apartment?'

'Still working on it.'

'You couldn't do it yesterday?'

Fletch shook his head. 'Sunday. Neighbours were in all day.'

The American grimaced. Not a lot anyone could do about that. So no point in getting pissed at Fletch. The Londoner was one of his best associates, and if it hadn't been possible, well, it hadn't been possible. Besides, it was hard not to like the guy. Fletch was as good with a rifle as he was with his fists, but he knew how to control his aggression. Seven years with the Special Boat Service had taught him how to kill but it had also taught him how to be discerning. Violence was reserved for those who'd earned it. The American smiled. *Goddamn English. Too chivalrous for their own good, sometimes.*

Fifteen minutes later they were on the M4, heading towards central London. Fletch drove a silver Ford Mondeo, keeping a steady fifty miles per hour as he followed the Bridges in their blue Renault. Anita, the mother, was driving. Mark rode shotgun, leaving Melanie and her father to squeeze in behind.

They reached Chiswick, where the Renault swung left on to the North Circular.

'How much longer?' the American asked.

'In this traffic? Could be another half-hour. You want me to call the boys?'

'No,' the man replied. 'Not yet.' Half an hour was plenty.

He stared out of the window. Rush hour in the suburbs: as far removed from the jungles of

164

Papua New Guinea as it was possible to be. There was a subway station opposite. Hanger Lane. He thought he recognised the name. *Hanger Lane gyratory*. That was it. A bottleneck that featured in just about every traffic bulletin he'd ever heard in England. It was beginning to cloy now too. Seven twenty-five on a Monday morning and west London was on its way to work.

The blue Renault was three cars ahead and they lost it briefly when the van in front stalled at an amber light. Fletch had to drive fast to find it again, using all three lanes as he picked a path through the traffic.

Ten minutes later, a left turn into Willesden was followed by a slow climb up the high street. Mark Bridges lived on Exeter Road, half a mile further east, but he wasn't going home just yet. The man watched as the blue Renault parked in a side street. The family clambered out, stretched and then crossed the road to a restaurant next to Willesden Green station. It was called Shish: some sort of chain outlet, pretending to be an authentic ethnic joint.

'Breakfast,' Fletch said. 'That's a good idea.'

'You want something, I'll keep an eye out while you're gone.'

Fletch parked the Mondeo outside a parade of shops where they could see both the restaurant and the blue Renault. Then he hauled himself out of the driver's seat and went to buy coffee from a café further up the road. The American

165

stayed behind and began reading the newspaper that his associate had left on the dash.

The meal lasted forty minutes. The boy and his father ate eggs Benedict, while the mother settled for a pastry. The girl, Melanie, was evidently struggling with jet lag. She'd ordered some sort of rice dish but was pushing it around her plate as though she'd rather annoy it than eat it. They looked like any normal family: animated but not raucous; urbane but working-class enough for breakfast in a decent restaurant to still be quite a treat. The father settled the check in cash, and suddenly they were on their feet, heading back to their car.

The American never looked up from his newspaper as the family passed. He waited until they had left the building, then pressed two buttons on his phone in quick succession, while Fletch started the motor.

'Hello?'

'Are you out?'

'Almost.'

'What took you so long?'

'Neighbours,' came the reply. 'Had to wait for them to go to work.'

The American's voice was calm and steady. 'I'd say you've got three minutes. They're on their way.'

Nineteen

'It's our lucky day,' Mark said as his mother released the handbrake and signalled that she was about to park. Two workmen in grey overalls had just climbed into an unmarked white van and were vacating the space directly opposite his flat. That was twice in a row that they'd found a good place to park. With an easy run home and a large breakfast, the week could hardly have started much better.

His parents didn't stay long. His father had spent three of the last five days travelling and was keen to get home. They made arrangements for supper later in the week and said goodbye on the doorstep. Once inside, Mark put the heating on and sifted through his post while Melanie ran a bath. They unpacked their rucksacks and made two piles of dirty laundry on the kitchen floor. Mark put away his passport, checked his emails and then announced that he was going for a run in Gladstone Park. Melanie called out from the bathroom to say that she wouldn't be joining him. She felt like shit and she was going straight to bed. Mark didn't dissuade her. There was no point her trying to beat her jet lag by staying up all day. She needed all the rest she could get. She worked in a clothes shop on Carnaby Street and was due back on Wednesday; but Mark reckoned she would need most of the week to recover.

He changed, grabbed his keys and stepped out into the street. Gladstone Park was just under a mile away. There and back with two circuits of the park itself made a four-mile run: not a huge distance but perfect for stretching his legs after nearly twenty-four hours on a plane.

Mark set off slowly, letting his muscles warm up. It was a grey December morning, and the commuters buried their faces in their scarves as they walked. The white van that had been parked outside the flat was now in a bay at the end of the street. Inside, its two occupants were enjoying a flask of coffee, listening to music on headphones.

Mark inhaled the crisp air and watched his breath fog as he blew it out again. The plane's in-flight information system had told him that the temperature in London was 4°C. That was thirty degrees cooler than it had been at Teraruma. A stiff wind was blowing from the north and Mark found it invigorating. The holiday hadn't worked out quite how he'd planned but their safe return was reason enough to be cheerful. He had fulfilled his dream of seeing wild birds of paradise and he had spent precious time with his sister.

He had a post at a small surgery on the Finchley Road, where he would start work after Christmas. All in all, it was good to be home.

By the time he reached the park he was breathing hard. Sandwiched between Dollis Hill and Neasden, Gladstone Park wasn't one of London's most salubrious open spaces, but it had an attractive central avenue, boasting fine views across the suburbs to the national stadium at Wembley. Mark looked across the grass and saw seagulls, sparrows and rooks, all apparently busy with the start of the new week. A thrush teased a worm from a flowerbed and a blackbird trilled its alarm call as Mark thundered past. They were drab in comparison to their cousins from the southern hemisphere but no less mercurial. No less free. He didn't know if birds could experience exhilaration, but the gulls appeared more energised than usual as they carved parabolic shapes in the wind.

Mark's first circuit took approximately eight minutes, his massive bulk compensated for by a lengthy stride. He had the park to himself, except for a few dog walkers and a man sitting on a log who was almost as big as he was. Mark put him at six five and maybe twenty stone, none of which was fat. He wore black jeans, heavy boots and a brown leather jacket with the collar turned up. His arms were folded across his chest like a bouncer on a nightclub door. He gave Mark a polite smile as he ran past, a silent greeting to a kindred soul.

Mark pushed harder on the second lap, leaning into the wind as he powered up the hill. When he got home he would shower and then pop to the newsagent to see if they had any copies of yesterday's *Observer*. Carmen had received a phone call confirming that the piece had been accepted and despite his previous protestations, he was keen to see what she had written.

'Dr Bridges?'

Mark braked and almost tumbled as he turned to find the voice. A man sat on a bench, a few metres to his right. Mark had been in a world of his own. He hadn't even noticed that the guy was there.

'Dr Bridges? You mind if I have a word, sir?'

Mark stopped and put his hands on his head as he heaved more air into his lungs. The speaker had an American accent. He was smartly dressed in a winter coat and charcoal suit. His hair was short but thick, greying slightly around the temples. His face was expressionless, as though he was neither pleased nor inconvenienced to be there. He stood up in one effortless motion, not too fast, not too slow. He was compact, precise. Measured. As he drew closer, Mark noticed that his complexion was heavily pockmarked. The mobile headset hooked over his ear suggested that he was now in business, but the hollows in his skin told Mark that he'd probably done something else before. The man looked vaguely familiar but Mark couldn't quite place him.

'Ronald Ross,' the American said, offering his hand. 'I'm with the US Department of State.'

Mark shook the guy's hand but was too surprised to say anything. Ross passed him an ID card, which Mark examined briefly. It looked authentic enough. Well worn too. The photograph had been taken at least ten years ago, when the American's face had been less creased around the eyes.

'I'm sorry to intrude on your run,' Ross said, taking back his ID. 'I hope I haven't alarmed you?'

Mark shook his head. 'Why would you alarm me?'

The American shrugged as though a full answer wasn't necessary. 'I was just pulling into Exeter Road when you left your apartment. I couldn't catch you in the traffic but figured you were making for the park. That's a terrific pace you're going.'

Mark hadn't been running fast. Just steady. But he acknowledged the compliment with a nod, unsure what else to say. The US State Department in Gladstone Park. What the hell was this all about?

'I'll get to the point,' Ross said. 'You're a busy man, and so am I. This won't take long.'

Mark watched as the American's hand disappeared inside his suit pocket. The movement forced the lapels of his coat open, giving Mark a glimpse of his tie. Suddenly he knew where he had seen the man before.

'The police in Papua New Guinea have brought it to our attention that you discovered a crashed helicopter,' Ross said, as he pulled a map from his pocket. 'As I understand it, there are two bodies on board. Is that correct?'

'Yes,' Mark replied. 'But they're hardly bodies any more. Skeletons would be more accurate.'

'Well,' Ross continued, handing him the map. 'Skeletons or not, I've been tasked with bringing them home. It's been very distressing for their loved ones not knowing where they are. Not knowing if they really were dead. Not being able to have a proper funeral. But with your help we can put the situation right. You'd want the same, I imagine, if they were colleagues of yours?'

It was a smooth pitch, calmly delivered. Ross's diction was as exact as his appearance, his tone implying that he would get what he had come for. It had been clever to end with a question too. If Mark agreed, it would be harder to refuse his request. Not that he had any reason to refuse. It wasn't every day you got to help a veteran diplomat in his work. But therein lay the problem. A quick glance told Mark that Ross's map was the same Australian Army edition that Terry Landevelt and Inspector Kiuke had referred to. The most detailed available, but still largely useless.

'They were colleagues of yours?' he asked. 'From the State Department?'

'They had been visiting the Ok Tedi mine in the north of the country,' Ross replied, adroitly avoiding a direct answer. 'We assume that they ran into bad weather and crashed on their way back to Daru.'

Mark nodded. His skin was pink and steamed in the cold. He remembered reading about the Ok Tedi mine in his guidebook. Situated in the North Fly District, it generated more than a quarter of Papua New Guinea's export income. At one point it was thought to have been the largest copper mine in the world. Ross's story sounded plausible enough. There was money in copper. And no doubt a great deal of corruption too. Land rights, environmental pressures and the economics of supply and demand meant that it was an extremely political industry. The kind of industry that might have an impact on the global economy. The kind that might easily attract the attentions of the foreign-affairs agency of the United States Government.

'I'd like to help,' Mark said. 'But I'm not sure I can. I went through this with the police in Daru. I can't be specific about the exact location. I was lost. The problem with that map is –'

'That's what they told me when I spoke to them last night,' Ross interrupted. 'But you were tired then. You'd endured a tough time. Helluva thing! Understandably you were keen to get home. I think if you look again now, we might be able to find something on the map to help us. Perhaps a river or some other feature.'

'Who did you speak to?' Mark asked, a trace of suspicion in his voice. 'Inspector Kiuke?'

'I think so,' Ross replied. 'I forget the man's name. It was late, I was supposed to be having dinner with my wife in Knightsbridge. Yeah! Kiuke. That rings a bell. Nice guy. Very helpful.'

Mark drew a deep breath to calm his rising nerves. An alarm had just sounded in his head. Several things weren't quite right. Surely a government official would remember the name of a policeman he'd spoken to only last night? And if Ross *had* spoken to Kiuke, he would know that Mark had been lost in the uncharted area to the north-east of Tidal Island. He would know that the map was useless: that there *were* no features to guide them. The fact that he'd described Kiuke as a nice, helpful guy also sounded wrong, but Mark was willing to accept that he may have met the Inspector on an off day. The real reason behind his suspicion, however, had nothing to do with maps or personality. It had something to do with last night. And Mark knew damn well that the American hadn't been trying to get to dinner with his wife in Knightsbridge.

The lie had been unnecessary. A superfluous flourish from a man overconfident in his disguise. Ross may or may not have been with the US State Department but he wasn't telling the truth about his phone call to Daru.

Mark shifted on his feet, his willingness to cooperate cooling in the winter air. His mind was working overtime. Carmen had spoken of a strong human element to the story, and he felt guilty for doubting Ross's intentions. But then again, there were too many things wrong with the American's approach. Why here? Why now? Why not wait until he was home? Why not make a phone call to set up an appointment? Mark remembered his interview with Inspector Kiuke; remembered discussing the possibility that the helicopter had been smuggling some form of contraband.

'I'm going to have to speak to Kiuke myself before I can help you,' he said. 'He gave me strict instructions not to discuss the whereabouts of the helicopter with anyone. You won't mind, I'm sure?'

It was a test. And Ross failed.

'That won't be necessary,' the American said. 'I have clearance from a higher authority. Kiuke defers to me on this matter.'

Mark wiped his nose on the back of his hand. 'Goodbye, Mr Ross.' And with that, he turned and set off up the hill.

Two minutes later, he made the left turn that would put him on the homeward stretch for the park gate. Four hundred yards away he saw Ronald Ross walking across the paddock in the same direction. The American was taking the direct route and would get there first. Was he trying to cut Mark off? Or was he simply walking back to wherever he had parked his car? It didn't really matter. Mark wasn't going to be per-suaded. He wouldn't stop if the guy tried talking to him again.

Only he did stop. Three minutes later, as he completed his lap of the park.

Ross was standing in the middle of the path, blocking his route. And he had been joined by the man from the log whom Mark had passed earlier.

Twenty

As Mark drew closer, he noticed that the guy from the log was carrying a small backpack over his shoulder. He may have been giving away an inch in height but he more than made up for it in width. He had a small W-shaped scar under his left eye, as though someone had cut their initial into his cheek. His toecaps were steel, his nose squashed from too much fighting. There was a relaxed, unthreatening warmth in his eyes but there was no doubting that he was Ross's muscle: a bodyguard or enforcer. Mark would have to have his wits about him if the situation turned violent.

In the meantime, he was damned if he was going to run away. There were a few more people in the park now. The dog walkers had been joined by young mothers with pushchairs. A short distance to his left, a man in a tracksuit was practising t'ai chi under the naked branches of a plane tree. Beyond him, a father and son kicked a football. In the distance a police car wailed along Melrose Avenue, bathing the white suburban houses in a flash of brilliant blue light. Mark felt his confidence swell. This was his turf.

He was now certain that this whole encounter wasn't about repatriating the bodies. It was about retrieving whatever was inside the passenger's briefcase. If Ross was who he claimed to be, he should have had no objection to Mark calling Kiuke for clarification. Now Mark wanted some clarification of his own. It was time to put the American under pressure.

'OK,' Mark said, before Ross could open his mouth. 'Maybe I *can* help you, after all. Let's just clear up a few details to put my mind at ease. What time did you call Kiuke last night?'

'I hardly think that's import –'

'What time?' Mark insisted.

Ross glanced at his companion and then at the map in his hand. He furrowed his brow, the lines packed tight as corduroy as he weighed up his options. No answer; no deal.

'About eight o'clock.'

'UK time?'

'Yes, UK time.'

'So that would have been six o'clock this morning in Papua New Guinea.'

'I had to wake him up,' Ross said. 'Like I said, he was a very helpful guy.'

Mark hadn't met Kiuke for long but it had been enough to know that the Inspector wouldn't have taken kindly to such an early wake-up call. 'And you called from where exactly?'

'My desk at the embassy in Grosvenor Square. Third floor, last office on the left before the fire exit. Sitting in my chair, for Christ's sake, wearing a pair of chinos, a Timberland sweater and a pair of black boxer briefs, price £6.99 from Marks & Spencer. You happy with that, Dr Bridges? You want to know anything else about me? My wife's name? Where I'm from? What I had for dinner last night?'

Mark shook his head. It was the confirmation he needed. 'No,' he said. 'I'm done. I'm sorry about your colleagues but I really can't help you. And, for the record, I know where you're from and what you had for dinner.'

'You do?' Ross raised his eyebrows but his tone of voice remained flat, leaving Mark unsure whether he was amused or unsettled.

'I'm guessing you're from Maryland,' Mark said. 'Or that you've got friends or relatives there. Baltimore probably.'

Ross swallowed. 'My accent?'

'No. Your tie. The bird in the print is *Icterus galbula*, commonly known as the Baltimore oriole. It's the state bird of Maryland. If you didn't buy it yourself, someone bought it for you. Either way, you've got some sort of personal connection to the place.'

Ross nodded, clearly impressed with Mark's powers of observation. 'And my dinner?'

'You ate airline food at thirty thousand feet.

You were on an overnight plane, which means you couldn't have been meeting your wife in Knightsbridge. And you couldn't have called Kiuke. Not from the embassy, at any rate. Now if you'd kindly step aside, I'll be on my way. Your friend here is making me nervous, and I'm worried I might do something unpredictable.'

The man in the leather coat gave him a warm smile, appreciating the threat and letting him know that physical confrontation would always be welcome. Ross, meanwhile, stared at him, open-mouthed: the first crack in his previously unflappable demeanour. 'You saw me at the airport?'

'Yes,' Mark replied. 'In a mirror in the customs hall. You were standing right behind me. It was your tie that I noticed first. If I'd got a clearer look at your face I would have recognised you sooner. Tell me, did you serve in Vietnam?'

This time Ross was speechless. He glanced at his companion again. His face was flushed red. It may have been embarrassment, anger or a touch of both. He was being made to look a fool and he wasn't enjoying the experience.

Mark knew that he was playing a dangerous game. Antagonising the American might encourage him to resort to violence. It was a risk Mark was willing to take. Ross's accomplice was a big man, but Mark hadn't yet met anyone he needed to fear. Besides, it didn't look as though the guy was ready to start anything just yet. In the meantime Mark was indignant that Ross had tried to deceive him. If the American really *did* work for the US Government, his charade suggested that his employer was more likely to be the CIA. His posing as a run-of-the-mill bureaucrat from the State Department didn't fit with his impregnable poise. Here was a man who thrived on manipulation. A man who was skilled in tracking people down and lying to them to get what he wanted. A man for whom intelligence and information were the key weapons in his arsenal. Only now he was being beaten at his own game.

'What makes you think I served in 'Nam?' Ross had found his voice again. He was over the shock. His composure had returned.

'The date of birth on your ID card says you're sixty-four,' Mark told him. 'The right age for someone who served there in his early twenties. But it's those scars on your face that made me ask. They're consistent with chloracne.'

'So?'

'So, chloracne is usually a result of exposure to dioxins. One of the most toxic dioxins is TCDD, which acted as a contaminant in Agent Orange, the herbicide the US Army used to defoliate the jungle in Vietnam. The article I read said as many as sixty thousand US personnel had been affected. I'm guessing, but I reckon you might be one of them.'

There was a long pause. Another jogger trundled past, tinny dance music pulsing from

181

her iPod. 'Mekong Delta,' Ross said after she had gone. 'July 26, 1969. Chopper from the 336th Aviation Company dropped a load, right where I was working. I was lucky to get away with a skin infection. Others developed soft-tissue cancers, nerve disorders and urological defects. You learned that in med school, I take it?'

'For the second and last time: goodbye, Mr Ross.'

'How much did that set you back, Mark? Thirty thousand pounds?'

Mark stopped. He knew he should walk away, but he was immediately fascinated with where this new line of enquiry was going. Curious, too, to find out who these guys really were. Ross had used the word 'working' to describe his time in Vietnam. Not 'fighting', 'stationed' or 'holed up', but 'working'. It only added to Mark's growing suspicion that the American was a spook. Either that or he was simply an impostor. He noticed too that it was 'Mark, now, not 'Dr Bridges'. Ross was changing tack, switching to Plan B as their game of chess entered a new phase.

'I can help you with that debt,' Ross continued. 'You help me; I help you. Nice and simple. Everyone's a winner. Fletch, would you show Mark here how much we'd value his help.'

The man in the leather jacket unhooked the backpack from over his shoulder and tossed it over. He still hadn't uttered a word.

'It's yours,' Ross said. 'Fifteen thousand pounds in used twenties. Take it now with no obligation. There's another fifteen in the car, if you want it. All you need to do is show me on the map where you found that helicopter.'

Mark's stomach turned somersaults. He had no doubt that the money was inside. Fifteen grand! More cash than he'd ever seen in his life. And another fifteen to follow. Enough to settle his debts in one fell swoop. It was tempting. Really tempting. After what he and Melanie had endured, they almost deserved a reward. All he had to do was point to a white space on a map, for God's sake. No one would know. Maybe the guy really did work for the CIA and had a legitimate reason for his deceit. Maybe he really did just want to bring those skeletons home.

Mark hefted the bag in his hands, but the more he tried to justify taking the money, the more he knew he would never accept it. 'I might lie,' he said. 'I might show you the wrong place on the map.'

'You might, Mark. But the next time we met you'd be talking to Fletch, not me.'

Mark felt his uneasiness rapidly turning to anger. He didn't like being threatened and he didn't like being bribed. 'I don't want your money,' he said. 'And if Fletch wants me to recommend him a good orthopaedic surgeon for when we've finished our chat, then I'd be delighted to put him in touch with a friend of mine at the Chelsea & Westminster. In the meantime, if I ever see you again, I won't hesitate to call the police.' And with that, he pulled the pack into his chest and then threw it out at maximum speed.

Fifteen thousand pounds in used twenties weighs a little over three-quarters of a kilogram. The pack flew with the momentum of a basketball. Fletch tried to catch it but it was through his arms before he could raise them from his sides. The pack hit him in the solar plexus, driving the air from his lungs. He tried to stand still but it was no good. He teetered, then took an involuntary step back.

Mark skipped around him and began running towards the park gate.

Not fast; just the same steady pace he'd been using before.

Twenty-One

'Thirty thousand pounds! Are you out of your fucking mind?' Melanie sat on the sofa, a duvet pulled up under her chin. She had come through to the lounge to watch Mark exercise. Right now he was in the middle of his press-ups. As a child she'd often kept count for him, goading him to work harder with a well-timed insult or prod in the ribs. Since then her brother's strength had always been a source of fascination and pride. If he wasn't one of the strongest men in London, then she didn't know who was.

'The guy was a fake, Mel. He was lying to me.' Mark's hands were level with his chest, one and a half times shoulder-width apart. His stomach was braced to maintain spinal rigidity and he'd flattened his hips to ensure his shoulders and knees were perfectly aligned. He bent his elbows so that his T-shirt brushed the carpet between his thumbs. 'Remember what Inspector Kiuke told us about all the smuggling that goes on in that part of the world? If these guys *are* smugglers and I'd accepted money from them, I'd be up to my neck in trouble sooner or later.'

'Why?' Melanie protested. 'Where's the risk? Why would anyone find out? Used twenties, for God's sake! It's not like you're going to take the whole lot down to the bank.' She paused, then scoffed. 'Actually, knowing you, you probably would. You'd probably pay tax on it too, if you had half the chance.'

Mark glanced at his sister before lowering himself to the floor. The press-up was his favourite exercise. He could feel the repetitions working his pectorals and triceps. There would be ancillary benefits to his deltoids, serratus anterior and coracobrachialis too. That was one of the beauties of callisthenic drills. You didn't need expensive weights or equipment. You didn't even need a gym. You could do them at home and give all the major muscle groups a thorough workout. Sit-ups and squats were the others in his routine. 'OK,' he retorted, piqued by Melanie's wit. 'Why did he bring a pro-fessional thug with him?'

'Just because someone's big and ugly, it doesn't make them a thug, Mark. You of all people should know that. You've been fighting that prejudice since you were thirteen.'

'He threatened me.'

'*I'll* threaten you if you don't get back out there and do the bloody deal!' Melanie shook her head. Why did her brother have to be so risk-averse the whole time? It wasn't as though he couldn't look after himself, was it? She looked at him, exasperated. His arms were pumped hard as tractor tyres. He was now halfway through his fourth set of a hundred push-ups and he was hardly puffing.

Down on the floor, Mark huffed his frustration. He seldom won arguments against Melanie. It was like fighting a boxer with lightning-quick hands. Jab would follow stinging jab until he was finally outpointed. He began pushing faster. The jungle had taken a lot out of him but he could feel his strength returning. The power crackled in his muscles. It pulsed in his arms, across his shoulders and up through the small of his back. It was part of who he was. He would do another fifty reps before awarding himself a break. 'All right, smart-arse,' he said. 'If Ross *was* with the US State Department or CIA even, why didn't he want me to call Kiuke?'

'*I* don't know,' Melanie replied. 'Maybe his real interest in the bodies is classified. Maybe he thinks Kiuke can't be trusted to know what's really going on. The police in PNG have hardly got the best reputation in the world. Besides, if Ross *is* on official CIA business, why *shouldn't* he lie to you? That's what secret agents do. And let's face it, you're not exactly high on the need-to-know list for whatever's going on. He probably had clearance to pay you from Langley.'

'Not when he could have got the same

information for free from Kiuke. Besides, if it was legit, he would have wired the money into my bank account rather than chucking me a backpack full of cash.'

'Oh, don't be so naive!' Melanie collapsed back on to the cushions as though physically traumatised by her brother's suspicion. 'They're doing dodgy deals the whole time, that lot. Thirty grand! You're insane, you know that? Christ! I would have taken the first fifteen and done a runner.'

'No, you wouldn't,' Mark said, unsure when Melanie had become such an expert on the CIA. 'You would have pointed at the map and taken the full thirty.' He shot her a worried glance. The heating was on and she'd had a hot bath, but she had just begun to shiver.

'OK, so maybe I would. Big deal! Honestly, Mark, sometimes I worry about you.'

'And right now, I'm worried about *you*. You don't look well. I think I should take your temperature.'

'I'm fine,' Melanie replied. 'It's probably just a cold. That's the trouble with planes nowadays. Bloody air con sucks in everybody's germs and then pumps them out into a different part of the cabin. They should release those oxygen masks as a matter of course, just to stop people getting ill.'

'Look on the bright side,' Mark said. 'At least they might be first-class germs.' He gave her a warm smile and finally allowed himself to rest. It was going to be fun having Melanie around. He'd told her that she could stay as long as she liked while she sorted herself out and found a flat of her own. His spare room wasn't huge: enough for a single bed, chest of drawers and the pine wardrobe he'd bought off Ebay. But the lounge offered enough living space for them to spread out and relax. Not that Melanie was going to be spending much time out of bed this week. Her cheeks had lost their colour. Her hazel eyes, normally glinting with mischief, were now dull and bloodshot. At least the scratches on her limbs didn't appear to be infected. Mark had treated them in Port Moresby and most had grown healthy scabs.

He went to the bathroom where he retrieved a thermometer from his medicine cabinet. Melanie returned to bed. She didn't object when he placed the thermometer under her tongue, admission perhaps that she really was quite ill. Next, Mark went to the kitchen to pour her some orange juice, which he served with two ibuprofen tablets. He showered quickly and threw on his dressing gown before returning to Melanie's room some three minutes later.

He removed the thermometer and read her temperature. It was 102°F. 'Are you still taking your Malarone?'

Melanie closed her eyes. 'Shit,' she said. 'No, I forgot. I haven't taken it since I was rescued.'

Mark grimaced. 'Mel, I reminded you specifically when we got to Port Moresby.'

'I know. You're great. I'm rubbish. So what's new?' She sighed and looked out of the window. 'Sorry. I didn't mean that. Am I at risk?'

'Yes,' Mark said. 'I'm afraid so. Your absolute risk of getting malaria was probably quite low, but the fact that you were bitten and haven't been taking your tablets increases your chances significantly. I'm hoping that the intravenous chloroquine that Dietmar gave you at Teraruma was enough to keep it at bay but malaria's a pernicious little bastard. It's been mutating for decades and many strains are now resistant to chloroquine. That's why it was important you kept going with the Malarone. It contains atovaquone and proguanil, which haven't been round as long, so the parasites haven't yet figured out a way around them. Where are your tablets?'

'In my washbag in the bathroom.'

Mark went to fetch them. 'Take two now,' he said. 'And another at bedtime. Then one a day until they're gone. In the meantime, I'm writing you a prescription and going straight to the chemist.'

'What for?'

'Ciprofloxacin.'

'In English?'

'It's an antibiotic. It'll help with your fever and diarrhoea.'

'Great,' Melanie said. 'Thanks for mentioning that. So when will I know if I've got malaria?'

'Another three or four days at the earliest. But it could be nine or ten. The chances are that you're fine. I think you should try to sleep, though. I'll see you later.'

Mark returned to his own room, dressed and grabbed his keys.

He was on his way out of the flat when the telephone rang. He hurried back to the lounge and lifted the receiver, keeping his voice low so as not to disturb Melanie.

'Hello?'

'Dr Bridges?' A woman's voice. Elderly. Frail and distressed.

'Speaking.'

'Oh, hello. My name is Elsie Chuter. I'm so glad I've found you. It's taken me four goes but I've reached you at last!'

The relief in the woman's voice was unmistakable. 'How can I help?' Mark asked.

There was a pause on the line as the caller drew a deep breath. 'I read about what happened to you and your sister in Papua New Guinea. There was an article, you see, in yesterday's paper. It mentioned a Dr Mark Bridges of north London. Well, I asked the operator to keep trying until I got the right one. It is you, isn't it?'

'Yes,' Mark replied. 'It's me.' Now that he had qualified he would have to remove his name from the next edition of the telephone directory. Otherwise his phone was going to be ringing at all sorts of antisocial hours. His current listing didn't mention that he was a doctor but his patients at the Finchley Road surgery would soon put two and two together. Mark still hadn't seen Carmen's article. Fearing that he would be too late if he waited until after his shower, he'd gone straight to the newsagent at the end of his run. But the newsagent had sold out of papers yesterday, and there had been no surplus stock in any of the other three places he'd tried.

'The article said you discovered a helicopter with . . .' Mark heard Elsie Chuter hesitate as though she was fighting back tears. '. . . with two bodies on board.'

'Yes. That's right.' Mark was growing increasingly curious. His initial hunch that the woman was seeking medical advice was quickly being dispelled.

'Well,' she said. 'I'm rather afraid that one of those poor men might be my son.'

Twenty-Two

Mark sat down, confused but intrigued. It was still only ten o'clock in the morning but already this was turning out to be one of the strangest days of his life. He had only been back in the country for a couple of hours and this was the second time someone had contacted him about the helicopter. 'What makes you think that?' he asked.

Mrs Chuter drew a deep breath. 'My son is an anthropologist. He's been studying shamanic culture in some of the world's most remote tribes. He went to Papua New Guinea a year ago and no one has seen or heard from him since. The newspaper said you were in the Middle Fly District, and I'm sure that's where Tom has been working. The article mentioned a notebook, you see, and Tom always kept a record of his findings. I'm sorry, Dr Bridges. I'm probably being silly, but I have to know if it's him. I wondered if I showed you a photograph, perhaps you might recognise him?'

Not likely, Mark thought. There wasn't anything left to recognise. The moths, termites, bats and blowflies had devoured the men's features long ago. But who else could the passenger's notebook have belonged to, if not an anthropologist? Mark remembered the drawings of flora, fauna and indigenous tribes. Remembered, too, how most of the explanatory text had been written about the natives. Papua New Guinea was an anthropologist's heaven. Wontok had been living proof that there were still people inhabiting its forests who were largely unknown to the outside world. People whose rites and customs would fascinate anyone with an interest in primitive society. People whose biology, even, might answer lingering questions about man's recent evolution.

Mark was now certain that he was talking to the passenger's mother. Conscious, too, that this had become a delicate situation. 'I'm afraid I haven't seen the article yet. What exactly did it say?'

'I've got it here,' Mrs Chuter replied. 'Now, wait a minute! Yes, here we are. "Dr Bridges discovered two bodies inside the helicopter. Neither the pilot nor his passenger could be identified, although a notebook found in the luggage suggested the latter might have had a professional interest in the local environment." Well dear, I'm afraid that sounds just like my Tom.'

Mark heard a sniff on the end of the line. Tom Chuter might not have been the only anthropologist to have been working with a notebook in Papua New Guinea, but his mother's grief was real and it demanded Mark's attention.

'I'd like to help you, if I can, Mrs Chuter. If you tell me where you live, perhaps I could visit? We could have a chat and maybe reach a conclusion, one way or the other.' He chose his words carefully. As a doctor he had been trained in handling bereavements and he knew better than to cause further distress over the phone.

'I live in Grantchester,' Mrs Chuter told him. 'It's a small village outside Cambridge. Very pretty. You'd like it, I'm sure. Do you have a car?'

'No, but don't worry about that. I'll take the train and then a taxi.'

'I'd offer to pick you up, but I don't drive any more. It's my knees, you see. Osteoarthritis. I can't work the clutch. Terrible nuisance it is! When do you think you might be able to come?'

Mark made the decision in a heartbeat. He wasn't working. He had the whole day ahead of him. Jane lived in Cambridge so he had made the train journey many times before. It was only forty-five minutes from King's Cross. His priority was to help Mrs Chuter learn whether her son was alive or dead, but a visit to Grantchester might also help him to understand why Ronald Ross had just offered him a sackful of cash. It was a long shot, but if the man in the helicopter *was* her son, as now appeared likely, Mrs Chuter might be able to shed some light on what he'd been carrying in his briefcase. Mel would survive without him. Sleep was what she needed most, and she would get more of that if he wasn't crashing around the flat.

'Well,' he said. 'I'm not working today, so I could come more or less straight away.' He glanced at his watch. 'Shall we say twelve thirty?'

'Only if it's not too much trouble, Dr Bridges. I don't want to be any bother. It's just that –'

Mark could hear her sobbing again. 'It's quite all right,' he told her. 'Now then, do you live alone?'

'Yes,' Mrs Chuter replied. 'Ever since September when my husband passed away. Pneumonia it was that got him.'

Mark shook his head. To lose a husband and son in the space of a year was hard. Very hard. It was going to take its toll. 'Do you have any relatives you can call? Or some friends perhaps, who could join us?'

'You think it's him, don't you? Oh my God, it's Tom! My poor Tom!'

'I don't know,' Mark lied. 'Not without looking at your photographs. And even then, I might not be able to help. But, whatever happens, it could be a draining afternoon. I think it would be a good idea to have someone there to look after you. Just in case.'

'No,' she said, crying openly now. 'There's no one. It's just been me on my own since Walter left me. Except for Henry, of course.'

'Who's Henry? A friend of yours?'

'Well, he's Tom's friend really, but he'll look after me. He always does.'

'Good. Now, Mrs Chuter –'

'Elsie, dear. Call me Elsie.'

'I don't want you jumping to any conclusions. Just because the helicopter crashed in the Middle Fly District doesn't mean that's where its passengers were from. We don't know whether the accident happened at the beginning of its flight, the end, or somewhere in the middle. Your son could have been hundreds of miles away when it began its journey.' Mark stood up and began pacing the room. Was he being sensible or making it worse? Protecting her from unnecessary anguish or giving her false hope? The notebook was a massive clue but it wasn't absolute proof. 'What's your address?' he asked, deciding that he would have to keep an open mind.

She told him and Mark scribbled it down amid an outpouring of thanks for his help. He told her that it was no trouble, said goodbye and was about to hang up when an idea occurred to him.

'Mrs Chuter?'

'Yes, dear?'

'Do you mind if I bring a friend?'

'Of course not,' she said. 'I'll buy some biscuits especially.'

*

At the end of the road, in an unmarked van, a man in grey overalls removed his headphones and turned to his colleague. 'You got that? Twelve thirty in Grantchester.'

'Got it,' his colleague answered. 'I'll call the gaffer now. I'm sure he'll be interested to know that Melanie's going to be on her own all day.'

Twenty-Three

The journey to Grantchester took a little under ninety minutes. Carmen drove, having picked Mark up at quarter to eleven. There was much to discuss and the miles disappeared quickly enough, despite the morning traffic.

Mark had thought that Mrs Chuter might appreciate some female company during what was going to be a traumatic meeting. Initially he had called Jane. They had broken up on amicable terms and it would have been good to see her. Jane worked at Addenbrooke's Hospital in Cambridge and she would have done a fantastic job of consoling the hapless old lady. But, not surprisingly, it was too short notice. Jane was free in the afternoon but was on duty all morning. There was no way that she could escape. She'd sounded surprised to hear from him, the hope in her voice telling him that it had been a bad idea to call.

So then he'd rung Carmen, tracking her down

via the features desk at the *Observer*. He'd had mixed feelings about inviting her to join him but had finally convinced himself that it was the right thing to do. He wasn't comfortable with the possibility that she might make news out of Mrs Chuter's misery, but it was *her* work that had created the lead in the first place. She had asked his permission before writing about him so no doubt she would be equally sensitive in this instance. Carmen had been hoping that the identity of the helicopter's passengers might lead to a follow-up story. It would have been unfair to withhold the development from her.

Or so Mark had persuaded himself. The fact that he found her bright and beautiful had nothing to do with it. A professional favour. That was all it was. He would have asked her if she'd been thick and ugly. Let's face it, he'd reasoned, driving seventy miles to tell an old lady that her son had rotted in a rainforest on the other side of the world, wasn't the best way to woo someone. Besides, Carmen had given no indication that she was interested in him. She'd twice preened her hair when she'd come to his tent that night near Tidal Island, but so what? That was hardly evidence of attraction. It could just as well have been gamesmanship. A subtle ploy to help her get what she'd wanted. *We journalists are not always renowned for our scruples.*

Mark glanced at her out of the corner of his eye. She was wearing what Mel would have called comfort clothing. A cream-coloured fleece accentuated her tan while a pair of tight jeans reminded him what a great pair of legs she had. Her feet worked the pedals in a pair of thick-soled pumps: casual but snug. Her driving was fast and alert, with no sign of jet lag. She seemed in high spirits, no doubt excited at the prospect of developing her story.

'So who do you think he was?' Carmen asked, continuing their conversation.

'I don't know,' Mark replied. 'Kiuke's going to escalate it to his superiors in Port Moresby, and they'll make contact with the State Department. My guess is that Ross *used* to work for them and is now just using his old ID as cover. Either that or he's CIA.'

'And what about the visit to the Ok Tedi mine? Do you buy that?'

'Maybe. Kiuke seems to think that the mine is one of the few places in PNG that *does* attract regular helicopter traffic. He's going to check if there's any record of a Bell JetRanger landing there in the last eighteen months.'

'Sounds like he is all over it.'

'Yes,' Mark said, realising that he could smell the conditioner in her hair. 'He was certainly very interested in my encounter with Ross. I guess it's more interesting than sorting out a clan war in some far-flung village. Turn left here.'

After dashing to the chemist to collect Melanie's Ciprofloxacin, Mark had called Inspector Kiuke while he had been waiting for Carmen to pick him up. It had taken him fifteen minutes to find the number for the police station in Daru but only one to confirm that Ross had been lying. Kiuke had not received a call from anyone about the helicopter, let alone from the US State Department. Mark's experience in Gladstone Park only increased the Inspector's suspicion that the helicopter had been smuggling something. Naturally, he was now keen to track Ross down. He'd thanked Mark for the information and confirmed that he would enlist some support from New Scotland Yard. In return, Mark had promised to be available for a police interview as soon as Kiuke could set one up. Then he'd placed Meleanie under strict instuctions not to answer the door while he was away, and to call the police if Ross turned up on their doorstep.

'Pretty little place,' Carmen said a few minutes later as they drove into Grantchester.

'Couple of good pubs too, by the look of it. She should be just up here on the left.' Mark looked out of the window as the houses flashed by. Many were large and all were in good repair. This was clearly one of Cambridgeshire's more expensive villages. It was no less grey or cold in this part of the country, but the lights on the Christmas trees inside promised colour and warmth. Mark looked at the date on his watch. Ten days to go. Maybe tomorrow he would get round to buying some presents.

Elsie Chuter lived in a row of neat terraced cottages overlooking a meadow above the River

Cam. Mark knocked lightly, careful not to dislodge the garland that was pinned to the wood. He stood well back so that she wouldn't be too alarmed when she opened the door.

In the event, he needn't have worried. Carmen's article had prepared her.

'Dr Bridges?' she asked. 'My! You *are* a tall one! The paper said you were, but goodness me! I bet the air's a bit thinner up there, isn't it?'

Mark smiled politely. He'd heard it before. He'd heard them *all* before. 'This is my friend Carmen,' he said. 'She's the reporter who wrote the article in the *Observer*. I thought it might be nice to have another friendly face with us, in case Henry couldn't make it.'

'Oh,' Mrs Chuter replied, 'don't you worry about Henry. He's always here since Tom went away. Delighted to meet you, Carmen dear. Don't stand there getting cold! Come on in. I'm so grateful to you. If it hadn't been for your article, I would never have known about poor Tom.'

They followed her inside. Mark ducked to avoid hitting his head on the lintel. He hadn't known how Mrs Chuter would react to having a journalist present but so far the signs were encouraging. No hostility and no mistrust.

She was exactly how he had imagined. Small and frail with stooped shoulders and a question-mark spine, characteristic of osteoporosis. Her hair was cropped short, primped into tight white curls. She had a long, scrawny neck and the skin

203

drooped from under her chin, flapping like a turkey's wattle whenever she moved her head. Her eyes, Mark noticed, were puffy and red, testament to the many tears she had no doubt shed. She wore a white blouse over a tartan skirt, together with stockings and slippers. She led the way into her cottage. Using the wall as support, she shuffled, back hunched, towards the kitchen. Eighty-five, if she was a day.

'I'll put the kettle on,' Mrs Chuter announced. 'You go through to the front room.'

Mark followed Carmen into the lounge, where they settled into the sofa and took in their surroundings. There was no sign of Henry but perhaps he was on his way. The room was neat and tidy, like the row of cottages itself. Despite her afflictions, Mrs Chuter clearly still found enough strength to do the housework. A few china ornaments glistened on the mantelpiece. Below them, an electric fire glowed orange in the wall. There were a handful of Christmas cards on the coffee table but no tree. Mark spotted three family photographs on the dresser at the far end of the room. He decided that he would wait for Mrs Chuter to show them herself.

She joined them a few moments later. Mark sprang to his feet to relieve her of the tray she was carrying. She'd made a pot of tea and had assembled a stack of biscuits on a small china plate. As if on cue, Mark heard his stomach rumble. It was lunchtime, and he was ravenous.

'Help yourselves to sugar, dears, while I fetch the photographs.'

Mark watched as she hobbled to the far end of the room. He felt his heart go out to her. She was putting on a brave face, but he could tell that she was bracing herself for the worst. How must it feel, he wondered, to know that you were moments away from receiving the most devastating news imaginable? He sighed. A damn sight worse than knowing that you were moments away from delivering it, and that was bad enough.

In truth, Mark wasn't yet sure how he was going to deal with this. He was hardly going to tell the poor woman that the man in the helicopter was now nothing more than a skull and bones. And besides, how could he be certain that it *was* Tom Chuter? Mark was no forensic pathologist, and matching a photograph of flesh and blood to a pile of bones was certainly beyond him.

'Before you show us the photograph, Mrs Chuter, why don't we see if it really was Tom's notebook that I found? If you've got something with his handwriting on it, I'll see if I recognise it.'

'Oh,' she exclaimed, 'that's a good idea. Wait here! I think there's a postcard in the kitchen.'

'I will go,' Carmen said. 'You sit there and enjoy your tea.'

'Thank you, dear. It's on the fridge. From Australia, I think. Tom stopped there on his way out to Papua New Guinea.'

Carmen returned a moment later and passed the postcard to Mark.

One glance was all he needed.

In the space above his mother's address, Tom Chuter had drawn a sketch of a young Aborigine girl cuddling a koala bear. The drawing's style and the handwriting were unmistakably the same as in the passenger's notebook.

'Well?' Mrs Chuter's hand trembled as she poured the tea. She couldn't look at her guests.

'It was his,' Mark said. 'I'm sorry. But the notebook was definitely his.'

Across the room, Elsie Chuter tilted back her head and groaned. For a brief moment her eyeballs rolled, giving her a corpse-like appearance. Then her neck seemed to give way and her face collapsed into her hands. Carmen leaped to her feet and put an arm around her shoulders.

'I'm sorry,' Mark repeated. 'I wish it wasn't, but I'm afraid it was.' He didn't want to watch her crying, so he leaned forward to collect the two photographs that she had left on the coffee table.

The first was mounted in a pine frame. It showed Tom Chuter standing in the cloisters of a university college. The building in the background boasted a fine row of neoclassical columns. The lawn in the foreground was immaculately kept. Chuter was dressed in a suit and academic gown. The fact that he was clutching a scroll suggested that he had just been awarded a doctorate or some other erudite qualification. The photograph had been mounted on white card bearing a colourful crest of arms.

'Where was this taken?' Mark asked, hoping to give Mrs Chuter something else to focus on.

She spread her fingers and peeped through the gap in her hands. 'Trinity College,' she said through her tears. 'Just down the road, in Cambridge. That's the Wren Library in the background. Tom was a research fellow in the Department of Social Anthropology. He was hoping that his latest paper might help him to become a professor.'

'How tall was he?' Mark asked, conscious that he had just used the past tense.

'Not tall,' Mrs Chuter replied. 'But then again, I suppose not many people *are* compared to you. About five-nine, I think.'

Mark closed his eyes. He seemed to remember that the passenger had been wearing big army boots, which might have implied that he was taller than five feet nine. Mark desperately wanted to remember something, anything, to give the old woman hope. But even as he picked up the second picture, he knew that he was clutching at straws.

The second photograph was a portrait: a close-up of Tom's face. He would have been in his late teens or early twenties when it was taken. And he was shockingly handsome. His eyes were wide and doe-like with effeminate lashes, but their deep green colour lent him a feline quality. His blond hair sat over his brow in a straight, short fringe: the height of fashion if you were in a boy band but childlike if not. A beauty spot adorned his clean-shaven cheek.

Carmen still held Mrs Chuter's hand as she leaned forward to glance at the picture. 'Wow!' she exclaimed. 'He is a good-looking man, Mrs Chuter. Incredible eyes!'

'Oh, I know, dear. Quite the most handsome man in the university, he was. Do you think it's him, Dr Bridges? Do you recognise him?'

Mark drew a deep breath. He looked long and hard at the portrait, desperate to spare this poor woman more anguish. But it was no good. He was going to have to tell her that her son's body had decomposed beyond all recognition.

'Mrs Chuter,' he began. 'When my sister and I found the helicopter, it was completely over-grown. It had probably been there –'

He stopped. There was something about Tom Chuter's face, his head.

Mark tilted the photograph in the light. Paused. Tilted it back the other way. Held it up. Put it down in his lap again.

'Mrs Chuter,' he said, after a moment's reflection. 'I need to ask you a question.'

208

Twenty-Four

Elsie Chuter's face was tight with expectation. Her hand trembled on her knee. Tears pooled in her eyes but something in her visitor's voice had given her hope. Carmen retook her place on the sofa. She looked equally tense as she waited to hear what Mark had to say.

'Tom's head?' he asked, passing the portrait back to his host. 'I hope that was an accident, not an assault?'

'He was fifteen,' Mrs Chuter replied with a slight nod. 'Goodness me but that boy's given me some scares in his time!'

'What happened? If you don't mind me asking?' Mark had noticed the scar peeping out from under Tom Chuter's fringe. The cicatrix, in turn, had drawn his attention to the shape of the anthropologist's brow. And that's when he'd noticed it. In the corner, above the man's eye. A slight swelling like a lens beneath the skin. The bump was very subtle, discernible only when

Mark had altered the angle of the light falling on the photograph.

'It was a swimming pool,' Mrs Chuter said, swallowing painfully. 'The bigger boys were teasing him. He was pushed. It was the shallow end, of course. He tried to turn it into a dive but there wasn't enough time. The lifeguard said he'd never seen so much blood.'

'And the surgeons fitted a cranial plate to repair his fractured skull?'

'Yes,' she said. 'The operation took five hours. It's titanium, I think.'

'In which case, Mrs Chuter, I can tell you with absolute certainty that neither of the bodies on that helicopter was your son.'

Hope flashed in the old woman's eyes. 'How do you know?'

'The bodies have decomposed. They're just skeletons now. I got a good look at both skulls and there's no way I would have missed a titanium plate.' Mark was smiling as he spoke. There was no need to gloss over the gory details now that they could cause no pain.

He watched the change in Mrs Chuter's face. Grief turned to doubt and confusion but then, finally, she allowed herself to believe. She raised her eyebrows and dropped her jaw in a silent gasp of joy. Then she stood up and hobbled towards him, pecking with arthritic fingers at the tissue up her sleeve.

'Thank you,' she said. 'Oh, thank you both! It's not him? You're sure it's not him?'

Mark smiled sympathetically. It wasn't so long ago that he'd experienced the same swirling emotions following the news of Melanie's rescue. 'I'm sure,' he replied.

'Oh, thank heavens!' She held out her hands to him. Mark gave them a reassuring squeeze. 'Something good has come of it at last. That accident was the source of more trouble than you can possibly imagine.'

'What sort of trouble?' Mark asked, helping her back to her chair. 'Headaches?'

'No, dear. If only it were that simple. Sadly, I mean family trouble. Walter, you see, always said it was the knock on his head that turned Tom queer.'

'Tom is gay?' Carmen stole another look at the photograph, as though it might somehow provide an answer to her question.

'Yes, dear. Although that word meant something quite different in my day. I never loved him any less for it, but Walter could *never* accept it. He took it very badly. Began calling Tom names, teasing him and what have you. His own son, would you believe? Tom was always a shy boy – complicated, you might say – but his father's bullying drove him to become even more distant. I've often wondered if that's why he developed an interest in travel. As soon as he was old enough, he began spending as much time as he could overseas.' She paused, a faraway look in her eye. 'Of course, he won't know his father's dead. Won't know that Walter apologised.'

Carmen poured another cup of tea. It was clear that Mrs Chuter needed to talk. Having driven all this way, they could spare a few more minutes. 'Tom doesn't know that his father is dead?'

'No, dear. How could he? He hasn't made any contact with me for over a year. He left very suddenly, you see.' Mrs Chuter shook her head. 'Sad. So very sad! "Tell Tom I'm sorry." Those were Walter's final words. I was with him when he went. If only Tom could have heard him. But here I am getting all upset again, when we should be celebrating. Dr Bridges, dear, have another biscuit.'

Mark helped himself. He'd never refused a custard cream in his life, and he wasn't about to start now. 'I'm pleased it's good news,' he said. 'But it does beg a question as to how Tom's notebook came to be in the helicopter. Was he working with a colleague perhaps? A friend he might have lent his notes to?'

'Oh, no!' Mrs Chuter exclaimed. 'I very much doubt it. He was far too protective of his work for that. And with good reason too.'

'Oh?' Carmen asked. 'Why is that?'

'A long story, dear. I don't want to keep you.'

'We are not in any rush, are we, Mark? Unless you don't want to tell us, Mrs Chuter? If it is none of our business, don't be afraid to say so.'

Mrs Chuter waved her hand. 'Nonsense, dear! In fact, I'm rather touched by your interest. And what mother doesn't like talking about her children?' She smiled, took another sip of tea and returned the tissue to her sleeve. 'Tom had been to Papua New Guinea several times before, you see. He loved it there. Always preferred it to South America, he said. Anyway, about three years ago he came back from one of his trips, terribly excited. He'd discovered a new tribe, you see. A hundred people living in the rainforest somewhere in the Middle Fly District. That's why I thought it must be him in the helicopter. I recognised the name of the area in your article. Anyway, Tom was convinced that they were the smallest tribe in the world: a unique community with all sorts of interesting characteristics. Well! You can imagine what a discovery *that* was for a Cambridge anthropologist! He raced back to England and presented his findings to the faculty, and they granted him an immediate sabbatical. Before we knew it, Tom was back out there, living with the tribe, studying their customs and what have you.'

'And he went alone?' Carmen asked.

'Yes. The paper he was going to write at the end of the year was to be his masterpiece, you see. He was rather hoping that his work might be enough to make him a professor. I still think of him as my little boy, but he's forty-nine next year. I know I shouldn't. He's one of the most respected anthropologists in the country.'

'So what happened?' Mark asked, eyeing another biscuit. It was one o'clock and the eggs he'd eaten for breakfast were beginning to feel like a long time ago.

Mrs Chuter smiled approvingly, clearly enjoying their company. Then she drew a deep breath before beginning the next instalment of her son's story. 'Tom has never been a happy soul. But when he came back from his sabbatical he was even more troubled than usual. I asked him about it but he wasn't very talkative. All he told me was that he'd made an important discovery during his time with the tribe.'

'A discovery?' Carmen asked. 'What sort of discovery?'

'He didn't say but it must have been something significant because I've never seen him in such a state. I remember, his reticence upset me for quite a while. Tom and I were always very close, you see. He always swore never to keep secrets from me, so it was a difficult time. I felt like he *wanted* to tell me but, for whatever reason, he couldn't. I watched it plaguing him, but, of course, I was powerless to help.'

'Was it something anthropological, perhaps?'

'Quite possibly, dear. He was torn, you see. Sitting on the horns of a professional dilemma, he said. He didn't know whether to publish his findings or keep them quiet. In the end, he decided on the latter. Whatever it was he'd discovered, he obviously thought that it should remain a secret. It could have been the making of him, but he turned a blind eye.'

Mark sat back in the sofa, fascinated by what he'd just heard. His list of questions was growing longer by the minute as he connected the dots. An intrepid anthropologist. A significant discovery. His notebook in the possession of an armed man.

One thing was now clear. Tom Chuter's secret was something tangible, not academic. And it wasn't a secret at all. Ronald Ross knew what it was. Knew too that it was locked inside a briefcase on a crashed helicopter in the middle of the jungle. Knew that it was worth paying £30,000 for information that might enable him to recover it.

'Tom's now back in Papua New Guinea?' he asked, keen to hear how the story ended.

'Yes, dear. So far as I know.'

'So what made him return? If he'd just had a year off, presumably the faculty would have wanted him back on its staff?'

'We *all* wanted him back! The university, the faculty, the college. Not to mention me and Henry. Even Walter said it couldn't be right for him to be spending so much time with those wretched fuzzy-wuzzies!' Mrs Chuter shook her head apologetically. 'His words, dear; not mine.'

'When did he leave?' Mark asked.

'Just over a year ago. Last September it was. Very sudden. He didn't say goodbye or anything. The first I knew of it was that postcard. Read it, if you like, dear, and tell me what you think. There's something rather final about it. He's quoting Scott, I believe.'

Mark picked up the postcard from the coffee

table and turned it over. He'd only glanced at the handwriting and sketch before. Now he gave the text his full attention.

Darling Mum. Am in Cairns en route to PNG. Things not good with Simeon – not to mention Dad, who won't miss me now I'm gone. The air in England never suited me. And where I'm going they have the ultimate protection against bad air!!! Take care, dear girl, and don't wait up! I'm just going away and I may be some time. I fear I have let slip the keys to Eden, and must protect my people. Your loving Tom. PS please look after Henry. You'll find his conversation a lot more intelligent than Dad's.

' "Turned native" is what Walter said. And I rather suspect that he was right.' Mrs Chuter took the postcard from Mark and passed it to Carmen. 'It *is* Scott, isn't it?'

'Lawrence Oates,' Mark corrected. 'But he was on Scott's expedition. "I'm just going outside, I may be some time." It's almost the same as what Tom's written.' He didn't add that Oates had been speaking ironically. The explorer knew full well that he would never survive the Antarctic temperatures outside the expedition tent. As far as last words went, they were beautifully weighted. So what had Tom Chuter intended to imply? That he was returning to

PNG to die? Or was he simply saying that he wasn't coming home? And what did he mean by 'the ultimate protection against bad air'? That was an odd turn of phrase. The three exclamation marks that followed flashed at Mark like beacons. A clue perhaps?

'And you haven't heard from him since?' Mark asked

'No, dear. Nor has anyone else. The university has had to let him go. No choice but to fire him. He was supposed to be lecturing, you see, but he never turned up at the beginning of term.'

'Who is Simeon?' Carmen asked.

Mrs Chuter swallowed painfully and glanced at the ceiling. 'Simeon Creasey was Tom's special friend. His partner; although I have to say I find that term rather misleading. Heaven knows, they were hardly playing tennis together!'

Mark and Carmen exchanged smiles. 'Do you think Simeon knew what Tom had discovered?'

'I don't know, dear. It's possible, I suppose. Although I hope that Tom would have told *me* before he told anyone else. I've tried contacting Simeon on many occasions but he refuses to communicate. I rather suspect he blames Walter and me for driving Tom away.'

'You?' Carmen exclaimed. 'How could anyone blame *you*?'

'Oh, dear, you know how it is. No one's ever good enough for Mummy's little boy. It never bothered me that Tom was gay but I never liked

Simeon. He told me once that I *smothered* Tom. Quite what he meant by that, I have no idea, but we never saw eye to eye. And Walter, of course, would have nothing to do with him.'

'He might talk to *us*,' Carmen ventured. 'Do you know where we might find him?'

'He's a pharmacologist,' Mrs Chuter said. 'I think that's right. Not a pharmacist – they're something different. He's got a lab in the Science Park, if I remember correctly. On the edge of town towards Milton. You could try the main switchboard there.'

'Well,' Mark said, picking a crumb from the floor. 'It won't do any harm to ask. Is there anything I can do for you before we go?'

'No thank you, dear. Kind of you to ask, but I get by on my own.'

'You're sure?' he asked, standing up. His grandmothers were both dead now, but he remembered his visits to them well. There was *always* a fuse or a light bulb to change.

'Quite sure, thank you. You've done enough as it is, coming all this way. But you must meet Henry before you go. I told him you were coming, and he's dying to see you.'

Mark looked at Carmen, confused. Who was this Henry character? And why had Tom asked his mother to look after him in his absence? Carmen shrugged and raised her eyebrows before following Mrs Chuter into the kitchen.

'He's out the back, dears. In the shed. The light's on, and you'll find it nice and warm in

218

there. You go and say hello, while I straighten up in here.'

The kitchen door comprised two large panes of frosted glass. Elsie Chuter unlocked it and ushered them through, closing it behind them to keep out the cold.

Carmen went first, stepping on to a patio that overlooked a small garden. The redbrick shed was at the end of a short path.

'A dog,' Mark said. 'I bet you a fiver it's a dog.'

'You are on,' Carmen replied, flashing him a smile. 'Tom is a cat person. You could see it in his eyes.'

'Why would anyone keep a cat in a shed? Let's make it ten quid.'

'Good point,' Carmen conceded. 'But it is still not a dog.'

Her hand was on the shed door. She opened it and stepped up over the threshold but then stopped dead in her tracks. 'You are kidding me!' she whispered.

'What?' Mark asked, still unsighted.

Carmen stepped to one side, giving him a clear view of the interior. 'Give me £10 and say hello to Henry.'

Twenty-Five

Mark peered into the shed. The cage occupied most of the back wall. It was too small for the parrot inside but then again, *any* cage was going to be too small for such a magnificent creature. Mark recognised it immediately from its plumage. Henry was an African grey parrot: a species renowned for its cognitive powers and intelligence.

A large window allowed what little sunlight there was to penetrate the gloom, giving Henry a teasing glimpse of the trees at the bottom of the garden. An electric heater provided warmth, while an elaborate feeder and full water bottle confirmed that this was a well-cared-for pet. Mark nonetheless felt the hairs on the back of his neck bristle. He was momentarily disappointed with Elsie Chuter. People who caged birds were right up there with people who threatened him in public parks. Then he remembered that Henry was Tom's bird, and that his mother had been left with no choice but to care for it. That, in itself, was something of a problem. African greys could live to be sixty years old, which meant that Henry was going to long outlive his guardian.

Mark hung back, reluctant to enter such a confined space. He watched Carmen's expression as she crossed the shed. He was thinking about the tattoo on her shoulder, and was curious to see how the sight of a caged bird would affect her. So far she appeared to be no more distressed than he was.

'Hello, Henry,' Carmen said as she approached the cage.

'Hello, Henry!' the parrot echoed.

'You are beautiful, aren't you?'

The parrot squawked, apparently thrilled with the compliment. *'Pretty lady!'* it cawed. *'Pretty lady!'*

Mark smiled. *Clever bird!* But he knew that flattery was the least of the species' talents. He had once read an article about an African grey called N'kisi who allegedly commanded a vocabulary of more than seven hundred words. Apparently it had also mastered the past tense and even spoke in complete sentences. Mark leaned against the door frame and folded his arms. It would be interesting to see if Henry was in the same league. Already the bird's enunciation was startlingly good.

'Pretty lady! Give us a kiss!' The parrot shuffled along his perch, leaning forward and bobbing his head. He was totally grey except for his yellow

eyes, black hooked beak and a shock of crimson tail feathers.

Carmen laughed with delight and put her fingers through the chicken wire to pet the bird's flank.

'I wouldn't,' Mark said. But he was too late. Henry lunged forward and nipped Carmen's index finger, causing her to suck in her breath.

'Ouch!' she said, withdrawing her hand. 'That was *not* very friendly!'

'Count yourself lucky,' Mark said, failing to hide his amusement. 'If he'd really got hold of you, he could have broken your finger.'

'Well, it would have served me right,' Carmen replied, clenching the bitten digit in the palm of her other hand. 'I should have known better. He was only protecting his toys. Do you think he is rare or endangered?'

'I'm not sure. CITES Appendix II, probably.'

'Really? Appendix II? And what the hell does that mean?'

'Sorry,' Mark said, reddening. 'CITES is the Convention on International Trade in Endangered Species. Appendix II lists species that are considered "Near Threatened", which means that trade of wild-caught specimens is restricted because the wild populations can't sustain trapping for the pet trade.'

'Wow!' Carmen pulled the corners of her mouth down and nodded: an inverted grin that suggested she was impressed. 'Did you read that in a book?'

'No.' This time Mark smiled as he realised that she was teasing him. 'A magazine, actually. Anyway, how about we go and find out what was in Tom's notebook? I don't know why, but I've got a funny feeling that Simeon Creasey might know the answer.'

He turned and was about to walk back to the kitchen when Henry shrieked something that made him stop.

'Notebook! My notebook, Henry!'

'Hey, Mark!' Carmen called. 'Come back! Did you hear what he just said?'

'I did,' Mark replied, turning on the patio. 'And I wonder why he chose that particular word to repeat? See if you can make him say it again.'

Carmen was about to speak but Henry beat her to it.

'Notebook! My notebook! They stole it, Henry! They stole my notebook!'

Mark was back at the shed in an instant. He stepped inside, indifferent now to the claustro-phobia that he knew would follow. 'He's repeating Tom's words. Someone must have –'

Mark never got to complete his sentence. Henry's reaction was shocking in its violence. The bird took one look at him and launched itself, talons first, at the cage.

'Thief!' he screamed. *'Thief! Thief!'* Henry spread his wings and hopped on his perch, sporadically lunging at the wire. He hadn't reacted that way to Carmen. Mark was in no

doubt that it was his presence in the shed that had set the bird off.

'*Thief!*' Henry called again. This time he flew at the cage with such ferocity that he lost a couple of breast feathers in the wire.

'Thief?' Mark said, taking a step back. 'I'm not a thief. I'm not going to take anything.' He just had time to glance in the cage before making his retreat. There were several perches and a mirror, together with a miniature treasure chest nestling in the sawdust on the floor. It was a hand-carved block of oak, the size of a bar of soap. The sort of thing you might keep earrings or cufflinks in. 'Relax, Henry! I'm not going to steal your treasure,' he said as he left the shed.

'I don't think that is what he is suggesting,' Carmen said, joining him outside so that Henry could calm down. 'It sounded to me like he thought *you* stole the notebook. If it was the chest he was worried about, he would have reacted the same way to me; but all I got was a little nip.'

'Why would he think *I* stole it?'

'I don't know.'

'Do I look like a thief?'

'Henry seems to think so.'

'Thanks a bunch. I wouldn't . . .' Mark paused. *A species renowned for its cognitive powers and intelligence.* He remembered what else he had read about N'kisi, the loquacious parrot from his magazine article. On one occasion it had been introduced to Jane Goodall, the world's preeminent primatologist. Recognising her from some photographs it had seen in *National Geographic*, N'kisi's first words to her had been, '*Got any chimps?*'

'What's up?' Carmen asked.

'I'm tall,' Mark replied.

'Yes, you are.'

'And big.'

'If you say so, Dr Bridges.'

Mark smiled. *Dr Bridges*. He liked that. She could call him that all day if she wanted to. 'Those are my defining characteristics. Visually, at least.'

'So?'

'So, if Henry thinks I stole the diary, there's a chance that the actual thief was the same build as me.'

Carmen shrugged. 'Maybe.'

'Better than maybe. If the notebook *was* stolen, it would certainly explain how it came to be in a helicopter without its rightful owner. I think I know who took it.'

'Who?'

Mark smiled again as he remembered the strange day he was having. 'I'll tell you in the car. Let's say our goodbyes and see if we can find Creasey. I'll call Directory Enquiries to get the number for the Science Park. We'll see if we can set up a meeting.'

'No,' Carmen said. 'Much better to surprise him. If you call, it gives him an opportunity to say no.'

'But at least we'll know if he's there.'

'We have just driven seventy miles, Mark. Another few won't hurt. Put him on the spot and we get to see his reaction.'

'That's a good point.'

Carmen winked. 'I'm full of them.'

Henry had already settled behind them. Mark's departure and the closure of the shed door had swiftly brought his distress to an end. They told Mrs Chuter what had happened and promised to update her with any news, if they were successful in speaking to Creasey. She thanked them again for their visit and waved them off from the doorstep, her spare hand using the wall for support.

Carmen drove an old VW Corrado but it was well maintained and it had them on the ring road around Cambridge in a matter of minutes. Mark had racked the seat back as far as it would go but his knees were still wedged against the dashboard. He yawned as Carmen pushed north towards Milton, his jet lag increasing with every passing minute. He would need to eat if he was going to stay awake.

They stopped at a sandwich bar on the edge of town but ate in the car as they drove.

Mark was just finishing his bacon and cheese ciabatta when his telephone rang. The caller introduced himself as Detective Inspector Calum Deakin from New Scotland Yard. Deakin explained that he had been tasked with trying to find Ronald Ross, following an alert from

Inspector Kiuke in Port Moresby. He was keen to meet with Mark as soon as possible to run through the encounter in the park and collect a description. The American Embassy in Grosvenor Square had also denied any knowledge of the man, and now there were several organisations interested in discovering his true identity. Mark looked at his watch and agreed to meet Deakin back at his flat at five o'clock.

'So,' Carmen said, once he had hung up. 'You said you knew who stole the notebook.'

'No. I said I *thought* I knew who stole it.'

'So come on then.'

'Well, assuming we're going to take a bird's word for it –'

'Which I think we are, given the violence of his reaction.'

'Agreed. Then I think it was a simple case of mistaken identity.'

Carmen's jaw dropped in mock astonishment. 'No shit, Sherlock! And there was I thinking you really *had* stolen it.'

Mark shook his head and rolled his eyes.

'Creasey?' she asked.

'No, not Creasey.'

'Who then?'

'A guy called Fletch. Ronald Ross's sidekick. I met him this morning in the park. He's the same height and build as me. When I walked into the shed, Henry thought I was Fletch and freaked. I think he witnessed the crime.'

Carmen pursed her lips. Mark wondered what

it would be like to kiss them. 'Interesting theory,' she said, nipping past a slow-moving van. 'So where does it lead us?'

'It goes something like this,' Mark answered. 'Tom Chuter discovered some sort of secret while he was living with his tribe in PNG. He recorded it in his notebook, along with information on the tribe's whereabouts. The importance of the discovery precipitated a professional dilemma, so –'

'*Precipitated*? Good word!'

'Thank you. So when he returned to England he was unsure whether to publish his findings. In the end he chose not to, but not before he had told someone else all about it.'

'They say a secret is something you tell one other person.'

'Precisely. Always a big mistake. Tom's confidant couldn't keep the secret to himself and told Ronald Ross, who subsequently dispatched Fletch to steal the notebook. Henry witnessed the crime, remembering that Fletch was a big man. Fletch then gave the notebook to the man in the helicopter, who used it to track down the tribe and steal their secret. Only the helicopter crashed on its way back from the jungle. We found it, you wrote it up, and Ross's team read the article and tracked me down. Now they're offering £30,000 for information that will lead them to the briefcase.'

'And you think Simeon Creasey is the confidant?'

'It could have been anyone,' Mark said, suppressing a yawn. 'But since it clearly wasn't either of Tom's parents, I'd suggest that his lover is certainly a candidate.'

'Well,' Carmen said, as she turned right into the Science Park. 'Here we are. Let's hope the double-crossing *culeado* is in.'

Twenty-Six

Christ on a bike! Now what?

It was one o'clock. Melanie had been asleep.
She would have liked to have been up and about,
spending some of her newfound wealth, but the
truth of the matter was that she was ill. Even
listening to her iPod was beyond her. Ronald Ross
had left two hours ago but it felt like two minutes.
Another visitor was the last thing she needed.

The doorbell rang again. Longer and louder.

'Keep your wig on!' Melanie yelled, and then
groaned as the effort made her sway.

She yanked the duvet aside and wrestled her
dressing gown over her shoulders. The rucksack
lay on the end of the bed, where she could feel
the weight of the money on her feet. Mark's loss
had been her gain and she was free from guilt.
She had done nothing wrong. And no one would
ever know.

Thirty thousand pounds! Not bad for a
morning's work.

Melanie had known who it was the moment she'd heard the American accent on the intercom. Known too that Ross had come to persuade her holier-than-thou brother to change his sanctimonious little mind. Well, this time he was going to be in luck. Mark had left for the day, and Ross would find her a much more accommodating collaborator.

The meeting had lasted a matter of minutes. Melanie had nodded politely while Ross had introduced himself and spun his yarn about recovering the bodies on behalf of the bereaved families. Then she'd shaken her head and muttered something about police confidentiality until the American had finally clicked his fingers to summon the bag. Fletch had shown her the cash. She'd riffled through the wads as though inspecting the notes for fakes. The money *might* have been counterfeit but there was a touch of class to Ross that led Melanie to trust him. Thirty thousand pounds was clearly a drop in his ocean. She'd even thought about asking for more, suspecting that his budget would stretch to at least double. Then she'd changed her mind, acknowledging that she was taking enough risks already. Mark had left for Grantchester with a warning to be vigilant in case Ross came to the flat. A degree of caution, she'd conceded, wasn't inappropriate.

Melanie had found Teraruma on Ross's map and explained that they'd paddled north, about thirty minutes upriver, before turning right along one of the Fly's many tributaries. They'd stopped in the unmarked village of Hulale and then fled five or six hours east. Or mostly east, if Mark's navigation had been anything to go by. That had put them on the edge of the unmapped area, which was as much as Melanie had been able to share.

Ross had produced a pencil from inside his jacket pocket and had traced her directions over the map. He had drawn a large circle around the approximate area of the crash site, and then folded the map away, evidently satisfied with what he'd just heard.

'You might like to keep this meeting to yourself,' he had said as he'd given her the second fifteen grand and then shaken hands on their deal.

'And you might like to fuck off before my brother comes home,' she'd countered with a grin.

'Your brother's in Grantchester,' Ross had replied. 'He won't be home until later.' And with that, he'd turned and exited the flat, leaving Melanie confused but too damn rich to care.

Now she stood by the intercom again, wondering if they'd come to take the money back. 'Hello?' she said, her voice much weaker than usual.

'Delivery for a Miss Melanie Bridges.'

'Leave it inside the door, please.' She pressed the button and heard a distant buzz as the latch released on the door downstairs.

'You'll need to sign,' the voice said.

'Can you bring it up?'

'Not without your help. It's heavy.'

'Christ!' Melanie said. 'I'll come down.' She hung up the receiver, tightened the cord around her gown and began trudging downstairs to the hall. A delivery? She wasn't expecting anything but with Christmas only ten days away, it might be an early present. Not that she needed another one of *those* after her bonus earlier.

The courier was standing in the hall. He was black and rangy with high cheekbones and dreads bunched tight under a blue beanie. He wore a padded lumberjack shirt for a jacket and was whistling 'Jingle Bells' while he waited for her with his clipboard.

'Where is it?' Melanie asked.

'Still in the van. You mind giving me a hand?'

Melanie sighed to let the guy know that going outside was a major inconvenience. She could see his white van parked opposite the door. It was bitterly cold but she was curious now, as she put the front door on the latch.

Melanie led the way on to the pavement, with the courier close behind. The van was a white Transit, its side door gaping open. She could see a large box on the floor against the far wall. It was brown, sealed with masking tape. A white sticker with the word FRAGILE in big red letters provided a vague clue to the nature of its contents.

'Here,' the driver said. 'Let me go first.'

He walked around her and hopped lightly into the van. He crouched as he pulled the box towards him, and then stepped over it so that he could push from the other side.

Melanie took a step forward. The guy's face was now only inches away from hers. His eyes were bloodshot from a hard weekend. She could smell fried onion on his breath. The wind whipped around her ankles, causing her pyjamas to balloon like windsocks. The sooner she got the bloody box inside, the better. Mark could carry it upstairs for her when he got back from Grantchester.

Melanie put her hands onto the box, her wrists sliding from her sleeves like delicate pistons. The guy smiled, and she knew then that she was in terrible trouble. It was the satisfied grin of a man pleased with his plan. A trace of surprise in there, too, as though he hadn't expected it to go *that* well.

By the time Melanie reacted, it was already too late. The courier's hands clamped on to her wrists and hauled her violently inside the van.

Twenty-Seven

The Cambridge Science Park was founded by Trinity College in 1970, with the objective of encouraging closer ties between the university, industry and the world of scientific research. Having expanded rapidly since its inception, it now covered one hundred and fifty-two acres and was home to more than ninety companies and their five thousand staff.

Mark and Carmen drove through it in silent admiration. The architecture was crisp and clean, surrounded by landscaped gardens and miniature lakes. Although many were nearly forty years old, the buildings retained a futuristic edge, which was enhanced by the logos of their tenants. Companies like 3i, Celldex, Genapta, Logotron, Neurascript, Pharmorphix and Xaar. Mark read the names, wondering what on earth they all did. He had three good A-levels and a degree in medicine but he knew that he would be out of his depth among the employees here. The park was home to some of the finest minds in the country: researchers and pioneers pushing the boundaries of science. These people didn't need to think outside the box because they weren't aware that there was a box in the first place.

Mark twisted his head as the Corrado flashed past another laboratory. Hypoxium Limited. What were they working on? A cure for cancer? A teleportation device? The elimination of global warming at the flick of a switch? This was an exhilarating place. The future was just yards away, morphing inside those buildings.

The temperature had dropped in the last hour and a thick fog was rolling in from the fens. Carmen stayed in the car while Mark entered the park's main reception building. Two minutes at the front desk were all he needed to discover that Simeon Creasey was the proprietor and managing director of a firm called Plasmavax Limited. The receptionist didn't know what they did – something to do with biotechnology, she thought. She gave Mark directions to unit 321 and sent him on his way with a lascivious smile and a colour-coded map of the campus.

Carmen drove the short distance to Creasey's lab and parked in the nearest vacant bay, some thirty yards from the building. She walked close to Mark's side as they crossed the car park, using his body to shield herself from the wind.

Mark had done most of the talking with Mrs Chuter but he sensed that Carmen would take the lead here. The sympathy and softness she had shown in Grantchester had given way to professional steel. There was briskness in her stride and a belligerent look in her grey eyes. The plot had thickened. She was now on the trail of a much bigger story. And poor old Creasey was guilty until proven innocent. But how would she persuade him to talk? Would she introduce herself as a journalist? Or as a friend of Mrs Chuter? Would she play good cop or bad?

'I will handle this,' she told him, as if reading his thoughts.

'I believe you,' Mark said.

Inside, the premises were immaculate. Chrome-plated furniture, tinted glass and polished wood were softened by fresh flowers and green plastic plants that reminded him of the jungle. Plasmavax comprised a reception desk, three offices and a kitchenette. Further back, at the end of a short corridor, a set of double swing doors led to a no-doubt state-of-the-art laboratory. Mark guessed that the whole enterprise employed no more than seven or eight people: a highly specialised organisation that had thrown all its resources into one niche of medical research.

The reception desk was staffed by an austere woman in her late forties. She had a matronly manner and wore her hair Princess Leia-style, in matching buns either side of her head. She was the gatekeeper to Creasey's empire. Mark knew instantly that she was going to be a formidable obstacle.

'Good afternoon,' she said, her tone as

challenging as a sentry's on a barracks gate. 'Can I help you?'

'Yes, please,' Carmen replied. 'We are looking for Mr Creasey.'

'*Doctor* Creasey,' the woman corrected, passing them the visitors' log so that they could sign in. 'Do you have an appointment?'

'No. We don't. But we do have some important news regarding his lover, Tom Chuter. We won't take a minute of his time, and it would be in his best interests to talk to us. My name is Carmen Beckwith and this is my companion Mark Bridges.' She gave the receptionist a conspiratorial wink. 'He is a doctor too.'

Mark watched the expression on the receptionist's face and tried not to smile. Carmen's frankness had left the woman dazed. He could see her trying to make sense of what she'd heard; as though she had long suspected that her boss was gay but was still uncomfortable to hear it confirmed. And why the doctor? That couldn't be good news, could it? Doctors never were. 'He's not in,' she stammered. 'He's gone to the canteen for –'

At that moment the door opened and a man in a lab coat walked in behind them.

'Ah, Dr Creasey,' the receptionist clamoured. 'You've got some visitors.' She shuffled some papers on her desk and then tapped her keyboard, like a newsreader trying to look busy at the end of her bulletin. 'They say it's personal.'

Like his premises, Simeon Creasey was neat

and tidy. Dapper even, in his blue shirt and bright red tie. His hair was parted on one side, combed over his head in a heavy brown lick. A trim moustache bordered a puckered mouth, with not a hair out of place. A milky complexion suggested that he moisturised at least once a day. Even the pens in his lab-coat pocket were neatly ordered according to height. He stepped forward with a welcoming smile and extended his hand to Carmen. 'Simeon Creasey,' he announced. 'How can I help you?'

Carmen shook his hand and returned his smile. 'My name is Carmen Beckwith. I would like to ask you a few questions about the theft of Tom Chuter's notebook.'

Mark had known that Carmen would be direct, but even he hadn't expected such a brazen assault. She'd cut straight to the chase, putting Creasey on the spot. It was a sly gambit.

Creasey wilted before their eyes, his blush confirming their suspicions. His mouth opened in silent panic. His eyes darted left and right, dropped to the floor, and then looked longingly at the sanctuary of his office. He ran a hand over his head, conscious that his reaction now made any sort of denial impossible. He looked like he wanted to say something but didn't know where to begin. Mark felt almost sorry for him. Carmen might as well have slapped him round the face for all the shock she had caused.

'Are you with the police?' Creasey eventually managed to ask.

'No,' Carmen replied. 'This is a private investigation.'

Creasey's face demanded more information but his receptionist had just answered the telephone and she announced the caller before he could speak. 'I've got Sean Capron on line one. He says he'll be here in ten minutes.'

'Good. Thank you, Jeanette.' Creasey drew a deep breath and turned to Carmen. 'You'd better come with me.'

They crossed the reception area to the first office on the right. Creasey closed the door and invited them to sit at a meeting table in the corner of the room. Mark cast his eyes around the office, taking in his surroundings. There was a whiteboard on one wall. It was covered in chemical equations and drawings of complex molecules. A rack of test tubes sat on the side of a low cupboard. Next to it a perspex beaker held a clutch of glass pipettes. There were a pair of goggles and some latex gloves on Creasey's desk. And there, on top of his in tray, was a copy of yesterday's *Observer*.

Twenty-Eight

Mark glanced at Carmen to see if she had spotted the newspaper. He needn't have bothered.

'I see you take the *Observer*, Dr Creasey?'

Creasey looked over his shoulder at the paper and nodded.

'There is a story on page eight,' Carmen continued. 'I don't know if you read it. It is about Dr Bridges here, who recently got lost on a birdwatching trip in Papua New Guinea.'

'No,' Creasey said. 'I must have missed it. Are you going to tell me who you are or do I have to guess?'

'I am a journalist,' Carmen replied, unfazed by his sudden growth in confidence. 'I wrote the article.'

A flash of comprehension in his eyes. 'And what, if I may ask, has this got to do with Tom's notebook? Or me for that matter?'

'Tom's notebook contained details of a

secret,' Carmen explained. 'Something he discovered during his time with a remote tribe in the far west of Papua New Guinea. Something significant.'

They watched his face for signs of a reaction but Creasey had regained his composure. He nodded slowly, his expression impassive.

'And you want to know what it is?'

'Yes,' Carmen replied. 'I sense it is important. I think it could make an interesting story.'

'Oh? And why is that?'

'Call it a hunch. Female intuition.'

Creasey smiled. 'And you're hoping I'm going to tell you what it is?'

'You were his lover. I imagine you talked occasionally?'

Creasey leaned back in his chair and stared wistfully out of the window. 'Yes,' he said. 'I was. But we were going through a bad patch when he left.'

'How bad?' Carmen asked, needling him in the hope that he would let something slip. Mark hadn't seen this side to her before. If they hadn't been working so well her tactics would have been cack-handed at best. But she spoke with such confidence and authority that she was all but commanding the information out of him.

'If you must know, I suspected him of having taken a wife among the tribe he was studying. Tom always had bisexual tendencies and if it meant better integration with the people he was studying, then going straight wouldn't have been too much of a hardship. I haven't heard from him in over a year, so whatever we once had is now over. He never told me anything about a discovery.'

'But the notebook *was* stolen?'

Mark could see it in the man's eyes. A calculation. Like he didn't want to talk but knew that his blush earlier had already given them their answer. A denial now might imply that he had something to hide.

'Yes. The day before Tom left. He was terribly upset. How do you know all this?'

Carmen drew her lips tight across her face in a pained expression. 'Sorry. Let us just say a little bird told me. Now, do you know who took it?'

Creasey shook his head. 'I have no idea. Tom and I were out for dinner. When we returned to his room, it had been ransacked and the notebook stolen.'

'Was anything else taken?' Mark asked.

'No. Not that I know of. Why?'

'Quite a specific thing to steal, don't you think? It suggests to me that the thief knew exactly what he wanted. Knew what he was getting.'

'If you say so.'

'Well they hadn't come for the TV or DVD player, had they? Did Tom report it?'

'No, he didn't. The police, I imagine, have better things to do than look for people's notebooks.'

Carmen folded her hands and leaned forward

over the table, keen to reassume control of the interview. 'And Tom went back to Papua New Guinea to warn the tribe that their secret was out?'

'Who knows?' Creasey said. 'It could have been Papua New Guinea. It could have been Brazil, the Congo or Cleethorpes. Like I said, I haven't heard from him in over a year.'

'And you did not think to tell his parents that he had left?'

'Oh please!' Creasey blurted, suddenly annoyed. 'Those two were the cause of more unhappiness for Tom than anything else. He always said that it was just his father but in my opinion his mother was just as bad. Never let him grow up. He's fifty next year and she still talks of him as if he were five. She smothered him. Never gave him a chance to think for himself. Interesting, isn't it, how closely related those words are? "Mother" and "Smother". Nothing between them except the sound of a hiss. And as for that bigot of a father –'

'He's dead,' Mark said.

Creasey paused. Pulled his mouth into a grimace. 'I'm sorry to hear that.'

'Perhaps the notebook might have been a priority for the police if they'd known what was inside?'

'Perhaps,' Creasey agreed. 'I wouldn't know. But I suspect that the study of anthropology isn't as high on their list as you seem to think.'

'You could have read it,' Carmen challenged.

'You thought Tom had taken a wife back in Papua New Guinea. You were jealous, so you read his notebook for confirmation.'

Creasey blushed but his tone conveyed anger as much as guilt. 'I'm sorry, Miss Beckwith. I'm not going to sit here and be accused of lying. Or of stealing my ex-partner's property, which you are blatantly insinuating with these ridiculous questions. Frankly I would have expected something a little less ham-fisted from an experienced reporter. But evidently you're not that experienced at all. Tom and I are history. Whatever your interest is in his notebook, it has nothing to do with me. I can't help you. Now, if you'll excuse me, I'm expecting a visitor for an important meeting, so I'll have to ask you to leave.'

Carmen stood up. 'What did Tom discover in Papua New Guinea, Dr Creasey?'

Creasey shook his head and opened the door.

'Protection against bad air,' Mark added, recalling the postcard on Elsie Chuter's fridge. 'Does that mean anything to you?'

Creasey's eyes narrowed. Half a second later the corner of his mouth twitched as though he was reining in a smile. 'Jeanette will see you out.'

There was nothing to be gained from arguing. Creasey was lying, and they both knew it. But so what? What could they do? There was no way to prove that he had arranged the theft of Tom's notebook. No way to prove that he knew the secrets inside. It was the end of the road.

Mark suddenly felt tired and grumpy. He was disappointed, and not just for Carmen. Before this morning he hadn't really cared what was inside the case. But since then his curiosity had quickly grown. Tom's secret was beginning to niggle. Beginning to peck away at him like a finch on a feeder of nuts. How could he not care what was inside the case when someone had offered him £30,000 to locate it? He should have looked, damn it. Should have kicked the fire extinguisher loose with his foot. If he'd snapped the plastic handle it would have fallen forward, releasing the pressure on the case. The keys had been right there on the floor.

He picked up a Plasmavax brochure on his way out of the office and followed Carmen down the steps. They returned to the car, quiet and dissatisfied. For a minute they just sat there, deep in thought. It was only two o'clock but it had already been a long day. Jet lag hung over him like a heavy cloud. Even Carmen seemed to have lost her ebullience.

'We should start heading back,' Mark said after a while. 'I've got to meet Detective Deakin at five, and this fog will slow the traffic down. Are you OK to drive?'

Carmen nodded and started the engine. 'Not much of a story,' she said. 'It is intriguing but it is hardly news. Not unless we can find out what Tom discovered. You don't fancy going back to Papua New Guinea, do you?'

Mark yawned and shook his head. 'Not

without a better reason than that, I'm afraid.'

'Spoilsport.'

She was about to drive off when Mark suddenly put a hand on the wheel. 'Stop,' he cautioned, his voice an urgent whisper. 'Don't turn around.'

Carmen peered at him like he was mad. 'What is going on?'

'A visitor.'

Mark looked again, staring into the rear-view mirror to confirm his hunch. He was alert now, his jet lag swept away on a tide of adrenalin. The suit and winter coat could have belonged to anyone but the measured gait was unmistakable. It was him, all right. There. Thirty yards away on the other side of the car park. Ronald Ross trotting up the steps to Simeon Creasey's office.

Twenty-Nine

'Well,' Mark said. 'That closes *that* little loop. Creasey and Ross know each other, which means Creasey is almost certainly our mole, regardless of what he's just told us.'

'One big happy family,' Carmen agreed.

'One big organisation, certainly.'

'You don't think they are the only ones involved?'

'No,' Mark replied. 'Ross isn't calling the shots. He's just an agent: a lieutenant dispatched to do the dirty work. I've got a hunch that he's ex-State Department. Or ex-CIA, or ex-military. Or maybe he used to be a cop. Either way, I don't think he's the kind of guy with enough wealth to own his own helicopter. If he *was*, he wouldn't bother to fly all the way from America to chase me around Gladstone Park. He'd hire someone exactly like him to do it on his behalf.'

'Good point.'

'Which makes me think that he's working for

someone or some*thing* bigger. A company perhaps. Or maybe even a government. Maybe it really does have something to do with the copper mine he mentioned this morning. But whatever it is, I think we've moved on from drugs and birds' eggs. If you can find out who he's working for then you really will have a story on your hands.'

Carmen nodded. She drummed her fingers on the steering wheel. Then, suddenly, her hand was on the car door and she was swinging her legs outside. 'That's a good idea,' she said. 'I'll be right back.'

'Wait!' Mark called. 'Where are you going?'

'To find out who he works for.'

'What? You think you can just barge in and ask him?'

'Why not? It worked with Creasey.'

'Creasey was a flake. Ross is made of sterner stuff. He'll eat you for breakfast.'

'Lunch,' Carmen corrected. Then she smiled, apparently amused by the look on Mark's face. 'Relax! I'm just going to check the visitors' log in reception. He might have signed in under a company name. I will pretend I have come back to leave a message for Creasey and take a quick look while I am talking to the lovely Jeanette.'

Mark ran a hand over his chin. It was a reasonable plan. Harmless too. Carmen wasn't going to confront the guy. Or even come into contact with him. He would be tucked away in Creasey's office, discussing the fact that he'd just missed them. She could be in and out in seconds and Ross would never know.

Only he wasn't called Ross, was he?

Carmen was already halfway across the car park when Mark lowered his window and called her back. 'His real name is Sean Capron,' he said. 'At least that's the name he would have used when he signed in.'

Carmen looked at him and raised an eyebrow. 'How do you know?'

'Remember when we first met Creasey? Jeanette took a call while he was introducing himself. "I've got Sean Capron on line one. He says he'll be here in ten minutes." That's him. That's the meeting that Creasey was waiting for.'

'Could be another alias,' Carmen suggested.

'Could be,' Mark agreed. 'But why use an alias if they already know each other?'

'Lots of reasons. What if this is a purely commercial relationship? He might have bought the notebook. He might not have wanted Creasey to know who he is or who he is working for.'

'That's possible,' Mark conceded. 'But if that's the case, how did Creasey find him?'

'Through an intermediary.'

Mark grimaced. Carmen was right.

'Don't look so upset!' she teased. 'For the record, I think you are right. I just like the look on your face when you have to acknowledge that you might be wrong.' And with that she turned and jogged across the car park.

Mark watched her go, her long legs carrying

her effortlessly over the asphalt. *Beckwith*. It was the first time he had heard her surname. *Carmen Beckwith*. Half Chilean, half English. Exotic and urbane. He remembered her tears and her embrace at the news of Melanie's rescue, her concern for Elsie Chuter, and her brutal dismantling of Simeon Creasey. Mark had been wrong about that. Carmen hadn't been using shock tactics. In fact, she hadn't been using any recognised interview technique at all. Deceit and guile were beyond her. She had waded in with all guns blazing because that was the only way she knew how. She wore her heart on her sleeve; passion present in everything she did. Mark shifted in his seat. That was the way to live, wasn't it? To *feel* everything. To engage with everything. To be riled by stuff. To celebrate other people's joy. To free the bird from its cage.

The Plasmavax marketing literature was in his lap. Its cover was blue and glossy and carried an artistic shot of Creasey's lab. Above the photograph, the 'l' in the company name had been replaced with a vertical syringe. Mark opened the brochure and found his eyes drawn to a paragraph entitled 'About Us'. He read it closely, wanting to understand the detail.

- We recognise that the most significant advances in medical technology are often made by individual researchers and small, non-commercial laboratories. However, lack of funding and the absence of

251

rigorous business acumen result in many such discoveries never reaching their intended markets.

- Plasmavax was founded in Cambridge in 2002 to address this issue. We advise on all aspects of the commercialisation process from procurement to pricing, branding to licensing. Whether you require assistance in gaining regulatory approval or simply want to meet the right development partner, Plasmavax will ensure that your products reach their full commercial potential.

- Last year we introduced our clients to companies such as GlaxoSmithKline, Johnson & Johnson, Bayer, Hoffmann-La Roche, and Gammell Pharmaceuticals, where they generated combined revenues in excess of £300m.

Mark flicked through the rest of the brochure quickly. There was a case study about a team from Surrey that had made inroads into developing a vaccine for Chagas disease. Another from Newcastle University that had engineered several new recombinant proteins. Towards the back, there was a prominent testimonial from a molecular biologist who had successfully licensed a new artificial insemination technique to Pfizer. The smile on his face suggested that he could now retire to his own island in the Caribbean.

Mark closed the brochure. An incubator. Wasn't that the term? Plasmavax nurtured its clients' technologies and then sold them to the world's pharmaceutical giants. And no doubt Creasey took a healthy percentage along the way.

Movement in the rear-view mirror caught Mark's eye. He glanced up in time to see Carmen leaving the building. She was hurrying, and he knew instantly that things hadn't gone according to plan.

His hunch was confirmed a moment later when Sean Capron appeared on the steps and began following her down. At first it looked as though the American was calling her back, but then Mark realised that he was speaking to someone on his mobile phone. Mark watched and waited. Capron wasn't running. Perhaps there was no cause for alarm, after all. Then, out of the corner of his eye, he spotted someone else crossing the car park at lightning speed. It was Fletch, moving between the vehicles like a galloping bear. Carmen hadn't seen him. And he was going to cut her off long before she made it back to the Corrado.

Mark swore and unclipped his seat belt. He opened the door and squeezed out of the car. Carmen must have spotted the concern on his face because she glanced over her shoulder and saw Fletch. He was bearing down on her with clenched fists and pounding feet. Trouble. Big trouble. She had a couple of seconds before he caught her. And the way he was moving was indication enough that he hadn't come to talk.

'Mark!' Carmen had her mobile phone in her hand. She lobbed it towards him, sending it high over the ground.

Mark took two steps forward and one to his right, watching it spiral end over end through the fog. What did she want him to do? Call the police? If so that was going to have to wait until he had dealt with Fletch.

It was a good throw. The phone landed in Mark's hands with a satisfying slap as he pouched the catch high on his chest. He immediately transferred it to his pocket and turned his attention back to their assailant.

Fletch had stopped running. It was the phone he was after, not Carmen. And the fact that it was now in Mark's pocket had given him pause for thought. He advanced cautiously, slipping the leather jacket from his shoulders. Behind him, Capron was making methodical progress through the cars, his steps as unhurried as they had been in Gladstone Park.

Mark felt the adrenalin explode in his stomach. His veiled threat in the park had been a bluff. He wasn't a fighter, but he had all of three seconds to become one. There would be no posturing. No melodramatic one-liners. It would be all-out violence from the start. Fletch was concentrating. This was work for him. Twenty stones of hired muscle coming to retrieve that phone. How many bones had he broken? Mark wondered. How many heads had he cracked? How many doctors had he created new patients for?

Carmen had made it. Mark reached out a hand and pulled her towards him, spinning her behind his back. 'Get in the car and start the engine,' he ordered. 'I'll join you in a minute.'

He took a step forward. He had no idea what he was going to do. Fletch tossed his jacket to the ground and held out his hand for the phone.

'Give it 'ere!' he said in a cockney accent.

Mark shook his head. And suddenly it was on.

Thirty

Fletch cocked his arm and swung.

The punch was a haymaker. An arcing blow, aimed at the doctor's chin. It was a tried-and-tested weapon. A one-stop solution that fixed ninety per cent of the problems it encountered. Occasionally, very occasionally, he would be required to follow it up with a left. As a kid he had sparred at a gym in Crystal Palace. At nineteen he had measured his power at four hundred pounds per square inch, which put him on a par with Tyson and Lewis. Bridges was a solid lad, but that wasn't going to make any difference. It didn't matter how big or tough you were. If you got caught with a punch like that, you were going down.

Or so Fletch thought. Had it connected, his fist would have knocked the doctor's head clean off his shoulders. But it didn't. It stopped two inches short.

Bridges had stood his ground, clueless but

unflinching. He hadn't tried to duck or to counter with a punch of his own. Instead he had simply held up his hand to protect his face. Fletch's fist had slammed into it and stopped. Completely. Like a baseball thudding into a catcher's mitt.

Now Bridges closed his fingers and squeezed. When he had the grip he wanted, he began to twist Fletch's wrist. Fletch turned, a compliant dancing partner performing a twirl. He gasped more in surprise than pain. How was it possible? How could anyone be *that* strong? There had been no give in the doctor's arm. No judder, no jolt. No movement back as it had absorbed the momentum of a jackhammer travelling at seventy miles per hour.

Fletch continued to twist. He didn't want to but he had no choice. He tried to spin from the hold but his arm was suddenly behind his back in a half nelson. The pain in his shoulder was unlike anything he'd experienced before. He tried to kick back, aiming at his opponent's shins. But that, too, was futile. Bridges was too tall, his reach too great. There was no way to get near him.

Fletch felt himself being lowered gently to the ground. He relaxed, signalling his submission. Resistance was futile. And too damn dangerous. A punch to his temple from a man that strong would leave him dead. He sank to his knees, and shrugged at his boss. The look on Capron's face said it all. It hadn't been a fight. It hadn't even been a contest.

Fletch felt Bridges press down on his shoulder. The guy's hand was like a piston. It was broad and heavy. It forced him on to his chest with hydraulic ease. There was nothing violent about it. Nothing hurried. It relied solely on phenomenal force.

'Stay there,' Bridges said.

And Fletch did.

'You were right,' Carmen said as she sped out of town. 'He signed in as Sean Capron, but he had left the "company name" box blank.'

'So what happened?' Mark asked. 'I thought you weren't going to confront him?'

'I wasn't initially.' Carmen flashed him a guilty grin. 'But I was standing in the reception area and I thought I have come this far, why not go the whole way?'

'And what exactly did that entail?'

'I figured it might be useful to have some photographs for my story, so before Jeanette could do anything, I crossed the corridor to Creasey's office, opened the door and told them to smile. Then I got the hell out of there. Capron is past his best-before date. He was never going to catch me. I did not know about the other guy, though. Thanks for intervening.'

'You didn't give me much choice.'

'No, but you would have stepped in anyway. You're not hurt, are you?'

'My hand's a bit sore.'

Carmen laughed.

'What's so funny?'

'The second-biggest man I have ever seen in my life just threw his best punch at you, and you complain that your hand is sore?'

'It is,' Mark replied. 'That really hurt.'

'You sound like you had a scrape in the playground.' She paused. 'I don't know. It just sounded funny, that's all.'

Mark looked at her confused. 'Did you see the size of him? Besides, like I told you the other day, I'm just an ordinary bloke from Ealing. When someone hits me, it hurts.'

Carmen shook her head and concentrated on the road. 'Do you think we should call the police?'

'Not much point,' Mark replied. 'I'm meeting this guy Deakin at five. I'll tell him all about it then. Capron isn't going to hang around the Science Park waiting for the cops to arrive. But that doesn't really matter, anyway. Creasey's the managing director of a well-established business. He's not going anywhere in a hurry. If the police want to find out more about Capron, all they've got to do is talk to Creasey.'

Carmen was silent for a moment, evidently mulling something over. 'Deakin is coming to talk to you about Capron, right?'

'Yes. Inspector Kiuke wants to know if he's running some sort of smuggling racket. And I imagine the State Department will be interested in knowing why someone's walking round London with thirty grand in a rucksack, pretending to be one of their employees. I'll give him a description and tell him whatever I can to help.'

'I imagine a photograph would be useful.'

Mark looked at her, wondering where this was leading. 'Yes, I'm sure it would.'

'In which case, I will trade it,' Carmen said. 'Deakin can have a copy of the snap on my phone in exchange for telling me anything he learns. He has got a much better chance of finding out who Capron is and who he works for than I do, but I still want my story.'

Mark rubbed his knees and twisted his legs, trying to make himself comfortable. 'Will the police cooperate with the press during an investigation? I don't know if that's normal. It sounds a bit of a long shot to me.'

'Features, Mark! Not news. I'm not going to break the story until I have got all the facts. It will be a retrospective. With photographs and interviews. I won't get in Deakin's way. If a crime has been committed then the perpetrators will probably be behind bars by the time I can sell it to a newspaper. Besides, I cannot get anything published until I know that there is definitely a story there.'

'There's a story all right. I've just been assaulted in a car park. By someone who works for someone who works for someone with his own helicopter and enough money for thirty grand to be small change.'

They sat in silence for a few minutes as the

Corrado flew down the motorway towards London. Outside, the fog had thinned but the cars still had their headlights on. Mark closed his eyes and felt his head nod with sleep. He jerked awake and opened the window. It wasn't fair to doze. Carmen's jet lag would be just as bad.

'Deakin will give me what I want,' Carmen said half an hour later as they approached the M25.

Mark glanced at her out of the corner of his eye. I believe you, he thought.

They arrived back at his flat just after four o'clock. The fog was thinner further south and they had beaten the rush-hour traffic. Beaten the commuters home too, which allowed Carmen to park directly outside.

Mark had his keys in his hand but noticed that the front door was ajar. He lived on the second floor of a Victorian terraced house. The woman on the ground floor worked in insurance in the City, while the first-floor flat was let out to a South African by a landlord who lived in Hong Kong. Neither neighbour would normally be home at this time of day. Perhaps Melanie had gone out and failed to close the door behind her? It wouldn't be the first time. But she was ill, and she was supposed to be resting.

Mark climbed the stairs wearily. His confrontation with Fletch had left him exhausted. It felt as though weeks had passed since they'd arrived back from Papua New Guinea, but it had only been this morning. He wanted nothing more than to crawl into bed and succumb to his jet lag. Carmen, too, had begun to tire. How she had managed to drive so well was a mystery. At least they had an hour in which to recharge their batteries before Deakin arrived. That would give him time to check Melanie's temperature and see how she was.

Mark arrived at the top of the stairs. The first butterflies immediately appeared in his stomach. It wasn't just the street door that was ajar. The door to his flat was wide open too.

Thirty-One

'Mel?' Mark hurried inside the flat. There were only five rooms. It took a matter of seconds to confirm that the place was empty. Where was she? Had she gone to the shops?

'Is everything all right?' Carmen had followed him in and seen the worry in his face.

'I don't know,' he replied. 'Mel's not here.'

He returned to her room. The bed was unmade, as though she'd just tumbled out of it. Her favourite trainers were still on the floor, along with her coat and scarf. Her iPod was right there on the bedside table. So too was her mobile phone. Something was definitely wrong. She would never leave home without those two items.

Mark flicked the duvet back as though she might be hiding underneath. And that's when he saw it. The same rucksack that Fletch had thrown at him in the park.

'Oh Christ, Mel! What have you done?'

Mark sat on the bed and opened the pack. Carmen joined him, standing in the doorway with a pained expression on her face. The money was inside. Big wads of used twenties, exactly as Capron had promised.

So what had happened? Where was she? That Capron had returned and offered Melanie the same deal was not in doubt. Mark had warned her not to open the door to him but she had clearly ignored his advice. She'd agreed to the terms, of course, but then what? Capron had driven to Cambridge to tell Creasey that they now knew, approximately, where the helicopter was. So did that mean Capron was working for Creasey? Was Plasmavax the organisation pulling the strings?

'I don't get it,' Mark announced. 'Where's she gone? Why would she leave £30,000 on her bed and leave the flat wide open?'

Carmen said nothing but Mark knew what she was thinking. The same as him. 'OK,' he conceded. 'It's a possibility. But why would Capron abduct her if she'd already told him what he wanted to hear? Why kidnap her but leave the money behind? Why not tell us that he'd taken her and use that as leverage to get the phone from you? It doesn't make sense.'

'There is probably a perfectly logical explanation,' Carmen said. 'Maybe she has gone to your parents. You said she was feeling ill, so perhaps they came to pick her up.'

Mark stood up from the bed and walked to the

living room. Melanie had a difficult relationship with their parents. The family home in Ealing would be an unlikely place for her to convalesce. And in any case, she almost certainly wouldn't leave all that money unhidden and in an unlocked room. Still, it was worth a try.

His hand was on the telephone, ready to lift the receiver, when it rang suddenly, causing him to jump.

'Hello?'

'Hello, Mark. Welcome home.'

Mark held his breath. He didn't recognise the voice. 'Who is this?'

'No one you know,' the voice replied. 'No one Melanie knows either, although we have at least met.'

Mark's heart leapt. He put the phone on loudspeaker and sat down on the sofa, fighting hard to control his rising fear. The man hadn't said much but there was unmistakable menace in the tone of his voice. He spoke slowly, in a broad Australian accent.

'She's a fiery little thing, isn't she? Plenty of spunk. Not mine, I hasten to add, but if she doesn't calm down, I might be tempted to change that.'

Mark felt his hand bunching into a fist. 'Who the hell are you, you sick bastard? And what have you done to my sister?'

'Calm down, mate. Everything will be fine. But I need you to do something for me first. If you want to see Melanie again, that is. If you don't – and frankly the way the little bitch is carrying on, I wouldn't blame ya – then just hang up now.'

'Who are you?' Mark shouted. 'And why have you taken her? What's she done? What the hell is this all about?'

Carmen entered the room and sat down next to him. She put a hand on his shoulder. She had heard the opening exchanges of the conversation and her face was drained of colour.

'You don't need to know who I am. But we'll have an opportunity to meet when you bring me what I want.'

'How much?' Mark asked. He was confused. Angry. Scared. Why would anyone want to kidnap his sister?

'Ah,' the man chuckled. 'If only it were that simple! Not money, mate. I've got enough of that for the time being. But it won't last forever. Which is why I want something that'll help me earn a lot more. I need you to run a little errand. I need you to fetch something for me.'

Mark exhaled loudly and stared at the ceiling. He knew what was coming next. It could only be one thing. 'The briefcase?'

'No, you fucking klutz! Not the briefcase. I want what's *inside* the briefcase. You can keep the bloody briefcase for all I care. Use it to put yer stethoscope in.'

'Why me?' Mark asked. 'Why don't *you* go? Melanie can show you where it is on the map.'

The man laughed. 'Me? I'm not welcome in

that part of the world any more. Too many people looking for me. Besides, how the hell am I going to find it? The newspaper said it was in the middle of bloody nowhere. No, mate. You found it, you bring it back! You've got a week.'

'A week?' Mark protested. 'That's impossible. It takes two days to get there and two to get back.'

'Which leaves you three days to find it. You'd better leave now.'

Mark's head was swirling. The thought of returning to PNG was crazy. He'd never find that crash site again. Not if he spent the rest of his life wandering through the Middle Fly District. The Australian was stark raving mad. He had no idea what he was proposing.

'I want to talk to Melanie.'

'You can do. But from Port Moresby. When I know you've arrived, and you're taking me seriously, *then* you can speak to her. There's a Singapore Airways flight out of Heathrow tomorrow morning. It hooks up with Air Niugini after a short stopover at Changi. You can be in Port Moresby in just over thirty-two hours from now. Check in to the Airways Hotel when you arrive. I'll call you there at nine o'clock in the morning, local time, the day after tomorrow.'

'Wait!' Mark said. 'What if I can't get a flight? The plane might be full. It's Christmas, for God's sake!'

'That's your problem, mate, not mine. Travel first class if you have to.'

'And delays?'

'Delays are out of your control. We'll push the call back if we need to. But I'll be watching the flight arrival times. I'll know if those planes are delayed or not. You lie to me and pretend you got stuck en route, then your little sister's coming home in pieces.'

'You lay a finger on her, and I swear I'll break every bone in your body.' Mark stood up and began pacing the room.

'Ah, cut the crap, will you? I'm serious here, mate. I won't hesitate to hurt your sister very badly if you don't do what I say.' He paused and chuckled down the line. 'Did I say *badly*? I meant *well*. I'll hurt her very well. I'm a bad man, mate, and the sooner you realise that the better. Now I want you to go to your fridge.'

'What?'

'Your fridge, mate. The big white box in the kitchen.'

Mark began moving towards the kitchen. He felt sick. He didn't want to go. Didn't want to play this twisted wacko's game.

'I'm there.'

'Good,' the Australian said. 'Now I've left something there. A small deposit to let you know how serious I am. There's a blue Tupperware box on the third shelf. You call the police or you decide not to fetch the case, and the next thing I leave will be too big for the fridge. You understand me, mate?'

'You're dead.'

'Excellent! That's the spirit! Goodbye, Mark. I'll talk to you in Port Moresby.'

Mark put the phone down. Carmen had followed him into the kitchen and watched him through her fingers.

He reached inside the fridge. Took the blue box from the shelf. There was something inside it. Not very heavy. Mark drew a deep breath. Put the box down. Picked it up again. Took another lungful of air. Finally, against every instinct in his body, he opened the lid.

What he saw caused him to retch and grab the table for support.

Thirty-Two

It was a woman's finger. The little finger of her left hand. Mark looked at it just long enough to know that it was real. The blood on the stump had congealed but it was still sufficiently fresh for him to know that it had been severed in the last few hours. It appeared to be slightly on the small side to be one of Melanie's, but then again, its diminutive size was probably due to the loss of blood.

Mark staggered to the sink, where he retched violently. Nothing came up. He turned in circles, unsure what to do. Then he returned to the sink where this time he was sick. He wasn't squeamish. It was the knowledge of what Melanie had gone through that was making him ill.

Worried that he might faint, he picked up the phone and returned to the lounge. He collapsed on the sofa. Behind him he heard Carmen's sharp intake of breath as she inspected the contents of the Tupperware box. If she hadn't been here, Mark might have believed that this was all just a delayed hallucination from Wontok's truffles. Certainly the experience was just as disorientating. He was out of control. Unable to think, or act, in a decisive way.

Mark couldn't believe it. What had they done to deserve this? Why had they become victims of yet more trauma? His anger grew in his chest, boiling like lava in the heart of a volcano. The water purification tablets had saved their lives but otherwise that helicopter had been nothing but trouble. The briefcase was like Pandora's box: a receptacle for all the world's evils. He never wanted this trouble. He had gone out of his way to avoid it. He hadn't opened the briefcase. Hadn't taken Capron's money. Hadn't wanted any part of it. And yet the trouble had found him, following him across the world like a wraith. Mark glanced at his hands. They had balled into fists.

Carmen came and sat beside him. She put an arm around his shoulder and told him that she was sorry. Mark didn't know if she was apologising for Melanie's misfortune or for writing the article that had unleashed this situation in the first place. He unhooked her arm and dropped it to the couch. He was short of breath. Her proximity was making him claustrophobic.

To say that it was all Carmen's fault was ridiculous, but Mark needed an outlet for his anger. She had mocked him for being melodramatic when he'd said that he didn't want his name in the papers. And look where it had got them. Sean Capron, Elsie Chuter, and now this Australian creep – three people he never knew existed before this morning – had all tracked him down and contacted the flat. And all thanks to Carmen's article. *Dr Mark Bridges of north London*. That was all it had taken. That and a listing in the telephone directory, which he should have removed a long time ago.

Mark turned towards her but bit his lip. He had only himself to blame. He could have refused. Could have told Melanie not to give Carmen an interview. Could have asked for them to remain anonymous. It was the same as his decision to allow Gile and Peri to take them to Hulale in the first place. *Weakness*. And a desire to be amenable. He should have put his foot down. Should have trusted his instincts. His fault. Definitely *his* fault.

'Do you want to me leave?' Carmen asked, her grey eyes pooling with tears.

'I don't know,' Mark snapped. 'I need time to think.'

'It might not be hers.'

'Oh please,' he said with a venom that surprised him. 'You don't know what the hell you're talking about. This is all your –' He stopped. Put his hands on his head. 'I'm sorry. Just give me a minute, will you?'

Carmen gave him a brave smile and returned to the kitchen. Mark didn't know what she had done with the finger but he heard the tap running as she filled the kettle for tea. It occurred to him then that the flat was a crime scene. They had already put their fingerprints all over the fridge and the Tupperware box, obliterating any that might have been left by Melanie's abductor. And there was a second issue too. He had been warned not to call the police, but DI Deakin was due to arrive in forty minutes. If the kidnapper was watching the flat, he might infer that Mark had called the cops, and inflict further torture on Melanie.

'We need to leave,' he said. 'We need to get out fast. We might be destroying evidence.'

Carmen agreed, staring guiltily at her hands like Lady Macbeth. They left the flat as they had found it, with the door open and Capron's money lying on Melanie's bed. There was no sign of a struggle, but Mark wanted the police to see what he had seen. A trained eye might spot something that he had missed.

They were halfway down the stairs when he felt his phone vibrating in his pocket. It was Detective Inspector Deakin, calling to tell him that he would be twenty minutes late.

'No,' Mark corrected. 'You'll be early.'

It didn't take long to relay what had happened. Mark tried to hold his voice steady as he ran through the details. It wasn't easy. Mention of the finger caused his pulse to rocket.

Deakin listened, asked a few questions and then told him to choose a location well clear of the flat where they could meet as soon as possible. Mark suggested his parents' place in Ealing, whereupon Deakin confirmed that he would be there in a shade over ten minutes. The meeting that had delayed him was no longer a priority.

Mark hung up. He reassured Carmen that she should join him. Then they set off towards Kilburn High Road, where they hailed a cab for Ealing.

Thirty-Three

Deakin was waiting for them when they arrived. He had parked some fifty yards from the house in an unmarked car. He saw them climbing out of the cab and flashed his lights to attract their attention. Mark and Carmen walked to meet him, introducing themselves in the street.

'Detective Inspector Deakin,' he said, shaking Mark's hand. 'Do your parents know what's happened?'

'Not yet,' Mark replied.

Deakin was short, squat and muscular, his broad shoulders testing the seams on his suit to their limit. He had a scowl on his face but the urgency in his voice confirmed that he was taking the situation very seriously indeed. If he hadn't been in law enforcement he might have passed for a bouncer but not much else. He looked hard and experienced: two qualities they would need in spades if they were going to save Melanie's life. Mark liked him immediately.

'And they're definitely in?' Deakin asked.

'They're *always* in.'

'In which case, I'll give you five minutes,' Deakin said. 'That's not much, I'm afraid, but time is of the essence. Stick to what you know. Don't jump to any conclusions. I want clear heads when I come through that door. It's not easy for you. You have my sympathy. But the calmer you all are, the quicker I'll be able to get on with the job of finding your sister.'

Mark nodded. He wasn't looking forward to this. His father would still be shattered after back-to-back long-haul flights. And as for his mother . . . He already knew that it would be more than she could take. To lose Melanie, find her and then lose her again in the space of a week was unfathomable. An insane turn of events that would leave her mentally and emotionally destroyed.

'I will stay here,' Carmen suggested. 'I can give you a head start on what has happened.'

'Good,' Deakin replied. 'And at some stage I still want to hear about this Capron character, but we'll deal with him later.'

'I can help you there too,' Carmen told him. 'I have a photograph.'

Mark left them to it and walked to the house. His parents lived in a red-brick semi. There was a paving drive at the front, with just enough space for two dustbins and the blue Renault. He pressed the bell and drew a deep breath. The combination of jet lag and shock had rendered him so exhausted that it felt as though he was floating on a cushion of air.

His father answered the door. Knew instantly that something was wrong.

Mark wasn't surprised. His anguish must have been plain to see: tight in the scrunch of his brow. Tighter still in the clench of his teeth.

'What's happened?'

'Melanie.'

Tony Bridges closed his eyes, only opening them again a few seconds later. 'Tell me,' he said, stepping to one side so that Mark could enter the house.

'She's been abducted.' It sounded ridiculous. Untrue.

Incomprehension flashed across his father's face. Then he turned and began walking towards the lounge. 'Have you called the police?'

'There's a detective waiting outside. He's talking to Carmen at the moment. It's a long story, Dad, but I'm going to have to make it quick. Is Mum in?'

'She's gone to Blockbusters. We were going to watch a film and hit the sack early.'

'She's not going to be able to handle this.'

'Let me worry about that. Tell me what happened while I get us a drink.'

Mark gave his father a brief overview of his extraordinary day, knowing that he would soon go through it in more detail with Deakin. His father poured two large tumblers of Scotch. They each took a long swallow. Another soon followed when Mark told him about the finger. His dad never interrupted. Never asked a question. Just waited for Mark to tell him what he knew. Then he sank into an armchair and put his head in his hands.

Carmen and DI Deakin arrived exactly five minutes later. They sat in the lounge while Mark took them through it, starting with his run-in with Fletch and Capron in Gladstone Park. He was confident that Sean Capron and the Australian didn't know each other but the briefcase was a common thread and he wanted Deakin to know it all.

Mark's mother arrived home twenty minutes later. '*No Country for Old Men*,' she called from the hall. 'It's that Coen brothers film. Won a couple of Oscars, I think.' Then she walked into the lounge, took one look at the man in the suit and whispered a single word. 'Melanie.'

Deakin was calm and efficient with an insatiable thirst for tea. His questions were direct and he made little attempt to mask the gravity of the situation. He was like a doctor discussing a potentially fatal disease: sincere and sympathetic but bluntly matter-of-fact.

Mark's mother fainted when she heard about the finger so Deakin called for a female constable to come and provide moral support. At the same time he called the chief inspector at Kilburn police station and demanded the immediate assembly of an incident room and a team of three detectives. Mark and his father exchanged a hopeful glance. It was progress. The first tangible step in bringing Melanie home alive.

The female constable arrived ten minutes later. Deakin made the introductions before asking a few final questions. 'OK,' he said, when he had finished. 'Here's what's going to happen. It's possible the kidnapper is still watching the flat, so we'll send someone in undercover: an electrician pretending to read the meter, or something like that. He'll be a forensic detective. He'll look the place over and get the finger sent off to the lab in Virginia Street. He'll take Melanie's toothbrush or hairbrush too and they'll check to see if there's a match in the DNA. If necessary he'll call in more officers and they'll go over the place with a fine-tooth comb. Plain-clothes officers will begin making door-to-door enquiries in the next hour to see if anyone saw anything. They'll pretend to be investigating a burglary. That way, if the abductor is still watching the flat, he won't be overly concerned if he starts enquiring about what's going on. In the meantime, PC Bennett here will stay with you to make sure you're all OK. Now then, does Melanie know your mobile number by heart?'

Mark nodded.

'So we have to assume that he could coerce it out of her, if he wanted to contact you away from home.'

'He won't,' Mark said. 'The next call isn't

going to be until the day after tomorrow in Port Moresby.'

'We don't know that,' Deakin said. 'Not for certain. He may change his mind. Now then, no one is to talk to the media. Miss Beckwith, I want your word that you're not going to take this to the papers.'

'You've got it,' Carmen replied. 'My story is irrelevant now. I'm not interested. The only thing that matters is finding Melanie.'

'Good, because if you were to . . .' Deakin stopped. Looked deep into her eyes and decided he could trust her.

'What should *I* do?' Mark asked. It was a question that had been eating him up for much of the last hour. 'Should I stay here or go to Papua New Guinea to fetch the briefcase?'

Deakin sucked in his breath. 'No. I wouldn't advise it. It's up to you, of course, but I'd prefer it if you remained somewhere where we could reach you at short notice. This is a serious situation and we'll be assigning significant resources to it. We're going to move heaven and earth to get your sister back. I don't think you jetting off to the other side of the world is going to have much bearing on events.'

'But it's such a specific thing he wants. I don't see any way round it.'

'If we can find him, we can negotiate,' Deakin said.

'I've already offered him money,' Mark countered. 'He said he wasn't interested.'

'And you don't know what's inside the briefcase?'

'No,' Mark replied. 'I've got no idea.'

Deakin sighed then smiled encouragingly. 'He's given you a week. A lot can happen in that time. Someone may have seen something. If Melanie was wearing pyjamas in the middle of the day, then that's going to strike people as unusual. If you go back to New Guinea it's going to be harder for him to reach you. He may change his mind.'

'What are the chances?' Tony asked. 'I mean, normally, when this sort of thing happens? How long till you find her?'

'I can't answer that,' Deakin said. 'No promises and no guarantees. In most hostage situations the first forty-eight hours are critical. The chances of a successful outcome drop dramatically after that. *But* . . . This is different. He's given you a week. That plays into our hands. Gives us a lot more time to find her.' He stood up and fished three business cards from his wallet. Fanned them out like he was about to perform a magic trick. 'Here are my details. You can call me 24–7. And I want to be the first person to know if he makes contact again. We'll be working with BT to identify the number he called you from. Any more calls from that number will give us a decent lead.'

'I don't think he'd be that stupid,' Mark said.

'No,' Deakin replied. 'Probably not. But even if he's using throwaway mobiles, we might be able to triangulate his position. Now then, I'll call you later and let you know how we get on at the flat. Be patient, have a little faith, and don't drink too much of that Scotch. Stay vigilant too. Any strangers outside the house or suspicious-looking vehicles in the street, then I want to know. OK?'

They shrugged and nodded. They weren't OK, but what else could they do except follow the man's advice?

Carmen left a few minutes after Deakin. It was an awkward goodbye. She looked pained. A combination of concern for Melanie coupled with a hopeless feeling that it might be all her fault. Mark could tell that she wanted to give him a hug. For reassurance and perhaps to apologise. That was her way: expressive and uninhibited. Irretrievably Latin. But Mark stood back. He was confused. He wanted to hold her. Wanted to feel her body against his. Wanted to press his nose against her neck and inhale her scent. But he couldn't do it. This wasn't the time. He didn't know what he felt. Didn't know what to say. Couldn't bridge the space and silence between them. If it hadn't been for Carmen, Melanie might –

Mark said goodbye and closed the door. Then he swore at himself for being so bloody *English*.

Thirty-Four

It was a tense evening. The worst of Mark's life. Harder than the night on the mudflat because this time he had to share it with his parents. It should have been easier with three of them but Mark couldn't stand to see their anguish. His mother was beside herself. She was unable to settle, scuttling from room to room, desperately seeking a distraction. All the time she reminisced angrily about the trouble that her daughter had caused as a child. As though the abduction was Melanie's fault. As though Mel had brought it upon herself. Mark's father had tried to calm her but had given up when she'd spun from his embrace. Now he sat in his armchair, silent; cut to pieces by his inability to do *anything* about the situation at all.

Mark felt much the same way. Only his pain was made worse by a sense of responsibility for what had happened. He was Melanie's big brother. He was supposed to look after her.

Supposed to protect her. He stood up and glanced at his jacket, hanging on a peg by the door. After his rescue at Dugudugu he had been ready to head straight back into the jungle, energised, he recalled, by Carmen's optimism. But London, if that's where Melanie was being held, was a more daunting prospect than the rainforest had ever been. No unmapped or uninhabited areas here. No snakes, crocodiles or hallucinogenic fungi. He could choose from any number of publications that would identify every street in the city. And yet where would he start? Which borough? Which postcode? And what if she had left London? Then what? Which county? Which farmhouse, barn or caravan was she now in? *No.* The jacket could stay where it was. This time there really wasn't anything he could do except wait by the phone for news.

It rang at half-past ten. Detective Inspector Deakin with an update from the forensic pathologist. Mark's father took the call. His reaction told them all they needed to know. Tony Bridges was six feet four inches tall. Fit and strong with not a single grey hair on his head. He had been an inspiration to Mark throughout his life. His gentleness, his manners, his calmness under pressure and quiet authority all influencing Mark in how he chose to behave. To see him now, chest heaving uncontrollably as he sobbed for his daughter's pain was the most distressing thing that Mark had ever seen.

'It's hers,' Tony said. And this time his wife

allowed herself to be held. 'The DNA's a perfect match. The bastard took her finger.'

Silence followed. There was nothing to say. This sort of thing didn't happen to them. It happened to other people. People on the news.

Mark's mother had made the bed in his old room. He trudged up the stairs some twenty minutes later. His parents were still sitting on the couch, staring vacantly at the wall. Ignoring Deakin's advice, he'd had another Scotch but its effects had been negligible. Had he not been jet lagged there would have been no way that he could have slept, but he was hoping that sheer exhaustion would get him through the night.

Mark had been expecting nightmares but he slept untroubled for the first four hours, waking again at half-past three. It felt strange to be in his old room. It was barely recognisable from his childhood. Everything had been cleared out apart from a few books and a photograph of a falcon that his parents had bought years ago on a holiday in Scotland.

He spotted his grandfather's sketchbook, gathering dust in the bookcase behind the door. It had been years since he'd looked through it. It called to him now, a familiar diversion that might take his mind off Melanie.

Mark turned the pages carefully, conscious that this was a family heirloom. The paper was brittle in places, slightly damp in others. His grandfather had worked in watercolours, with a meticulous eye for detail. The raggiana bird of paradise was there on the first page with its maroon breast, yellow collar and emerald throat. Mark and Melanie had seen several specimens in Varirata National Park at the beginning of their trip. Next came the resplendent Princess Stephanie's astrapia with its blue-green and purple head, silky plumage and long central tail feathers. The superb bird of paradise, black-billed sicklebill and Queen Carola's six-wired bird of paradise followed: three species that he and Melanie had missed. Mark turned another page and found himself looking at the King of England's bird, the only unauthenticated species in the book. It was the size of a crow; jet black except for its fluorescent pink throat and wingtips. Mark remembered Wontok's neck decoration. Had his grandfather really dreamed up this species?

Next came the magnificent bird of paradise, complete with Melanie's vulgar addition. Noel Bridges had drawn it perched high in a tree, fanning its feathers while it displayed to a clutch of females on a nearby branch. Beneath it, his grandfather's rucksack and hat nestled against the tree's trunk, skilfully painted so that their shadows eked across the page.

Melanie had been seven when she'd done it. A calculated act of revenge after she and Mark had rowed about something trivial that he couldn't even remember now. She had used a blue biro, scratchy at first but then gloopy with ink, to add some art of her own. By the time she had finished, it looked as though the bird was defecating on the rucksack. A trail of droppings falling with ballistic precision from its anus to the bag below.

Mark shook his head but couldn't suppress a smile. *Mel!* It didn't come any more immature than that. They'd all been so angry at the time. Especially Mark's father, for whom the sketch-book was a nostalgic treasure. But at least Noel Bridges never knew that his work had suffered such abuse. He'd died of malaria long before Melanie was born.

Mark turned the page again. The glossy-mantled manucode was another species he and Melanie had seen at Varirata. He ran his finger lightly over its feet, marvelling at how accurately his grandfather had captured the scales on its talons.

Mark paused. Listened.

A noise downstairs.

He slipped out of bed, hoisted his jeans over his hips and then felt his way along the corridor in the dark. Moments later he entered the kitchen, where he found his father making a pot of tea. He placed two mugs on the tray, telling Mark that his mother was also still awake.

Tony Bridges was wearing blue pyjamas and a towelling robe, with a pair of leather slippers on his feet. He looked up, forced a smile but said nothing, perhaps not trusting his voice. His eyes were red through lack of sleep or tears. Mark didn't know which. His father had taken it badly, his hand shaking as he retrieved the milk from the fridge. Mark had always thought that his dad was invincible but right now he looked old and suddenly frail. He may have been tall but the muscle was beginning to go and there were the first signs of a stoop in his shoulders. The milk bottle looked heavy in his hand. He shuffled his feet when he walked. His hair was tousled, the skin on his face looser than it had ever been before. His lower lip had just begun to quiver.

Mark had never seen him so dejected; so beaten. And in that moment he knew exactly what he needed to do. He crossed the kitchen in a single stride. Grabbed his father by the shoulders and enveloped him in a tight embrace.

'Dad,' he whispered. 'I'm going back. I'm going to get that briefcase.'

His father pulled away and looked at him, a glimmer of hope in his eye. 'You think?'

'Yes, I do. This guy is serious. He's already taken Mel's finger. I've got no reason to doubt that he'll carry out his threat to hurt her again if I don't comply. If we've got the briefcase then at least we have something to negotiate with. He doesn't want money. Whatever's inside is unique. It's the only thing that's going to satisfy him.'

Tony Bridges nodded. 'I agree. Your mum and I will look after things here.' He paused. Filled the teapot with boiled water. 'How will you find it?'

'I'll get the locals to help me. But I've got to get a plane ticket first.'

'We'll pay.'

'No,' Mark smiled. 'Melanie will pay. There's thirty grand sitting on her bed. Assuming Deakin lets us keep it, we might as well spend it on something useful.'

He left his father in the kitchen and walked to the study, where he fired up the computer and found Singapore Airlines on the Internet. It felt good to be acting. To be doing something again. More importantly, it felt like the right decision. This whole mess was a result of him *not* trusting his instincts. He was damned if he was going to make the same mistake again.

But it wasn't going to be straightforward. Finding the briefcase was only half the problem. Finding it *first* would be the hard part. Melanie had told Capron where the helicopter was. Even if she couldn't have been specific about its location she would have mentioned Teraruma and Hulale. Either of those places would have given Capron a base from which to launch his expedition. And he was a man with a considerable expense account at his disposal. Possibly even another helicopter.

Capron must have known that Mark and Carmen would call the police after their run-in at the Science Park. Most likely he had already left the country. Maybe he had access to a private jet that would get him to Papua New Guinea in half the time it was going to take Mark. If he got there first, Mark would be left with nothing. And Melanie would almost certainly be killed.

Economy was full for the next flight to Singapore, so Mark booked himself a seat in business-class. The Christmas holidays appeared to have had little impact on demand for tickets to Port Moresby, but Mark reserved premium seating on the connecting flights to Daru and Suki, thanking Melanie for her generosity. Then he found the home page for the Airways Hotel and booked a day room so that he could take the kidnapper's call.

There. The decision had been made. He was going. And the race for the case was on.

PART III

Thirty-Five

Melanie lay on her mattress trying not to cry. She focused on the noises outside and concluded that it was now the second night of her abduction. It would have been easier to tell the time if there had been a window. But there wasn't one. The room was bare except for the mattress and a toilet in the corner, its cistern dripping. A solitary light bulb emitted a weak glow directly above her head but the switch to turn it off was nowhere to be seen.

She was in some sort of subterranean cell, the size of a student bedsit. There was no plaster on the walls, and the bricks were black with grime. A lead pipe ran up the wall in one corner and Melanie had been relieved to discover that it was hot. The floor was a rough concrete screed, covered in dust. Opposite her, the door was steel, with no handle nor any keyhole to peep through. It did have a hatch, however, through which she had been passed a couple of meals.

The sandwiches had been served on paper plates and there had been no cutlery to steal for a weapon. Melanie hadn't been hungry on either occasion but she knew that she needed to eat to maintain her strength. She had forced the food down and guzzled the water, acknowledging that it made a passable distraction from the pain in her hand and the ever-worsening fever that racked her limbs.

The railway above her head had been in constant use, except for five or six hours yesterday when she'd managed to sleep. The frequency and rhythmic clatter of the trains suggested a tube line, which meant that the quiet period was due again soon. The fact that she was probably still in London had brought comfort of sorts but it had been tempered by the instant realisation that escape was out of the question. No windows, no weapons. No air ducts or manholes to slip through. And even if there had been, she doubted she'd get far with only one hand.

Melanie didn't remember anything about the amputation of her finger. After the courier had hauled her into his van, she vaguely recalled a second man waiting in the shadows with a syringe. He had plunged the needle deep into her thigh. The anaesthetic had rendered her unconscious in seconds. *Thank God!* She hadn't felt a thing. Hadn't known whether they'd hacked or sawn. Hadn't known which of them had done it, or where they'd put the damn thing once it was off.

Melanie had woken up with a dull ache in her left hand. When she'd seen the bandaged stump she'd only just made it to the toilet before she was sick. The pain had come in waves then: great throbs of agony, pulsing through her hand and up her arm like an electrical current. The knowledge of what had happened had sent her into shock. She'd sat on the floor shivering and gibbering like a senile drunk. She had cried for a very long time. Cried for Mark to make it better. To break down the door and to fix her hand. Hour after hour the tears had come until she was so exhausted that she'd had to rest.

Then, slowly, she'd started to pull herself together. She had asked herself what Mark would have done in a situation like this. And she had heard the answer as clearly as if he'd been sitting next to her and had told her himself. *Think!* That was what Mark did. All the time. *Think.* That's how he had made it out of the rainforest. Not because he was bigger and stronger than anyone she'd ever met, but because he had used his brain. Every time he had sat on a log to rest, he'd first checked underneath it for snakes. He had trapped rainwater. He had protected himself from mosquitoes using just the mud on the ground. And he had used the sun to keep them moving in a straight line. Nothing remarkable. Just common sense. Common sense that she didn't have. She couldn't even get the name of the country right, for Christ's sake! Papa New Guinea, she'd called it. Like Papa Smurf.

So, in the absence of her iPod, Melanie had resolved to think. To take a leaf out of her brother's book. To ask herself questions and test hypotheses rather than simply letting the thoughts fly through her mind like birds in the jungle. And she'd soon found that she knew far more about her situation than she'd realised.

Firstly, she knew that the courier and his accomplice hadn't been working for Ronald Ross. Ross and Fletch had been inside the flat. If they'd wanted to, they could have picked her up and carried her outside. Could have knocked her over the head and taken back their money as soon as she'd told them what they'd wanted to hear. No, she'd done a deal with them and they'd left with exactly what they'd come for. Besides, Ross was too classy to own a place like this. He would have treated her better. With more respect.

So she had been taken by someone else. A gang, because there had been more than one of them. She hadn't seen the courier again. He was an underling; an employee of the Australian whom she'd heard barking orders in the corridor outside her door.

The fact that they had bandaged the wound and treated it with some sort of purple disinfectant suggested that they had at least some interest in her welfare. There was very little blood too, so maybe they had stitched the wound? Melanie didn't dare remove the bandage to look. They were feeding her, which meant that they weren't going to kill her. *Yet.* And they had taken her finger in order to threaten her family, so they clearly wanted something in exchange for her life.

There could be no doubt that this was connected to the contents of the briefcase. Why else would someone abduct her? A twenty-two-year-old shop assistant from Ealing? None of her family had any wealth. Her dad did loft conversions. Her mum was a housewife. Mark would be earning good money once he started work after Christmas, but right now they were just an ordinary working-class family.

But if it was the briefcase they wanted, why hadn't they asked her where to find it? Why hadn't they whipped out a map like Ross had done? She would have told them in a flash where the helicopter was. She wouldn't even have asked to have been paid. Would have given them her £30,000 if it meant that she could have kept her finger.

That was as far as Melanie had got. And the dead end had brought another bout of despair. Now she sat on the mattress battling tears. Her limbs felt heavy. Another day and a half had passed since she'd last taken her Malarone. *Great!* As if being abducted and having her finger cut off weren't enough, she was now about to break out with malaria. *Stupid bloody pills!* Why couldn't they just give you a jab in the arm like they did for yellow fever and hepatitis?

The rasp of approaching footsteps caused her

to jump. Melanie heard the bolt being slid back. Hours ago she'd beaten on the door with her good fist, swearing blue murder at the top of her voice. In a rare return to her usual self, she'd even threatened to kill them. Now she feared reprisals.

'I'm coming in,' a man said. 'If you stay calm, I won't hurtchya. You understand me, darlin'?'

Melanie nodded. It was the Australian. She could tell by his accent. She had no intention of struggling. The manner in which she had been subdued in Exeter Road had left her in no doubt that this man and his gang were capable of immense cruelty.

'I can't hear you, sweet 'art! Speak up!'

'Yes,' Melanie said. 'I understand.'

Then she heard the metallic scrape of the door opening over the concrete screed. She shrank back on the mattress, leaning into the wall as her captor entered the room. He wore designer jeans and a blue blazer over a black shirt. Melanie couldn't see his face because he was wearing a balaclava. It was an intimidating item of clothing: the favoured headgear of terrorists and criminals all over the world. The man's lips protruded through the cut-out, chapped slightly by the cold outside. He wore a gold chain around his neck and a matching bracelet on his right wrist. Apart from the balaclava he looked as though he might have been on his way to a drinks party. The Australian wasn't in Ross's league but he was still smarter than Melanie had expected.

A professional hood. A predator rather than pond life.

He walked forward, stopping a yard in front of the mattress. He put his hands on his hips as though contemplating what to do with her. Fearing that she was about to be raped, Melanie began to cry.

'Shuddup!' the Australian snapped.

Melanie did as she was told. 'Where are we?' she dared to ask. She had been alone for more than twenty-four hours, silent except for her sobs. Now the need for contact was overwhelming. She didn't care if the man had kidnapped her; she just needed to talk.

'My place,' the Australian replied.

'Are you going to kill me?'

'I don't know yet. It all depends.'

'On what?' Melanie felt her stomach lurch in fear. Her palate flooded with saliva, warning her that she was about to be sick. She swallowed and concentrated on steadying her breathing.

'Whether I get what I want or not.'

'The briefcase?'

'No, you klutz! Not the fucking briefcase. Jesus! Why does everyone think I want the briefcase? If I wanted a briefcase I'd go to Harrods and buy one. I want what's *inside* the briefcase.'

'I can tell you where it is,' Melanie told him.

'I'm sure you can, darlin'. But that's not gonna get it *here*, is it?'

'Why not?' Melanie whined. 'I don't understand. What's going on?'

The Australian sighed and squatted down opposite her. His eyes were cold and unblinking in the balaclava. He moistened his lips with his tongue. It was shockingly pink against the black material surrounding it.

'Your brother's going to fetch it for me.'

'Mark?'

'He's the only person who knows where it is. Except for you, of course. But I figured he was the right man for the job.'

'But . . .' Melanie's mind reeled. The implications of what she'd just heard were giddying. 'What if somebody's already found it? Or moved it?'

The Australian's lips twitched in anger. 'Who the bloody hell's gonna find it? If the newspaper was right, it's in the middle of bloody nowhere. It was there for over a year before you fellas turned up and nobody found it then, did they?'

Melanie shrugged.

'I'll keep it simple,' he continued. 'If Mark tells me he can't find it, then it's curtains for you. Failure isn't an option. You understand?'

Melanie spluttered as she fought back tears. The calmness with which the Australian spoke was as terrifying as the words themselves. 'You'll do it? You'll really kill me?'

'Of course I'll bloody kill ya! I've got any number of people I could lock in here. I don't need *you* cluttering the place up. But let's look on the bright side, eh? We're gonna call Mark a few hours from now. I'll let you have a quick word. Tell 'im you're being well looked after, and that –'

'Christ!' Melanie interrupted. 'You want me to sound happy?'

'Why not? It could be a whole lot worse, trust me!'

'Great!' she scoffed. 'Why don't I sing him a song while I'm at it?'

'Sing! Whistle! See if I bloody care. Just don't clap your hands. That might smart a little.' The Australian sniggered and stood up to leave. Then he put his hand in his jacket pocket and tossed her a packet of painkillers. 'Here. Take these. They'll help with the pain. I'll see you in a couple of hours.'

Melanie watched him go and felt some of her bravado return. The meeting had gone pretty well. No more torture. No more pain. And the analgesics were a blessing too. *Christ!* She positively liked the guy for that. Maybe he *was* human, after all. It was going to take more than a couple of Nurofen to recover fully from the trauma of an amputated finger, but the tablets were better than nothing. Next time she would try to keep the conversation going for a little longer. Try to establish some sort of rapport with the guy. If she could get him to *like* her, that might buy her a stay of execution in the event of things going wrong.

Melanie put her head in her hands and tried to think. Something new was troubling her. Something to do with Ross. Hopefully he was no longer in the picture but could she afford to take that risk? She cast her mind back to his final words after they'd done their deal. 'Your brother's in Grantchester. He won't be back until later.' How had Ross known that? He could have been watching the flat and seen Mark leave, but how would he have known that her brother had gone to Grantchester? There was no way that he could have followed him there and returned in time for their meeting.

Melanie stood up and stretched. The movement sent a bolt of pain shooting through her stump. There was only one answer. Ross had bugged the flat. He'd had a full twenty-four hours between the *Observer* being published and their return from Papua New Guinea. That would have given Fletch, or whoever, plenty of time to plant a device. The bug would then enable them to keep track of their movements. To work out who would be where, when, so that they could make their approach. *Of course!* That was how Ross had known to find Mark in Gladstone Park. Not because he'd happened to turn up just as her brother was running out of the door. *Honestly! What a load of bollocks!*

Melanie returned to the mattress. She had something very important to tell Mark. But the flat had been bugged, and there was an outside chance that Ross or his men would still be listening, hungry for any additional intelligence that would increase their chances of success. She tore at the sheet of painkillers with her teeth and good hand, and swallowed four of the white pills inside. She had got them into this mess, so she would damn well get them out. *Think*, she told herself. *Think!*

Thirty-Six

Mark arrived in Port Moresby at dawn on Wednesday 16 December. He had now flown more than twenty thousand miles in four days and he barely knew which planet he was on let alone which hemisphere or time zone. He had travelled business class all the way. The extra legroom had allowed him to snatch short periods of sleep but his body was still confused. It had been dark when it should have been light. And they'd served him with a three-course dinner when all he'd wanted was some fresh fruit for breakfast. The eight-hour stopover in Singapore had passed particularly slowly. And with no appetite for sightseeing, he had remained inside the airport, fine-tuning his plan.

Mark had called DI Deakin at four o'clock in the morning, waking him up to inform him of his decision to retrieve the briefcase. Deakin hadn't tried to dissuade him. The fact that the finger was Melanie's placed the Australian firmly in the driving seat. A man capable of mutilation was possibly, if not probably, capable of murder. It was therefore eminently plausible to believe that he would kill her if he didn't get what he wanted.

Mark had asked for permission to return to his flat, which Deakin had granted, telling him that the forensic team had finished its search. They had taken the knapsack full of money, and confirmed that the notes were genuine. They were now trying to trace the cash. As long as it hadn't been stolen, Deakin could see no reason why Melanie shouldn't be allowed to keep it.

Mark had exercised, then set about packing: three T-shirts, a pair of jungle trousers, his walking boots, swimming shorts and wash bag. He'd still had enough Malarone to last five days, but he'd written himself a prescription and scooped another week's supply from Boots at Heathrow. The rest of the rucksack had been filled with anything and everything that might assist him in the jungle. A first-aid kit, a torch, a penknife. A water bottle, mosquito repellent and sun cream. Binoculars. Sleeping bag. The forest had been too dense to pitch a tent, so he'd found an old tarpaulin in the attic that would serve as a rain sheet when tied between the trees.

The plan, if it was worthy of that name, was to find the mudflat where he had spent the night. Melanie had eventually been spewed back into the Fly River a few miles north of Tidal Island. Mark would make his way there from Suki, where he would enlist Terry Landevelt's help in hiring a local guide to ferry him upriver in a dug-out canoe. They would explore the tributaries one by one, recognising the mudflat from its teardrop shape and branch of driftwood. Then they would paddle three hundred yards upstream to where Mark had been attacked by the croco-dile. Once there, he would transfer to the tributary's west bank and begin looking for the abandoned rucksack on foot. Then, if he found *that*, it shouldn't take too long to find the last of the crosses he'd notched into the trees as he and Melanie had walked away from the crash. The trail, if he could find it, would lead him directly back to the helicopter.

There would be obstacles every step of the way. Communication with the guide, for example, would be a major barrier to success. And the jungle would have grown in his absence, possibly obscuring the crosses on the trees. If it had rained, the river would have risen, sub-merging at least part of the mudflat. But while the odds were stacked against him, Mark retained a degree of optimism. His flights hadn't been delayed. If he could get to Suki by evening, he would actually be ahead of schedule. This next leg of the journey however, might yet be the biggest obstacle of all. Flights within Papua New Guinea were notoriously unreliable. Planes could be cancelled with just a few minutes' notice and delayed for several days. This was usually a major inconvenience for the expats but would often be greeted with delight by the locals, for whom an overnight delay meant an opportunity to enjoy the amenities of a decent hotel at the airline's expense.

The international terminal at Jackson Airport was a white two-storey building that gleamed in the morning sun. The low volume of traffic meant there were only two luggage carousels, and the flight from Singapore was the first of the day. Mark's bag came through quickly, the plane having parked just a few metres from the terminal.

Mark entered the arrivals hall and began making his way towards the hotel-transfer desk. There was a clock on the wall opposite: 06.45. Another two and a quarter hours until the abductor called. That allowed plenty of time for a shower and a shave, followed by a swim to unwind from his journey. As he approached the desk, he was surprised to see Inspector Kimpeau Kiuke chatting to a trim Caucasian guy in an expensive-looking linen suit. The policeman saw Mark coming and took a step forward, extending his hand.

'Welcome back,' he said. 'Detective Inspector Deakin has told me all about your situation. You have the full support of the Royal Papua New Guinea Constabulary.'

'And Her Majesty's Foreign Office,' the guy in the suit said. 'I'm Philip Mitcheson from the British High Commission. We've been working with Interpol and the Australian Government to make your mission here a little easier.'

307

Mark didn't know what to say to that. He felt like a VIP: a visiting dignitary on some sort of ambassadorial mission. All that was missing was the red carpet. Kiuke's face was one big smile now, a far cry from the cantankerous mask he'd worn in Daru. Mark guessed that the change in the policeman's demeanour was a reflection of the investigation's growing importance. Working alongside the High Commission and Australian Government, Kiuke would be under more scrutiny than usual. A courteous tongue and a helping hand would demonstrate that PNG's police weren't all as unsophisticated as the Australian press liked to report.

Mitcheson, meanwhile, looked friendly enough but his charm was forced, as though he was trying too hard to impress. He was bald with a long, equine face that glowed with too much sun. Or Shiraz. He was in his mid fifties, dispatched to the far reaches of the empire to end his long and undistinguished career. Not that Mark minded about any of that. On the contrary, he was feeling decidedly optimistic. Deakin had been busy. The situation had been escalated and strings had been pulled. Interpol was working behind the scenes and, for some reason he didn't yet understand, the Australian Government had also been consulted. Mark now had resources and allies. A team. Capron and Fletch were out there somewhere, but at least now it was a fair contest.

'Thank you,' Mark said. 'I wasn't expecting a welcoming committee.'

'Let's find a drink,' Mitcheson suggested. 'I'll bring you up to speed on what we've learned while you've been travelling. Twenty-eight hours is a long time in a case like this. Then we'll give you some time to relax at the hotel before joining you for the call at nine.'

They found a café in the corner of the terminal where Mark ordered a bottle of water.

'There's no news on your sister's whereabouts,' Mitcheson began. 'But one of your neighbours recalls seeing a white van parked opposite your house around lunchtime. She didn't get the number plate but the Met are checking CCTV footage of the area to see if anything shows up. It isn't much of a lead but it's better than a kick in the teeth.'

Mark grimaced. Small acorns. Mighty oaks. You had to start somewhere.

'In the meantime Inspector Deakin tells me that his team found a bug in your flat.'

'A bug?' Mark asked. 'Like a listening device?'

Mitcheson nodded. 'Four in fact. One in the kitchen, one in the living room, and one in each of the bedrooms. Deakin reckons it was a backup plan. If the bribe didn't work, then Capron had a surveillance team eavesdropping on your conversations, in case you ever mentioned the helicopter's whereabouts. He's thorough. I'll give him that.'

Mark sighed as he remembered the two workmen in their van outside his flat. Pictured them in their headphones drinking their coffee as he'd run past. Imagined them telling Capron that he was on his way to Gladstone Park. 'So what do we know about him?' he asked.

'Quite a lot, in fact,' Mitcheson replied. 'Interpol has been sharing the research. It turns out he *used* to work for the CIA but retired eight years ago. Since then he's been running his own PSC. A small operation in Baltimore.'

'PSC?' Mark asked. 'What's that?'

'Private security contractor. It's a cross between a security firm and a private militia. Some of the big players in the industry have several hundred ex-soldiers on their books. They send them to places like Iraq, Sierra Leone and Afghanistan to protect commercial assets and VIPs. It's the sort of work that attracts a lot of soldiers from the Special Forces. The pay, as you can imagine, is a lot better than in the regular army.'

'So they're mercenaries?' Mark asked. 'Is that legal?'

'It's complex and depends where they are. Often it's not, but much of the time they're operating in war zones, where "legal" is the least of their worries. Anyway, Capron isn't in that league. According to the CIA, most of his work is fairly routine. Private detective stuff, close protection, that sort of thing. He employs a full-time team of four in Baltimore but no doubt he has access to a number of contractors that he can bring in at short notice to help out where it's needed. Like here, for example. Or London.'

Mark thought of Fletch with his Cockney accent: a freelance member of Capron's network. It was all beginning to make sense. Except for who was paying the wages. Simeon Creasey may have been running a successful business but there was no way that Plasmavax could afford its own private army. 'So do we know who he's working for?'

Mitcheson smiled. 'No. But we've got a damn good hunch.'

Thirty-Seven

Mark leaned forward. All around him the airport hummed as people went about their business. Expats walked briskly towards their air-conditioned cars while locals shuffled by in sandals or bare feet. It was prohibited to chew betel nut inside the terminal, but Mark still noticed a trail of stains on the floor: big russet splodges where someone had spat out the nut's flesh. It was a gruesome sight. As though several people had been shot and then fled the building, leaking blood as they'd run.

'Who?' he asked, turning back to Mitcheson. 'Who's pulling the strings?'

Mitcheson wiped a hand over his pate. 'All the signals point to Gammell Pharmaceuticals. You've heard of them, I assume?'

Mark nodded. He had indeed. Seen their name in the Plasmavax brochure too. Gammell was one of the world's leading pharmaceutical companies: a multibillion-dollar operation headquartered in Baltimore. It ranked sixth on the list of the world's largest privately owned companies. And if the statistics in last month's *New Scientist* were anything to go by, then it commanded an eleven per cent share of the global market for therapeutic drugs. 'What makes you think it's Gammell?'

Mitcheson sniffed and poured himself another glass of Diet Coke. 'Like I said, it's just a hunch, but it's based on the fact that the Vice President of Global Research & Development is none other than Sean Capron's brother-in-law. His name's Frank Wanstead. Quite an impressive guy by the sound of it. Fingers in all sorts of pies. As well as his work at Gammell, he also does a lot for charity and sits on the board of the local baseball franchise.'

Mark smiled as he remembered Capron's tie. He was pretty certain that Baltimore's baseball team was called the Orioles.

'The fact that Gammell is privately owned', Mitcheson continued, 'makes it easier for someone like Wanstead to act improperly. He's got no public money to misspend. No shareholders to worry about. No Sarbox regulations to comply with. And, to cap it all, he's also a non-executive director of Capron's company.' Mitcheson put his drink down and rubbed his thumb and forefinger together to suggest the transfer of cash. 'Helped him to get started when he retired from the CIA.'

Mark didn't know what Sarbox regulations

were – some sort of accountancy rules probably – but that didn't matter. The chain was
now complete. Simeon Creasey had read Tom
Chuter's notebook in a fit of jealousy.
Recognising the commercial value of the secret
inside, he'd contacted Gammell Pharmaceuticals and struck a deal with Frank
Wanstead. Wanstead had then hired his
brother-in-law's firm to steal the secret from the
tribe. Simple as that. With everyone getting
paid along the way.

Mark winced as he realised how wrong he'd
been not to have shown more interest in the
contents of the briefcase. It wasn't birds' eggs,
cash or drugs – at least not the recreational kind
– it was something with medical value. Something sufficiently revolutionary for Wanstead to
hire a small firm of mercenaries to steal it.

But what?

'Does "the ultimate protection against bad
air" mean anything to you?' he asked.

Kiuke shook his head. 'Should it?'

'Chuter wrote it to his mother on a postcard
he sent from Cairns. He said that where he was
going "they had the ultimate protection against
bad air". I think it might have been a clue.'

'Sounds like a cure for flatulence,' Mitcheson
smirked. 'Why would he tell his mother?'

'They didn't have secrets.' Mark paused,
uncomfortable with the banality of the conversation. 'Apparently.'

Mitcheson and Kiuke both noted it down.

Then they sat in silence, mulling it over. Mark did the same.

A cure wasn't a bad guess. Neither was a serum. Nor a toxin. And if it *was* something medical, maybe it was wrong to think of Creasey, Capron and Wanstead as the villains of the piece. If the case contained a scientific breakthrough, weren't their motives ultimately altruistic? Mark took a sip of water. No, that was probably stretching it. Their motives were undoubtedly financial, but if they could bring this thing to market, it might help millions of people all over the world. And if *that* was the case, then perhaps Tom Chuter was the real culprit for wanting to keep it under wraps?

Life was never straightforward, Mark thought. Never black and white. Just shades of grey. Except for Melanie's abduction, of course. That was as black as it came. No altruism there. No mitigating circumstances. So who had taken her? A rival firm? Unlikely. Drug companies were often in the news, embroiled in scandals that involved pricing, testing or the side effects of their products. But abducting a twenty-two-year-old girl and amputating her finger? No, he couldn't see that being signed off in the minutes of the last board meeting.

'Leave it with me,' Mitcheson said, interrupting Mark's train of thought. 'In the meantime, the information I've given you is all we've got. So far Capron hasn't done much wrong.'

'Except impersonate a State Department official and plant those bugs in my flat.'

'Yes,' Mitcheson agreed. 'And no. The former might earn him a rap on the knuckles back home but I doubt it's even an offence in the UK. And as for the bugs, we still need to prove that he was responsible. If we can't, we're going to have precious little that incriminates him.'

'What about the theft of the tribe's secret?'

'Who said they stole it?' Mitcheson challenged. 'Far more likely that they bought it. They wouldn't have had to offer very much to change the lives of the entire community. With annual revenues of over $30 billion, they could buy the entire country if they wanted to. PNG's GDP is only fifteen billion. All they'd need to do is flex a little financial muscle.'

And send a Special Forces mercenary with an automatic pistol to encourage them, Mark thought. 'So what about the theft of Chuter's notebook?'

'Immaterial. Chuter never reported it to the police, did he?'

'I was assaulted,' Mark said, desperate now to find something to pin on Capron.

Mitcheson shrugged. 'Again, that's a matter for the Cambridgeshire constabulary. Do you want to press charges?'

'No,' Mark sighed, realising the hopelessness of the situation. 'It was nothing. I've got more important things to do. Has there been any sign of Capron here? We have to assume that he's come back to retrieve the briefcase.'

'Not yet.' Kiuke spoke for the first time in several minutes, his face suddenly animated now that the conversation had returned to matters under his control. 'We have sent a description of him to every airport in the country, but so far we have no record of his arrival. A man like that, with his experience, he could be very difficult to . . . intercede.'

'Intercept,' Mark corrected with a warm smile.

'Inter*cept*!' Kiuke replied. 'Exactly! Now, may I suggest that we run you up to the hotel? We have arranged a room with a speaker phone in it so we will be able to hear what the kidnapper has to say.'

'Will you be able to trace the call?' Mark asked.

'It depends. Probably not. Between here and Scotland Yard we should be able to identify the number, but tying him down to a specific location is going to be difficult if he is using a cellphone. The best we can do is get an approximate area for the origin of the call by triangulating the network masts. In the meantime, the room at the hotel is all paid for. Anything you need, you just ask.'

'Thank you,' Mark said.

'My pleasure to help you. And when you have spoken to your sister I have arranged for transport to take us back to Western Province.

You will have the benefit of an expert guide to assist you in your search for the briefcase.'

Mark smiled appreciatively. *An expert guide*. He liked the sound of that. Mitcheson paid for the drinks and moments later an unmarked car shuttled them to the Airways Hotel.

The hotel was situated in a gated compound overlooking the airfield. Backing into a hill, it had been constructed as a number of tiered storeys, with a pool, bar and restaurant on the upper level. A scale model of an aeroplane, decorated in the Air Niugini livery, soared over its botanical gardens. The hotel was the best in the country: a five-star oasis that would be unimaginable to the majority of Port Moresby's citizens.

Mitcheson and Kiuke adjourned to a meeting room while Mark checked in. His room had a double bed, wooden floors and an air-conditioning system that would have kept the Sahara cool. A digital alarm clock on the desk told him that it was 07.24. An hour and a half to go. He took a long shower and then made his way up to the pool. It was beautifully designed, with a commanding view over the distant waters of Bootless Bay. Opposite, on the far side of the airfield, the jungle-clad foothills of the Owen Stanley mountain range steamed in the rising sun. Somewhere out there was the Kokoda Track, a pass made famous by the Australian infantry, who in 1942 had fought a series of running battles there against the advancing Japanese.

It was still early. There was only one other person in the pool. Mark threw his robe on the nearest deckchair and strode to the deep end. He wasn't a great swimmer but the temperature was perfect and he needed exercise to loosen his joints after all those hours on the plane.

He swung his arms back and rose up on his toes. Then, just as he was about to launch himself forward, the other bather turned around at the far end of the pool. Mark already had too much momentum to pull out of the dive, and he was now too surprised to execute it properly. He fell forward, his chest smacking the water in an ungainly flop.

Ten thousand miles from home, he hadn't been expecting to see someone he knew.

Thirty-Eight

'That is the worst dive I have *ever* seen!' Carmen said as Mark swam towards her. 'What were you trying to do? Empty the pool?'

'You took me by surprise,' Mark replied. He didn't know whether to be embarrassed, confused or irate. 'How did you get here?'

'I flew.'

'You flew?'

'Well, to be honest, between you and me, I cannot actually fly so I took the plane. Same as you.'

Mark reached her in the shallow end and found his hostility beginning to cool. Carmen was in a playful mood. It was impossible not to be enchanted by her smile. 'You were on the same flight?'

'Right behind you all the way. Only I was slumming it in economy. They told me I got the last seat, which is presumably why you had to travel in business class? I must have booked just before you. Once we were on the plane, you were too busy eating your caviar to notice me.'

She stood up as he approached, water cascading from her elbows as she smoothed her hair back over her scalp. She was wearing a lime-green two-piece, a stunning choice for her figure and tan. Her breasts filled her bikini top, which was tied provocatively in a single bow behind her neck. She was so natural, Mark thought. No inhibition, but no coquetry either as she wrung the water from her ponytail.

'So why have you come?'

'I want my story,' Carmen replied. 'And I thought that you could use some moral support.'

Mark knelt down on the bottom of the pool. The water was four feet deep but it still only reached his chest. This wasn't fair. She was putting him in an awkward position. Carmen hadn't kidnapped Melanie, but it was her story that had given the abductor his lead. And now, here she was, all smiles and perfect breasts, telling him that she had come to offer moral support. Was that true? Or had she come to further her career on the back of his family's trauma?

Mark scooped the water with his arms, following her as she made her way to the side of the pool. Was it possible that someone so guileless could be so mercenary? 'All right,' he said. 'So how did you know that I was coming back? Who told you? Deakin or my parents?'

'Neither,' Carmen replied. She swam the last

few yards and slipped from the water in one easy motion. 'I knew you would come, the moment the kidnapper made his demands. The first time I met you at Tidal Island, you wanted to go straight back into the jungle to find Melanie. I knew you could not sit around doing nothing. Your parents were there to liaise with the police. I knew you would rather try and fail than wait for the phone to ring. You could never have lived with yourself if you had not given Melanie a chance.'

Mark stood up and waded towards her. She was sitting on her hands, leaning back to catch the sun on her face. She smiled at him. A peace offering. Nothing flirtatious, just a friendly gesture of reassurance. Mark hitched up beside her. For a few minutes they just sat, side by side in silence, admiring the view. Down in the valley a light aircraft eased off the runway and climbed into the blue, its engine too small to be heard from this far away.

'What's this *really* all about?' Mark asked after a while. 'It's not just the story, is it?'

Carmen lowered her eyes. Sighed and kicked the water with her feet. 'No,' she said. 'Not at all. If it happens, it will be a bonus. But that is not why I am here.'

'And it's not to see me, is it? You could have waited until I got back.'

Carmen shrugged. 'Partly. What I said about moral support was true.'

'So what am I missing? Why *are* you here? The

ticket must have cost you a fortune. It's Christmas. You should be at home with your family.'

'Ah, yes. My family.' This time Carmen laughed, scoffing at something she found ironic. She closed her eyes and tilted her head up, as though absorbing energy from the sun. Mark said nothing. Waited. And it was another thirty seconds before she was ready to speak.

'I had a sister,' she began. 'She was called Alondra. In Spanish it means lark. You will know about the lark. It is one of the freest of all birds. It likes to sing. It likes to hover on the wind; so high that sometimes you cannot see it. Its song is the sound of summer: of walks on hilltop meadows with a warm breeze rippling through the grass. That was Alondra. She had the voice of an angel and she loved to sing.'

Mark saw her pause and swallow. Then her eyes flashed with defiance as though, for once in her life, she wasn't going to let her emotions get the better of her. He glanced at the tattoo on her shoulder. A drop of water slid from the bird's wings, running down her arm through the broken bars of the cage.

'When she was nineteen she returned to Valparaíso to visit our grandmother. It is a port city, north-west of Santiago. That is where my mother and her family came from. It was Alondra's birthday so she and her friend Ximena went to a nightclub to meet boys. The club was in the cellar of an old shophouse. There was a gas explosion. A wall collapsed. Then the whole building came down. Most people managed to escape but those by the bar did not. Alondra was one of them.'

'Carmen,' Mark said gently. 'You don't have to tell me this.'

'I do,' she said. 'You asked. And it is important. So that you understand me.' She pulled her hands from under her thighs and hugged herself as though she was cold. 'Witnesses say that the people under the rubble were screaming. The building was on fire and to scream was to draw smoke into your lungs. Alondra was trapped; unable to move. By the time the emergency services arrived the fire had gutted the building. Most of those under the rubble were dead. They had either died from their injuries, burned to death, or – the lucky ones – had been asphyxiated by the smoke. Seventeen died.'

Carmen paused while a member of the house-keeping staff walked past with a bundle of starched tablecloths. She waited until he was out of earshot before continuing.

'But not Alondra. She survived. She was burned. She had suffered terrible injuries to her neck and spine. She was in hospital for nine months before they could move her, and then it was not to go home but to a specialist unit in Santiago. She was quadriplegic, and she had lost the skin on her face. She was alive but she had no life. She could not breathe without the help of a respirator. She could not feed or dress herself. She could not go to the toilet. When we visited her she was often too distressed to talk. Her body had become a cage. She could not escape it. Could not fly and sing as she had done before. She stayed like that for three years. *Three years*, Mark! A prisoner of her injuries. Lying motionless, accumulating bedsores. I could not imagine what it was like for her. I remember once, more than once, wishing that she had died under the rubble. She ended it when she was twenty-two: the same age Melanie is now. She persuaded a nurse to leave a syringe by the bed. Fentanyl. You know it?'

Mark nodded. Fentanyl was one of the most powerful opiates in any intensive care unit. Used as an anaesthetic and analgesic it was approximately eighty times more powerful than morphine. Great in small doses. Lethal in large.

'We think it was Ximena who gave it to her, but we will probably never know. She is free now.' Carmen turned to face him, a solitary tear rolling down her cheek. 'So you see, Mark, I know what it is like to lose a sister. A younger sister who means the world to you. When I heard that Melanie was still missing after Steve and I found you, I wanted to cry. I could see your pain. I could *feel* it. I wanted to help you to find her. And I want to help you again now. *That* is why I have come.'

Mark reacted before he knew what he was doing. His hand reached out and cupped

Carmen's face. Then, without thinking about it, his thumb brushed her cheek, mopping up the tear. 'Thank you,' he said. 'Thank you for telling me.' He lowered his hand, suddenly conscious of the intimacy between them. 'And thank you for coming.'

Carmen stood up and walked to the nearest deckchair where her towelling robe was waiting.

'There have been some developments,' Mark said, keen now to repay her openness. 'Things you'll need to know for your story. I'm going to swim a few lengths and then maybe I could tell you over lunch.'

'Breakfast,' Carmen corrected. 'I will order you some coffee. How do you like it?'

'Black,' Mark replied. 'With just over one and a half sugars.'

'That is admirably specific. And how many stirs would the doctor like?'

'Seven clockwise followed by five the other way.'

Carmen laughed. 'Anything else?'

'Maybe later,' Mark said, before slipping into the water and launching into his best front crawl. *When this is all over.*

He joined her fifteen minutes later. 08.06 on the clock above the bar. The exercise had refreshed his mind and helped him to rediscover his appetite. They sat in their towelling robes, chatting as they ate. Mark updated Carmen on what he'd learned from Philip Mitcheson, happy to share the details now that he knew that her story wasn't the real reason why she was here. She was welcome to write whatever she liked and he wished her every success.

When they had finished they returned to their rooms to dress. Mark made time for two hundred press-ups and a quick shower before Carmen knocked on his door at 08.40. She was followed minutes later by Mitcheson, Kiuke and Kiuke's driver: a junior-ranking policeman in plain clothes who hung back as they rearranged the furniture around the phone. Mark introduced Carmen and she repeated her promise not to break the story until the case had been closed.

Mark found himself getting increasingly nervous as the minutes counted down on the alarm clock. 08.57 now. He wasn't going to have much time with Melanie. He knew that if he tried to elicit information on her whereabouts then the Australian would hurt her. The best that he could do would be to find out how she was, offer her some advice for looking after her hand, and then give her as much reassurance as the Australian would allow.

08.58 on the alarm clock. Mark stood up and walked to the window. He peeled back the net curtain, startling a lizard that had been sunbathing on his balcony. In the distance a mirage hovered over the runway, the tarmac shimmering in the heat. It would be eleven o'clock at night back home. Where was she? How much fight did she have left? How was that fever? He swore as he suddenly remembered Melanie's Malarone and Ciprofloxacin. They'd been right there on her bedside table. *Still*, he thought, malaria was probably the least of her worries.

The room was hushed. They were all feeling the tension. Mitcheson sat with his shoulders slumped, cleaning under his nails with a piece of paper he'd torn from the jotter pad. Kiuke was speaking to his deputy in Pidgin, his voice quiet and low.

08.59. Mark put his hands on his hips and exhaled loudly. What if the bastard didn't call? What if he'd changed his mind as Deakin had suggested he might? What if it had been a sick joke to make him travel halfway around the world?

Carmen stood up from her chair and joined him by the window. She put a hand on his shoulder and gave it a squeeze. When he looked down he noticed that her fingers were crossed.

Mark glanced at the alarm clock. The red digits glowed back at him, the cursor between them blinking the seconds away. Then, suddenly, all four numbers changed together.

09.00.

And the telephone rang.

Thirty-Nine

Philip Mitcheson had positioned a Dictaphone next to the receiver. He pressed RECORD as Mark leaned forward to answer the call. The volume on the speaker phone had been turned up. The crackle of static interference on the line was startlingly loud. Carmen, Kiuke and his driver all sat back in their chairs hardly daring to breathe. As Mark withdrew his hand he noticed that it was shaking slightly.

'This is Mark.'

'G'day, mate. I trust you had a pleasant journey?'

'Where is she?'

'I'm pleased you listened,' the Australian continued. 'That was wise. Very wise. Melanie's not very well at the moment and the last thing she needs is more pain.'

Mark felt his stomach turn. A mixture of anger and nerves that made him want to slam his fist into the desk. 'Let me talk to her.'

'Patience, mate. I need to explain the rules first. You get ten seconds. No more. Any attempt to find out where she is will result in me hurting her. Not that she knows, of course, but rules is rules. When you're done, we'll be hanging up. I imagine you've told the police what's happening, so you can tell 'em from me that this phone will be destroyed the moment we've finished speaking. No point trying to trace the call. Waste of time for everyone. Next time we speak will be on Monday. I'll call you at home to arrange the exchange. You'd better be back and you'd better have what I want. Doesn't matter how good a doctor you are, mate. You fail me and I guarantee you, you won't be able to make yer sister better. Now, then, say "I understand".'

'Screw you.'

The Australian chuckled. 'Excellent. I knew you'd get it, bright boy like you! Hold on while I enter the little bitch's kennel. Here's yer sis. Ten seconds only. Time starts now.'

'Mel?'

'Mark, is that you?'

Hearing her voice was momentarily confusing. It knocked him. It was like a fist reaching inside his chest and squeezing his heart. Mark had been bracing himself for tears. For hysteria, terror and panic. But while Melanie sounded weak, she also sounded controlled. *Prepared*. Like she had something to say.

'Are you OK?' he asked.

'Yes,' she replied. 'Magnificent. Listen!' And

then she began to whistle. Three long notes, followed by a short one and then a series of little whoops. Not very tuneful. Not very melodic. She did it again but this time her lips failed her and she ended up blowing.

Mark felt a lump rise in his throat. Christ, he was proud of her! Melanie had been abducted. She had been mutilated by a psychopath and yet there she was, whistling in the guy's face to signal her defiance. Mark couldn't help but smile. Her resilience gave him hope. She had come through her ordeal in the jungle and she would come through this. Hysteria, terror and panic? He would never underestimate his sister again.

'It's going to be OK, Mel. Keep your hand up. Drink as much water as you can and do whatever he says. I'm in PNG and I've got –'

'Time's up, mate.' The Australian spoke with ill-concealed relish as he snatched back the handset.

'Wait!' Mark yelled. 'I haven't finished. She needs help, for God's sake! Have you treated her hand?'

'This ain't a hospital, doc.'

'Let me speak to her,' Mark commanded. 'I need more time.'

'More time?' the Australian challenged. 'I said ten seconds. That's what you got. You're not breaking the rules are you, mate?'

Mark snorted, bridling at the implicit threat. 'You hurt her and I'll break every bone in your pathetic little body.'

'What? Like this?'

There was a pause on the line. Then Melanie screamed.

It started quiet and low, a sob of dread as she realised what the Australian was going to do. Then, as he inflicted the punishment, she opened her throat and shrieked the agony from her lungs. Mark heard her gulp, draw more air and then blast it out, her voice rising then cracking as the torture continued. This was followed by a click and a monotonous tone to signal that the line had been disconnected.

For a fraction of a second Mark sat rooted to the spot in disbelief. Then, realising that she had gone, he leapt from his chair, strode two paces to his right and drove his fist through the fitted wardrobe. The wood split. So did the skin on his knuckles as the cupboard disintegrated. Coat hangers jangled and then clattered to the floor inside.

Stupid! Bloody stupid! What had he been thinking? He knew that the Australian was dangerous. Knew that he was serious too. Bait a snake and you're likely to get bitten. Only he hadn't been the one to get bitten, it was Melanie.

Mark wrenched his arm from the wardrobe, blood seeping from a deep cut that began below his elbow and finished at his wrist. For the first time in two years, he wanted to *really* lose his temper. Wanted to psyche out. Wanted to 'go schizo', as Melanie would have called it. He wanted to flail his arms at anything and everything; to take the hotel room apart at the seams. He wanted to smash the cupboard into kindling wood and hurl the safe through the window. He wanted Mitcheson, Kiuke and the driver to be his enemies so that he could fly at them and fling them against the walls. He wanted to feel their kicks in his stomach and their punches on his face; wanted to know that he was in a fight so that he could give a free rein to his aggression. He wanted the kidnapper to be in the hotel so that he could rampage through it like an unchained beast. He wanted the staff to be members of the Australian's gang so that he could swat them to the far corners of the country as he sought out their boss. He wanted to flatten the phone, break the window and batter the walls.

But Mark did none of these things. Instead he closed his eyes and took a deep breath. Sucked the air through his nostrils and blew it gently out of his mouth. Five times he did it. Then, when he was ready, he turned to face Kiuke.

'I'll pay for the cupboard,' he said. 'Now let's go and find that briefcase.'

Forty

Mitcheson said goodbye on the hotel steps. He promised Mark that he would send his recording of the conversation back to London in that night's diplomatic bag. Deakin would arrange for it to be analysed in case there was any background noise that might provide a clue to Melanie's whereabouts. Mark, Carmen and the two policemen then piled into Kiuke's car, and the driver shuttled them back to the airport. The scheduled flight to Daru wasn't until three o'clock in the afternoon but Kiuke's intervention had made Mark's timetable redundant. Clearly there was alternative transport waiting up ahead.

The car passed through a barrier and skirted the terminal. Soon it was on the perimeter road, speeding past the cargo area. Mark still felt sickened by what he had done. He had never hurt Melanie in his life. Now his idiocy had caused her excruciating pain. Threatening the Australian had been the most stupid thing he had ever done. Deakin had warned him to cooperate; warned him not to antagonise. Mark shook his head in disgust. He had been weak. He had lost control. He had chosen brawn over brains and the consequences had been dire. What had the bastard done? Broken a bone? Taken another finger? Cut her? Beaten her? Burned her?

Mark stared out of the window, hoping for a distraction. When that didn't work, he tried consoling himself with the fact that Melanie had sounded weak but upbeat. What was the word she had used? *Magnificent*, that was it.

Mark had no sooner repeated it to himself than he felt a jolt of adrenalin in his stomach. Since when had Melanie ever used a word like that? Magnificent? Not *great*, not *fine*, not *wicked*. A slightly odd choice for anyone, but coming from her it should have jarred his bones.

He sighed. He had been too engrossed in the call to have noticed it at the time. 'She was trying to tell me something.'

'What are you talking about?' Carmen asked. She was sitting on his right, behind the driver. Her hand held the comfort strap above the window. Her bicep flexed as the car traversed a pothole in the road.

'Melanie was trying to tell me something,' Mark repeated. 'A clue to where she's being held.'

Now Kiuke twisted his head so that he could see Mark from the front seat. 'Tell me,' he said.

'When I asked Melanie if she was OK, she

replied "Yes. Magnificent." "Magnificent" isn't a word that girls in their early twenties usually use. Especially not Mel. It was a signal. An alarm. Her whole tone of voice was businesslike, as though she really had something to say; something to impart. As though she knew she only had one chance to get it right. Then she'd told me to *listen!* It was a command. The word and the whistle were clues.'

Neither Carmen nor Kiuke spoke but Mark knew that they had already warmed to his theory. Knew that he was on to something.

'We should have kept the tape,' Mark said. 'How did that tune go?'

'It wasn't really a tune,' Carmen replied. 'More like a series of notes.'

'Yeah, well that's music according to a lot of the bands that Mel listens to.'

Mark paused. Felt his heart skip a beat.

Was that it? A song or a band with the word magnificent in the title? Maybe Mel had been pointing them towards a lyric that would help them to find her? Under the bridge, sitting on the dock of the bay, behind the green door, that kind of thing? He smiled as the penny dropped. Why not? Melanie had an encyclopaedic knowledge of music so the possibilities were endless. She couldn't tell him outright for fear of reprisals, so she'd coded her message into her favourite medium.

'Kimpeau,' Mark said, addressing the Inspector. 'Can you get a message to Deakin? He needs to analyse Melanie's iPod. Tell him that it's on her bedside table. Somewhere on there, there's a song or a band called "Magnificent". It'll be something recent. Something she's been listening to a lot. Something she'll expect me to have heard. He needs to check the lyrics.'

Kiuke nodded in the rear-view mirror. He made the call instantly, instructing his team in Daru to contact London straight away.

Mark was happier now. It was another break-through. Perhaps the most significant yet. *Ha!* He wanted to give his sister a big hug; tell her what a genius she was. Instead, he gave Carmen a little nudge with his elbow. It was rewarded with a smile.

Mark glanced out of the window as the car followed the perimeter fence towards the end of the runway. He tried to recall the notes that Melanie had whistled. Three long, one short, then a series of little whoops like a radio being tuned. Who was it? Bowling for Soup? OPM? Or someone he'd never even heard of? He began racking his brain, trying to remember all the songs that she'd sung on their holiday. But it was hopeless. There were too many. It wasn't obvious and he had no idea where to start. He sighed and ran a hand through his hair. He wasn't going to get it. Not in a million years. He would have to leave it to Deakin.

'That's our ride over there,' Kiuke announced from the passenger's seat.

Mark followed his outstretched finger. In the

distance, well away from the runway's apron, he saw a military helicopter shimmering in the sun. It was slightly bigger than the one it would be hunting, and wore camouflaged paintwork from nose to tail. A Land Rover with a steel drum in its well had pulled alongside. A soldier was hand-pumping the aircraft full of fuel.

'Have you been able to trace the JetRanger back to Gammell Pharmaceuticals?' Mark asked. 'If we can prove that they've lost one, it would be another link to Capron.'

'Not yet,' Kiuke replied. 'That is something Interpol is still looking into.'

The car parked a few moments later. They clambered out on to the burning tarmac. Mark and Carmen retrieved their rucksacks from the boot and then joined Kiuke, who was talking to a Caucasian soldier wearing jungle fatigues.

'This is Sergeant Fox,' Kiuke said. 'He is an instructor with the SASR, the Australian SAS. He is on secondment to train our own Special Forces but he will be your guide for the next forty-eight hours.'

'I'm grateful for your help,' Mark said, shaking Fox's hand. *Australian SAS.* So that was why Mitcheson had been speaking to their government. Deakin had been right. The authorities really were moving heaven and earth to find Melanie. No doubt Kiuke had played his part in setting this up, too. The JetRanger had crashed in his jurisdiction. He wanted to know what was on-board as much as anyone.

'Pleased to meet ya, Lofty,' Fox said. 'I'm sorry about yer sister, mate. But we'll do our bit to get her back.'

The SASR sergeant was short and wiry. His hair was curly and unkempt, his face bronzed from years in the sun. When he put his hands on his hips the sinews in his forearms stiffened like cables on a suspension bridge. You only had to look at the guy to know what he was about. Stamina, tenacity and gutfuls of courage. Not a strong man, but still as hard as they came. He was badly named, Mark thought: far more terrier than fox.

'Now then,' the soldier continued. 'Who's the girl? Nobody told me about a woman.'

'You do not need to worry about *me*,' Carmen said with a tilt of her nose. 'I can look after myself.'

'I dare say you can, sweetheart. We're hardly going to fight a war. But that's an extra mouth to feed and I don't like the look of that camera. You on safari or something?'

'Something,' Carmen replied.

Fox was wearing sunglasses but Mark saw his eyebrows lift above the frame in surprise. He turned to Kiuke, who nodded as if to say that Carmen's presence had been approved.

'Fair enough,' he said. 'But if I see you taking a picture of me, I'll destroy the camera. If I so much as end up in the background with my head turned, I'll use the bastard thing for shooting practice, you hear me?'

She nodded. 'My name is Carmen Beckwith. Pleased to meet you.'

'Carmen, eh? What's that? French?'

'Spanish. I'm half Chilean.'

Fox nodded, his eyes no doubt admiring her figure behind his mirrored lenses. 'Half Chilean, huh? Fair enough. Heat shouldn't be a problem for ya then. I'm Sergeant Fox and you can call me Sergeant Fox. This is Corporal Mamando, who'll be operating the radio. I'll introduce you to the pilot once we're airborne.'

Mamando was the soldier who had been refuelling the helicopter. He nodded and passed behind them, where he picked up the rucksacks and slung them in the chopper. He had strong cheekbones and muscled arms: a proud Melanesian in his early twenties. He looked more of an athlete than Fox but lacked the sergeant's brash manner. He was deeply embarrassed when Carmen shook his hand, fixing his eyes on the ground and grinning like a bashful schoolboy.

'Right,' Fox said. 'Chilli! Lofty! Let's get this show on the road!'

They climbed in one by one. The seats were rudimentary. Since Fox and Mamando didn't bother with seat belts, neither did Mark, Carmen or Kiuke. They sat three abreast, facing inwards on either side of the cabin. There was plenty of space: room enough for another ten troops or six stretchers. The doors were open and they remained that way as the helicopter climbed into the sky.

Mark felt his spirits soar with it. It was still only half-past nine in the morning. He was way ahead of schedule. He had a helicopter, a pilot and a patrol of two men at his disposal. He had an armed sergeant from the world's most highly trained regiment to lead the search. In three or four hours they would be above Teraruma. Another ten minutes would put them over Hulale. And from there they could begin their search in earnest, flying east over the jungle, peering through the canopy for signs of the wreck.

Mark glanced at Carmen and flashed her a reassuring smile. Sean Capron and Fletch were going to have to move pretty fast now. If they didn't, they were going to lose. The American may have had a twenty-four-hour head start, but Mark felt confident that he'd already closed the gap. He knew better than to count his chickens before they'd hatched, but to hell with it! A little of Carmen's optimism, a little of Melanie's chutzpah wouldn't go amiss. If everything went well, there was no reason why he shouldn't be holding the briefcase before the end of the day.

Forty-One

It was an exhilarating way to travel. A thousand feet up, with the doors wide open. Fox clearly wasn't going to lecture them on safety. If they fell out, it would be their own stupid fault. Their rucksacks had been lashed to the webbing that hung from the walls, and now served as footrests in the aisle. Despite the ventilation, the helicopter still reeked of oil and gunmetal. Mark savoured the smell, enjoying the sense of purpose that permeated the cabin. Looking down on the palm trees, he felt as though he was filming *Apocalypse Now*.

Conversation was impossible without shouting, so Mark contented himself with watching the scenery pass underneath. They flew northwest over the township of Nine Mile with its ANZAC war cemetery. Beyond it, the city's suburbs came to an abrupt end. Steep mountains and verdant jungle took their place. Smoke rose from the occasional longhouse but signs of civilisation became scarcer by the minute. No bitumen roads. No pylons or telephone wires. No agriculture, industry or infrastructure on any meaningful scale.

The United Nations and International Monetary Fund classified Papua New Guinea as a developing country, which was a polite way of saying that it belonged to the Third World. Looking down on it now, Mark could understand why. What little cultivation he saw – coconuts, bananas, yams and sweet potatoes – was all being farmed at a subsistence level. And this was the fertile part of the country. Further inland, up in the highlands, the soil was of much poorer quality: heavily leached and vulnerable to accelerated erosion. Even in the city it was hard to make a living. The largely transient population resorted to any means possible to earn a buck. Many of the streets, for example, had no names because thieves had stolen the signs and sold them for scrap.

The helicopter wheeled left towards the coast, causing Mark's stomach to lurch. Beside him, Carmen involuntarily clutched his knee for support. Then, suddenly, they were over the sea, heading west over the Gulf of Papua. Further offshore, the coral reefs formed ragged scars in the blue.

Fox, Mamando and Kiuke were all napping, so Mark fastened his seat belt and followed suit. He had been expecting to doze rather than sleep but as they descended into

343

Daru some two hours later, he woke with a vicious jolt.

They dropped Kiuke at the airstrip, where a car was waiting to run him into town. The helicopter would pass that way again on its return to Port Moresby, once the contents of the briefcase had been retrieved. In the meantime, the Inspector had plenty of loose ends to investigate while Fox supervised the search. Mark chatted to him on the leg up to Suki and learned that he had led anti-smuggling operations in Australia and Fiji. Fox had a camera of his own and would work the JetRanger for any signs of criminal activity. He knew where to find the helicopter's identification numbers and he would make a preliminary assessment of the cause of the crash. If Kiuke still deemed it necessary, they could send a specialist investigator to answer any lingering questions once the immediate pressure was off.

Another hour put them down at Suki, where they took on more fuel. The villagers came to stare at the scene, wandering on to the grass landing strip with puzzled expressions. Mark got out to stretch his legs. He ducked under the blades as they spun above his head. Two kids ran towards him but stopped just short, squealing with delight as they pushed each other forward. Mark knelt down and held out his hand. Up in the Tari basin, he and Melanie had met children who had never seen white skin before. Their reaction had been the same as that of these two scamps: wide-eyed fascination and a playful desire to hold his hand. The youngest boy ran forward and brushed his fingers against Mark's palm. Then he shrieked and hid behind his friend, a huge smile lighting up his face.

Mark saw Fox beckoning him back. He stood up, causing the kids to run hollering to their mothers. Fox ushered him to the co-pilot's seat and gave him a set of headphones so that he could communicate with the pilot. Mark hopped in and the chopper rose, dipping its shoulder in the direction of Teraruma.

It was a short flight. Just long enough for Mark to learn that the helicopter was a Bell UH-1H Iroquois: one of four in active service with the Air Operations Element of the Papua New Guinea Defence Force. A cousin of the crashed JetRanger, the 'Huey' was one of the most popular utility helicopters in the world.

'Teraruma,' the pilot announced a few minutes later.

Mark peered through his door as they flew overhead. The Katzers' compound occupied three acres on the edge of the Fly River. It really was an isolated spot: surrounded by jungle, accessible only by boat. Mark could see the main lodge, staff quarters and generator shed, neatly arranged like a model village. Further right, the hammocks in the garden swayed in the helicopter's downdraught. Beyond them, the pirogues rocked nervously on their moorings. All the buildings had been constructed using local bush materials. With hand-dug latrines and a reliance on rainwater for washing, cooking and drinking, this was the very definition of eco-tourism. The vision, confidence and courage that must have been required to establish a bird-watching lodge in such inhospitable country were inspiring.

One of the cooks came to investigate the racket. She was followed by a white woman, whom Mark recognised as Beatrice Katzer. Did they have guests? he wondered. Or were they closed now for Christmas? Had the murders of Gile and Peri led to cancellations? He waved through the glass. Beatrice waved back although Mark doubted that she could tell who he was.

'Over to you,' the pilot said. 'Where do you want me to go?'

'Follow the river north,' Mark told him. 'We want the third or fourth major stream on the right. It should lead to a village.'

'Roger that!' the pilot said, and the Iroquois dipped its nose and swung away upriver.

They found Hulale after only ten minutes. Having made forays down the first few tributaries, Carmen had spotted smoke rising from the jungle, a mile or so to the east. Now the Iroquois created panic and fascination in equal measure as it flew overhead. Several villagers stopped to point at the sky, while others ran for the shelter of their huts. Children peered from doorways, scarcely believing their eyes. Apart from the Defence Force's search for Mark and

Melanie, this was probably only the second time they had seen such a machine. Elsewhere, an old man, naked except for his penis gourd, sat in a clearing, plucking a chicken. He looked up disdainfully, too old and too wise to worry about the intrusion.

Seeing the village again brought back gruesome memories for Mark. This was where it had all gone wrong; where this whole wretched adventure had begun. It looked peaceful enough now: hard to imagine that it had been the scene of such carnage.

The Iroquois circled the village twice, giving Mark an opportunity to orientate himself. He felt momentarily ashamed to have brought such a modern, Western disturbance into the villagers' lives. But their treatment of Peri and Gile meant that his sympathy was short-lived.

'There!' Mark called. 'That's where they were killed. We must have entered the jungle where those pigs are tethered.'

The pilot acknowledged the reference and swung his craft over the forest.

'We went east,' Mark said. 'About five hours' slow walking. Then we spent the night before travelling a similar distance the next day. All in all, I guess the crash could be anywhere between seven and fifteen miles from here. How long will that take to search?'

This time the pilot just smiled. He had a map on his knees: the same Australian Army edition that seemed to be de rigueur in this part of the world. Despite being devoid of relief data, the blank area did at least have grid marks. Each block was five kilometres long by five kilometres wide. Mark watched as the pilot drew a square over the area east of Hulale: four blocks long by four blocks wide. It didn't look huge on the map but it was, he realised, equivalent to four hundred square kilometres down on the ground. And in a uniform landscape of thick rainforest, that was quite some search area.

Mark shook his head as he acknowledged the enormity of the task. Everything had run so smoothly since his arrival in PNG but they were now at the business end of the expedition. He should have known better than to think it would be easy. Talk about trying to find a needle in a haystack! All he could see were green treetops in every direction. Still, he mused, they had five pairs of eyes, three hours of daylight, and a full tank of fuel to help them.

The Iroquois dropped to three hundred feet: high enough to cover a wide area but low enough for its crew to peer between the trees. Fox and Mamando sat on opposite sides of the aircraft, their feet resting on the helicopter's skids. They carried binoculars in one hand. The other gripped the webbing to prevent them from falling outside.

Having flown to the centre of the pilot's square, the Iroquois was now working its way out in an ever-expanding spiral. Mark quizzed the pilot and learned that this was an established search-and-rescue pattern, favoured by coast-guards. Cruising at a slower than normal speed of one hundred and fifty kilometres per hour, the Huey would cover slightly less than one square kilometre every minute. That implied that they still had up to seven hours' flying ahead of them, which made the prospect of an overnight break increasingly likely.

The next forty minutes brought nothing, but at least the circles were getting bigger, which contributed to a more stable ride.

'I don't know whether to actively look,' Carmen said. 'Or wait for something to catch my attention.'

Mark knew what she meant. It was hard to concentrate when everything looked the same. He glanced at the instrument panel and saw that the needle on the fuel gauge had dropped. Behind him, Fox and Mamando perched silently on their skids, scouring the jungle with binoculars and grim expressions. They were like eagles, he thought, sitting in their eyrie, waiting to swoop.

Another hour brought the first breakthrough. But it wasn't a good one. It was Mamando who spotted it. High ground, some three miles north-east of their position. It was a plateau; a rocky outcrop, devoid of trees. And there, perched in its centre, was a brand-new JetRanger beneath a camouflage net.

Forty-Two

Mark's lips tightened against his teeth as the Huey circled the outcrop. This was a potentially decisive blow. He could scarcely believe their misfortune. Even through the camouflage netting, he could see that the JetRanger was empty. Capron was already down there. On foot, invisible, and closing in on the briefcase.

'Can you sabotage it?' Mark asked. 'To make sure it can't get airborne again.'

'I could,' Fox smiled. 'But I'm not gonna. We don't know for certain who it belongs to. And we don't know whether anyone's done anything illegal. I'd like to, mate. Believe me. But I can't go around vandalising private property without the necessary clearance.'

'What if it's entered the country illegally?' Mark asked.

'That's Kiuke's problem, not mine. I'm here to help you get that briefcase, and that's what I'm gonna do. We'll call Kiuke now and get him

350

to look into it. In the meantime, we're not gonna find the crash point here, so we might as well get back to the job in hand. That thing's not gonna take off without us seeing it. If we need to follow it, we will.' And with that, he tapped the pilot on the shoulder and instructed him to resume their search.

Mark sank back in his seat. Behind him Corporal Mamando raised Kiuke on the radio, before handing it to Fox to relay the message. What if Capron had already found the briefcase? What if the American was already on his way back to the outcrop? Mark sighed. There wasn't much he could do except trust Fox's judgement. The soldier was probably right. Now that they had found his getaway vehicle, it was going to be difficult for Capron to leave the country unnoticed.

The Huey resumed its search pattern. Round and round they went, scouring the trees for a flash of white paint or the glint of sunlight on metal. The forest canopy was largely even, extending below them like green baize. The trees were mostly cajuputs, interspersed with the occasional eucalyptus, acacia, teak and palm. Beyond those, Mark was unable to identify the species. He fared better with the birds, of course. Imperial pigeons, orange-breasted fruit doves and parakeets all erupted from their roosts to protest against the disturbance. Further on, a Papuan hornbill glided over the treetops, its yellow beak clearly visible against the green below. Mark felt the same sense of guilt that he had experienced over Hulale. This was Eden: a vast paradise of virgin forest. And here they were, polluting it with the roar of their machine. The Huey had already scattered the birds. Down on the forest floor the lizards and tree kangaroos would be scampering to escape its din.

Carmen had come forward. She was leaning on the back of Mark's seat. She looked over his shoulder, her cheek an inch away from his. She was closer now than she had ever been before. He could smell her scent. He could feel her breath caressing his neck.

Mark realised then that Carmen had been with him more or less constantly since that morning in the Land Cruiser. She had been there when he and Melanie had been reunited. Been there when he had met Elsie Chuter and Simeon Creasey. She had been there in the car park and again when the abductor had made his demands. She had been there when he had discovered Melanie's finger, and when Deakin had briefed his parents. Then she had flown halfway round the world to offer him her support. She was his teammate, his partner. She didn't need to say anything. Her presence alone was enough to give him hope.

'Think lucky!' she shouted.

Mark smiled. He wanted to lean to the right and rest his skin against hers. To make contact and thank her for her support. To plant a delicate kiss on her beautiful cheek.

'Be lucky!' he yelled back.

Another twenty minutes passed. Now it was Fox's turn to spot something unusual. It was a break in the trees, running through the jungle like a fissure in a rock. The pilot swung towards it and minutes later they confirmed it as a tributary of the Fly. The waterway wasn't marked on the map, despite being nearly thirty feet across.

Mark felt a surge of hope when he saw it. It was serpentine and brown, much like the river that he and Melanie had floated down. 'Let's follow this for a while,' he suggested. 'Downstream first, back towards the Fly.'

'What are we looking for?' the pilot asked.

'A mudflat shaped like a tear in the middle of the stream.'

The pilot nodded and increased his speed. The tributary was an obvious landmark. There was no need for the caution that he had exercised before. When they arrived above the confluence of the Fly a few minutes later, Mark refused to be downcast.

'Turn around,' he said. 'Back to our starting point and then the same distance upstream.'

The pilot smiled. The thrill of flying clearly hadn't worn off. Mark got the impression that he would have gladly flown along the river all day, if that was what was required. The Huey passed the point where they had first picked up the river and continued its journey upstream.

They didn't have far to go.

'There!' Mark yelled. 'That's it!'

The pilot immediately turned around and they circled the mudflat at a slower speed. Mark nodded. The teardrop shape was unmistakable. And there, in the middle, was the branch of driftwood that he had used to drive away the crocodiles.

'Turn around,' he told the pilot. 'We want to be three hundred yards upstream. That's where we came out of the forest. So now we've got our entry and exit points. The crash should be somewhere in between.'

'How straight did you walk?' the pilot asked.

'I don't know,' Mark replied. 'But let's give it a try anyway.' It was hard to keep the excitement out of his voice. He had pushed Melanie to the back of his mind while he concentrated on what he had to do. Her abductor had set him a challenge and Mark realised that he was enjoying taking it on. A quick glance over his shoulder told him that Carmen shared his enthusiasm. Even Fox looked slightly less mean than usual.

The Huey dropped to its search altitude as it banked west towards Hulale. At one point Mark thought he could see the creek that he and Melanie had followed but he couldn't be sure. They arrived over the village a few minutes later. Still no sign of the JetRanger.

'Let's try again,' Mark called. 'We might have walked in a slight dog-leg but it's down there somewhere. It has to be.'

The Huey turned. Mark returned his gaze to

the canopy below. Very occasionally he caught sight of the forest floor but most of the time it was impossible to penetrate the vegetation. A white helicopter, for God's sake! How hard could it be?

They were just over halfway back when Mark became aware of someone standing behind him. He turned, expecting to see Carmen, but it was Fox. And he was tapping the pilot on the shoulder.

'What?' Mark shouted. 'Have you found it?'

Fox grinned and clapped a hand on his shoulder. 'Back there,' he yelled. 'About half a mile to starboard. Couple of trees growing funny. Like they'd been pushed out of place.'

The helicopter looped around. Mark followed Fox's outstretched hand. He saw it too now: a clump of semi-felled trees; slightly lower and less dense than the surrounding canopy.

Moments later he caught a flash of the JetRanger's fuselage and he knew that they had found it.

Forty-Three

Melanie had been dreaming when the noise awoke her. A sound like a drill coming through the wall. She was still dog-tired and in desperate need of rest, but on this occasion she was grateful for the disturbance. She had been strapped inside the crashed helicopter, handcuffed to Zak. A mosquito had laid its eggs in her hair and the larvae were wriggling through the roots. Her entire scalp had been moving. She'd known that she'd needed to open the briefcase to survive but she hadn't been able to move. Then the larvae had hatched into mosquitoes. They had begun biting her. On her eyes, her lips, her ears. *Wow!* she thought as she propped herself up on the mattress. *That was one pretty fucked-up dream!*

Melanie held her breath and listened. She wasn't dreaming any more. The noise was real. It was definitely a machine of some sort. And it was no more than a foot away, on the other side of the wall.

She moved as quickly as she dared. The stump of her amputated finger throbbed chronically under her bandage. She had grown used to the pain until that sheep-shagging Australian motherfucker had squeezed her hand while he had been on the phone to Mark. The pressure had forced the blood towards the wound, where it had ruptured one of the stitches. Now the bandage was stained maroon with her blood. She had been guzzling painkillers at the rate of four every four hours but they were woefully inadequate for the agony she was suffering.

Worse still was the knowledge that she had developed malaria. The fever had been with her from the beginning. Now, in the last twenty-four hours, she had exhibited a number of other symptoms. She had been repeatedly sick in the toilet. Her limbs felt like lead and had twice locked in rigors. There was a non-stop ache across her lower back. Her diarrhoea was relentless. Then, as the last of the night's trains had rumbled overhead, she'd experienced her first bout of chills. Being locked in a brick basement in the dead of winter was enough to make anyone cold but this was different. It had come from within. As though her very bones were sheathed in ice. The lead pipe was too hot to lean against but too thin to heat the whole room. Melanie had tried hugging herself with her good arm but had been unable to generate any warmth. The violence of her shaking had taken her by surprise. Her whole body had shivered back and forth like a skyscraper in an earthquake. And every tremor had sent new pain to her stump.

It had lasted a full five minutes before it passed. Melanie had collapsed to the mattress, sobbing in the certain knowledge that there was far worse to come. Then, while she had been waiting for sleep to dull the aches, she had counted back the days to her first unprotected night in the jungle. Mark had told her that malaria had an incubation period of seven to fourteen days. It was now ten since she had first missed her Malarone. Dietmar's chloroquine, meanwhile, had clearly been insufficient to stave it off.

It frightened her because she didn't know much about it. She knew that malaria was potentially fatal but she didn't know *how* it killed. Something to do with the liver? The blood? The brain? She had seen reports on the news: millions of African babies, with twisted limbs and flies in their eyes, waiting for death to end their suffering. Melanie felt sick with guilt. It had been her privilege to have had access to medication and she had abused that privilege. She was supposed to have taken the drug for a full week after her return from Papua New Guinea, yet she had swallowed just two pills since her rescue from the river. *What a waste.* She deserved to be ill. Unthinkable that those poor kids in Africa and Asia would ever be so profligate.

Now the noise on the other side of the wall

offered her a glimmer of hope. She knelt on the mattress and put her ear to the bricks. The noise was getting closer. It was at knee-height. A scraping, whirring, high-pitched whine. Like a drill. *Shit the bed!* It *was* a drill! Someone was drilling through the wall! She could hear the bit chewing through the brick.

A smile appeared on her face. The first in several days. Someone had found her! Someone had come to get her out! Melanie pressed her ear against the wall again only to jerk it away a few seconds later as the bit spun through the brickwork. She watched as it withdrew, taking dust and debris with it.

'Who's there?' she whispered, adrenalin masking her pain.

There was no reply. Instead, the drill started again. It was quieter this time as it met with less resistance. A minute later another bit came through the pilot hole, widening it by several millimetres. The process was repeated twice more. By the time the fourth bit appeared, the hole was half an inch in diameter.

Melanie knelt on the mattress with her mouth by the hole, waiting for the bit to be withdrawn. 'Who *is* that?' she whispered.

'A friend,' came the reply.

'Are you the police?'

'Not exactly, love. No.'

'So who are you, then?'

'My name's Fletch,' the voice said in a Cockney accent. 'We met three days ago.'

Fletch! Ronald Ross's bodyguard! The guy who had given her the backpack full of cash. What the hell was he doing here? 'Are you going to get me out?' she asked, trying to keep her voice as low as possible.

'Not yet. But longer term I think you're going to be fine. Providing you do exactly as I say. You OK with that?'

'I don't have a lot of choice, do I?'

'Not a whole lot, love. No.'

'OK,' Melanie said. 'I'm listening.' She looked at her hands in the gloom and realised that they were shaking; only this time it was with hope and excitement.

'I'm going to send a probe through the wall,' Fletch told her. 'On the end of it, you're going to find a metal disc about the size of a five-pence piece. It looks like an earpiece from a set of headphones but it's actually a mobile listening device.'

'Like the one you planted in our flat?'

'Similar,' Fletch chuckled. 'Only a lot smaller. And a lot more expensive too. Take it and hide it. Then, when you get the opportunity, I want you to plant it on the guy who's abducted you. Not the black guy from the van, but the ringleader. He'll be the one with the Australian accent. Dark hair, bushy eyebrows. About six feet tall.'

'Don't worry,' Melanie said. 'We've already met.'

'Slip it into his pocket but choose one that he

might not use very often. If he's wearing a jacket, go for the outside breast pocket. If he's wearing jeans, try the back pockets. You'll have to get close, so you'll need to be creative. You got that?'

'Yes,' Melanie said. 'I think so.'

'Good. Don't do it right away. Wait until they move you for the exchange with your brother. If they don't move you, it's because we've beaten Mark to the briefcase. If *that* happens, there won't be any exchange, but we'll let the police know where you are. Either way, you're going to be all right.'

'Wait!' Melanie hissed. 'I don't understand.'

'You don't need to,' Fletch countered.

'You're going to leave me here?'

'For a while. But, like I said, you'll get out eventually. You're our insurance policy, you see. If we get the briefcase, we call the police and they come to fetch you out. If Mark gets the briefcase we pick it up when he comes to exchange it for you. That's why it's important that you plant the bug. It'll tell us where to be and when.'

'Christ on a frigging bike, mate! You're no better than the scum who took me!'

'Shh!' Fletch said, raising his voice very slightly. 'You'll attract attention.'

Melanie sighed, conceding that this was no time to throw a tantrum. 'Where am I?' she asked.

'You're in the East End, love. In a lock-up under the Central Line. But I'd keep that to yourself if I were you. Might go badly for you if the Aussie knows I've been in touch.'

'Where are you? Can anyone see you?'

'I hope not,' Fletch replied. 'There was a camera but we disabled that earlier. Gotta go, love. Hang tough and you'll be right as rain in a few days' time. Make sure you cover up this hole, all right?'

'I need medication,' Melanie said. 'I've got malaria.'

There was a pause. For a moment she feared that he had gone. Then his voice, rough but sweet as rain.

'I'll see what I can do. It won't be tonight though. I'll catch yer later, alligator.'

'In a while, crocodile.' Melanie sank back on the mattress, her confidence booming. She still didn't know who Fletch and Ronald Ross were, but right now they were the only friends that she had. She didn't understand how Fletch had found her either, but frankly, she didn't care. She sighed. Her situation had improved dramatically but her life was still undoubtedly on the line.

She shifted her position so that her back covered the hole in the wall. Hopefully Fletch would return tomorrow with some medication. In the meantime, there was nothing to do except wait. And hope that Mark had understood her message.

Melanie had thought that she'd been speaking to her brother in the bugged flat, which is why she'd taken the precautionary measure of speaking in code. As it turned out she needn't have bothered. Mark's final incomplete sentence had told her that he was already in PNG, which made it highly unlikely that Ross was listening. *Typical! Fucking typical!* Melanie shook her head. This wasn't the first time that she'd tried to be clever. And it wasn't the first time that she'd cocked it all up.

Forty-Four

There was nowhere for the Huey to land but when Mark glanced over his shoulder he saw Corporal Mamando unpacking ropes, harnesses and karabiners from a black kitbag. The trees around the JetRanger had been forced apart by the crash, leaving a hole in the canopy they could drop through. There was no sign of Capron. Fox was still talking to the pilot. Moments later he beckoned for Mark and Carmen to join him in the main cabin.

'Right,' he began. 'Chopper's gonna descend to twenty metres, just above the tree-line. We'll jump the last bit.'

'Jump?' Carmen yelled. 'You must be joking.'

'Just a bit of jargon, sweetheart. You call it abseiling; we call it jumping. Either way, we get to the ground by sliding down this rope. There's no wind, so it'll be nice an' steady. Once we're down, the chopper's gonna return to Suki, take on more fuel, and come back in an hour to pick us up. We've just been training the boys how to do this so there's plenty of equipment on-board for everyone. You can stay with the Huey or you can come with us. Choice is yours, but if you come with us, it's on the understanding that you're responsible for your own safety. I'm here to help Lofty get that briefcase, not to hold your hand. You injure yourself on the way down, that's your problem. You break a leg and decide you want to sue, Canberra will deny we were ever even here. You got that?'

Carmen nodded. 'I'm coming with you.'

'All right,' Fox beamed. 'Good on ya! Mamando will go first, then you, Chilli, then Lofty. I'll bring up the rear. Assuming you don't let go of the rope we should be back in Daru in time for tea and medals. Here, try these harnesses. Step into them like a pair of pants and tighten them around yer arse with those straps.'

Mark and Carmen did as they had been shown, before Mamando attached a descender to each of their harnesses. Fox gave them a quick briefing, demonstrating how to control the speed of their descent with the friction hitch. The descent line was a low-stretch rope, covered in an abrasion-resistant sheath, but Mamando gave them a pair of gloves each to protect their hands from burns.

The gloves were clammy and stank of sweat. Mark was too pumped to care. He glanced at his watch. Two fifteen in the afternoon. Eight hours ago he hadn't even arrived in the country. Now here he was, about to abseil into the jungle to retrieve the case. Apart from the pain that he had caused Melanie and his subsequent destruction of the wardrobe, things couldn't have gone much better. Nerves jangling, he stole a glance at Carmen. Her eyes were ablaze with excitement, her face flushed with adrenalin.

Mamando fastened the descent rope to a winch on the ceiling and then hurled it out of the open door. He had a VHF radio on his back, and a black headset hooked over his ear. He clipped himself in and was gone, stepping out of the helicopter as calmly as if he had stepped off a kerb to cross the road. Seconds later there was a tug on the rope, signalling that he had arrived safely on the ground.

Carmen's turn. Fox held her elbow, shepherding her to the exit.

'Wanna change yer mind, Chilli?'

'No,' she replied. 'But don't be embarrassed if you do.'

Fox grinned and clamped the rope into her descender. Then he adjusted the strap on her camera, feeding it on to her back where it was clear of the line. He put a hand on her shoulder and coaxed her gently round so that she was ready to step backwards into the blue. Mark caught her expression as she went. It was one of total concentration as she recalled everything that she had just been taught. The enjoyment would come in a moment, as soon as she had reached the ground.

Carmen leaned back with her toes on the threshold and waited for the rope to take her weight. Then, when she felt the harness tighten around her thighs, her confidence blossomed. She eased the tension on the brake and slipped a yard down the line. She did it again, slipping further so that her head was now level with the Huey's skid. Then, suddenly, she was gone. All Mark could see was the tension on the line and open sky beyond.

'Six seconds!' Fox shouted as he watched her go. 'That's pretty good for a first-timer. We were doing this yesterday and one poor bugger was on there for three minutes before we could get him down. Froze solid. Does it again next time and he'll be out on his arse! Right. Your turn, Lofty. Remember what I told ya: nice and relaxed and let the rope do the work. If you feel it running away with you, just pull your right hand up, like this! You all set?'

'Ready,' Mark replied. He waited for Fox to connect the descent line to his harness and then leaned back until the rope absorbed his weight. It was a thrilling moment, perched over the treetops like a falcon waiting to swoop. The sky throbbed as the Huey's blades beat the air above his head. He pushed off with his toes and opened the brake: experimentally at first but then faster as his confidence grew. Each drop was longer than the last and he covered the final fifteen metres in one smooth slide. He bent his knees to cushion the impact of his landing and braked hard with his right hand so that he arrived lightly on his feet.

Mamando gave him a high five and then disconnected him. Seconds later, Fox slid down the line at breakneck speed. It was only when he had reached the ground and walked away that Mark realised Fox hadn't been wearing a harness.

'That's called fast-roping, Lofty. We'll try that next time.'

'Right,' Mark replied. 'Just as soon as you've taught us how to get back up.'

Overhead, the helicopter keeled left towards Suki. The rope still dangled from its midriff like a black umbilical cord. For a moment they just stood there, waiting for its noise to fade. Then, slowly, the sounds of the jungle took over. The cry of a bird, the croak of a frog, and the chirrup of a thousand unseen bugs.

Mark glanced around the clearing, taking in the scene. It hadn't changed much. The gunnera leaves that he had laid as a groundsheet were beginning to turn brown, but otherwise it was exactly as they had left it. There was no sign that Capron had beaten them to it. No sign that anyone had been there at all since he and Melanie had walked away nine days ago.

Mark turned towards the JetRanger. Entwined in the vegetation, it looked just as incongruous as it had when he and Melanie had first stumbled across it. A grotesque curiosity that had dropped from the sky like a creature from another planet. It had lost none of its mystery either. The two blackened windows that made up its windscreen now looked like the eyes of a monstrous fly. Inside, the skeletons still guarded its secret. Mark didn't believe in ghosts or spirits but the fact that two men had died here gave the clearing an eeriness that made his spine tingle.

'Whaddya waitin' for, Lofty?' Fox asked as he began walking towards the wreck.

'Nothing.'

'You want me to go?'

'If you like,' Mark replied, grateful to avoid a certain bout of claustrophobia. 'The briefcase is on the left-hand side of the main cabin. It's pinned to the seat by a fire extinguisher. You'll have to smash the handle to free it. The keys are on the floor by the passenger's boots.'

'OK,' Fox said. 'Leave it to me. I'll see you in a second.'

Carmen had already taken several photographs of the crash but now she stopped to follow Fox inside. Mark watched her go, admiring her pluck. Whatever she might have said earlier about her motives, there was no mistaking the professional zeal with which she approached the wreck. He didn't hold that against her. Abseiling into thick jungle to inculpate one of the world's largest pharmaceutical companies was enough to concentrate any reporter's mind. Investigative journalism didn't get much better than this.

Corporal Mamando was examining the JetRanger's fuel tank. Mark settled on a fallen tree trunk while he waited for Fox and Carmen to return. He had begun to develop a bad feeling about this. A sense of doom. It had all been so easy. *Too* easy. It didn't look as though Capron had got there first, but the American was out there somewhere. Mark hadn't yet thought about what he would do if the briefcase *wasn't* there. He had no contingency plan. It would be down to the police to arrest Capron before the deadline expired. And if they did, what pressure could they exert on him? The American had done nothing wrong. It was a straightforward case of finders keepers. He would pass the prize to his client, whereupon Gammell Pharmaceuticals would deploy a powerful team of lawyers to protect it. And Mark would be left with nothing. The kidnapper's threat made the hairs on the back of his neck shiver. *Failure isn't an option.*

Mark glanced across the clearing. A red bird of paradise had landed on a branch to his left. It flew away again the moment he turned his head. The sun was well past its zenith now, its beams probing the trees as it slipped through the sky. A solitary ray, as sharp as a laser, picked out a fern and projected its silhouette on to the trunk of an acacia behind. Mark heard voices from inside the helicopter. Carmen appeared in the door, jumping lightly to the ground.

'Well?' Mark asked.

'It is there,' she replied with a grin. 'Fox will bring it out in a minute. He is just examining the rest of the cabin to make sure there is nothing else hidden in there.'

Mark felt a wave of relief wash over him. They had beaten Capron to it. The prize was theirs. It was another massive step towards bringing Melanie home. Carmen joined him on the log, her thigh pressing against his due to lack of space. They waited in silence and suddenly there was Fox, bounding from the helicopter with the briefcase in his hand.

Mark leaped up, euphoria and adrenalin rushing in his veins. He and Carmen moved away to make room on the log. This was it. The moment of truth. The answer to the riddle on the postcard on Mrs Chuter's fridge. The reason for Melanie's abduction. And the collateral for her release.

Mark wiped his sleeve over his forehead. Sweat stung his eyes. His heart pounded his chest. Beside him, Carmen stood with her camera at the ready, poised to take the picture that would end days of speculation.

Fox balanced the briefcase on the log and tried the key. Then he withdrew it and stuffed it in his pocket. 'It's not locked,' he said. His thumbs were on the brass catches. He slid them to the right and the clasps sprang up with a satisfying click. He gripped the leather panel. Raised it. Took a step back.

A flash of beige suede as the lid came up. Then more as the main compartment was finally revealed.

What the –?

Mark looked again and felt instantly sick.

Apart from a passport, magazine and a couple of pens, the briefcase was empty.

Forty-Five

Mark stared at the empty briefcase in disbelief. He hadn't come all this way for a passport and an old biro, had he?

'I thought there was something wrong,' Fox said. 'The moment I saw the case.'

'What do you mean?' Mark asked.

'The fire extinguisher was there all right, but the handle had already been smashed. I didn't have to break it at all. Just chucked it on the floor and picked up the case.'

'Capron!' Mark spat. 'He's beaten us to it.' He put his hands on his head and stared at the treetops. Closed his eyes and thought of Melanie. How could they negotiate her release if they had nothing to exchange? It was sickening. The consequences of their failure, too awful to contemplate. The irony was palpable. By trading details of the crash point, Melanie had inadvertently sold the one thing that would have guaranteed her safety.

Mark exhaled loudly through puffed cheeks, trying not to lose control of his emotions. 'We need to get back to the outcrop as fast as possible. We'll cut him off as he tries to leave.'

Fox nodded. He signalled to Mamando, who immediately raised the pilot on the radio.

'He is refuelling,' Mamando said. 'But he will be here in twenty minutes.'

Mark swung his boot at a clump of nettles. Twenty minutes? That was going to feel like an age. Capron's JetRanger was at least seven miles away, but who was to say that he wasn't already closing in on it? Twenty minutes could make all the difference. Mark knew nothing about the speeds of the two helicopters, but the JetRanger looked faster than the Huey. If it came to a chase he didn't fancy their chances. And if Capron could enter the country undetected, then why shouldn't he leave it that way too?

Mark returned to the log. If Capron escaped it would be up to Deakin and his team of detectives at Kilburn nick. What progress were they making? he wondered. Deakin would have retrieved Melanie's iPod by now. Some junior detective would be scouring the downloads for a reference to the word 'Magnificent'. If it wasn't immediately obvious, the poor guy was going to have to listen to the lyrics of every single track. And with well over a thousand songs in Mel's library, the task could easily take two days.

Beside him, Fox had taken the passport from the briefcase's pocket and had flicked to the back page. Now it was his turn to shake his head as he studied the owner's photograph. 'Well, well, well!'

'What?' Carmen urged. 'Who is it?'

Fox grinned. 'According to this, he's called Andrew Dickson.'

'But that is not his real name?'

Fox shook his head. 'He's called Chris Bartlett. He and his brother Charlie were with the regiment. Served with us for four years. Then Charlie got thrown out and Chris left too. Last I heard, he was working close protection in the private sector.'

'That figures,' Mark said, grateful for the distraction. 'If he's ex-Special Forces, he fits the profile of one of Capron's mercenaries. It would make sense to use an Aussie for this job rather than flying someone in from the other side of the world.'

'Why was his brother thrown out of the regiment?' Carmen asked.

'Drugs,' Fox replied. 'We have mandatory random testing twice a year. He was selected and failed. Cocaine, I think it was. When they dug a little deeper they discovered that he'd been dealing it to junior ranks in other regiments. Pretty bloody dumb, if you ask me. As if what we do isn't exciting enough. A lotta the boys come from troubled backgrounds. For most of them the army's a way of escaping their past, but some never manage to move on. Charlie was one of them.'

'And Chris left too?' Mark asked. 'Why?'

'Something like that happens, and the rest of us take a pretty dim view of it. Brings shame on the regiment. Dishonours the cap badge. Chris was guilty by association. He knew he was never gonna hear the end of it if he stuck around. He coulda toughed it out, but it would have been a helluva a ride. There's some real hard cases where we come from. In the end he packed it in. Good riddance to the pair of them, I say!'

'So where's Charlie now?'

'Hell do I know, Lofty? It was over fifteen years ago. In jail. On the beach. Smoking crack in some whore's bedsit, for all I care.'

Mark was about to ask another question but he was silenced by the sight of Corporal Mamando holding up his hand in the universal stop sign. Then, slowly, he moved his index finger to his lips in a demand for quiet.

Everybody froze. Mamando made another signal to Fox, who nodded and slowly unclipped the holster on his thigh. Mark and Carmen exchanged glances. They had heard nothing. Seen nothing. Yet the reaction of the soldiers told them that there was something out there. Something far more dangerous than the possum that had scared Melanie.

They waited, hearts thumping like drums in their chests. Fox had the weapon in his hand now. Mark watched him release the safety catch with his thumb. It was the same make of pistol he and Melanie had found in Chris Bartlett's bergen. Mark scoured the jungle for movement but all he saw was layer upon layer of lush green leaves.

'Down.' Fox said it quietly: a solitary command that left no room for questions.

Mark grabbed Carmen's hand and pulled her to the mud. Fox was a metre to the right, with Mamando a few yards behind. Mark had no idea what the threat was or where it came from. All he knew was that the log made pitiful cover. Sometimes it wasn't an advantage to be the biggest member of the group. He was as clear a target as a pink barn door. Legs splayed, he held his breath and pressed himself into the dirt, trying to make himself as small as possible. But there was no need. It was too late. The voice that called out from the jungle was as calm and measured as when Mark had first heard it in Gladstone Park.

'Everybody relax,' Capron said. 'We've got you covered. To prove it, we're going to put a round between Mark's legs. If you don't move, you won't get hurt. If you retaliate, or run, you'll be shot. On three. One. Two. Three.'

It was over before Mark had really registered what was going on. A shot rang out: the sharp, resonant crack of a semi-automatic rifle. Mark heard a thud and a felt a simultaneous tremor as the round smashed into the mud between his calves. It was an expert shot. A couple of inches either side and he would have been hit. Carmen was shaking beside him, so he put his arm over her shoulders and pressed down. His heart was in his mouth.

'All right,' Capron said. 'I want you all to stand up. Nice and slow. You! Short-ass with the Browning! I want you to toss it forward into those nettles to your left. You do anything else, and we'll shoot you.'

Mark peered into the foliage but he still couldn't see Capron. The American had learned a thing or two about camouflage during his time in Vietnam. Fox, meanwhile, was concentrating on a spot some fifteen yards to the right of where Capron's voice had come from. He had brought the Browning to bear and was aiming it into the bush. Mark saw the sergeant's eyes narrow as he glanced quickly at Mamando. Something passed between them, and Mark knew instantly that they had no intention of cooperating. Capron's warning shot may have been harmless but it had also been highly provocative. Fox was a soldier whose raison d'être was to meet fire with fire, to combat hostility with as much force and aggression as he could muster. Having been fired upon once, there was no way that he was going to let this pass without a fight. Mark swore silently and rolled on to Carmen's back just as Fox started shooting.

Forty-Six

The Browning was a single-action, 9 mm Hi-Power. Fox squeezed off the first two rounds from his original supine position. The third was fired from a crouch. The fourth at a run, as he charged the thicket in front. Carmen screamed. The jungle crackled as bullets tore through the vegetation. There was a muffled grunt from the forest before the rifle replied twice in quick succession. Mamando had rolled to his right and was sprinting towards the cover of the helicopter. He had almost made it before he was dropped by a single shot to the head. Mark saw a geyser of blood spurt from his scalp like lava from a volcano. Then the rifle fired again, its bark sheer and decisive. Fox managed one more shot before he fell, collapsing awkwardly as though he had slipped on ice. His left hand reached behind him to break his fall but his wrist was too weak to take his weight. Mark winced as he heard the sergeant's radius snap. Fox arched his back, his mouth gaping in silent pain. His body convulsed once but then settled motionless on the ground, the Browning still in his hand.

Silence followed.

Carmen had pressed her face into her hands. Her whole body was shaking with shock. Mark rolled off her and heard her gasp as she fought to get the air back into her lungs. There was a rustle of branches opposite as someone moved through the jungle. Mark felt stalked. Every cell in his body pulsed with energy. He could feel the blood pumping in his ears. It was visceral. He had never felt so alive.

Mamando was undoubtedly dead but Mark wasn't sure about Fox. The sergeant wasn't moving but there might still be something he could do. 'Don't shoot!' he shouted, climbing slowly to his feet. He put his hands up and took a step forward. 'I'm going to check Fox.'

'Stay where you are!' Capron called back. 'He's dead. They both are. Should have known better.'

Mark saw the leaves moving in front of him. Capron emerged from the forest. He was dressed in khaki slacks, military boots and a long-sleeved green shirt. He wasn't sweating. He wasn't flushed from exertion, or shaking from the exchange. He looked as calm and unhurried as he had in Cambridge. He gripped a long-barrelled assault rifle in his shoulder, aiming it at Mark's chest. He was poised and professional, leaving nothing to chance.

'You can put that down,' Mark told him. 'I'm not armed.'

'I underestimated you once before,' Capron replied. 'I'm not going to do it again.'

'You will never get away with this,' Carmen hissed. She had stood up and was hiding behind Mark, her voice quivering as she came down from her adrenal rush. 'We know who you are, and who you are working for. We will testify against you.'

Capron shook his head, a half-grin appearing in the corner of his mouth. 'Self-defence. Your man fired first. It's not going to court but if it did, you'd perjure yourself if you said anything to the contrary.'

'That's debatable,' Mark said. 'What about the round you put between my legs? Besides, Mamando wasn't armed.'

'Impossible for us to know that. Men running, bullets flying all over the place. He could have had a concealed weapon. We did what we needed to do.'

'You still killed an innocent man.'

'Not personally. My partner did. A fraction of a second before that trigger-happy sonofabitch with the Browning killed *him*.'

Mark examined Capron's pockmarked features, unsure whether to believe him.

'Take a look when I'm gone,' the American continued. 'He's back there. One in the throat, one in the jaw. He's a mess. Nothing you can do for him either. That Browning's got a muzzle energy of five hundred joules. You wouldn't even find all the pieces to put him back together.'

Mark looked around the clearing, scarcely believing that three men had died in such a short space of time. He shook his head, momentarily speechless.

Capron lowered the rifle, confident now that his competitors didn't pose a threat. The shock must have been plain to see on their faces. 'You've just witnessed a firefight between two highly trained commandos,' he explained. 'These guys don't piss around, Mark. They shoot to kill.'

'How long have you been here?' Carmen asked.

'Not long. That Huey told us where to find you. We just followed the noise.'

'Where were you?'

'About a mile west of here. I guess we were doing OK but we still might never have found it without your help. Now then, I'll just collect the briefcase, and I'll be on my way.'

'You're welcome to it,' Mark replied. 'It's emp –' Then he stopped. Capron still wanted the briefcase. Didn't know that it was empty. Which could only mean that someone *else* had removed the contents. A third party they didn't know about. But who? How many other people knew about Tom Chuter's secret? How many other people had read Carmen's article and set off to find the crash site? Had Chuter himself found it and taken it back to his tribe? What about Steve from Save the Children? He had shown an almost obsessive interest in Mark's story. Or Dietmar Katzer, who had been at the police station in Daru when Mark had shown Kiuke the approximate location of the crash on the map.

Capron walked to the fallen tree trunk and looked inside the briefcase. He poked the pockets and flaps with the muzzle of his rifle and then sent the whole thing crashing to the ground in disgust.

'Where are they?'

'Whatever *they* are, we haven't got them.'

Capron's face creased in annoyance. 'I haven't got time for games, Mark. And neither has Melanie.'

Mark stared at him, his eyebrows knitted tight in confusion. He didn't understand. Couldn't keep up. 'How do you know about Melanie?' he asked. 'Have *you* got her?'

'No. Charlie Bartlett's got her. But if you give me what I need, I'll tell you where he's holding her.'

Mark felt the anger stir within him. This was what Capron did best. Manipulate people with his superior intelligence and data. *Charlie Bartlett?* Yes, it was possible, wasn't it? First there was the Australian accent. Second, his profile as a convicted drug dealer and ex-SASR soldier meant that he was probably capable of perpetrating a violent abduction. And if Chris, his brother, had been employed to retrieve the briefcase, that would explain how he knew what was inside. The two had talked and Charlie had spotted an opportunity to get rich quick. Chris, it appeared, had been moonlighting on Capron. Retrieving the briefcase and dividing its contents for two different customers: Gammell Pharmaceuticals and his brother, Charlie.

Mark felt some of the tension in his shoulders ease as another piece of the puzzle clicked into place. The picture, though, was still far from complete. 'How do you know where she is?' he asked. 'You could be bluffing.'

'I could be, but I'm not. We planted a bug in your flat before you got back from Papua New Guinea. My boys were still listening after Fletch and I had done our deal with your sister. We needed to know if she was going to call the police. A couple of hours later she was abducted by someone posing as a courier. My guys were parked just up the road. They knew something was wrong when the courier returned to your flat and Melanie didn't. I guess that was to leave you her finger. My guys followed the van to –'

Something flashed through the air.

Capron hissed in surprise and jerked his hand to his neck as though he had been stung by a bee.

The dart had struck him between his hairline and collar. It was two inches long. The shaft was made of bamboo, the flight of bird's feathers. Capron spun around with the rifle on his hip. A second dart sunk into his thigh. He reeled several paces to the left, thought about firing, but decided against it. A thick trail of blood dripped down his neck as he discarded the rifle, conceding the fight before it had even begun.

Mark and Carmen remained stock-still in the middle of the clearing as Wontok and seven of his tribesmen emerged from the jungle.

They were all naked. All armed.

Forty-Seven

Mark placed an arm around Carmen's shoulders as the tribesmen approached. They carried spears, blowpipes and stone axes. Two had bows and arrows. They edged forward, weapons at the ready, as though stalking dangerous prey. They had white quills through their nostrils and reed armlets around their biceps. Several of the older men wore necklaces of what appeared to be human teeth. One young man had a series of ugly welts on his back: thick chevrons of scar tissue, resembling a crocodile's scales. He was the most excitable member of the group, a young warrior eager to demonstrate his prowess in battle. Mark glanced away to avoid catching his eye.

It was a wise decision. Seconds later the young warrior shrieked and ran at Capron, his spear gripped tight in his fists. Capron may have been wounded but the instinct of survival was still strong. He read the attack, ducking right just as the tribesman lunged. Then, as the Papuan's momentum carried him past, Capron let fly a backhanded punch, which caught him full in the throat. The young warrior was lifted off his feet. He collapsed to the ground, dropping his spear. Capron must have been a formidable fighter in his youth, but at sixty-four and with two darts in his body, the exertion proved too much. He sank to his knees, drained of all strength.

A few yards away, his young assailant was in considerable pain. He cried out, but with his larynx badly damaged he soon realised that it was safer to suffer in silence. Mark saw him glance at his discarded spear only for Wontok to pacify him with a sharp command.

Mark turned his attention to Capron. The American's lips were drawn tight over his teeth, his mouth twisted in pain. He had removed the darts from his neck and thigh and was trying to stem the bleeding with his fingers. The missiles had clearly been tipped with some sort of poison because his actions were fumbling and drunken. When he tried to stand, he managed only to stumble a few paces before collapsing to the ground.

Wontok spoke quickly as he issued instructions to his men. Mark tried smiling as he had before, but his greeting was met with a scowl. There was no rapport now. This was a war party. The time for diplomacy had long since passed. Mark felt ashamed. He had broken their unspoken bond. Only a week ago, Wontok had saved his life. The elder had asked for nothing in return except, Mark had sensed, the right to privacy. Now Mark had reneged on that most simple of deals. He had returned to the forest, bringing men and machines with him. Their helicopter had shattered the peace. Their gunfire had sprayed death and destruction through the jungle. Mark shrugged apologetically. He wanted to explain that it wasn't his fault. That Melanie had been kidnapped. That he'd had no choice but to return. He kept smiling. It was the last thing in the world that he felt like doing but he wanted Wontok to know that he posed no threat.

'What are they going to do?' Carmen asked.

'I don't know,' Mark replied. 'But if they wanted to kill us they would have done it by now. Try to stay calm. Keep smiling. Don't catch that young one's eye if you can help it. He may be hurt but he looks like trouble.'

Wontok spoke again, his speech punctuated with occasional clucks of his tongue. He was having difficulty coordinating his men, many of whom were examining the JetRanger with fascination and fear. Wontok raised his voice. This time the tribesmen responded. Several disappeared into the forest, returning a few minutes later with two large bamboo poles. The stems were thick, green and strong. Another man, the eldest of the group, had cut a six-metre vine from a nearby tree. Now he sat on the ground, one end of the plant looped over his big toe. He began peeling away the bark with the blade of his axe. When he had finished, he spliced the creeper into strips and then wove them together to make rope.

Mark and Carmen watched in silent admiration. Capron, too, was quiet. His bleeding had stopped but he was only semi-conscious now as the poison ran riot in his veins. He offered no resistance as the tribe trussed him to the bamboo poles and then hoisted them on to their shoulders. He hung upside down like a shot pig. His head lolled as the Papuans trotted into the jungle.

Wontok waved his spear at Mark and Carmen, instructing them to move. They did as they were told, following Capron in single file. Wontok walked behind them with two of his companions bringing up the rear.

The pace was fast. Mark and Carmen had to trot every twenty yards to make up the gap with the group ahead. If they didn't, they felt the tip of Wontok's spear against their spines. Further in front, Capron was now in a terrible state. He was pulling on his bindings, straining his neck to prevent the blood from rushing to his head. He was delirious but battling gamely to make himself more comfortable. Mark felt a begrudging respect for the man. Sixty-four and tough as old boots. His face was racked with pain but there was no sign of fear. He hadn't uttered a sound since the first dart had struck.

There was no path but the tribe moved

effortlessly through the jungle, clearing a passage for the prisoners behind. The only sounds were of men breathing, leaves brushing against skin, and the occasional knock of a spear on wood as someone hurdled a fallen tree.

They rested for the first time after an hour. Carmen had already begun to tire. The long flight from Europe and the adrenalin that she had expended earlier had left her mentally and physically drained. She hadn't yet complained but Mark could see the first signs of doubt creeping into her eyes. As though she wasn't sure how much more of this she could take. Mark was feeling the strain too but he refused to show it. He wanted Carmen to know that she could rely on him to get them home.

Wontok gave them each some water from a gourd he carried over his shoulder. It was just before four o'clock in the afternoon. The sun had lost some of its warmth but it was still thirty-two degrees in the shade. Mark could hear the Huey in the distance, its rotor blades throbbing like the beat of a distant drum. The pilot would try to raise Mamando on the radio and would get no response. He might even see the corporal's body, poleaxed in the middle of the clearing. Then what? He would contact Kiuke and they would return with more men, possibly tonight but more likely in the morning when they had more daylight ahead of them. In the meantime, the Huey could fly directly overhead and the pilot would still never see them through the trees. The helicopter may have been a weapon centuries ahead of the tribe's Neolithic axes, but right now the Papuans held the upper hand.

On they went, swatting mosquitoes and tearing off leeches. They were heading east towards the tributary. Mark calculated that they were likely to reach it some two miles north of where he and Melanie had been attacked by the crocodile. The tribesmen sang as they marched. The main group hummed a percussive bass line while Wontok and the rope-weaver chanted descant lyrics over the top. Only the young warrior was silent. His throat had begun to swell, his black skin taking on a purple hue that Mark feared was indicative of internal bleeding. Mark listened as he walked, captivated by the tribal harmony. He didn't need to understand the words to get the gist of it. The Papuans were masters of their art. Their song was undoubtedly one of triumph over their enemies.

Mark had always thought that singing was the purest art form. You didn't need anything else to do it. No instrument, no pen, no brush, no materials. It came from within. And it was used to communicate emotion. Not meaning but *feeling*. He thought of Alondra and the horror of being trapped inside a body that no longer worked. Of her not being able to sing. For someone who loved music, it must have been the ultimate torture. The ultimate loss of freedom. Even slaves sang.

Several metres ahead, Sean Capron appeared

to have regained some of his strength. The poison had been temporary; strong enough to incapacitate him but not enough to be fatal. He was more alert now, his eyes scanning the phalanx for information that might later aid an escape.

Mark watched him examining each of the tribesmen in turn. He was working: assessing their personalities, running inventories of their weapons and then combining the two sets of data to identify the weakest links in the chain. Mark realised then that Capron's professionalism could be the difference between life and death. Not only did the American have experience of jungle warfare, he also knew where Melanie was being held. Like it or not, he was their ally. Mark knew that he was going to have to free Capron at the first opportunity. Without him, they might never escape from the forest alive.

Another hour brought another rest. It was dusk and the birds were beginning to roost. Now it was their turn to sing. Mark and Carmen sat on the ground, deafened by the noise.

'It is incredible!' Carmen whispered. 'It's like the air itself is resonating.'

Mark knew what she meant. The song was all around them. The babble of warblers, the whistle of shrikes, the squawk of parrots and the *peet-peet-peet* of a white-shouldered fairy wren. It was as though they could reach out their hands and pluck the notes from the sky. Even the tribesmen were silent, appreciating the birds' superior performance.

Then, amid the cacophony, Mark heard the song of another bird. Heard it and smiled. Slowly at first and then wider as the penny dropped. He couldn't see it but he didn't need to. It was the song of a bird that he knew as well as any. A bird he had grown up with in his bedroom in Ealing. And in that moment he knew who had removed the contents of Chris Bartlett's briefcase. Knew, too, where he would find Tom Chuter's secret, if only he could engineer the opportunity to retrieve it.

Forty-Eight

'What's up?' Carmen asked, glancing nervously at their captors. 'Something has tickled you.'

'No,' Mark replied. 'Something's just slapped me round the face and told me to wake the hell up.'

'What are you talking about?'

Mark looked at Capron lying on his side between the two poles. The American had heard their exchange and was eavesdropping for more information. *Too bad!* Mark wasn't going to give him any. 'I'll tell you later,' he said, and before Carmen could protest, Wontok had ordered them to their feet for the last leg of their journey.

They reached the river some twenty minutes later. It had taken Mark and Melanie eight hours to find it but the Papuans had got there in just over two. The tribe had constructed a simple ferry to get themselves across. It comprised a raft and a length of interwoven vine that had been lashed around a tree either side of the water. A second rope attached the raft to the vine and then it was simply a case of hauling themselves across, hand over hand, until they arrived on the other side. Mark and Carmen went on the second crossing, joining Capron just as the first bats appeared for their evening feed. Soon the air was thick with mosquitoes. They flew in Mark's ears, eyes and nostrils, their whine making his flesh crawl. He buttoned his shirt to the neck and scooped a handful of dirt, applying it to his face and hands as he had before. Then he did the same for Carmen.

With the threat of malaria humming once again in his ears, it was impossible for Mark not to think of Melanie. If she *had* developed the disease, it would be beginning to break about now. And without proper treatment her condition would deteriorate rapidly. Charlie Bartlett was hardly likely to take her to hospital, was he? Unchecked, the parasites that had been present in the mosquito's saliva would invade her liver. Once there, each one would attack a cell, eating its contents before asexually reproducing itself forty thousand times. The cell would burst, releasing more parasites into her blood, whereupon the whole process would start again. Her body would react by raising its temperature in an attempt to boil the invaders to death. She would shiver to generate additional warmth and then, having overheated, she would break out in a cold sweat as she sought to cool down. The parasites would ride her bloodstream, arriving in her brain. Then they would attack again. Within a few days she might carry over a billion of them, each one eating her up from the inside out. Melanie would be locked in an uncontrollable cycle of fever and chills, sweats and shakes, until finally her brain shut down.

It sounded awful – and of course it was – but if it happened, Melanie would be just one of three million people who died from malaria every year. Children were perishing in their thousands every single day in Africa, Asia and South America. The scale of the disease was phenomenal. A death every thirty seconds since before man was even human, leaving some scientists to conclude that malaria had killed one out of every two people who had ever lived. Alexander the Great, Attila the Hun, George Washington and Abraham Lincoln had all experienced its grip. Since then the world's more affluent countries had succeeded in eradicating it – but not without a fight. Spain could not declare that they had defeated the disease until 1964. Victory in Greek Macedonia was only won as recently as 1975. Now, though, it was largely a Third World disease: out of sight and out of mind for those in the developed West. Bill Gates and other benefactors had ploughed hundreds of millions of dollars into finding a vaccine, but so far the parasites had proved to be smarter than even the brightest human brains.

Mark looked at Capron. Trussed to his poles the American was unable to defend himself against the mosquitoes. His hands and face were flecked with insects. He never made a sound but the relief in his eyes was unmistakable as they moved away from the water and back into the forest.

They arrived at Wontok's village just as it was getting dark. It was a neat settlement, comprising just thirteen buildings. There was a central long-house with two clusters of six houses set back on either side. All were constructed from timber, bamboo, sago bark and leaves. They stood on stilts two metres high: a design that allowed the air to circulate underneath while reducing the opportunity for snakes and other creepy-crawlies to enter.

The women and children, Mark noticed, occupied the houses to the right, segregated from the men on the left by a distance of almost fifty metres. They peered nervously from their door-ways, mouths slightly open in confusion and fear. Naked above the waist, the women wore grass loincloths to preserve their modesty below. One old woman sat by an unlit fire, suckling a piglet on a withered tit. She smiled a greeting across the clearing, her toothless gums pink against her chestnut face.

Mark and Carmen were led to the central longhouse and ordered to sit. Capron lay next to them, still bound to the bamboo poles. The war party stood over them while Wontok climbed the gangplank and disappeared inside the house.

While they waited for his return, the women

and children plucked up courage and made their way to the clearing. It wasn't long before Mark, Carmen and Capron were surrounded. Men followed from the other direction. One of the first to arrive was leading two pigs on a tether. He hammered a stake into the ground on the edge of the clearing and then joined his friends, leaving the animals tied to their post.

There were perhaps ninety people now. Mark guessed that the entire tribe had gathered to witness the proceedings. It was an intimidating atmosphere: volatile, though not overtly hostile. The women had grown in confidence, whispering, pointing and occasionally laughing as they inspected the day's catch. They seemed to find Carmen particularly interesting, the hue of her skin a source of considerable debate. Only the children stayed silent, holding their mothers' hands, wondering what on earth was happening, and who these aliens were.

Wontok emerged a few minutes later. He ran down the gangplank, leaving the route clear for someone else to descend.

Mark watched as a second man appeared in the doorway. He was Caucasian but almost as tanned as his subjects. His hair and beard were long, blond and thickly matted, framing his face like a lion's mane. His skin was tough and dry, coating his delicate bones like leather. He, too, was naked, although the end of his penis was encased in a painted egg-shell *kotek*. He wore a leather thong around his forehead and a single pink feather on a cord around his neck. There were scars on his arms and legs. Judging from the regularity of the pattern, they were not the result of an accident. He looked wild. Unpredictable. Feral almost. A man who had turned his back on the developed world from which he had once come.

He descended the gangplank slowly, his neck stretched as he peered at his prisoners. He appeared to be slightly nervous, as though these were the first white people he had seen in a while. He reached the ground and stood before them, clucking his tongue. Up close, Mark could see wrinkles in his brow, betraying his age. But for all the man's wildness, it was his eyes that demanded attention. Doe-like with effeminate lashes, they were a brilliant green. And they blazed with the same intensity as they had in his mother's photograph in Grantchester.

Mark waited until the man was directly opposite. 'Dr Chuter, I presume?'

Forty-Nine

Tom Chuter sat down, hoisting his ankles on to his thighs in the lotus position. The tribe followed suit, jostling for position and demanding hush as though they would understand every word of the conversation that was about to take place. Chuter held up his hand. For a moment the only sound was the trill of insect song pulsing through the forest.

'Yes,' he began. 'I am Dr Chuter. And who are *you*?'

'My name is Mark Bridges. This is my friend Carmen Beckwith.'

'Carmen?' Chuter asked, twitching his nose. 'Do I smell Spanish blood?'

'Half Chilean,' she corrected. 'On my mother's side.'

Chuter nodded. 'Chile. The most beautiful country on earth. Home of the Araucanian Indians. The Mapuche and Huilliche I have always found particularly interesting. Fearsome warriors but also highly skilled silversmiths.'

'And potters,' Carmen added.

'Indeed,' Chuter said. He closed his eyes as though meditating. With his long hair and tanned nudity he might have passed for a yogi. 'And to what do I owe the pleasure of your acquaintance?' he asked, opening his eyes and looking at Mark.

Mark sighed loudly. 'Trouble that I want no part of. It's a long story.'

Chuter smoothed his hair behind his ears, revealing the scar where his cranial plate had been fitted. 'No one has to be anywhere.'

So Mark told him. Starting with the murders of Peri and Gile and finishing with the shoot-out at the crash site. He spoke of their trip to Grantchester and their subsequent meeting with Simeon Creasey. His account was honest and thorough. He could see no reason to lie. The only detail that he withheld was the news of Walter Chuter's death. That was a personal message that could wait for a more appropriate time. The story took more than half an hour to tell. Chuter listened without asking a single question. He had clearly learned a great deal of patience during his time with the tribe, trusting Mark to cover everything that mattered in his own good time. Capron was equally intent as he learned where and when the police had been involved. Carmen, too, was an attentive listener. This was the first time she had heard about Mark's previous encounter with Wontok,

401

and she flashed him a scowl to register her hurt.

'Creasey!' Chuter spat, when Mark had finished. 'I knew he was a snake. I never told anyone what I'd discovered, but somehow I always knew that he'd read my notebook.'

'He thought you'd taken a wife,' Mark explained. 'He was jealous. He read it, looking for something to use against you. I think his discovery of the secret was accidental.'

'Be that as it may,' Chuter replied, 'there was nothing accidental about what he did next, was there? Simeon was always a vain old queen. And insecure too. He thought I had bisexual tendencies, which was nonsense. A wife? Ha! Even if I wanted to, I could never get married. Addu unions involve a complex system of sister exchange. I have no one to offer in return for a bride. Not that I would ever dilute their blood with mine. No, it's simpler than that. Homosexuality, you see, is unheard of here. Most likely it would be highly taboo. The fact of the matter was that when I returned from my sabbatical, I discovered that I had lost all interest in sex. After a year of enforced abstinence, I had inadvertently become celibate.' He paused and waved his hand theatrically. 'But let us not concern ourselves with such tawdry matters. If the briefcase was empty when you found it, where are the contents now?'

'I'll trade,' Mark replied. 'You tell me *what* they are, and I'll tell you *where* you can find them.'

On his left, Capron jerked his head towards him. 'You've got them?' he asked.

'No,' Mark replied. 'But I know who has.'

The American narrowed his eyes, suspecting a trick. He was still bound. There wasn't a damn thing he could do but wait and listen. The frustration seemed to be causing him more pain than Wontok's poison-tipped darts.

Opposite them, Chuter stroked his toes and laughed. 'All this time and all this way, and you still don't know what you're chasing?'

'No,' Mark replied.

'But you found my notebook?'

'Yes, I did. But I never had time to read it. Melanie was dangerously dehydrated. I had to find water. It's the same reason why I never opened the briefcase when I first saw it. Do we have a deal?'

Chuter's nose twitched as he considered the proposition. 'Allow me to consult with my council,' he said. 'This is a decision that affects the whole tribe. I cannot take it alone.' He stood up, uttered something in the Addu language and then re-entered the longhouse. Wontok and the rope-weaver followed. Then, three other elders pushed their way through the crowd and trotted silently up the ladder.

They were gone for two hours. Mark and Carmen sat patiently on the ground, stretching occasionally to make themselves comfortable. The tribe waited with them, the long delay of no consequence to anyone. Whispered conversation

403

competed with the grunt of the pigs as the Addu speculated on what would happen next. Capron, meanwhile, must have known that he was temporarily safe because he had closed his eyes and appeared to be dozing. Quite how he found the mental fortitude to relax was astonishing. The young warrior with the scarred back stood over him, determined to administer whatever punishment was coming his way. But if he wanted his revenge, he would have to be quick. The blow to his throat had been even more severe than Mark had first thought. Now, four hours on, the youth was having difficulty breathing as the swelling closed around his trachea. He was unsteady on his feet too, his brain starved of its regular oxygen quotient.

Night had fallen by the time the elders returned. The skies were clear and the stars blazed above the clearing in unfamiliar, close-knit constellations. Chuter reassumed his pose in front of his prisoners, flanked now by two members of the council. His right fist was bunched as though concealing something. Wontok had remained behind. Mark could hear him chanting in the longhouse. The rhythmic creaking of the reed floor suggested that he was dancing too. The tribe fell silent. Capron opened his eyes and rolled into a sitting position.

'Look around you,' Chuter began. 'And tell me what you see.'

Mark and Carmen turned their heads, glancing at the assembled tribe. Their eyes had adjusted to the dark but it was still unclear what Chuter was driving at.

'Men, women and children,' Mark replied, choosing his words carefully. 'A small tribe of forest dwellers, enjoying a peaceful existence.'

'The children. Yes! What about them?'

Mark looked again, but Carmen got there first, her time with the Fly River Children's Health Project making the difference obvious. 'They are all healthy,' she said. 'There's no malaria.'

Mark glanced at the nearest child: a girl of four or five. A bulge under her tummy button suggested umbilical herniation but otherwise she looked fit and strong. So too did the rest of the kids. A few showed minor facial deformities, a result perhaps of incestuous unions, inevitable among such a small and isolated population. But none appeared to be suffering from the same afflictions that had blighted the kids in Terry Landevelt's hospital. No running noses, no weeping eyes. No contorted limbs, racked with fever. No coma from cerebral malaria. Carmen was right. Mark felt his stomach leap as the penny dropped.

Bathed in moonlight, Tom Chuter rattled his fist and then unfurled his fingers.

Mark knew now what he was going to see, even as they appeared in the anthropologist's palm.

Fifty

Mark leaned forward for a closer look. His hunch had been correct. There were four of them. Four black truffles, identical to those that Wontok had fed him a week ago.

'What we have here', Chuter explained, 'is a natural vaccine against malaria. Protection against one of the world's most lethal diseases. Eat it, and it provides lifelong immunity. It is without parallel. A panacea. A miracle. A magic bullet. In terms of its potential impact on the world, only a cure for AIDS or cancer could come close to rivalling it. Gold dust, of course, to a company like Gammell Pharmaceuticals.'

Mark stared at the truffles in awe. No wonder that Capron had gone to such lengths to retrieve the briefcase. Commercialisation of the fungus's properties would create an instant market worth billions of dollars. Brian Selby, the doctor at Tidal Island, had said that he'd always thought a natural vaccine was more likely than a synthetic one. And here it was, growing just a few miles from his hospital.

Chuter turned to Carmen. 'You look sceptical. Why? For years quinine was the most effective cure for malaria, and that is what exactly? An alkaloid derived from the bark of the cinchona tree. The world is full of natural medicines: cortisone can be produced from the diosgenin in yams; digitalis, which they use to treat heart conditions comes from the dried petals of foxgloves. Even penicillin was derived from the secondary metabolite of a mould.'

'It's the same with a lot of recreational drugs too,' Mark added. 'Cocaine, cannabis and opium all originate from plants. The main component of LSD comes from a fungus that forms on rye grain. That's why Charlie Bartlett wants the truffles, isn't it? For their side effects? With a monopoly on supply, and the spores to grow his own, he could become a millionaire many times over.'

'Ah, yes!' Chuter smiled. 'The side effects!' He rattled the truffles in his fist again. 'The Addu call these *kerili-bawaya*. I doubt that they are true truffles, but they are certainly a form of fungus and, I assume, from the same family as truffles. Kerili is a benign tree spirit. He provides shelter, shade and nutrition. It is his influence that protects the children from disease. Bawaya, on the other hand, is a river spirit: a mischievous imp who colours our dreams and tempts us with impure thoughts. His is the narcotic influence that Charlie Bartlett wishes to peddle on the streets of London.'

Mark glanced at Capron to see how the American had reacted to the knowledge that his mercenary had been running a side operation. Chris Bartlett was the fulcrum on which the whole thing pivoted. Employed by Capron to retrieve the fungi for Frank Wanstead, he had been given the notebook to enable him to find the tribe. Reading it, he had learned of the fungus's narcotic properties and realised that he could get paid twice if he also delivered a sample to his brother.

'We consume the *kerili-bawaya* only when a child is born,' Chuter continued. 'A protection ceremony that lasts for several days. The shaman meanwhile may eat it at any time to contact the spirit world and pass on counsel to the rest of the tribe. That is what Pindu is doing now. He took some at the beginning of our meeting. He will join us shortly to let us know what he has seen.'

Mark glanced towards the longhouse. Wontok – or Pindu as he was really called – was now firmly under the fungus's spell. His silhouette flashed past the open door, his thighs stomping like pistons as his dance grew more frenzied. His chanting had become less musical, interspersed with peals of crazed laughter. Deep in the hut's shadows, he appeared to be swiping at invisible shapes in the air.

'The fungus grows underground,' Chuter explained. 'But only the shaman knows how and where to find it. It is a secret passed down from generation to generation. If the shaman dies before he has divulged his knowledge to his successor, the secret will die with him. That is why the shaman is always the first to feed, and the first to choose a wife when he comes of age.'

'So how did Chris Bartlett manage to get his hands on some?' Carmen asked. 'Did he steal them?'

'Not initially,' Chuter replied. 'He and his pilot offered us cash first. Two hundred thousand dollars, if I remember correctly.'

'Two hundred thousand dollars!' Carmen whistled under her breath. 'That's a lot of money.'

'Where you come from, yes. But here, for us, it is utterly meaningless. The Addu do not understand money. They have no currency. They are entirely self-sufficient, trading with no one. The forest is their supermarket and they shop for free.'

'So you refused the offer?' Mark asked.

'Of course we refused! Gammell Pharmaceuticals only knew about the fungus because they had stolen the notebook. I was determined that they were not going to profit from such underhand tactics. I told Bartlett and his sidekick to go away and never come back.'

'But they didn't?' Carmen prompted.

'No. They resorted to scaremongering to get what they wanted. They fired their machine guns into the air.' A deep frown appeared on Chuter's face as he glanced over his shoulder to the longhouse. 'The bullets came down over the women's huts, killing one of Pindu's wives. An accident, but manslaughter all the same. The tribe was terrified. They had never seen weapons like those before. They feared the involvement of magic. Ninety-three people stampeded into the forest, tearing their hair, running for their lives. Bartlett, meanwhile, calmly jammed his gun under Pindu's chin. I have no doubt that he would have shot him, had I not persuaded him to surrender his cache of *kerili-bawaya*.'

'And they would have got away with it,' Mark mused. 'Had it not been for the accident.'

'Ah, the accident!' Chuter smiled and translated for the benefit of the tribe, who immediately fell about laughing.

'That was you?' Capron asked.

'Yes,' Chuter replied, his upper lip curling in a canine snarl. 'I'm afraid so. We did what we needed to do to prevent the fungi from leaving. Your men were good. We only had to see them move to know that they had spent many years in the jungle. But how could they compete with the Addu? A people born to the forest? We had heard the helicopter arrive the previous day. We knew where it was. There is a plateau eight miles north of here, where you were dropped yesterday. It is the only place within twenty-five miles of here that you could possibly land a helicopter. Bartlett's mistake was to leave it unattended. Our warriors were still cowering in the forest and we knew that we would suffer terrible casualties if we initiated a fight. The tribe refused to follow, but Pindu wanted his revenge. He and I outflanked your men on their return to the JetRanger. We were unarmed so an ambush was out of the question. Then I saw the fuel cap on the fuselage. I couldn't believe it. It was the same as on a car, only you didn't need a key to open it. There was just a spring-loaded metal flap with a screw cap underneath. By the time Bartlett and his pilot returned we had shovelled two kilograms of soil into the tank. The engine started well enough but they began to experience problems a few minutes into their flight. We watched them go, knowing we could never keep up. We heard the crump as it crashed but we figured it was well into Hulale territory, so we never made an effort to find it. Until yesterday, when Mark and Carmen arrived in *their* helicopter. Pindu climbed a tree and marked the spot where you abseiled down. Our men set off immediately, less fearful this time because the element of surprise was on their side.'

Chuter rocked back, his slender limbs tense now with aggression. Overhead, a shooting star fizzed across the sky before diving into the leaves of a distant tree. The tribe was growing restless, agitated by Pindu's ravings. The whispers around the semicircle became loud conversations. Children were crying, hungry for their supper. A scuffle broke out between two adolescents, forcing the aged rope-weaver to wander

411

menacingly into the crowd. Even the pigs were unsettled, snaffling the ground, tugging on their tether.

Mark knew that the change in mood was a bad sign. Knew too that his next question was potentially antagonistic. But he had to ask it. It was the only thing left that he didn't understand. He examined Chuter's face, looking deep into his eyes for a clue that would explain his extraordinary behaviour. Walter Chuter had been right. Tom had turned completely native. There was no doubt that the anthropologist had become a bona fide member of the tribe. He had taken on many of their mannerisms: clucking his tongue, jutting his chin and avoiding eye contact whenever he spoke. Only his hair was different: long, blond and matted, where the Addu's was short, dark and coarse as steel wire. His vocabulary was still erudite but his syntax had become increasingly rambling as the effort of speaking English again began to take its toll.

It wasn't hard to understand why he felt so at home here. His postcard from Cairns had said it all. *The air in England never suited me.* Back there, he was a loner; a misfit. A man his own mother had described as complicated. Bullied by his father, falsely accused by his lover, and driven to nervous exhaustion by the weight of his discovery, he had since found a niche in which he could thrive. He had travelled the world and eventually found kinship among a people who couldn't judge or upset him. Here he had status.

Respect. A sense of belonging, and full-time immersion in his passion for anthropology. It must have been an irresistible combination: as liberating and intoxicating as the fungi themselves. All of which was understandable but none of which explained the enormity of his biggest decision.

'Why?' Mark asked. 'Why didn't you share your secret with the rest of the world? Why didn't you publish?'

Chuter's green eyes flashed with anger. His left hand played with his hair, curling the locks around his fingers. 'I will answer that question in a minute,' he said. 'But first you must fulfil your side of the deal. I told you what you were looking for. Now you must tell me where I can find them.'

'Fox has them,' Mark said. 'He had a couple of minutes alone in the helicopter before he brought the briefcase out. Time enough to smash the fire extinguisher and hide the fungi in his pocket. They'll be on his body somewhere. But if you want them, you'll have to return to the clearing tonight. The police will know we're missing. If they haven't already done so, they'll return tomorrow to collect the bodies.'

Chuter closed his eyes and rocked back and forth on his haunches. Then he translated and the council spent the next few minutes in heated debate. On Mark's right, Capron shook his head, ruefully acknowledging that he had been seconds away from searching Fox's body when he had been struck by Pindu's darts. Conversation among the rest of the tribe became increasingly vocal as everyone expressed an opinion on what to do.

Then, suddenly, there was silence. Pindu appeared in the door of the longhouse. His eyes were glazed and his mouth slightly ajar. His movement down the ladder was languid and relaxed. The most visceral hallucinations had passed. He was now enjoying the all-enveloping euphoria that Mark remembered from his own experience. Once he had reached the end of the gangplank, Pindu began patting his head with his hands. His semi-erect penis twitched hungrily between his legs – a display that was met with total indifference by the tribe. Then he sat down, taking his place among the council on Chuter's right. His speech sounded muddled as he related his discourse with the spirits.

The tribe waited patiently until he had finished. His final pronouncement drew a ripple of excited approval, which sent a shiver the length of Mark's spine. There was a short conversation between the elders before Chuter turned his attention back to his prisoners.

'We will recover the fungi at dawn,' he announced. 'The Addu do not leave their village after dark because that is the time when the *karkahua* – the demon spirits – are most active. Only the shaman may move freely at night but Pindu says that your presence here has angered Kerili. Not even he will leave the village until it is light. Besides,' and here Chuter glanced mischievously at Capron, 'the spirits have decreed that there is to be a feast.'

Fifty-One

Sean Capron returned his captor's look with a cool, unblinking glare. It was wasted on Chuter, who had already turned his eyes to the ground. On Mark's right, Carmen blanched, her hand held over her mouth as she digested the horror implicit in the anthropologist's words. *A feast*. It could only mean one thing.

'You asked me why I won't allow the fungus to leave,' Chuter continued. 'I will tell you. You look only to the future, where you see teams of scientists analysing the *kerili-bawaya* in a laboratory. You see botanists, biologists and pharmacologists like Creasey, deconstructing its DNA so that they can synthesise a vaccine from its genes. You see only what you perceive to be advancement and progress. You see only where we are going. And in doing so, you are blind to the past. Blind to where we have been and where we have come from. Blind to the fact that it is *regression* not progress that would yield improvements to our quality of life. Look around you! See the simplicity! The purity! The beauty of life at its most basic! Anthropology unlocks the mysteries of our evolution but it also holds the key to our salvation.'

Mark shook his head, unimpressed by Chuter's bombastic logic. 'But think what a vaccine could do. Think of the millions of lives you could save.'

'But at what cost?' Chuter snapped back. 'Not without turning Papua New Guinea into a mine. I have already told you that the *kerili-bawaya* grows underground. Right now, Pindu and his son are the only people on the planet who know where to find them. If I published my findings, Gammell or others like them would tear the country to pieces. They would bring bulldozers, uprooting the forest in search of profits with which to fatten their shareholders. Perhaps they would strike a deal with the government, offering a profit-share scheme so that Papua New Guinea could generate some wealth from its newfound resource. But what good would that be to the Addu, who do not know that such things as government and money exist? They would be driven from their land. They would be forced to make contact with people from other tribes. People with different customs, beliefs and laws. The change would be bewildering. Terrifying even. Then, slowly, they would become dependent on their new way of life. If they had accepted payment for their fungus they would

417

learn to need things that they never knew existed. They would learn greed, envy and materialism. Within a matter of months they would cease to live as we see them today. Within a generation they would disappear altogether. The purest example of human existence anywhere on the planet destroyed because of what *I* had written.'

'You must at least have thought about it?' Carmen protested. 'You must have been aware of the bigger picture? The greater good?'

Chuter scoffed angrily and clucked his tongue. 'Stupid girl! What? You think a decision like that was easy? You think I took it lightly? You think it didn't keep me awake at night, driving me half insane? Yes! Of course I was going to publish! It would have been the making of me. I would have become a professor. I could have travelled the world, lecturing on my discoveries. I could have written books and appeared on television chat shows. Had I wanted to, I could have profited from the vaccine myself. I had taken a sample of *kerili-bawaya* home with me and hidden it in a safe place. All I had to do was give it to Creasey and we would have been millionaires in a matter of weeks.'

'So what happened?' Mark asked. 'Why did you change your mind?'

Chuter leaped up only to crouch down opposite him. He was like a toad on a lily pad; his face just an inch away. His eyes may have been beautiful but his teeth had begun to rot, his gums blackened by bush tobacco and lack of care. He stank of embers, earth and stale sweat.

'The theft of my notebook happened! Just three days before I was going to publish my report. And in that moment my priorities changed. The secret was out, and not in the controlled manner in which I had intended. The Addu had never asked to be discovered. Now they were about to be invaded. White colonialists would come and bribe them from their lands. And all because of me. You tell me to think of the millions of lives I could save, to which I reply: name two of them! In the real world, Mark, we think of our nearest and dearest first. Our natural instincts are to protect our own before we show others any altruism. That protective instinct is as primitive and base as life itself. I had lived among the Addu for a year. They were my family, my friends. They were my *tribe*. And now my notebook was going to destroy them. These are real people. The millions you want to immunise are faceless, nameless statistics. How could I put them first?'

'Faceless and nameless?' Carmen challenged, her voice sharp enough to match Chuter's rising hysteria. 'Just a few miles south of here there is a field hospital run by Save the Children. When I left last week, there were twenty-four kids in there, many of whom will already be dead. I can name every single one.'

Chuter waved his hand in contempt. He was getting more distressed with every passing minute. Pindu had closed his eyes and was smiling as he rode the narcotic rushes in his blood. The council sat unmoved but the crowd were responding to the anthropologist's frenzy, fizzing now with hostile energy.

'You do not understand because you *cannot* understand. The Addu are one of the last uncontacted peoples on earth. Perhaps one of twenty such communities on our planet. My colleagues in Cambridge will tell you that the Sentinelese are uncontacted. That the Brazilian Jururei, Bolivian Ayoreo and Colombian Nukak all fall into the same category. They will list the Wapishana and Wayãpi, the Awá, Akuntsu and Akulio as uncontacted. But that is not true. These tribes resist contact but they have at least encountered men from the developed world. You can find reference to them in journals. You can read about them on the Internet. Not a great deal, I grant you, but at least they are known. Take the Korowai, over the border in Indonesia, for example. For many years they were erroneously believed to be the last practising cannibals. So much has been written about them that they are now a tourist attraction in their own right. But not the Addu. You will not find their name anywhere. Not in any textbook; nor any documentary. They had no name for themselves so *I* called them Addu myself. It is a word from their own language that implies "special" or "favourite".'

'You are claiming that they are a lost tribe?' Carmen asked.

'Lost?' Chuter spat. '*Lost*? I would never be so patronising. Look around you, Carmen! It is *you* who are lost. The Addu know their way through this forest better than you will ever know your way around London or Santiago. They are unique. Unlike any other people on earth. Their social practices show no signs of external influence *whatsoever*. They have not discovered agriculture. Only recently have they learned to breed pigs. They speak their own language. Like the Korowai, they still practise cannibalism and, by necessity, incest. They have weapons but few tools. Only a handful know the art of making fire. The young man over there with the scars on his back . . .' He waited for Carmen to nod. 'His name is Birahl. He was cut by his parents sixty-six times. His father then rubbed nettles into the wounds so that his skin would blister like the scales on a crocodile. It was a coming-of-age ceremony but one that was unique to him. I still don't know why. The Addu are as close to our early ancestors as we can ever hope to find. They are just as unique, just as valuable as a vaccine against malaria. And *that* is why they must be preserved.'

'You make them sound like an endangered species,' Carmen said, shooting Birahl a worried glance. The young man looked as though he was about to faint, his throat having swollen to the size of a tennis ball.

'They *are* an endangered species. That is my point! Tribes are disappearing all over the world. We save the rhino and the panda and the whale but we do nothing to protect our own kind. Look at what is happening to the Tagaeri in the Ecuadorian Amazon. They are disappearing because their forest is being destroyed so that ranchers can graze cattle to provide the beef for McDonald's restaurants. Many of the Onge people from the Andaman Islands, once thought of as the smallest tribe on earth, are thought to have perished in the tsunami of 2004. That leaves the Addu: ninety-five of us, living in two settlements in an enclave of unexplored forest. But even we are now under threat. Just by coming here you expose us to germs against which we have no immunity. Something as innocuous as the common cold could prove catastrophic and decimate our population.'

'You seem to be forgetting something,' Mark interjected. Chuter was at fever pitch. Antagonising him further could have disastrous consequences but the debate was in full flow, and the anthropologist hadn't yet demanded that they be quiet. He must have been clever to have been a lecturer at Cambridge but lack of practice meant that his argument was riddled with hypocrisy. '*You've* contacted them,' Mark said. '*You've* exposed them to germs, and I'm assuming that it was under *your* orders that we were brought to the village.'

'Yes!' Chuter exclaimed, beaming suddenly as though proud of an astute student. 'Clever boy!

You are right. And that irony is precisely the point I am getting to. My whole life had been about finding a people like this. But the moment I found them, they ceased to be what I was looking for. They ceased to be an *un*contacted tribe. The fantasy had been destroyed and they had become *real*. When they first saw me, they ran for their lives. They thought I was a ghost: an ancestral spirit returned to haunt them. They threw themselves to the ground, chanted and cried. If I came too close they threatened me with their weapons. The only reason they didn't kill me is because they feared supernatural reprisals. It was only when Pindu here followed me into the forest and watched me defecate that they realised I was a man like them. Only by prodding and smelling my shit did they know that I was not a *karkahua*. Even then it took weeks before they would accept me. That first contact was the zenith and nadir of my career. I discovered them and, in doing so, I changed them forever. I stole their innocence. They became tarnished; polluted by knowledge like Adam and Eve in the Garden of Eden. They knew that other tribes existed because they had fought them for land and hunting rights, but they knew nothing of white men, clothing, or travel. My intrusion forced them to rethink their entire concept of the world.'

Silence followed. Carmen was about to say something but Mark silenced her with a cautionary glance. Chuter was too far gone.

Further contradiction would be a dangerous waste of time.

'You can trust us not to tell anyone,' Mark said. 'But I must ask that Pindu gives me some fungi to trade for my sister. Bartlett won't accept anything else. If I fail him, Melanie will die.'

Chuter put his hand to his head and rubbed his titanium plate, an involuntary gesture that betrayed years of psychological abuse. 'I'm afraid you have misunderstood me. I have just spoken at length about the need to protect this tribe. For them to remain a secret. The only way I could undo the harm I had done was to *un*discover them. To swear myself to secrecy. To destroy my notes, live among them and never return in case I let slip their existence. Similarly, I cannot have you write about them in your newspaper. Or talk about them in your pub.'

Chuter stood up, a faraway look in his eyes. He said something to Pindu, who addressed the crowd. Within seconds people began to break away as though tasked with various jobs. Chuter made his way up the gangplank. He stopped at the entrance to the longhouse and turned to look at Mark. 'This', he said, spreading his arms, 'is what it means to be human. I will not sacrifice it for your sister or that which you call the greater good. And it is for precisely that reason that I can never let you leave.'

Fifty-Two

Mark and Capron exchanged glances. They were both thinking the same thing. Chuter wasn't going to be reasoned with, which meant that they would have to fight their way out. Either that or they were going to be killed and, quite possibly, eaten.

Mark tried to remain calm as he remembered what he had read in his guidebook. Papua New Guinea had long been synonymous with tales of missionaries being devoured by savage natives. But the outbreak of kuru among the Fore tribe in the 1950s had contributed to cannibalism's rapid demise. Kuru, a fatal cousin of Creutzfeldt-Jakob disease, had been linked to the consumption of human brains during Fore funerals. It had spread rapidly, particularly among women and children, who took on the role of cleaning their relatives after death. Recognising the scale of the epidemic, the Australian administration had out-lawed ritual anthropophagy in 1959, and kuru had all but disappeared within a generation. Since then there had been isolated reports of cannibalism among remote tribes but little hard evidence to suggest that it had continued much beyond the seventies. Various factions of the media had tried to rekindle the myth that it was still widespread, but their claims had been rebuffed by sceptical anthropologists, who accused them of groundless sensationalism. Mark stared up at the longhouse. Had Chuter been bluffing? Were the Addu really going to eat them? Or would they prefer the pigs?

'I've got a knife,' Capron said. 'It's in a sheath, strapped to my ankle. When the time comes, I want you to take it out and cut my bindings.'

Mark looked at him again and experienced a flutter of hope. Capron was serious. The Addu hadn't searched him. Why would they, when they were unfamiliar with clothing and what it could conceal?

'Not now,' Capron said. 'But soon. We may only get one opportunity, so be ready. I'll tell you when. It's on the outside of my left calf. Four firm strikes. Two between my ankles, the other two between my wrists. Do my ankles first, so I can run if necessary. We'll take the poles with us as weapons. You got that?'

Mark nodded but the hope that he had felt earlier had already vanished. Chuter had returned to the longhouse but the war party still stood over them with their weapons ready. All except Birahl, who was now unable to stand. He sat on the ground, chest heaving as he desperately tried to suck air down his ever-tightening trachea. Clearly he was no longer a threat, but that still left six armed men, with perhaps thirty more in the crowd behind. Even if Mark could set Capron free, there was no way that they could escape with the odds stacked so heavily against them. *Fight their way out?* How? What the hell with? He had never fought anyone in his life. He had restrained Fletch in the car park, but even then he had not been able to muster any real aggression. Perhaps it would be different when his life was on the line? It would have to be, wouldn't it?

Mark experienced a wave of sadness as the hopelessness of their situation sank in. He had failed. Failed Melanie. Failed his parents. It had been Carmen's choice to join him but he felt responsible for her too. She sat next to him, a terrified expression on her face as she watched the activity in the clearing.

The women were doing most of the work while the men stood over their prisoners. Mark glanced over his shoulder and identified the start of the trail that led to the ferry. If they could get beyond the village boundary then the Addu might not follow for fear of encountering the forest's evil spirits. In the meantime, there was nothing else to do except join Carmen in watching the scene unfold.

The group of women were digging a pit in the clearing outside Chuter's longhouse. They scraped away the earth using wooden paddles and heaped it to one side. When they had finished, they repeated the process until there were five pits. Each one measured approximately four feet long by three feet wide and one deep. They looked like shallow graves for children. A second group appeared shortly afterwards, their arms bulging with wood. Kindling was laid in each of the pits, and then the rope-weaver was summoned to make fire.

Mark, Carmen and Capron watched in silent fear as the pyres roared to life. Once they were alight and burning well, the women heaped a number of large stones among the embers. Each stone was roughly the size of a cantaloupe. And within half an hour most were already white-hot.

Behind them the rest of the tribe were becoming increasingly excited. There was animated conversation and occasional laughter. The children scampered around the fringes of the crowd, fighting or playing chase. One boy ran forward and slapped one of the pigs on its flank. It squealed and tried to bolt but only tripped on its bindings, causing the second animal to stumble into its rump. The crowd clucked their tongues, the expressions on their faces making it clear that tonight's feast was a very special occasion. The little boy, meanwhile, was grabbed by a member of the war party and vigorously beaten with a blowpipe.

The women in the cooking detail returned a few minutes later, this time carrying armfuls of sago fronds: broad, paddle-shaped leaves, which they laid on the ground like mats. Each one was sprinkled with a handful of chopped vegetation, which Mark assumed to be some sort of forest herb.

'What are they doing?' Carmen asked.

'Preparing dinner,' Mark replied grimly.

If they *were* going to be eaten then the cartoon image of the missionary being boiled alive in the cannibal's pot was ludicrously inaccurate. The Addu didn't have any pots. Instead, they were going to dismember their victims and wrap their flesh in the sago leaves. The leaves would then be buried in the mounds of earth and the heated stones lain on top to create an oven, so that the meat could be baked in the ground.

Chuter returned from the longhouse a few minutes later, still naked except for his *kotek*. 'This is fascinating,' he said, indicating the preparations behind him. 'Truly fascinating! I never dreamed I could witness something so extraordinary. Incredible to think that it still goes on.'

'Stop them!' Carmen pleaded 'You have the power. They will listen to you.'

Chuter shook his head. 'I am an anthropologist, Carmen. I must observe and learn. Pindu tells me that this is rare, even by their standards. The last time that they ate someone was over three years ago. A hunter from Hulale, who strayed too far from his territory. I always thought that cannibalism derived from a need for more protein in the diet but Pindu assures me that it is spiritual and has no nutritional value. Unlike the Fore and the Korowai, the Addu only practise exocannibalism: consuming people from outside their own community. Like many tribes in Papua New Guinea they adhere to a strong code of *payback*. If you are wronged, you revisit that wrong on your enemy twofold. Similarly, acts of great kindness are rewarded bountifully. You will find the same creed among the Gogodala people to the east, the Huli in the Highlands, and even among the Trobriand Islanders in the Solomon Sea. Capron, here, will be eaten to complete his humiliation. The Addu believe that by consuming him they are reducing him to the status of an animal – the ultimate insult to a hated enemy. You, Mark, will be eaten for your strength. Pindu says that your flesh will make his children grow big and strong like you. You should consider it a compliment. A sign of respect.'

'You're bluffing,' Mark said. 'They're going to eat the pigs.'

'No,' Chuter exclaimed. 'Wrong! Wrong! Wrong! This is real. For too many years people like you have tried to dismiss cannibalism as a slanderous, fictitious taboo. But we now have irrefutable biomolecular proof that it was commonplace throughout our evolution. In Colorado, the desiccated faeces of seven Pueblo Indians have been shown to contain protein, unique to the human heart. That evidence dates to the twelfth century, but only last year UN observers in the Congo reported instances of cannibalism in South Kivu. Chimpanzees do it. Over seventy other species of mammal do it. Nothing could be more natural.'

Mark shook his head in contempt but said nothing. What was the point? The guy was demented. Obsessed. Lost. A latter-day Kurtz who had abandoned all reason. Even if he wasn't bluffing, his refusal to intervene made him no better than the psychopaths who advertised on the Internet for people to eat.

Chuter had barely finished speaking when two of the tribesmen picked up the bamboo poles and hauled Capron into the clearing beside one of the fires. There had been no signal from Chuter, nor any from Pindu, who continued to chase hallucinogenic shapes around the longhouse.

The stones were hot. The tribe was ready. Capron was meat. His slaughter was going to be as unceremonious as a pig's.

Fifty-Three

The warriors began by cutting the bindings around Capron's wrists. Mark was about to throw himself at the American's ankles to free the knife. But just then the rope-weaver began shouting, demanding Chuter's attention.

Everyone stopped, arrested by the alarm in the old man's voice. It quickly became clear that the source of his distress was Birahl, the young warrior with the scarred back. His throat had finally swollen to such an extent that he could no longer breathe. He lay on his side, his eyes bulging with panic. He was suffocating. One look told Mark that he had less than a minute to live.

Mark was moving before he'd even considered that he might be endangering himself. He knelt on the ground by Birahl's shoulders and manoeuvred him gently on to his back. A murmur passed through the crowd, and several of the warriors raised their spears. They were placated by a raised hand from Chuter.

'There's a knife on Capron's ankle,' Mark told Chuter. 'Let me have it.'

Capron glared at him accusingly, disgusted that Mark had disclosed the whereabouts of his secret weapon. Then, realising that cooperation might work in his favour, he swung his ankles towards the anthropologist. Chuter withdrew the knife from its sheath and passed it to Mark.

'I need a short length of bamboo,' Mark said. 'The thinner the better, but we don't have time to be choosy. Get someone on it, now.'

Chuter hesitated for just a second before issuing the command. It was repeated by the rope-weaver, whose distress suggested that he might be Birahl's father.

Mark gripped the knife in his right hand and took several deep breaths. The warriors were hollering now, convinced that he was going to kill their man. They stood over Mark, the tips of their spears already piercing the shirt on his back. Mark shot Chuter a glance. The anthropologist eased the tension with a few calming words but the warriors' eyes remained full of mistrust.

Mark turned his attention back to his patient. He was a GP, not a surgeon. He had never done anything like this before. He was operating on autopilot, recalling things that he had learned from watching a consultant in Accident & Emergency. He placed his left index finger on Birahl's throat, running it lightly over the traumatised area until he felt the thyroid cartilage of the man's Adam's apple. He applied gentle pressure as his finger moved lower, feeling for the next little ridge. This was the cricoid cartilage, and the space above it the cricoid membrane.

Mark never hesitated as he made the cut. There wasn't time. Birahl was dying. Capron kept a sharp blade but Mark needed only the knife's point to make his incision in the membrane: half an inch wide by the same deep. There was a trickle of blood but not too much. Mark exhaled loudly, relieved to know that he had picked the right spot. He tossed the knife aside. Pinched the cut with his thumb and index finger. He tried again but it still wouldn't open so he wiped the dirt from his little finger and forced it gently into the hole.

The crowd gasped as more blood oozed through the incision. There were whispers and cries of fear. Mark looked up in time to see a member of the war party passing him a stem of green bamboo. It was the right width but far too long. Mark took it and snapped it over his knee. Then he used the blade to smooth the splintered edges. When he had finished he tossed the knife away. It was supposed to look casual but he threw it as close to Capron as he could. With the crowd engrossed, the American might just have an opportunity to use it.

By now, Birahl had passed out. Unable to breathe, his eyes had closed and his chest had finally stopped moving. It was going to be close. Very close.

'You've lost him,' Chuter said, and the panic in his voice caused even the rope-weaver to reach for his spear.

Mark ignored them both. He took two deep breaths to steady his hand. Then, slowly, carefully, he withdrew his finger from the hole in Birahl's throat, and replaced it with the bamboo. There was a third spurt of blood. Then the wound closed around the tube, holding it fast and upright. Mark leaned forward. The jungle, the village, the tribe had all ceased to exist. Carmen, Capron and the precarious nature of their predicament were all forgotten. He could hear nothing except the sound of his heart pulsing in his ears. *OK*, he said to himself. *Here goes.*

Mark put his lips to the bamboo and blew twice in quick succession.

Nothing happened.

He waited five seconds and then blew again: just once, but slightly longer this time.

Still nothing. Birahl lay limp and inert.

Mark counted to five and blew again. This time the man's chest rose in response. There was a hiss as he sucked in air, followed by a low whistle as he blew it out a few seconds later.

Mark collapsed back, light-headed with adrenalin. Birahl was now breathing of his own accord. Mark closed his eyes and took a few deep breaths of his own. There was pandemonium all around him. At first he thought that the tribe's clamouring was in approval of his surgery but then he realised that something equally dramatic had just unravelled behind his back.

Capron had used the crowd's preoccupation with the tracheotomy to attempt an escape. The American had clearly retrieved his knife and cut through the bindings on his ankles. He had made it past the pigs and under the longhouse before he had been shot. Now, when Mark finally spotted him, he was lying face down with an arrow between his shoulder blades.

Then, suddenly, he disappeared from view as the tribe closed around him. Carmen refused to look as they dragged him away to a nearby hut. Mark stood up but Chuter shook his head. The point of a spear between his ribs soon persuaded him to sit back down.

It took twenty minutes for calm and order to return.

The council reconvened in the longhouse, leaving the rest of the tribe to disperse back to their huts. The owner of the pigs led his animals to the same hut that Capron had been taken to. A series of squeals, snorts and grunts confirmed their slaughter. Birahl, meanwhile, had been carried to the far side of the village, wheezing through his pipe.

Mark and Carmen were still in the clearing an hour later when Chuter returned from the longhouse with Pindu and the rope-weaver. With Capron dead, the guard had been relaxed, but they'd still had three armed men for company.

Now the senior members of the village council stood before them, each wearing a different expression. Pindu was grinning inanely, high as a falcon hunting a rabbit. The rope-weaver was also smiling, although his eyes were filled with gratitude rather than hallucinations. Chuter, meanwhile, made no attempt to conceal his disappointment.

'When I returned here last year,' he began, 'I made a vow. I told myself that I would *never* interfere in tribal matters. I would only observe. You have noticed how the Addu have already elevated me to a position of status and respect. This, I assure you, was not of my own choosing. By the time they realised that I was not a ghost, they were already in awe of me. But, I try to ignore this and impose as little change as I can.' He clapped the rope-weaver on the shoulder. 'This is Menna. Birahl is his son. It is Menna's wish that you go free.'

Mark sighed with relief. Beside him, Carmen closed her eyes and offered up a silent prayer.

'It is not *my* wish,' Chuter continued. 'But I must honour my vow and allow these people to live as they would without me.'

Mark nodded. No way was he going to thank the guy. Not when the cooks had just returned from the killing hut, the sago leaves now wrapped and heavy like big green calzone. Nor was he going to tell Menna that the tracheotomy was a temporary solution and not a very good one at that. There had been no time to sterilise the knife. No time to clean the bamboo or the wound. Birahl couldn't live the rest of his life with a tube in his throat. If he didn't die from haemorrhage or infection, then his smashed larynx and crushed oesophagus were sure to prevent him from eating. He needed proper emergency surgery but Chuter would never allow him to be evacuated.

Mark took Carmen's hand and led her towards the ferry. He walked quickly. He didn't want to spend another second with Tom Chuter. And he didn't want to smell the meat that had just begun roasting in the Addu's ovens.

Fifty-Four

They spent the night on the ferry itself: a bamboo raft that strained against its mooring as the river washed underneath. They took it in turns to watch while the other slept but they saw nothing to cause them alarm. No Addu; no crocodiles, no *karkahua*.

They left before it was light, conscious that Chuter would soon send his warriors to retrieve the *kerili-bawaya* from Fox's pocket. Mark untied the raft from its mooring and they sped downriver, spinning on the current. They collided repeatedly with the mangroves as the tributary meandered towards its confluence with the Fly. Eight times Mark took to the water to heave the raft back into the flow. Then, after a mile, Carmen spotted a broken branch that he was able to use as a punt pole. It made their progress smoother, his corrective prods guiding them past the crocodiles that watched hungrily from the shallows.

When they reached the mudflat two hours later, Mark leapt off and dragged the raft to the bank.

'Where are you going?' Carmen asked. 'Tidal Island is that way.'

'We haven't got what we came for yet,' Mark replied.

'The fungi?'

'Exactly.'

'But I thought you said that Fox had them? We should have crossed the river opposite the village.'

'I was bluffing,' Mark replied.

Carmen looked at him confused. 'So where are they?'

Mark smiled and began to whistle. Three long notes, followed by a short one. Then a series of little whoops. Not very tuneful. Not very melodic.

'Melanie's song!' Carmen exclaimed. 'You know what it is?'

Mark nodded. '*Magnificent*, Carmen. Listen!' He repeated the whistle before offering her an explanation. 'Mel never did very well at school but she's as bright as they come. Far more intelligent than her numbskull brother. That whistle . . . It's not a track from her iPod, it's the call of a bird. The magnificent bird of paradise. I taught it to her on our holiday.'

Carmen said nothing, still not comprehending.

'The fungi are just up here,' Mark replied. 'In Chris Bartlett's rucksack.'

'You had them all along?'

'Not me. Melanie. That shot she fired with the pistol wasn't at a possum at all. It was at the fire extinguisher, so that she could free the briefcase's lid. That's why it was already smashed when Fox got there. That's why he didn't need the keys to unlock it. Melanie had already done that for him. Her reference to the magnificent bird of paradise was to draw my attention to the rucksack. When we get home, I'm going to show you a sketch that my grandfather painted in 1933. It's of a magnificent bird of paradise sitting in a tree above his backpack. Melanie defaced it with a stream of droppings that landed right on the bag.'

Carmen laughed. 'Why though?'

'She knew that if I thought of the magnificent bird of paradise I would think of the painting and the rucksack at the same time. Only I hadn't considered her capable of leaving such a sophisticated clue. Mel thought that she was speaking to me at home, in the bugged flat, and assumed that Capron's men would still be listening. If Capron knew that he had been double-crossed there could have been severe reprisals for us further down the line. At the very least, we could have expected another visit from him when he came to get his money back. But, more importantly than that, if she'd told me outright where the fungi were, she would have compromised my competitive advantage. If Capron was listening, he would know that I had come to PNG to retrieve the vaccine, and he could simply have followed us here or had us picked up at the airport as we tried to leave. And if Capron had got his hands on the fungi, we would have returned to England empty-handed, and Mel would be killed.

'So why *did* she take them? And why didn't she tell you earlier?'

'Why?' Mark repeated. 'You've met her, Carmen. You know what she's like. I made the mistake of telling her that there was a briefcase handcuffed to a dead guy's wrist in the helicopter. She put two and two together, concluding that it must have contained something valuable. She and Zak had borrowed heavily to buy their own place and she was in considerable debt. As for not telling me, she knew that I would never approve. Like I told you when we first met: Mel and I are chalk and cheese.'

Carmen smiled. 'Yes, you did. And I told you that she was harder than you were. Lying to Capron and Fletch took a lot of guts.'

'I don't think she actually lied,' Mark ventured. 'Capron asked me where the helicopter was, not where the fungi were. I assume he asked Mel the same question. She was just extremely economical with the truth.'

'It was still very brave.'

'Or clever. Or stupid,' Mark agreed. 'She certainly ripped them off. Still, after what she's been through, I reckon she deserves every penny. I spent just over £4,000 on my ticket here, which still leaves her a decent amount to play with.'

Carmen nodded, but they both knew that Melanie wasn't safe yet. The realisation spurred them on. They picked their way over the mangroves, sloshing upstream until they found the point where Mark and Melanie had first entered the river.

The rucksack was still there, hanging on its branch, exactly as Mark had left it. He hoisted it down and laid it on the ground. Then he rummaged deep in the main compartment, recalling that Melanie had been doing the exact same thing when he had charged back into the clearing after hearing the shot.

The *kerili-bawaya* were in a vacuum-sealed cellophane bag, similar to the one that had held Bartlett's dried apricots. There were perhaps twenty of them: shrivelled, flaccid and black. Many were still peppered with soil. Mark stuffed the packet in his trouser pocket before lifting the rucksack onto his shoulders. The glucose sweets and water-purification tablets were still inside. He and Carmen would need both on their journey back to the JetRanger. It was now seven o'clock in the morning. By the time they made it to the crash site, the clearing would hopefully be crawling with Kiuke's men.

The last of Mark's crosses was clearly visible on the trunk of a nearby tree. He strode towards it just as Carmen whispered his name.

'Mark.'

'Yes?'

'What bird is that?'

'Where?'

Carmen raised her hand and pointed towards the canopy.

Mark shielded his eyes. 'I don't see it.'

'In the tree that looks like a trident. About halfway up.'

Mark squinted. *Nope.* He still couldn't see it.

'There's a branch that curves over like an arch.'

'Got him,' Mark whispered. 'I think it's a . . .' He stopped. Felt his heart beat faster. The bird was the same size as *Corvus frugilegus*, the European rook. Similar beak, plumage and feet. Only its throat was different. A luminous pink, so vibrant that it looked as though it had been sprayed on with an aerosol.

'Have you got your camera?' he managed to ask. He was breathless. Shaking.

Carmen felt around her back for the strap. She tried to move as slowly and as quietly as she could, but the movement was still too much. The bird sprang from its perch and flashed away through the trees, its pink wingtips like sparks in the jungle.

'Fuck,' Mark said.

Kiuke had posted two sentries at the JetRanger, in case anyone should return. Mark and Carmen called out long before they emerged from the forest to make sure that they were recognised as friends. The trail of crosses had enabled them to make quicker progress than Mark had with Melanie. It was still only two o'clock in the afternoon. They were weak and hungry but the sight of the policemen injected them with new stamina for the final leg of their journey.

The sentries radioed Suki. Within twenty minutes they were back on the Huey travelling to Daru.

Mark wasn't comfortable lying to Kiuke, especially when the Inspector had done so much to make his return visit so easy. But having come this far he was in no mood to take risks. If he revealed that he was carrying a vaccine for malaria, Kiuke might – *just might* – decide that he wanted the fungi for himself. It was ungracious, groundless and insulting. It was suspicious and mean. If not racist it was certainly xenophobic – but with Melanie's life still on the line, Mark was prepared to be labelled all of those things. He remembered what Chuter had told him outside the longhouse. *In the real world, Mark, we think of our nearest and dearest first. Our natural instincts are to protect our own before we show others any altruism. That protective instinct is as primitive and base as life itself.* Once Melanie was safely home, Mark would happily reveal what had really happened.

In the meantime, with Carmen sworn to secrecy, he mentioned only that there had been a shoot-out in which each side had eliminated the other. Capron had run bleeding into the bush with a stomach wound and was now presumed dead. Mark and Carmen had run for their lives, and had been unable to find the helicopter again in the dark. Mark claimed that he had no explanation for the empty briefcase but suspected that Chuter was out there somewhere and had retrieved it himself while Mark had been back in England.

Kiuke looked sceptical to start with but sent them back to Port Moresby with his condolences that the trip had not been a success. He wished Mark good luck for Melanie's safe return and said that he would look forward to an update from Deakin. If he required any further statements from them, he would take them by phone.

Philip Mitcheson met them from the helicopter, and they took a taxi back to the Airways Hotel. They sat in the poolside restaurant, gorging themselves on the unlimited buffet while they spun a similar yarn. No point in changing their story just because it was a Brit from the High Commission. Mitcheson was just as likely – or just as unlikely, in fact – to want to profit from the fungi himself. But Mark had made up his mind. This was the only way that he was going to play it. Tomorrow, he would call Deakin and ask him to arrange safe passage through customs so that the fungi weren't confiscated as he passed through Singapore.

Mitcheson finally left at eight o'clock. Carmen disappeared for a few minutes while Mark had a third helping of pudding.

'We should check in,' he said when she returned. 'It's late and there might not be any rooms.'

'Great minds think alike,' Carmen replied. 'That is what I have just been doing. Come with me. I will show you.'

Mark followed her down the staircase and through the tiled corridors, admiring the sway of her hips as she walked. They arrived outside a room, a suite by the look of it. Carmen slipped her key card into the lock.

'Where's *my* room?' Mark asked.

Carmen glanced over her shoulder, and flashed him a smile. 'Didn't I tell you? They only had one available. We have to share. Our bags are inside. If you do not mind, I will go first in the shower.'

Carmen sat on the end of the bed in her towel, waiting for Mark to come out of the bathroom. She had ordered room service. There was a bottle of champagne in an ice bucket on the dresser. She smiled at her own mischief. There had been several vacant rooms, but hey, *we journalists aren't always renowned for our scruples*.

She lay back, staring at the ceiling. She had only known Mark for six days but what a six days they had been! She had lived. Really lived. She had seen things that she never thought she'd see. She'd unearthed a story that was going to make headlines all over the world. Better still, she'd met a man unlike any other. Six days wasn't long, but it was plenty to know that she wanted him. She wanted him now. She wanted him back in England.

Just an ordinary bloke from Ealing? *Dónde la viste!* When the time was right, she would tell him that there was nothing ordinary about him whatsoever. She would confess that she had watched him treating the kids in Landevelt's hospital. That she had witnessed the compassion in his face. She would tell him that she had seen the delicacy of his touch as he had handled syringes, pills and swabs with hands as big as bellows. That she had seen the awe and adoration in the children's eyes at Suki as he had climbed from the Huey to stretch. That she had seen his pain at Melanie's misfortune. That she had seen him catch a punch, for Christ's sake, and save a man's life with a piece of bamboo. Ordinary? How could you be six feet six, eighteen stone and as obsessed with birds as Dr Mark Bridges, and still be ordinary? How could you be so sensitive? How could you be so blind to the fact that a single woman found you so attractive?

Carmen smiled as the bathroom door opened. She felt comfortable making the first move. Why shouldn't she? If she waited for Mark to do it, she might be waiting six months.

She stood up. Stood before him and dropped her towel.

Mark was bare-chested, *his* towel almost indecent around his massive thighs. Drops of water fell from his hair, streaming down the muscles in his arms.

Carmen heard herself gasp as he scooped her up and laid her on the bed. It was like being lifted by a machine. She remembered that first night near Tidal Island when the candle had flickered, charging the office with something primitive and base. Then she had felt like a slave girl, clandestinely visiting the tent of a Spartan warrior. He was so strong. So big.

'Mark?' she whispered, half in fear. 'Promise me that you will not be *too* gentle.'

Fifty-Five

Flight SQ303 landed at Heathrow at 06.38 on Saturday 19 December. Having travelled business class, Mark was among the first to leave the plane. Carmen was somewhere further behind, still queuing to leave the economy-class cabin. Mark had offered to pay for an upgrade but the flight had been full and there had been no room for manoeuvre. Failing that, he had volunteered to swap seats but she had just laughed and told him to enjoy his extra legroom. Such had been his exhaustion that he had slept uninterrupted all the way from Singapore, waking up somewhere just east of Amsterdam. They had shared a cup of coffee before landing, but with Carmen stuck in row 58, they had agreed to meet up again at the baggage carousel once they had cleared immigration.

Mark made his way through the gate and began following the signs to arrivals. He carried a small rucksack over his shoulder. The fungi were inside, wrapped in a T-shirt for additional protection. He had slept with the bag under his seat, one strap looped around his ankle so that it couldn't be moved without his knowledge. Now he swung it off his shoulder and peered inside. The fungi couldn't possibly have gone anywhere but he couldn't resist the urge to check. Only the paranoid survive, he told himself as he stepped on to an escalator.

His parents would be waiting outside. He had called them yesterday from Port Moresby. Their news confirmed that his decision to retrieve the fungi had been correct. Inspector Deakin had been working around the clock to find Melanie but every new lead had fast become a dead end. The white van that Mark's neighbour had spotted in Exeter Road had indeed been caught on several CCTV cameras. It had been stolen from a plumber in Reigate the day before but was now smouldering in a Bedfordshire field, having been dumped and burned to purge it of evidence. Now, with only one more day until Bartlett's deadline, Deakin was working on a new plan. It looked as though the exchange would have to go ahead. The policeman was keen to ensure that Mark remained under surveillance the entire time. They had arranged to meet in Ealing at half-past ten to run through the detective's initial thoughts on how they should handle the day.

Mark knew that the next twenty-four hours were going to be as tough as any since the ordeal had begun. It would be a case of hoping, waiting and trying not to worry. He sensed that the hardest part was now behind him but there was still plenty of scope for things to go wrong. It was difficult to imagine what Bartlett would gain by double-crossing him, but the guy had already proved that he was a vicious piece of work, and Mark had resolved to expect the unexpected. He didn't know what tricks Deakin had up his sleeve but if they involved body-armour and the protection of Special Branch, then that was fine by him. No doubt Bartlett would have a few tricks of his own. Mark had already decided that wearing a wire was too risky. If Deakin wanted evidence to use against Bartlett in court, then he was going to have to glean it from afar.

Mark returned the pack to his shoulder. He pressed forward, walking through the crowd at his usual pace. It wasn't particularly fast but the length of his stride carried him past the majority of people with little effort. The moving walkway gave him additional speed. He was confident of reaching immigration before a queue could form. He stepped right to overtake the guy in front: a tall black man in a denim jacket and blue beanie. The man had been standing with his back to Mark, one hand on the escalator's rail, the other hanging by his side. Mark slowed down to squeeze past. As he did so the guy grabbed his arm, interlocking it with his own at the elbow as though they were lovers.

What the –? Mark had considerable momentum

but the guy sprang forward and began matching him stride for stride along the escalator.

'Have you got them?' he asked, his accent pure Jamaican.

The question was a like a punch in the stomach. It made Mark gasp for air. So much for expecting the unexpected. He tried to free his arm but the man had it pinched tight against his side. He had bloodshot eyes and thick dreadlocks under his hat.

'Who the hell are you?' Mark managed to ask.

'You can call me DJ,' the man replied. 'Now, tell me if you've got the drugs. Melanie's waiting.'

Mark felt his stomach leap but he kept on walking. It would be superfluous to ask DJ if Bartlett had sent him. Dangerous too. Revealing that he knew the kidnapper's identity could have disastrous consequences for him *and* Melanie. Bartlett clearly ran a highly efficient organisation. He must have had eyes and ears in Singapore to have known which flight Mark was on.

'Yes,' Mark replied. 'I've got them.'

'Good. Now listen carefully. I'm gonna take you to Melanie right now. If you run, if you draw attention to us, or if you don't do exactly as I say at all times, Melanie will be killed. If I don't call in every ten minutes the same thing will happen. Are we clear?'

'Crystal.'

'Good,' DJ said, releasing Mark's arm. 'Now give me your phone.'

'What?'

'Your phone, man. Give it to me!'

Mark reached in his pocket and did as he had been told. He hadn't even switched it on yet after the flight. 'I thought the exchange was tomorrow?'

'It was,' DJ said. 'But you're early. That suits us fine. Another day would have given you time to organise surveillance an' shit like that. This way we get to do it on our terms. Turn right here.'

Mark glanced at the sign above his head. TRANSFERS. TERMINAL 2. That was clever. DJ was taking him out through another exit to avoid whatever allies he might have had waiting in Terminal 3.

They walked in silence for the next few minutes, before taking a short ride on the airside bus to Terminal 2. They passed a bin in the corridor. DJ chucked Mark's phone inside without breaking stride.

'When we get to immigration, I'm gonna be standin' right behind you. You take longer than necessary an' I'll be on the phone to my friends. You open your mouth, you so much as give the guy a look, and Melanie will be dead before he returns your passport. You got that?'

'Got it,' Mark replied. No way was he going to screw things up now. He knew who the abductor was. So long as Melanie came home alive then it wouldn't matter if Bartlett got away. Not initially, at any rate. That wasn't Mark's problem. Once Melanie was safe, Deakin could then focus his resources on finding the Australian and his gang.

There was a short queue at immigration. Mark waited his turn before having his passport swiped. He was sent on his way with a silent nod. He turned in time to see the customs officer asking DJ a couple of questions, both of which were answered with a smile. DJ joined him moments later. With Mark's main bag heading to terminal 3, neither of them had any luggage to collect, and they passed through customs without incident. Mark imagined Carmen looking for him in the baggage hall, half a mile away. She would be calling his mobile only to find that it cut straight to voicemail. How long would she wait before she raised the alarm? Fifteen minutes? Half an hour? Their movements through the airport would be picked up by the security cameras but Mark was going to be long gone before anyone could organise a tail.

Once clear of customs, DJ walked briskly through the terminal. Up an escalator and outside to the set-down area opposite departures. Less than a minute later a grey Vauxhall Vectra pulled alongside. The passenger door opened from the inside. Mark climbed in, placing his bag in the footwell. The driver was Caucasian: unshaven with greasy hair and a hooked nose that reminded him of a vulture's beak. He didn't even acknowledge Mark as he eased the Vectra into the early-morning traffic.

It was just turning light outside: another grey day during which the sun would never penetrate the clouds. The driver had the radio on. The Met Office was forecasting snow. It was unlikely to last but the presenter announced that Ladbrokes had slashed its odds on a white Christmas to even money. Mark thought of Tom Chuter and his tribe, deep in the Papuan jungle. Ninety-five people who didn't know that such a thing as snow existed.

The Vectra drove smoothly up the spur road, sticking to the speed limit. DJ made a brief call on his mobile to confirm that things were running to plan. At the M4 they crossed over the roundabout and headed into Hendon, where they switched cars in an underground car park. Then they returned to the motorway, joining the clockwise carriageway of the M25 some fifteen minutes later.

The second car was a VW Passat: navy blue and unremarkable in every respect. Except for the pistol that DJ had retrieved from its glove compartment before Mark had taken his seat.

'Couple of hours,' DJ announced. 'Kick back an' enjoy the radio. I'll be watching you, man. Any funny business and it won't just be Melanie getting killed.'

Mark nodded. He had come to the conclusion that the change of plan was actually for the best. The sooner it began, the sooner it would be over. More importantly, if Melanie *had* developed malaria, as was eminently possible, then the extra twenty-four hours could prove crucial in saving her life.

It was an uninspiring journey. The traffic grew increasingly heavy as they passed first the M40 and then the M1. On they went, ignoring the M11, eventually leaving the motorway in favour of the A12 towards Brentwood. Neither DJ nor the driver spoke. Both were seemingly content to listen to the breakfast show on Radio 1. Mark wasn't overly preoccupied with their route. So far it had been easy enough to remember. And the fact that DJ hadn't blindfolded him suggested that the exchange was going to take place somewhere that would be of little significance to the police.

Instead, Mark took a leaf out of Capron's book and began assessing his captors for signs of weakness. He had no intention of escaping but if something went wrong later, he wanted to react without having to think. The driver didn't appear to be armed but he was more vigilant than his accomplice, and a heavier build. DJ had the gun and had shown extreme poise while passing through Immigration; but when Mark glanced in the rear-view mirror, the Rastafarian was struggling to stay awake. His head was lolling on a rubber neck. His eyelids stayed down longer each time he blinked. When he called Bartlett to report on their progress, his words were slurred with sleep. The fresh air was going to sharpen him up when they left the car, but his reactions would still be slower than those of a man alert from driving.

They left the A12 somewhere between Chelmsford and Colchester, passing through several small villages that Mark had never heard of. A brace of startled pheasant burst from the verge as the Vectra rolled smoothly on. More villages came and went.

Outside, the lanes became narrower, the landscape increasingly bleak and rural. There were fewer houses now too. Just acres and acres of open farmland, windswept fields and shivering hedgerows. Mark sensed that they were getting close. No prying eyes here. No uninvited guests. The nearest police station was probably fifteen miles away, and with Christmas just around the corner no one would be out looking for trouble at this time of day.

The Vectra left the main road a few minutes later, turning right down a dirt track between two fields. The driver slowed to five miles an hour to absorb the bumps in the ground. They passed a spinney on their left, its deciduous trees cowed and skeletal. Another turn along another track. Soon they were in deep countryside, invisible from the road. They rounded another copse. Suddenly Mark saw a second vehicle waiting for them ahead.

It was a black BMW X5: a muscular sport utility vehicle with thick tyres and tinted glass. Its number plates had been removed. Its doors were flecked with mud after its journey through the fields.

Mark breathed deeply to control his rising nerves. This was it. The end of the line. The final act of an adventure he'd never wanted.

The Vectra pulled alongside.

DJ ordered him out.

Fifty-Six

Mark climbed slowly out of the car, bringing the rucksack with him. No sudden movements; no sign of panic. He wanted Bartlett to know that he was calm; that he wasn't going to do anything stupid or brave. The fact that DJ hadn't already shot him and stolen the fungi gave him confidence that the Australian intended to honour their agreement. And with no police to spook them, it would hopefully all be over in a matter of minutes.

Mark looked hard at the BMW but the tinted glass made it impossible to see if Melanie was inside. Then the driver's door opened and Charlie Bartlett stepped out.

Mark hadn't really known what to expect. Until now Bartlett had been a voice: a psychotic menace on the other end of a phone line. Now here he was in the flesh. He was dressed in white jeans, brown leather loafers and a thick roll-neck sweater. He was unshaven, his eyes hidden by sunglasses. His hair was cut close to his scalp, not much longer than his stubble, and he moved with a fluidity that suggested he had kept himself fit since leaving the SASR. There was something smug about him. Maybe it was the overconfident grin. Or the sharpness of his attire. They were surrounded by muddy fields but Bartlett was dressed like an actor en route to lunch in an expensive wine bar. The sight of him made Mark's arms twitch with aggression.

'G'day, mate. You've made good time.'

'Where is she?' Mark demanded, his voice cracking with pent-up hate. Confronted with the man who had abducted and mutilated his sister, he was no longer sure that he could restrain himself. This was an unfamiliar feeling. And it wasn't at all unpleasant.

'She's in the back. Not very well, I hasten to add. She says she's got malaria and I'm inclined to believe her.'

'Bring her out,' Mark commanded. 'Let me see her.'

'All right, big fella. Easy now. Play this nice and cool and nobody will get hurt. Dazzler!' Bartlett turned and beckoned at someone inside the BMW. Mark waited with his heart in his mouth. Away to his left, a murder of crows cavorted in the wind above the spinney. One of the rear doors opened. A second man climbed from the car. Once out, he leaned inside again, the strain in his back making it clear that he was struggling with something heavy.

It took a while for Dazzler to lift Melanie out. She was clearly incapable of supporting her own weight. She emerged stiff and angular, creased over the guy's shoulder like a sheet of folded card.

Mark's heart missed a beat when he saw her. Melanie was rigid and ashen, locked in a rattling chill that confirmed his fears. Her hair was matted with sweat, four long strands stuck across her face like lashes from a leather whip. She was shivering violently. Her mouth was ajar, her teeth chattering loud enough to be heard above the crunch of Dazzler's boots. Her eyes were only half-open, lifeless and unable to focus on anything at all. Her left hand was bandaged. There was a patch of dried blood where her little finger should have been. She sagged as Dazzler attempted to carry her over. He heaved her up again but the angle was too awkward. Melanie collapsed to the ground, hitting her head against the BMW's wheel arch.

Mark could take it no longer. He reached into his bag, retrieved the packet of fungi and tossed it to Bartlett. He didn't wait for permission to move, he simply strode to the car and pushed Dazzler aside. He bent down and scooped his right arm under Melanie's shoulders. His left went behind her calves. He picked her up in one easy movement, cradling her to his chest. Holding her with one arm now, he repositioned her left hand on his shoulder so that the blood wouldn't flow to her stump.

Mark didn't bother with goodbyes. He just

walked straight at DJ and the driver of the Vectra, who were blocking his path. A glance from Bartlett must have reassured them, because they stood aside, allowing Mark to pass. He picked up his rucksack. Then he started walking in the direction of the road.

Mark couldn't remember the last time he had carried Melanie. She felt lighter than she should have done. He cradled her head in the crook of his arm so that his movement down the track didn't cause her too much discomfort. He had seen a farmhouse a mile before they had left the road. It would take him twenty minutes to reach it.

'Mark? Is that you?' Melanie spoke without moving her lips, her voice a pained mumble that somehow escaped her gnashing teeth.

'It's me,' he replied, fighting back tears. 'You're safe now.'

'I knew you'd come.'

Mark swallowed hard. He didn't know what to say. He felt his body relaxing as the adrenalin seeped out of his stomach, down his legs and away through his boots.

There had been a time in Cornwall. A family holiday when he had been seventeen and Melanie eleven. He had been teaching her how to bodysurf at Constantine Bay. They had been in the shallows: the waves only three feet high but still foaming as they roared up the beach. Melanie had soon got the hang of it, screaming as she rode the white horses. She had grown bolder, swimming further out in search of greater thrills. Mark had called her back, but she had spun out of reach, a defiant look on her face. The next wave had been the first in a new set: a timeless surge of energy that had begun somewhere on the other side of the ocean. Out of her depth and suddenly scared, Melanie had misjudged it completely. It had come down on her head, hustling her underwater and pounding her into the sand. Mark had reached below the surface. He had hauled her from the sea with one hand, before carrying her up the beach. Looking at her now, he saw the same little girl. Cold and bedraggled but less scared than she should have been because she knew that he had been there all along. It made him angry. It made him elated. It made his heart swell with love.

'I'm sorry,' Melanie said. Then she tensed in spasm, as though hit by a massive electrical current.

'Don't be,' he replied. 'Try to rest.' He clutched her to his chest but he was powerless to stop her shaking. Her malaria was at an advanced stage. Mark increased his pace. He needed to get her to a hospital fast. Which was closer? Chelmsford or Colchester? The owners of the farmhouse would know.

Mark had walked fifteen metres when he heard the first shot.

The rifle must have had a silencer because the report was more like a cough than a bang but it still caused him to flinch in surprise.

'Gotcha!' Melanie whispered.

Mark ducked, spinning in time to see the driver of the Vectra collapse to the ground. A second shot followed. DJ was thrown backwards by the force of a bullet in his chest. The crows above the spinney shrieked, the flurry of their wings like applause in the distance. Dazzler had thrown open the BMW's door and was crouching behind it for cover. He had drawn a pistol from his jacket, aiming it at the trees. He popped up, ready to fire, and the third round entered his face through the bridge of his nose. He rolled back, twitched once and then lay lifeless in the mud, his brains already oozing through the hole in his skull.

That left Bartlett.

Trained to the sound of gunfire, the Australian had reacted far quicker than his men. He too had a pistol. He fired twice at the spinney before breaking into a jinking run. He must have known that the cars were inadequate cover against such a skilled marksman because he was running towards Mark and Melanie. It was a canny ploy. With Mark in the line of fire, the sniper couldn't risk a fourth shot unless he was prepared to hit them both.

For a moment Mark stood rooted to the spot, unsure what the hell was going on. It couldn't have been the police shooting. They would have issued a warning. They would have tried to make an arrest, only opening fire if fired upon first. No, this was cold-blooded murder: a clinical assault to take the gang out.

Mark glanced towards the spinney. He saw the silhouette of a huge man emerging from the trees. He was carrying a long-barrelled rifle with bipod legs. *Fletch!* It had to be. Ever thorough, Capron must have established a contingency plan in case things went wrong in Papua New Guinea. Now that plan was being executed with ruthless efficiency. Capron's claim that he knew where Melanie was being held hadn't been a bluff at all. Fletch must have followed the BMW and set up the ambush while Mark was still en route. It had gone pretty well too. Three dead in under fifteen seconds and only Bartlett left to deal with before he could collect the fungi.

Bartlett was running hard. Mark watched him come. Saw him crouch low and pump his arms for speed. Saw too the smirk on his face as Fletch's ceasefire confirmed the guile of his decision. Unarmed, with nowhere to run, Mark took a deep breath and told himself to be calm. He looked, assessed the situation, and knew instantly what he needed to do.

He was gentle and unhurried as he laid Melanie on the ground. Then he stepped forward so that she was well behind him, out of harm's way.

'Put your hands up,' Bartlett commanded. He was just yards away now. He had slowed to a walk. The conceit in his face had turned to aggression as he aimed the pistol at his hostage.

Mark obeyed. He knew what was going to

happen. Bartlett was going to stand behind him and use him as a shield until he reached the cover of the copse behind. It wasn't a bad idea. With a fifty-four-inch chest, Mark was the biggest thing around: wider certainly than the tree trunks for which they would soon be heading.

Bartlett stepped behind him. He tried reaching around his neck but Mark was too big. Realising that it was no good, the Australian changed tactics. He grabbed Mark's pullover between the shoulder blades and pulled Mark against him so that he was obscured from Fletch's line of fire.

'OK,' he said, jamming the pistol against Mark's neck. 'Let's go!'

Mark took a step back. Then another. He was facing the cars. Bartlett was behind him, shielded behind his back. Melanie lay a yard to the right. Fletch had already reached the vehicles and was checking that the other men were dead.

Mark's shoulders were pressed tight against Bartlett's chest. They shuffled awkwardly back, locked together like mating crabs. They drew level with Melanie but her eyes were closed. She knew nothing of what was happening.

Twenty metres away Fletch was preparing himself for another shot. His rifle would be accurate at over a mile so there was no need for pursuit. He lay down and steadied the barrel on its legs. Maximum stability. Maximum accuracy. Could he hit Bartlett without hitting Mark? Or wasn't he worried about that? A round into Mark's chest would kill both men in the same second.

Bartlett pulled again. Mark dug his heels in, refusing to budge. There was a stiff breeze, but Fletch had proved himself an expert shot. And he was already closer than he had been when he'd killed the others. Mark felt his pullover constrict around his chest as Bartlett yanked on the material again. He held firm, hardly daring to breathe.

Bartlett swore as he realised that he could no longer coerce his hostage to walk. He moved the pistol away from Mark's neck, straightened his forearm and took aim at Fletch.

That changed everything.

Mark knew instantly that he had to react. If Fletch came under fire he would shoot back, regardless of the danger to Mark. He wouldn't hesitate to kill them both if that was necessary for his own survival. Mark still had his hands up but they had slipped down level with his shoulders. Bartlett's gun arm was an inch from his fingers, his wrist in the gap between Mark's hand and neck.

Mark struck like a snake, grabbing the Australian's wrist and forcing his arm up. Bartlett pulled the trigger but the pistol was already pointing harmlessly at the sky. The bullets cleared Fletch's head by metres.

Bartlett was a big man. Six feet tall with broad shoulders and a strong stance. But he was powerless to stop his hand being forced to one side as Mark turned to face him.

'Drop it,' Mark said. 'Or I'll break your arm.'

Bartlett ignored him, aiming a knee at his groin. Mark swivelled his hip, and took the blow on his thigh. Then he twisted his grip and heard something snap as he dislocated the bones in Bartlett's wrist.

Bartlett cried out and dropped the pistol, but he had been trained to fight and he threw a stinging left that crashed against Mark's cheek. Mark groaned as the shock wave flashed across his face, rattling his eye in its socket. His vision blurred then cleared again just as the second punch landed on his ear. It went black then quiet. For a second Mark thought he had been shot. Then he regained his senses. He still had hold of Bartlett's wrist and he pulled the Australian towards him.

Mark glanced at Melanie. There was fresh blood on her bandaged stump. The sight of it changed something inside him. He closed his arms around Bartlett's back, lifted him off his feet and began to squeeze. Mark didn't lose his temper. He didn't give in to his aggression. He was as cool-headed as at any time in his life. He just stared into the Australian's eyes and focused on summoning his strength. He called it from his feet, his calves and his thighs. He called it from his torso and the small of his back. He called it from the pectoral mass of his chest and his deltoids.

Strength. His gift. His essence. He felt it pool in his shoulders and flow down his arms.

Then he let it explode in his biceps.

Bartlett's face turned purple as the air was driven from his lungs. His arms were pinned to his side. He tried a headbutt but he was unable reach his target. Mark tightened his arms and gained an inch of slack. Now he clasped his left wrist in his right hand and locked his grip. He felt Bartlett's ribs crack then collapse. Saw his eyes bulge and his tongue forced from his mouth. Mark squeezed harder; felt the man's spine pop and knew that he would never walk again. The kicking on his shins stopped immediately. He let go. The Australian fell silently to the ground.

Fletch was still prone, his rifle trained on Bartlett. Mark knelt down and retrieved the bag of fungi from the Australian's pocket.

'Leave 'em,' Fletch warned, his voice carrying on the wind.

'Are you going to shoot me?' Mark called back.

'If I have to.'

Mark believed him. He opened the seal on the bag and raised his hands to signal his submission. Then he waited. Waited for Fletch to stand up. Waited for him to take his eye away from the rifle's sight.

Fletch eased back from the stock and placed his palms on the ground, ready to push himself up. It would take no more than three or four

Christmas with Mark and his family, and she was relieved to hear that Mrs Chuter would go next door to her neighbours after church. Carmen was an expert at lifting the old woman's spirits, leaving Mark time to reflect on what he had learned from DI Deakin earlier that morning.

There was no trace of Fletch but a man his size would struggle to go unnoticed for long. Privately, Mark hoped that the guy would avoid arrest. He had, after all, saved Melanie's life and eliminated Bartlett's gang. Meanwhile, an email from Philip Mitcheson had confirmed that the Australian Civil Aviation Authority had been helping Kimpeau Kiuke with his investigation. A specialist team had returned to the wreck and traced the JetRanger's serial number. The helicopter was registered to *Tatania IV*, a sixty-metre luxury yacht owned by none other than Frank Wanstead, Head of Research & Development at Gammell Pharmaceuticals. Analysis of the boat's movements revealed that she had travelled from Cairns to Bali fourteen months ago. It was a route that would have taken her through the Torres Straits, along the coast of Papua New Guinea. Launching from the yacht, the JetRanger would have had enough fuel to complete its mission without refilling inland. Her passengers, meanwhile, would have been able to enter the country without creating a record with immigration. *Tatania IV* had been back in the Torres Strait a few days ago. She had been seen leaving Darwin with a new JetRanger on her helipad, but the helicopter hadn't been there when the Australian Navy had subsequently boarded her off the coast of Daru.

The investigation was still in its infancy but Gammell Pharmaceuticals had distanced itself from any involvement in the affair. Wanstead had been suspended from the board pending the outcome of the enquiry, leaving Deakin to conclude that the American had been acting autonomously, without the backing of his company. He was, to use the Inspector's phrase, currently helping the police with their inquiries.

'You said yesterday that you needed to collect something,' Mrs Chuter said, stirring her tea and Mark from his thoughts.

'That's right,' he replied. 'Tom's secret.'

'Tom's secret?' Mrs Chuter looked puzzled. 'You know what it is?'

Mark nodded. 'The answer was right here all along.'

'It was?'

Mark stood up and crossed the room, pulling Tom's postcard from the fridge door. He turned it over, found his place and began reading out loud. '*The air in England never suited me. And where I'm going they have the ultimate protection against bad air!!!*' He stopped and handed the postcard to Mrs Chuter.

'I don't follow,' she said, straining to read her son's writing without her glasses.

'Tom discovered a natural vaccine against malaria. The word malaria comes from the medieval Italian *mala aria*, meaning bad air. In England, it was initially called marsh fever because of its association with the stagnant air that you find around swamps.'

Mrs Chuter looked confused. 'A cure for malaria, you say?'

'Not a cure,' Mark corrected. 'A vaccine. To prevent people from developing the disease in the first place.'

'Is that better?'

'Infinitely. It's the first rule of medicine that prevention is always better than cure.'

'And they don't have one already?'

'No,' Mark replied. 'They don't.'

'It must be rather important then?'

'You could say that.'

'Goodness me, well, you'd better take it!'

Mark smiled. 'I was hoping you were going to say that.'

Mrs Chuter was momentarily silent while the significance of Mark's revelation sank in. The visit had given her plenty to think about.

'They say a secret is something you tell one other person,' Carmen said, pouring her host another cup of tea. 'I think Tom felt bad about keeping his discovery from you. This postcard was his way of letting you know what he had found.'

Mrs Chuter picked up the card and peered at it again. 'Bad air? *Mala aria*?' Her brow furrowed as though she was struggling with a difficult crossword clue. 'Well, I must say, it was a little too cryptic for me. So where is this thing? I have a few boxes of Tom's possessions from his room at college, but I don't remember seeing anything that looked like a vaccine.'

'You wouldn't have done,' Mark said. 'Henry's got it.'

'Henry?'

'Where else would you hide your treasure other than in a treasure chest?'

Mrs Chuter raised her eyebrows in surprise. Then a look of understanding flashed across her face as the penny dropped. 'All that time and it was right here under our noses?'

'I'm afraid so,' Mark replied. 'I didn't need to return to Papua New Guinea at all. I could have just come to see you. It'll be a packet of fungi in the treasure chest under Henry's perch. They look like small black truffles. Would you mind going? Henry probably still thinks I stole Tom's notebook. I don't want to upset him again.'

'Very wise, dear,' Mrs Chuter replied. 'Tom and I are the only two people he'll let anywhere near his chest. Not even Walter, God rest him, could put his hand in there without being attacked.'

'Thank you,' Mark said. 'We'll wait for you here.'

She was gone for a couple of minutes. Mark and Carmen passed the time by returning to the living room to examine the photographs of Tom. Neither bore much resemblance to how he looked now. Only his eyes were the same: blazing with the same intensity as they had witnessed in the jungle.

'He was a little upset to start with,' Mrs Chuter said on her return. 'But I told him we wouldn't need it for long. Here you are, dear! I think it's better if *you* open it.'

Mark took the chest and drew a deep breath. It fitted neatly in the palm of his hand. He hoped that he was right. Hoped that he hadn't misheard as Tom had ranted about his initial decision to reveal his secret to the world. *I had taken a sample of* kerili-bawaya *home with me and hidden it in a safe place. All I had to do was give it to Creasey and we would have been millionaires in a matter of weeks.*

Not any more, Mark mused as he lifted the lid. Neither Chuter nor Creasey would be making any money from the vaccine now. A lack of evidence meant that the police had been unable to arrest Creasey for his involvement in the affair, but Carmen's story was going to cast a shadow over Plasmavax for many years to come. If the pharmacologist had any sense he would sell up before his clients deserted him and rendered his company worthless.

'Well?' Carmen asked.

'We're in business,' Mark replied.

There were eight of them, vacuum-packed in a cellophane bag. Mark lifted the packet out of the chest and placed it in his jacket pocket.

Earlier that morning he had called the head office of Save the Children and learned that Dr

Selby had returned to England for Christmas. When Mark had stressed the urgency of making contact he had been rewarded with a phone number. Selby had naturally sounded sceptical when Mark had explained what he would be collecting from Grantchester but the urgency in his voice had eventually won the physician over. Selby had agreed to a meeting at four o'clock that afternoon at the London School of Hygiene & Tropical Medicine. Three of his former research colleagues had subsequently agreed to join him. Their meeting would be the first step on a long and arduous journey to develop a commercially viable vaccine against a disease that killed a child every thirty seconds. Separating the two spirits, Kerili and Bawaya, would be the first of their challenges.

Would the sample be large enough to extract what they needed without having to return to PNG for more? Mark didn't know. Probably not. Which meant that some time in the not too distant future he might be called upon to disclose the Addu's location. He would demand conditions. He would seek written reassurances so that the matter was handled sensitively. But he would not lose a single night's sleep over his decision to tell. It was a straightforward case of numbers. The greater good.

Mark glanced at his watch. Half-past two. It was time to go. They would be driving in the opposite direction to the daily exodus from London, but the traffic would still be bad. Mrs

Chuter offered them another cup of tea but not even a second helping of custard creams could persuade Mark to stay.

'If things work out,' he told Mrs Chuter as they stood in the hall, a few minutes later, 'Tom will have been responsible for one of the greatest discoveries of the twenty-first century. I think, in time, it could make him very proud.'

'Thank you, Dr Bridges,' Mrs Chuter replied, a tear welling in her eye. 'It's certainly made *me* very proud.'

'Please. Call me Mark.'

'Thank you, Mark. You've made an old lady very happy.' She turned to Carmen and squeezed her hand, whispering conspiratorially, 'Look after him, won't you, dear. He's a rather extraordinary young man.'

'I know,' Carmen whispered back. 'I intend to.'

Mark smiled and rolled his eyes. 'Happy Christmas, Mrs Chuter.'

'Oh, it will be, dear. It will be. And the same to both of you!'

They left her smiling on the doorstep and began making their way back to the car. Mark was halfway down the path when he stopped and put a hand on Carmen's arm.

'What is it?' she asked, sensing something important.

'Listen!'

Mark watched as Carmen cocked her head and held her breath. It came to her a few seconds later, as the winter's first snowflakes tumbled from the sky. It was the voice of an angel; the rapture of a free spirit, invisible but irrepressible above the meadow opposite. It rose and fell, as clear and pure as a mountain spring. The liquid warbling twitter of a lark in full song.

Acknowledgements

Thank you to Dr Ayan Panja and Detective 'J' at Special Branch, who assisted me with my research for this novel. Any inaccuracies in the story are mine alone. Thanks to Joffy Conolly and John Capron, and to my agent Camilla Bolton and editor Oliver Johnson for their ideas and expert advice. My thanks also to Tim Robinson, Charlotte Haycock and Caroline Johnson. Above all, thanks to my beautiful wife, Sally-Ann, for so many happy memories of Papua New Guinea, and for her patience at home while my mind was still in the jungle.

Postscript

While researching this novel, I travelled to the Tari highlands in central Papua New Guinea, an area famed for its birds of paradise. There, I was fortunate enough to meet David Nicholson, an Australian financial management adviser who had taken a foreign-aid role with Papua New Guinea's Department for Community Development. Soon after completing *First Contact*, I received the shocking news that David had been murdered in his apartment in Port Moresby – another victim of the lawlessness for which the city is sadly renowned. David loved Papua New Guinea and contributed some of the Pidgin (Tok Pisin) that appears in the first third of this novel. I would like to take this opportunity to acknowledge his help, and to wish his family well. Papua New Guinea is all the poorer without him.

Double Cross

Patrick Woodrow

When Ed Strachan's parents were killed in a horrific car crash eighteen years ago, they left their son a miserly inheritance: the memory of a mangled nursery rhyme and a cufflink inscribed with a single set of coordinates.

But eighteen years later when a beautiful girl tries to poison Ed and steal the cufflink he guesses it may have greater significance than he had imagined. Christine Molyneux is just the first of many who will stop at nothing to get hold of it.

Ed is soon prime suspect in a complicated homicide and immersed in a mystery that goes back way before his parent's death. It is a mystery that lies hidden off a coral island in the South China Sea; that has already cost thousands of lives and that will cost many more before it sees the light of day again.

Fans of Clive Cussler will love Double Cross: a breathtaking mixture of mystery, action and undersea adventure.

'Exceptionally accomplished' Boris Starling, bestselling author of *Messiah*

'Utterly gripping' *Manchester Evening News*

'An author to be reckoned with' *Bangkok Post*

'A classic actioner with a chunky plot. You'd pay to watch the film they'll surely make' *Lads Mag*

arrow books

Jurassic Park

Michael Crichton

The phenomenal worldwide bestseller

On a remote jungle island, genetic engineers have created a dinosaur game park.

An astonishing technique for recovering and cloning dinosaur DNA has been discovered. Now one of mankind's most thrilling fantasies has come true . . .

'Crichton's most compulsive novel to date'
Sunday Telegraph

'Breathtaking adventure . . . a book that is as hard to put down as it is to forget'
Time Out

'Wonderful . . . powerful'
Washington Post

'Full of suspense'
New York Times

arrow books

Congo

Michael Crichton

Deep in the darkest region of the Congo, near the legendary ruins of the Lost City of Zinj, an eight-person field expedition dies mysteriously and brutally in a matter of minutes . . .

'Ingenious, imaginative'
Los Angeles Times

'Thrilling'
New York Times Book Review

'Dazzling'
People

arrow books

The Lost World

Michael Crichton

Something has survived . . .

It is now six years since the secret disaster at Jurassic Park, six years since the extraordinary dream of science and imagination came to a crashing end – the dinosaurs destroyed, the park dismantled, the island indefinitely closed to the public.

There are rumours that something has survived.

'Another monster hit by a giant of a writer'
Daily Express

'*The Lost World* moves at a spanking pace . . . recommended as first rate entertainment'
Specatator

'Gripping'
Sunday Express

arrow books

ALSO AVAILABLE IN ARROW

Airframe

Michael Crichton

The twin jet plane en route to Denver from Hong Kong is merely a green radar blip half an hour off the California coast when the call comes through to air traffic control:

'Social Approach, this is TransPacific 545. We have an emergency.' The pilot requests priority clearance to land – then comes the bombshell – he needs forty ambulances on the runway.

But nothing prepares the rescue workers for the carnage they witness when they enter the plane. Ninety-four passengers are injured. Three dead. The interior cabin virtually destroyed.

What happened on board Flight TPA 545?

'A compulsive page-turner . . . Crichton dazzles the reader'
Financial Times

'This is the first book in ages which I can honestly say I read at a single sitting'
The Times

'A deftly-woven tale of corporate skulduggery, media deceit and sleuthing that culminates in a genuinely gripping and surprising ending . . . an engrossing yarn'
Express

arrow books

THE POWER OF READING

Visit the Random House website and get connected with information on all our books and authors

EXTRACTS from our recently published books and selected backlist titles

COMPETITIONS AND PRIZE DRAWS Win signed books, audiobooks and more

AUTHOR EVENTS Find out which of our authors are on tour and where you can meet them

LATEST NEWS on bestsellers, awards and new publications

MINISITES with exclusive special features dedicated to our authors and their titles

READING GROUPS Reading guides, special features and all the information you need for your reading group

LISTEN to extracts from the latest audiobook publications

WATCH video clips of interviews and readings with our authors

RANDOM HOUSE INFORMATION including advice for writers, job vacancies and all your general queries answered

Come home to Random House

www.rbooks.co.uk